This book is dedicated to stimulus and entropy, without which the experiment fails.

PROLOGUE: THE FIFTH WALL, A DEFINITION

You'll probably recognize "breaking the fourth wall" as a technique in metafiction where a member of a story speaks directly to the audience. The member is a fictional character who leverages the power of breaking the fourth wall to produce a reaction in reality. Breaking the fourth wall is safe enough and sometimes appropriate given the circumstances, although on occasion it is quite dangerous. While the literary technique is what this act is most widely known for, it can also be used to describe any transaction between reality and fiction.

You've got a clear picture of the difference between reality and fiction, right? Easy.

- *Reality* is the collection of states, measurements, and circumstances which are presently descriptive of real existence.

Reality is simple enough. You only *think* you know fiction, though. See, fiction only *seems* like it's easy to understand. Here's the easy definition. The *real* definition:

- Anything which is not real.

But here's the *fictional* definition of fiction:

- *Fiction* is the collection of states, measurements, and circumstances which *are not* presently descriptive of real existence.

This is obviously where things get tricky. I didn't get it at first either, but let's just break it down together, bit by bit.

Now. When you have any sort of definition of fiction, of course it *must* be fictional. Otherwise it cannot possibly, by definition of reality, be a definition of fiction. Nothing which is descriptive of fiction can occupy reality, and this is including its own definition. That's why I've supplied you with a fictional definition of fiction, otherwise you wouldn't know what was real and what was - precisely - fiction. If I say something isn't real, when it very clearly is real, that's fiction - and it's what I had to do to the definition to make it proper.

So there's our definition of reality and fiction. What was next?

beats fist on head, eyes clenched

Right, yeah, the transactions!

So, what happens to a state in reality when it changes in any way?

It becomes a state in fiction.

The new state, which was previously fiction, replaces the previous state, which is newly fiction. So there are actually two transactions which take place simultaneously. One state moves from reality to fiction and another state moves from fiction to reality.

Too technical? Here's a pretty straightforward example:

- If you take lemons and make lemonade, the whole lemons are now fiction, and the lemonade, previously fiction, is now reality.

And another one:

- If I finish this beer, in a couple hours it will be fiction.

And here's a much more complex example which breaks the fourth wall, twice:

- Reading this sentence breaks the fourth wall, twice. Once in the classical definition for my acknowledgement of you as a reader in order to evoke a response in reality, and once because you've committed the act of reading it, thus pulling that very circumstance from fiction into reality.

And that's the thing - *we're breaking the fourth wall with literally every action*. Made me uncomfortable at first but now I get excited while lost in the very thought of it. It makes everything more significant, more present, more…

deep inhale

…*real*.

So since this change of states, measurements, and circumstances from fiction to reality and vice versa occurs constantly, it means that all fictional states, measurements, and circumstances have to already exist somewhere. Yeah, they gotta come from somewhere, right? They gotta exist, yet somehow, they can't be descriptive of real existence. How can something possibly exist and also not be descriptive of real existence? It is all possible due to *fictional existence*.

You know about fictional existence right? No?

See, there are two types of existence, fictional existence and real existence. Neither are descriptive of the other and they are consistently conducting transactions between one another by breaking the fourth wall.

You really didn't know about fictional existence? I wouldn't be too worried, although it's surprising. Wanna know why? Well, how are you with numbers? Let's say real existence is represented by the letter "R". R contains every state, measurement, and circumstance present in reality. Let us also say that fiction is represented by the letter "F". F contains every state, measurement, and circumstance which R does not contain. So to put that into an equation:

$F = \infty - R$

So, I said I was surprised because, proportionally speaking, fiction is *almost* infinitely bigger than reality. This is called the "Law of Proportions of Existence" and it is incredibly important for many reasons which I'm sure you probably already understand, being as smart as you seem. Oddly enough, this law is the reason why no one is perfect. See, if fiction is infinitely - well, *almost* infinitely - larger in size than reality, then the likelihood someone will attempt to advocate for a state, measurement, or circumstance from fiction, as reality, is almost infinite.

And of course, they will be wrong, because fiction is not descriptive of reality and vice versa yadda yadda you get it.

But enough about laws and fourth walls, you really wanna know some shit?

You wanna know what the *fifth* wall is.

sips beer

See, for starters, almost no living thing even knows about it. Makes sense - it's really far away from everything else, and it's deliberately difficult to get to for security reasons.

But I'll tell you anyways because there's no way they'll find out I told you. I'm off the clock.

I'll try to make it simple. The fifth wall could be defined as the very boundary that prevents fiction from mingling freely with reality.

Take your time.

Oh, right, people like mental images to help explain things, yeah? I'll give you one. So close your eyes a minute and imagine the following:

In a vast region of space there are a series of windows built into a wall of incomprehensible size which turns out to be a sphere - like a planet. A planet where the surface is made of dark, black drywall, and every three steps in any direction there are windows of different sizes and styles built directly into the drywall.

Behind every window is a different potential reality (which is just another way to say fiction). These windows let the fiction in and out. They are channels for safely breaking the fourth wall and facilitate each transaction from fiction to reality and vice versa. And that giant sphere of dark, black drywall? That's the fifth wall. All of these windows? Built into the fifth wall. From real far away you can see the light they reflect from off the surface of the sphere.

And you'll never know which light it is in the night sky.

Do not break the fifth wall, I'll have to deal with the mess.

Why? I work there, and just trust me it's a *real* pain in the ass.

CHAPTER 1 THINKING IN COLOR

It was around one in the afternoon on a Sunday. There was loud construction outside my apartment window. I fucking hate Sundays.

I live on the eighth floor of an apartment complex that used to belong to the University of Ohio and was what they used to call an "apartment style residence hall". It was condemned, and then not condemned, and then condemned again, and then not condemned again. That's when I moved in.

The diligent crew below, no doubt beleaguered by sweat and safety, continued blowing up the back parking lot to get to some such apparatus I know nothing about and have no sympathy for.

While attempting to reclaim my peace, pillow perched atop dome, a tinge of the dream I just had colored my thoughts. I remember being so lucid during the dream and understanding everything, but now I can't seem to form clear thoughts about it.

Something about fiction…? Partial images fade in and out, but they don't mean anything to me. Right then I was drooling on myself while trying to go back to sleep.

I woke up about thirty minutes later and didn't really have much else to do but lie there and stare at the wall. My goals for today: stay in bed until my back hurts, get up and think about showering, eat anything I can find, and stare mindlessly at the television until I either have to eat, piss, shit, or go back to sleep. What else are Sundays for? I would say that I felt sorry for animals other than human beings because they don't have a television, but they also don't have complex emotions and thought processes like humans do, and therefore do not feel the need to be entertained because they probably cannot have such a thought in the first place. Then again, what do I really know? I could have just made that up. Humans think animals are stupid because they don't have a written language or opposable thumbs (most of them don't) or cell phones and even if they did have cell phones, they couldn't use them because they don't have a written language or opposable thumbs (again, most of them don't). I can actually confirm the accuracy of this statement because I am: 1. A human, 2. I wouldn't have written it if I didn't have a laptop and opposable thumbs, and 3. Give a cat a fucking cell phone and see what it does with it. Perhaps stupid isn't the right word to describe how humans feel about the other animals, but we certainly feel like we are the highest form of life on the planet, and we can boss around all of the other species no problem. The human race may be one gigantic bio-bully, but this was just one thought in a sea of…well about three other thoughts and "What's on TV?" was about to be upgraded from a tropical storm to a hurricane. So the horrible time-wasting creativity-killer we know as television comes on and basic cable appears to be failing as usual. Nothing on but televangelists and obscure old bad movies that make me wish I remembered what channel the televangelists were on. Somehow this was actually depressing me further than I already was so I turned off the TV and laid down on the couch. My back was already killing me from sleeping for fourteen hours straight, so it looks like my first goal was accomplished. I scratched myself for about three minutes continuously and then got up to look in the fridge.

On my wonderful journey to the fridge, I started to notice my floor. The fibers were grotesque at their very best (thumbs up because I can do that). Everything started to look like it was disgusting garbage to me (I tend to ignore this, but the hangover was not kind to me today). Part of this I could contribute to my cat who sheds like she's making money doing it, but I realize the rest could be contributed to me not bothering to clean anything. The vacuum I have is terrible, merely providing a light breeze for the dirt, grime, and human skin particles that consisted of the majority of my carpet. The fact remained that I was fine with it, and continued to the fridge as if it were not an issue. The fridge light did not work. Well, it didn't work when I wanted it to. Every two months or so it would flicker on when I would put groceries into its yawning maw, but the light would cease shortly after as if the light were merely there to taunt me. It didn't matter anyways, there wasn't much food to shed light on today. I had about three slices of pizza left and I put those in the microwave to nuke them up to a decent temperature. I had always appreciated my microwave. The droning hum it provided was close to a major chord. There was no way for me to know this other than the fact that I am a music major in college, and a music composition major at that. This makes me a big nerd, and the only reason why I would bother to identify the noise my microwave was making. I liked to think that it was playing me a happy song while it was heating up my food, as if it were some ensemble of joyful birds from a children's movie. I always made certain to stop the microwave before its final inhuman beeps signifying that the timer was finished and my food was then way too hot to eat for another ten minutes. I save myself from this fate by stopping it one second short of the timer as if it were a bomb that was about to go off. The pizza was--imagine that--way too hot to eat (another thumbs up, because life is swell). I took the plate back to my couch-seat and sat there staring out the window at all of the glorious depression a Sunday afternoon had to offer. I wasn't very thrilled at the idea of going outside and even less thrilled at the idea that I had class tomorrow. What was a young man to do with his life? The pizza in his lap is too hot to put in his mouth and the sunshine pouring through the window all too taunting. I was never one to enjoy the outdoors. I hated mosquitoes with a passion and I'm nowhere near athletic because my heart is about ready to give out due to the copious amounts of soda I pour down my throat on a daily basis. Thinking of which, I forgot to get some while I was at the fridge! I stood up in the middle of my thought process and the damned pizza landed on my hairy feet with no warning. I watched it in slow motion like a child spilling milk or some other such disaster. My primal reactions immediately kicked in and I flailed my feet out from underneath me in a pissed off rage. I lost my balance and fell backwards. I hit my head on the coffee table and blacked out immediately.

I came to eventually while hearing a knock at my door. I had no idea what time it was, I just knew that the sun was still out at this point. It was beaming through my window. I had apparently been bleeding out of the back of my head because when I put my hand back there, there was a large wet scab. When I looked at my hand, it was stained with blood. The door was not my top priority, what time was it anyways?

"Hang on just a minute!" I yelled across the apartment, hoping whoever was at the door would just go away. My uncle came to mind. He told me a story of how a solicitor approached his door and saw him sitting at the kitchen table reading the newspaper. The solicitor knocked on the door so my uncle looked up from his paper at the solicitor, waved at him, and looked back down at his paper. The solicitor continued to knock on the door for another three minutes before walking away in frustration. In my current situation, however, the person knocking could not be a solicitor. The apartment complex has a large "NO SOLICITORS" sign above every entrance. I suppose it *could* be a solicitor, but he or she would have no right to be here, and I would let them know immediately. At this point, I wasn't too sure I was going to remain conscious much longer. I managed to stumble over to the door and looked through the grimy, minuscule peephole to see who it could possibly be. It was one of my best friends, Michael Alabaster, an American asshole of European descent with a sense of humor to rival any primetime writer. He had blazing red out-of-control hair and a beard that made him look much older than he really was (twenty). Of course all I could see through this damn peephole was a blob of flesh against the vomit green background of the walls in the apartment complex hallway.

"Who the fuck is it?" I said, trying to fuck with him.

"Just look through the fucking peephole Punxsutawney you fucking bastard," he said. Yes, my name is Punxsutawney. Punx for short, of course.

"I don't know you. State your name and business or I'm calling the cops," I said like a paranoid old white man. At this point, I unlocked the door and then locked it back before he could turn the handle. He was getting really pissed off and banged on the door very loudly. I was getting really dizzy at this point and decided it was a good idea to stop fucking around and possibly get him to take me to the hospital if things got any worse. I unlocked the door and let him in and he immediately punched me in the shoulder.

"Fuck you. I've been calling you for an hour." He said. I checked my phone and saw it was true: he had been calling me since five and was now six thirty.

"Sorry dude, I fell and hit my head. I passed out. I think I may need a doctor. I think I may need a doctor real bad," I said, trying to sound sincere.

"Look at the back of my head for me please." We walked into the light and he moved some of my hair around to try and see.

"Holy shit!" he said all of a sudden.

"Dude this looks like shit, are you okay?"

"No, I think I need to sit down for a while."

We walked into my living room and I got to take a look at the crime scene where I assaulted myself. My fucking cat was half-heartedly licking the pizza that was on the floor. The coffee table had been knocked over, and there was a moderately sized bloodstain on the carpet where I was.

"Ohhhhhhhh fuck dude, you must have hit that thing really hard. You need me to get you anything?" he said.

"Just some water for now. I just want to sit for a minute. Why did you call me thirteen times in one hour?" He started laughing at me, and brought my water over. Then he got this excited look on his face.

"Dude, I got it!" he exclaimed.

"Got what? What the fuck are you talking about?"

"Let me show you, hang on." He pulled out his wallet and then started digging around for something.

"I don't care that you bought condoms, Michael. Save them for your girlfriend."

"No you fucker, LOOK!" He brandished a small wad of what appeared to be aluminum foil.

"Is that…what I think it is?" I asked.

"Maybe." He smiled and walked over to my freezer and deposited the contents of the aluminum foil inside.

The last thing I remember was Michael showing me the folded foil. I apparently had passed out once again from the spill I took previously. When I came to, I was in a hospital bed. I had never been in the ER before due to my own injury, only for my friends or relatives. I was scared. Hospitals were places of death. After watching many shows based in hospitals, one comes to expect certain things about them that just aren't true. They are not glamorous places. The one I wound up in certainly wasn't flashy. The staff is bitter by and large, and none of them beautiful. Michael was there, he hadn't noticed that I'd come to yet, and I would like to keep it that way if I could. I was still scared, but I was scared AND angry. These two emotions coupled together make for a very confusing state of mind. He was texting or playing a game or something on his phone. Whatever, it wasn't important. I heard people out in the hallway speaking to each other. I couldn't understand what they were saying. My head was throbbing and I actually felt worse now than I did when I came to earlier. I wanted to vomit. As hard as I tried, I couldn't keep it back at all. I lurched forward and threw up all over the bed and myself. I started crying immediately. There was saliva and snot pouring out of my face. I looked down and realized that the contents of my stomach seemed to be pizza, even though I don't remember having any before yesterday, but it should have been digested by this point.

"Oh fuck! He's awake!" Michael said and leapt to his feet.

"Where am I?" I said knowing full well I was in a hospital.

"You're in a hospital, bud. You passed out shortly after I came over to your place. With that nasty injury and all, I took you to OSU Hospital even though you kept saying you would be okay."

"Jeez," was all I managed to say before I hit the bed again. It took all of my strength just to puke, and I was about to pass out again.

A doctor came over and started to check on me. I was so disoriented that I had no idea what he was doing, nor did I care. A couple of nurses came into the room as well to help clean up the mess I had just caused. I just wanted to go home again. I didn't ask for something like this to happen. No one ever asks for this to happen to him or her. The nurses left, but the doctor stayed and was scribbling on my chart. He looked really pissed off, just the opposite of what I had come to expect from television. He had a large quantity of unattended salt and pepper facial hair. I could only focus on him, and even then it was just for seconds at a time. Then my extreme disorientation would take over for a while. Things continued on this way until Michael finally broke the silence.

"Punx, they said you got a real bad concussion man. You should have made that bump on your head sound a bit more serious when I got to your place," said Michael. "They got you on some painkillers, but I didn't know if you were allergic to anything so I just told them to pump you full of their best stuff."

"I'm not allergic to anything. Did you say I kept asking you to NOT take me to the hospital?" I mumbled.

"Yeah bubsy. It was right after we went for that walk to Vermacelli's for some pizza. You were pissed that your cat ate yours. You kept stumbling and shit, but kept saying you were fine. I didn't give it another thought."

"Michael, I don't remember any of that shit. What the fuck time is it?"

Michael checked his phone. "Oh fuck I didn't even realize! It's six thirty AM on Monday morning, man. I've been here all night for you."

"Did you call my parents or my girlfriend?" I asked.

"No, I didn't even think about it until you just mentioned it. I thought we were going to be in and out of here. Been asleep since a few hours after we got here at seven almost twelve hours ago."

"Fuck you man. You should have gone through my phone."

It was at this point the doctor finally spoke to me. "You should be thanking this young man for bringing you here, he saved your life. You have a severe concussion that has rattled your brain quite hard. Memory loss is to be expected in the first 24 hours. You're lucky it hasn't been any more than that. For now, the only thing you need to be worried about is getting a lot of rest. We definitely need to keep you for the next 24 hours to see if any complications arise and perhaps a day or two after."

"Thank you doctor." I barely managed to say.

"You are welcome young man," and with that he disappeared out of the doorway and turned the corner.

"You don't look so good Punx. I'm glad I came over when I did. You may not have made it for long."

"Michael, where's my phone? I want to call my girlfriend and my parents," I said.

"Your phone is dead, I was going to tell you before the doctor started talking. I don't have your girlfriend's number in my phone."

"I don't have any of them memorized. Fuck technology," I mumbled. I felt like absolute shit mentally. The pain medication was working wonders, I was not in pain at all physically. I was, however, completely disoriented. I wanted to puke again, but didn't have the strength to do so. Everything was really blurry and soft, but I was seeing double. I felt like I had drank a handle of vodka and the only thing that happened was the double vision.

"Michael, I bet you have shit to do today. Just go home and get your shit finished and come back with my phone charger. Don't tell anyone that I'm in the hospital. Not even Victoria. I don't want her to worry about this until after I get a little better."

"Fuck school, I'm not going to class. You're more important. I will go back to your place and get a charger though. Everyone needs to know you're okay. Don't be a dumbass, I know that's difficult for you."

"I love you, Michael. Thanks."

Michael locked his phone and got up to leave. He walked past me and out the door in a similar manner to the doctor. I actually felt relief at this point in time. I'd been so tense for no reason other than the fact that I was in the hospital, but the doctor seemed confident. It looked like I would be getting back on track eventually and there was nothing to be done about it at the moment. I just breathed a sigh of relief and closed my eyes to try and sleep off the grandmother of all headaches.

I blame the drugs for the dream I had that morning. It started with me approaching a large blue truck that I had never seen before, but by the rules of the dream, I knew my family was in it, and they were. My dad was driving and was waiting to pick me up. My two sisters were in the truck as well. It had a back seat, and looked like a minivan on the inside even though there were clearly only two rows of seats looking from the outside. The interior of the car was absolutely covered in pink dolls and pink doll accessories as if a little girl had just exploded. Naturally by dream rules, these objects deserved no explanation, so I just hopped in and started riding along with my family. We wound up in what looked to be some small town in Italy or Spain (I know they're completely different, but come on, drugs people). There were people everywhere, but there were cars everywhere also. In fact, we were in dead standstill traffic. There was some commotion ahead of us, so I got out to see what it was. There were several pitch-black humanoids using super powers to freeze people, cars, and plants. I thought this was odd, but didn't really question it or feel any need to stop them or flee or, well, anything really. The dream then shifted to view a cartoon mayor being interrogated by the press about what was to be done about this crisis. He was clearly in distress because there were sweat drops launching from his forehead. He started to panic and turned away from the podium to scribble his thoughts down on a sheet of paper. An exclamation mark appeared above his head and he turned back around to show the press what he had come up with. The word "Cinnamon" was surrounded by a red explosion drawing that looked like it had come from a comic book. The next scene was from above looking down at the town showing dozens of planes carpet-bombing the city with cinnamon bombs to get rid of the freezing men. The men started to dissolve and all of the townspeople considered it to be a miracle. The traffic began to move again and we went along with it. The dream took a turn at this point, the focus of the dream shifted entirely. Perhaps I woke up and started a new dream, but I have no memory of it. Just darkness.

I started catching glimpses of two people. There was something important about them that I could not place my finger on. They were just flashes across my field of vision, but I saw them struggling against each other in almost hundreds of different time periods, most of which more futuristic than the one in which we reside. It was as if they were two eternally dueling forces choosing to manifest themselves physically as humans when they could have just as easily been anything else. One of them, a female, spoke to me without words. The closest translation was, "I could always think more clearly with one less bullet in my gun." The dream then cut to an unrealistic ritual, one that she apparently used to help her think more clearly and get answers to her problems. There were three beings involved. The two eternal dueling forces had a magnetic gyro wheel children's toy clenched tightly in their teeth. The third seemed to be mortal and was standing there willingly with his mouth wide open. The two eternal forces each had an additional item to the children's toy. The female force had a six-gun and was pointing it directly into the man's mouth about a foot away from him. The other force was a male and he had a vice grip in his hands, ready to pull something out of the man's mouth. I heard the woman say without speaking, "It had never not worked before, why not now?" The idea was to fire a bullet into the man's mouth. By the rules of the dream the magnetic gyro wheels would somehow prevent it from doing any damage to the mortal and then the bullet would be fished out of the man's mouth with the vice grip. The bullet would then have the solution to the problem at hand written on it. After seeing the setup of the ritual, I woke up repeating her thoughts in my head over and over again. I still do not understand the process to this day, and perhaps I never will. I did not recognize the man, and I felt sorry for him as if I was an audience member to his execution. The next thing I knew, there were people surrounding me. I was moving through a hallway on my back. The ceiling was passing by; the tiles and lights were unbridled blurs. There was something wrong with me. I was far more disoriented than ever before.

"Where am I…?" I managed to whisper. The doctor who saw me previously came down from above like a god. All of a sudden he was just there in my face trying to communicate with me. He started to speak, but I could barely hear or understand what he was saying. I managed to make out just a few words like "complication" and "surgery", neither of which were very reassuring at the time. I could only assume that I was the complication that needed surgery, and they were taking me into the OR. The last thing I heard before they anesthetized me was that same phrase from my dream, "It had never not worked before, why not now?" Only this time, it was the surgeon who said it, and she looked exactly like the eternal force from my dream. Her mouth didn't move when I heard it either. I was taken down hard by the anesthesia, and slept a deep sleep.

There was something amiss when I came to, something very amiss indeed. I was not in a hospital, or anywhere familiar. I wasn't even inside a building. I had been lying in the tall grass of a field. Each individual blade was a different color chosen from the standard set of colors: red, orange, yellow, green, blue, indigo, and violet. Additionally there were four more colors: black, white, gray, and brown. The wind was blowing and it was shaking everything around me. That is when I noticed the trees. These trees were so odd. The leaves at the top were all fashioned into a three-dimensional prism commonly found in geometry such as: spheres, cubes, pyramids, rectangles, and cylinders. Every tree had a leaf that reflected the two-dimensional base of the prism they were shaped into: the spherical trees had circular leaves, the cubical trees had square leaves, and the pyramid-shaped trees had triangular leaves. Jet-black one-dimensional branches, twigs, and trunks held all of these trees together, all barely visible against the multi-colored grass. The clouds were all shaped like something recognizable. I saw a train (which was actually quite magnificent and had the smoke stack spewing full steam), a game of chess (both sides were white so it was very disconcerting), and a baseball diamond (the game was getting called due to rain). I was further bewildered that I had yet to see another complex organism other than the plants anywhere around. There weren't any rodents, birds, or even bugs anywhere to be found. As far as I could tell there weren't any humans either. At least this way I figured there was no immediate danger. I was breathing oxygen, or so I thought. The gravity was very similar to Earth's, assuming I was on another planet. Then I noticed there were two suns and three moons in the sky. The suns were in a binary star formation, orbiting each other. One was an almost-white blue dwarf. The second closely resembled the sun I was used to seeing. Looking at the moons, one had its own asteroid belt, one looked to be covered in ice, and the last was in the process of falling apart. There were fragments of the third moon drifting around the largest piece of itself. After soaking in all of my surroundings and attempting to assess them, the first thing I thought should be done was to try flying as a test to see if this was real. I jumped up into the air and came right back down.

"Doesn't look like I'll be getting any flying done any time soon," I said to myself. At that moment, I realized that I was incredibly lucid, more so than I had been recently after sustaining that head injury. While this was an excellent discovery, the next problem I needed to sort out was whether or not I was going crazy, because there was certainly no place like this I had ever heard of. If I was in fact going crazy, that would be fine because then everything I was witnessing would be, well, normal by a crazy person's standards. If I hadn't lost my mind then I should really try to figure out where I was and how to get back home. I really started banking on the insanity theory, because it was starting to rain. And the way it did this was absolutely remarkable to me. I stopped and watched the show for what felt like hours.

The first thing I heard was thunder. This would have been a normal thing to hear during a normal rain shower. However, this wasn't a normal rain shower. A cloud shaped like a bass drum and a cloud shaped like a mallet were hovering just overhead. The mallet-cloud pulled back and beat the bass drum-cloud. A dense veil of rain started to pour out of the other side of the bass drum-cloud. The rain started covering everything it touched, and what it touched, it changed. Looking through the downpour, everything behind it was just white with a black outline as if it had been purged of its magnificent color. After noticing this, I got up and ran to look at the ground where the rain had fallen. All of the wet grass here was white with a black outline. The rain had bleached the color right out of the grass. I continued surveying the sky at this point. There were what appeared to be UFO-clouds racing each other, and instead of tractor beams, it was rain coming out of the bottom. This rain was having the same effect on its surroundings as that coming out of the bass drum-cloud. The clouds continued gathering near my location each one relinquishing water in a clever fashion: there were sponges wringing out, jets and cars leaving water trails, and buckets dumping their payload just to name a few. I looked off in the distance and there was a large cloud that was taking over the entire sky. It was an unbelievably enormous patchwork homemade quilt. It was producing no rain at this point, but it had almost completely covered the sky. In the distance I saw a rainbow form, and it faded from white to black as opposed to the standard color set. Befuddlement governed my perceptions. There was no explanation for what was happening; yet I didn't feel scared at all. I actually felt incredibly safe and I started to smile and then laugh uncontrollably as the quilt finally covered the sky. Everything around me was just completely preposterous. It was so preposterous that I had to express it.

"Everything around me is just completely preposterous," I expressed.

"Preposterous you say?!" A distant voice cut my euphoria in half. I had no idea where it was coming from, but it sounded very familiar.

"Up here child," sounded another familiar voice.

"Michael?" I yelled over the rain and bass drum-cloud thunder. I looked up just in time to see two characters sailing down from the sky through the rain and clouds. They were using umbrellas to glide gently to the ground. I knew these people. These people were my friends, but they were wearing completely absurd attire. One of them was clearly Michael, but he was dressed like an emperor. He had grown a two-foot beard and was wearing a crown covered in what appeared to be moon rocks. The other was my friend Winston Crenshaw. He was born in the UK and moved to the US when he was three. Somehow he managed to hold onto a slight Scottish accent. Winston was wearing a gentleman's tuxedo with dazzling cufflinks, a polished cane, spats for his shoes, and a black bowtie. His head boasted a monocle and top hat of unrealistic height. They were both being battered with the rain, and it was soaking away their color wherever the rain hit. Winston's tuxedo was now more white than black, and it was favoring a cow pattern.

"Dear boy, you're soaking *white*! Bwahahahaha! I could not resist such an excellent pun!" Winston pointed out. He was right: I had lost all of my color. I resembled a sketch on a napkin. After everything else that was going on, I didn't really pay much attention to this, and instead turned my attention towards how and why my friends just descended from the clouds.

"Winston, what are you doing here?! How is it you two are able to fly?! Where are we?!" I asked hurriedly.

"MY GOOD MAN, PLEASE CALM DOWN! One question at a time, please. Lovely weather we're having by the way. First of all, I am not certain who this Winston fellow is, but he sounds like a handsome devil if you mistook me for him! Ohohohohoho! Yes, quite handsome!" Winston said.

"Well if you don't think you're Winston then you must have lost it too!" I screamed over the rain.

"Introduce us Beedlebop, the boy is growing impatient with your jokes." Michael said to Winston.

"PLEASE DEAR BOY, REMAIN CALM! Allow me to introduce myself, er, ourselves, yes quite! I am Beedlebop, Connoisseur of the Preposterous, and this," Beedlebop then motioned to Michael, "is The Emperor of the Moon."

"Oh, well then. Which moon?" I asked mockingly.

"Every moon, dear child! I am certain you are fascinated by my title, but our time is brief," said the Emperor.

"ONE OF YOU! START MAKING SENSE OR I AM GOING TO REALLY LOSE IT!" I screamed.

"MY DEAR FELLOW, DO CALM DOWN, I WILL NOT ASK YOU AGAIN!" said Beedlebop. "You will have all of your answers shortly, but you must please present them in an orderly fashion! Now then dear boy, what is it you would like to make sense of?" The Connoisseur removed his monocle and polished it with a cloth.

"Okay, thank you. Now, where are we? What is this place called?" I implored.

"We are inside your very head mortal, we thought you knew that. Everyone knows that!" said the Emperor. He began laughing politely and started stroking his beard.

"So wait, what?" was all I could manage to say before the Connoisseur started in.

"What I believe our dear Emperor is trying to say," Beedlebop nodded towards the Emperor, "is that we are, if you will, a part of your very imagination. A sort of realistic branch combining your daydreams with creative ideas you have had throughout your lifetime. Now THAT is preposterous! I LOVE IT! OHOHOHOHOHO!" Beedlebop chortled.

"Okay well I'm almost willing to accept that." I said. "But does that mean I'm just asleep? What about my head injury?"

"This is something shrouded in mystery from the dawn of time," said the Emperor."

"The fucking dawn of time," I whispered to myself, exasperated. "So when was the dawn of time, Michael?!" I asked the ridiculous duo.

The Connoisseur was still examining his monocle lens. Without looking at me he checked his wristwatch and said, "Oh? Time began right around…when you woke up in the field a few feet that way," he motioned to his wristwatch with a white-gloved hand. The watch was a blank face with one arm slightly to the right of a picture of me in the field where 12 o' clock should be. I couldn't believe my eyes. This was completely unbelievable. "Fantastic watch isn't it? I picked it up just after the dawn of time. Isn't it just so…"

I cut him off with a raised hand, "Preposterous, yes. So this has to be just a dream, just…crazy drug and injury influenced dream. They say you can't feel pain in a dream," I said. I promptly pinched the shit out of myself. "FFFFFFFUCK! That hurts!" I was instantly disappointed. "Okay so this isn't a dream. I have no idea where we could possibly be."

"You should have listened to me the first time Sapien, we are inside your head," the Emperor said. Until now I hadn't realized but he was sitting on a throne that looked like it was made out of moon rock. It had craters, crags and valleys running all over it. He rose from his chair and glided over to me. "Dear mortal, you are doing what we call 'thinking in color', for lack of a better English term. It is not something many Sapiens are capable of, or can even comprehend in the first place. We've taken a special interest in you, boy. We want to make sure you use this talent…" he paused to looked at the rain, "…well."

"Okay I get it, I hit my head and now I have some special powers that no one else has. Is that it? Do I get to run around with an internal struggle like: 'why oh why can't I be normal'?" I asked sarcastically.

"Let me put it this way, dear Sapien: you will now be able to see things that others cannot. You have seen them all along, just as everyone has, but your mind will be able to interpret them differently now. Where your subconscious was but a faint whisper, it will now be a dull roar. The secrets to the universe will start to unfold before you one by one, and you will touch the lives of everyone who comes into contact with you. You created this world in which you are standing just as you have created the Connoisseur and myself. Do you now understand?"

Completely dumbfounded by the Emperor's speech, I merely stood there stammering. There was nothing I could say. What had happened to me? I worried about everyone back home and how this would work out. Would I be able to tell them? Who could possibly understand what ridiculousness I had just witnessed? I wanted to lie down and never think of anything ever again. I wished this had never happened to me, because I still didn't understand a thing. A few moments passed, and I started to notice that the rain was pooling in different areas around me. The Emperor addressed me once more.

"Dear boy, you are about to wake up. You have exhausted the amount in which you can think in color for the time being. The rain is taking away your creativity drop by drop. We're already becoming mere outlines against an outline forest against the outline horizon. Your subconscious hardly had enough time to create us to tell you about yourself and your transformation. Try to go back to sleep now. That is the only way you will awaken. Beedlebop!"

"My Emperor! Let us leave this place before we are completely erased! Excellent work, my boy! You will be seeing us later I have no doubt! Farewell!" And with that, their umbrellas took them back into the sky, above the clouds, above the white grass and the white trees, and above me. I laid face down in the grass and begged for sleep to overtake me. When it did not come I rolled onto my back and noticed an object falling from the sky directly above me. It was a piano, and I failed to avoid it colliding directly with me.

CHAPTER 2 THIS WHOLE EXISTING THING

I sat bolt upright in my hospital bed, and was immediately grateful to be somewhere I recognized. There were people in the room with me, but I didn't care in the least. I looked at my hands and slapped them. I ran my tongue along my teeth. I pinched myself. I slapped my face. I tried to burp. It was me again. Well, it was me again in context of being a human on Earth in the Milky Way. There were people tugging on me and trying to get my attention, and I still did not care. I waved my hands in front of my face. I was alive. I still had my hands, and my feet. I bet I could even walk if I stood up. There were bandages on my head, but I bet I would heal too. I had something many people didn't have. The most important of these is time. Even as I had multiple familiar faces trying to speak to me, the only thing I could think about was myself. I was fine with that, and they needed to be fine with it too. I still had time and they did too, so why spend it on me? My eyesight was bad; I didn't have my glasses on and had no idea where they were. I looked at everyone and asked them an obvious question just to get a rise out of them: "What are you guys doing here?"

Michael was the first person I noticed. He was no longer the Emperor of the Moon. He bore no crown. His beard was no longer of regal length. He was just eccentric Michael. The way I remembered, they way I liked. I missed him. Both of my parents were there too, which was a shock. My parents had been divorced since I was nine. I suppose after almost twelve years of not being with each other they could stand to be around each other long enough to make certain their only son was okay. Winston was here too, and he was looking quite different from his doppelganger, the Connoisseur of the Preposterous. Everyone seemed glad to see me, and I was very glad to see them after I had finally established this was real life. My mom finally rushed me and gave me a hug. I couldn't ignore everyone any longer.

"My baby boy I'm so glad you're okay!" my mom sobbed loudly into my ear. She was shorter than me. Everyone in my family was shorter than me. I'm not a giant, I only stand at 6' 3" but I still look down on my family's heads. I loved my mom. Hell, I even kind of liked her, but I used to hate her. I would like to think everyone in America goes through a parent-hating phase during their teenage years. I sure as hell did. My mother is a Christian. She does go to church, and I assume she reads her Bible, but ultimately I feel it does no good in furthering her as a person. But I don't know a thing about her individual experience. This is all speculation. However, I view her as the product of a religion that has been, shall we say, unkind. Regardless of our differences we manage to get along quite well now, and I am very thankful for this.

"Mom please! I'm still plugged up to these machines! Be careful!" I said.

"I'm so glad you're okay! The doctors thought you would never wake up!"

"One thing at a time please mom. After all, the doctors thought I would never wake up."

"You smart ass!" She was still crying and hadn't let go of me. She wanted to rock me from side to side, but I prevented that from happening. I was already wary of all of the tubes and cords coming off of my body, I didn't want the IV to come out or to knock something over.

"I love you mom, but I will die if you don't let go of me," I warned. I knew she would back off if I said I was going to die. Here is an excellent example of something I've picked up during my short time living: how to be manipulative. I'm not evil, I just know how to get people to do things that I would like for them to do occasionally. As far as I can remember I've never done this to hurt anyone. There would be enough time for hugs later, anyway. For now, I just wanted to get out of this damn hospital and re-establish my failure of a life (a weak thumbs up, because I can). She sat back down and continued to cry to herself while looking at me.

"We were worried about you bubs. Glad you're back," said Michael.

"Glad to be back bubsy," I said. I took another look at Michael at this point. Why did my subconscious piece him together the way it did in my head? There wasn't really anything regal about him. He was practically insane. One time I asked him "Do you ever think you're going insane?" and his response was just a very slow maniacal laugh. He didn't even say anything to me, just laughed. He was also driving at the time and I was in the passenger's seat. I wasn't worried though, that was just his style. Hell, it was my style too. Perhaps we were both insane. He would certainly think I am after I get to tell him what I saw while I was knocked out. This was the difference between thinking in color and dreaming, I suppose: I remembered everything that happened to me as if it happened in real life just a few minutes ago. I remembered it better than I remembered most of my days.

No one else was saying anything. I could just tell they were thankful that I was still around. I started contemplating all the reasons why someone would be sad if someone they were close to died. I suppose it is more difficult to examine such an occurrence when you are the person dying and you have to think about why everyone else is sad that you're not going to exist in your human form any longer. I've always heard people say that committing suicide is the most selfish thing someone can do. Suicide is a personal thing, and while it is a terrible tragedy when it occurs, it damn sure isn't selfish. Typically suicide occurs when the individual is not happy with their surroundings, and most often their relationships with other people. Sure the individual will take their own life, but there could have been a few steps taken along the way by others to prevent it. The world's view of suicide is far too narrow as well. By suicide's own definition, which is "the intentional taking of one's own life", a larger portion of deaths on the planet are suicide than we care to think of. Here are a few examples: smokers with lung cancer, obese people with any fatal obesity related disorder, and drinkers with liver failure. Nobody else made these choices for the individual. Great measures are taken to warn people of the risks associated with these lifestyles. The list goes on and on. Arguably I could suggest all victims of transportation-related accidents are suicidal too because they took the risk to drive or ride in the first place, but I won't go that far. My injury could have even been called suicide had I died under the circumstances, but only by me. This is just my opinion, and I'm aware it isn't the popular one, but I digress.

My father had gotten up to go get a nurse or doctor to come look at me, I assumed. He got up and left the room shortly after I woke up. My dad was a great man. I had my quarrels with him when I was younger as well, but they weren't as heated as those between my mother and I. When my parents got divorced we lived in a small town in the south of Tennessee a few miles away from the Alabama border. I don't know what the final straw was, but I remember riding in the car with my mother on the way to Nashville from Pulaski. She was arguing with my father on her cell phone. She closed it suddenly and said to no one in particular "We're getting a divorce." I started crying, and that is where the memory ends. I was so young when they were having problems, I don't really know why they didn't get along. They argued quite a bit. There are very few things I can remember from their relationship together, but I know what she says about my father is not entirely true, just as my dad has his own versions of stories. I have always asked both of my parents on separate occasions about their relationship, and I can only somewhat piece together what the truth is. Now, I am a far better judge of character. Both of my parents have their faults. Every human being has their faults, at least by other human beings' standards. I have my faults, and I love both of my parents equally and like them just the same.

In context of this whole existing thing, what relevance does my parent's relationship have regarding anything? The influence it has on me is obvious. The influence it has on my parents is obvious. As I look at other people though, it doesn't matter too much. Perhaps close family has been influenced in some small way, but my friends certainly haven't. People who haven't met my parents certainly haven't, and that is the vast majority of the world. If this is the case, why have I assigned so much importance to it? I'll never understand why humans are so obsessed with being humans and what their social status is. This far in my life I've only really been concerned with surviving and being entertained from time to time. I have no enemies that I know of. I'm sure I have people who don't like me, everyone does, but I don't care. The best way to control any other person's emotions is to greet them with apathy, unless they are trying to kill you at which point I suggest running. It is so simple to avoid conflict with other people, and yet it seems to happen way too frequently. At the risk of sounding like a hippie, I'm surprised we all can't get along.

My father came back into the room with the doctor who saw me previously. I wasn't really glad to see him, but I wasn't disappointed either.

"Hello young man, good to see you awake finally," the doctor said.

"Finally? How long was I out for?" I mumbled.

"Oh I meant nothing by it. It has only been about a day since the surgery."

"What was wrong with me?"

"You were growing steadily more disoriented and we decided to run some tests. There was blood pooling around that area where your wound was, and it was causing clots and pressure on your skull. We tried to act before there was any brain damage, and I believe we were successful. You have complete function of your eyes, yes?" The doctor looked at me like I was supposed to do a trick.

"Well I suppose I do," I said. I moved my eyes around a bit to show him.

"Excellent! Well we expect you to be able to go home tomorrow. Rest up for now. A nurse will be in later to check on you."

"Thank you doctor," I said. He nodded and walked out of the room. I could hear my mom start crying a little harder now that the doctor was gone. I found myself wanting to comfort her, but I didn't say anything. My method of comfort usually involves logic, which people don't really want to hear when something has made them very angry or very sad. I suppose I could tell her that I'm okay and that she shouldn't worry any longer, but her mind is probably firing of thousands of thoughts a second, and she won't be able to process all of them for now. She will calm down in time.

I was very hungry and really wanted a kickass cheeseburger, but that was probably out of the question. I imagined either my father or my mother would take me out to dinner once I got well enough to leave. Then I could eat whatever I wanted, most likely. I hoped this hospital visit wouldn't be expensive. My parents would probably wind up paying for it anyways. I didn't want them to, but I wasn't exactly in a position to pay for it myself. It made me think about what I would do for my child if I ever had one. Both of my parents have expressed that they love me unconditionally. I turned and looked at everyone and noticed my girlfriend wasn't there which I found odd.

"Where is Victoria?" I asked to no one in particular.

"She went to the cafeteria, Punx. Do you think she wouldn't be here?" said Winston. He had remained silent until now. I really liked Winston. There was no one like him that I could ever possibly think of. I've seen so many people and thought, "That person is so generic in their looks and mannerisms. They could just as easily replace any of thousands of others who do the same things and live the same way they do." At the University of Ohio, there is a plethora of these people. The only thing I can think on my way to class is how much all of these other students look and act the same to me. I understand that I do not know each individual on a personal basis. It may sound like I am forcing them into a box, but they're already inside the box, and they couldn't get out to save their poor generic lives. Winston is one of a kind. I have not been exposed to another human through real life, television, movies, or Internet who looks or thinks like he does. His mannerisms, his style, the way he carries himself, they're all so unique, so different from everyone else. He is genuinely one-of-a-kind.

"Winston, you silly bastard. You were in my dream I just had."

"Oh, do tell," he said. He crossed his legs and batted his eyes.

"You were dressed up like a proper gentleman for once. You had on a tux with the works. You had a top hat, a monocle, cufflinks and spats, dude. Fucking spats," I assured him.

"Sounds like a handsome devil to say the least!" he assured me, and he laughed. His words reminded me of the Connoisseur's. I shuddered a little bit at the coincidence. This always happens to me when something makes too much sense to be possible, and I love it.

"You and Michael were two real characters. He was the Emperor of the Moon. Go ahead and ask me which moon."

"All of them, bubs. For sure," Michael chimed in. I pointed at him with my hand shaped like a gun, closed one eye, and fired.

"You got it bubsy."

"You sound like you had a pretty sweet dream there Punx," said Michael.

"I'll be sure to tell you all about it later. It was more than a dream. I feel like it had significance. Something is different about me."

"You could have had some brain damage, so I can't decide if it is that or the drugs talking," taunted Michael. "I already asked, but they wouldn't give me any of the stuff they gave you."

"Really? They gave me some. I'm on it right now," said Winston. He promptly waved his arms around in the air like noodles and started making noises.

"Wooooooo loooooooo looooooo!" Winston said, because apparently that's what people sound like while under the influence of painkillers.

"So that's what I sound like to you lot then? Woo loo loo? I probably couldn't lift my arms above my head if I tried." I sounded like shit. I barely used my voice because I felt like if I got excited, I would just black out again.

It always intrigued me that when one speaks, one hears their own voice differently than everyone else around them. This is due to the fact that his or her ears are receiving the majority of the sound waves from the inside of their head. I can't count the number of times I've heard someone say "THAT'S what I sound like?!" after hearing a recording of his or her own voice played back. I used to be the same way. Hell I'm still getting over it, and I'm a singer. It used to be that I refused to sing songs I had written in front of anyone. Singing in the car however was no big deal. That wasn't my song on the radio, and it certainly wasn't my voice. I love singing in the car. There's just something incredible about going fast down a dark interstate coupled with the intensity of a song that really gets in your chest. It makes you think things you would have never thought before, like some sort of creative catalyst that only appears during rare times. Sometimes you feel things you have never felt before, and believe things that aren't true or possible. I've imagined my car leaving the ground and coasting through the sky. I've believed it would happen before on a few separate occasions, but it never did. Feeling is superior to believing, and thinking is superior to both of them. At least I've had the opportunity to feel something that isn't possible, and this isn't the only example. My imagination has always been overactive, but that is a bit of an understatement. Perhaps these people wouldn't consider me crazy if I told them about my dream. Perhaps they would. I decided I would tell at least Winston and Michael eventually. Up until this point, I had only jokingly mentioned what had been one of the most fantastic and horrifying experiences of my life. They would find out about everything eventually. I didn't want to tell them in my current circumstances anyways, they certainly wouldn't believe me.

Everyone had gotten silent after laughing at my previous comment. It was that special flavor of awkward silence that hangs in the air after a group of people laughs together but then has nothing interesting or particularly relevant to follow up with. Everyone was just sitting around waiting for me to get better. My mind was racing with thoughts that I couldn't actively piece together into something comprehensible. I kept thinking about these people sitting around me and why I was so special as to draw them together to be by my side. I kept trying to make sense of myself. What was I trying to tell myself while I was out cold? I wondered if it would happen again. The Emperor had called it "thinking in color", and I couldn't think of any better way to put it. Had I not woken up in this hospital bed, there would have been no way for me to know that what I saw didn't actually occur. I was relieved to once again be conscious, and I was thankful that I was still alive. Nobody had said anything for a while. I had my eyes closed for a moment while I tried to slow my thoughts. I was getting hungry. I opened my eyes.

"Hey mom could I get some food?" I asked. I looked over at my mom slowly. She wasn't there. No one was there. Everyone had left.

"What the fuck?" I asked my mom who wasn't there, as if it were her fault. I couldn't see anyone from my bed. My parents and friends were nowhere to be found. I really wanted to get up and find them, I thought it was a joke. I found the call button for the nurse and pressed it. I waited a few minutes and no one came. I pressed it again and waited. Nothing.

"NURSE!!!" I yelled out the door. No one was answering. No one was there. I started getting really worried. I started pulling diodes off of me and didn't dare to take out the IV, so I just took the stand with me when I got out of bed. I shuffled over to the door of my room and looked out in the hallway. There was no one there. I walked around for a few minutes and finally realized that there was no one in the entire hospital.

"Okay, fantastic I seem to be the only one left in the building." I said out loud to no one in particular. This was obviously another illusion brought about by a combination of painkillers and my head injury. At least I was able to differentiate between real life and this "thinking in color" business, or so I reasoned. I started walking around the hospital a bit longer. I seemed to be confined to the floor I was on, because I had no idea what the rest of the hospital looked like in real life. I suppose by this logic I could just imagine what the rest of the hospital looked like and then I could go anywhere I wanted. I promptly attempted this and got on the elevator. The hospital now had 500 floors and I could pick what was on any of them. I chose floor 372. The elevator rose up and up. I couldn't wait to see the arcade I had just come up with. The elevator stopped short, however. Floor 292. The doors opened and The Connoisseur of the Preposterous got on. He looked like shit. His clothes were torn and his shoes were scuffed. His monocle had a crack in it. He looked very upset.

"Beedlebop is that you?" I asked the Connoisseur. He heaved inside the elevator and fell back against the wall. His breath was very heavy. His words were strained. "This wasn't supposed to happen dear boy. It is far too soon, I'm afraid," he paused to cough.

"We're going to have to take action to prevent you from accessing this part of your brain for some time. You know it is raining outside? You remember the rain from the Geometric Forest I trust? We took a great risk visiting you then, just as I am now. You're in great danger dear boy, just as I am in great danger coming to you here. You have got to wake up again. You have to do it now," he then pressed floor 305 which was the next floor we would pass.

"Beedlebop, I don't understand. What is going on?" I asked. He was panting heavily by this point.

"You're not ready for this. I told the Emperor you weren't ready for this but he sent me anyways. I can't explain anything now dear boy, you have to wake up." He was continuously looking at me and then at the walls of the elevator and then at his wristwatch. He seemed very distressed.

"You keep telling me to wake up. I don't know how to do that. I don't know what is going on and I don't know what you mean," I said.

"There is no time to explain. I'm sorry dear boy," said the Connoisseur. He looked very concerned and not at all calm or friendly like he did previously. He promptly pushed me out of the elevator doors as soon as they opened.

"Just do it the way you did it last time dear boy! Wake up the same way!" said the Connoisseur. And with that he held the door close button down and was gone. I had to wake up apparently. Just when I thought things were going right, I was completely mistaken. The floor I was on consisted of just one room. It was my bedroom at my mom's house. The curtains were drawn, but I could hear the rain and thunder outside. I walked over to the window, drew back the dark curtains, and looked outside. I was on what appeared to be the 305th floor of a skyscraper in the middle of a large city. The rain was so intense that everything was white with a black outline, and it was starting to flood. I moved back from the window and walked over to my bed. I got under the blankets and tried to go to sleep. That's what I did last time to snap out of thinking in color, why wouldn't it work now? The rain and thunder was so loud, I had never been through such an intense storm before. I was having difficulty sleeping with all the noise. I tried for what felt like hours.

All of a sudden, something broke through the window across from me and landed on the floor. It was a small old piano keyboard. I suddenly remembered how I stopped it all last time and I knew what I had to do. I got out of bed and looked out the broken window. Everything was beginning to be consumed by the color-purging rain. I knew what I had to do in this moment. I jumped out of the window and turned in midair to look above me. A grand piano was falling from the sky faster than I was. I caught it and hugged it with my entire body on the way to the ground. I then realized too late that I had made a mistake, and would not be hitting the ground, but the flooding white water below that had claimed all of the color from this city. The piano crushed me between itself and the water and knocked all of the air out of my chest. I couldn't breathe at all. I opened my eyes under the water and saw something that I did not expect. Everything underwater had all of its color as if it had never been touched. I started writhing around the piano to try and make it to the surface and catch my breath. I managed to move it out of the way and breach the surface of the flood. The rain was still coming down really hard. I was horrified. I had always been afraid of open water ever since I was a child. I remember even being terrified of playing video games where my character had to swim in the ocean or to the bottom of a lake. The flood was pushing me to the right side of the building I just jumped from. I couldn't believe hitting the water didn't wake me. There had to have been something wrong just like the Connoisseur had said. I closed my eyes and tried to drown myself, but realized I could actually breathe underwater at this point. It was as if I didn't want to let myself wake up. I closed my eyes tightly and concentrated hard. All of a sudden I heard a large splash over the thunder and rain. I looked up just in time to see my handiwork before I was taken out by an upright player piano. There were possibly hundreds of pianos of all kinds falling from the sky, plunging into the water and destroying buildings. I was amazed for a split second before the player piano caught me on the crown of the head.

The blow brought me back to reality in a similar fashion to how it did before. I sat up immediately and looked at my hands. I made sure that I was aware of my functions and cognitive abilities. I looked around to see if everyone was still there. They were. My girlfriend Victoria was there too. We met in college and had been dating since November of freshman year. Our first kiss was the first time I ever got drunk. It was Halloween night. I had a lame costume on. It was supposed to be "late for work". I was wearing a button-up shirt with a tie half-tied around my neck. There was a little shaving cream on my face, and I had my right pant leg tucked into my sock. I really didn't want to buy a costume, and I already had these things so I figured, why not? Random acquaintances were giving me mixed drinks that they had concealed in large-sized fast food cups. We gathered at this particular spot on campus dubbed "the grate". Why "the grate" you may wonder? There was a large vent about 6 by 6 feet in the ground that was an exhaust path for the steam plant. A large steel grate covered it. Stoners, drinkers, frat douche bags, tripping kids (what we called people on LSD, mushrooms, or ecstasy), and sorostitutes (really shitty stupid sorority girls who think they're wonderful) would flock to this place late at night, particularly during the winter months because the steam coming out was about hot enough to give you blisters on any given summer day. Now back then I didn't mind the stoners, the tripping kids, and sometimes even the drinkers, but the random frat assholes and sorostitutes that would show up always pissed me off. They were usually drunk, very loud, remarkably uninteresting, incredibly confrontational, and just overall worthless. Despite how much I detested them, these types of people made up the majority of the population of the great University of Ohio, and I couldn't get away from them. Other people like me (not detestably generic) found their way to this little group of people we called The Night Owls. It was a group of people who (unjustifiably) terrified the majority of the generic mass, and those who either hadn't heard of us or were too drunk to be intimidated by a bunch of weird people smoking hookah would typically have their faces bit off after they got too close. There were only about five or six people considered the very core of the club, but there were upwards of thirty others who would visit once or twice a week. I don't really smoke hookah very much any more, but this was a very important part of my life, so it is worth bringing up. We thought we were the coolest. Our little group broke all the rules, and we felt invincible. The psychedelics and the drinking really didn't help our egos, and some of us took it too far, like me. I wound up tripping thirteen times during about a fifteen-week period. I never noticed at what point, but it permanently altered my sight. Recently it has been affecting me much more noticeably, and it is becoming unsettling. It is like my sight is governing what my mind thinks. Sometimes I can't concentrate and my body starts to feel like I don't own it and I shouldn't. Doing something as simple as scratching my arm makes me feel like I'm going crazy for absolutely no reason. I know this new head injury isn't going to do me any good and will probably go hand in hand with my already pseudo-insanity. Perhaps even these incredible delusions I call 'thinking in color' are just another sign of me going crazy. Perhaps one day I'll wake up and will just be inside my head for the rest of my life not knowing how to differentiate between what is real and what is imagination. I won't be able to contemplate why the people sitting next to my hospital bed would willingly give up their time to watch over me. I won't even be able to contemplate what going to work or class would be like.

I don't want to end up like this. I have always had a fascination with insanity and sometimes secretly wished I was for incredibly selfish reasons. The insane, while they are subjected to many types of medication and experimental procedures, are also freed of all responsibility from society. I wonder under what capacities I would be able to function under in a mental health institution. Would they let me have a guitar? A keyboard? A sheet of paper and a pencil? I would be able to sit and create all day, the one thing I've never been able to do even though I want to so desperately. I am constantly going on and on about creative projects I have in the works only to find that I haven't really gotten that far with anything that I'm talking about. And instead of driving to work more or harder on the project, I hide from it in hopes that it will either finish itself or dissolve into nothing as long as I can ignore it.

I've heard the phrase "context is everything" tossed around now and then, and I agree. Everything in our past and present shape us whether or not we have an active or subconscious grasp on it. Music is a prime example of this statement. Think about a single pitch sounding against a background of silence. Is this music? Is this a song? No, just a note. Play the next pitch and we have the beginnings of an idea. A few more and the idea is complete. Then there's a verse. Then another. Then a complete song. That first note that is played still has influence on the last note and helps to put it into context. Each note in the song pulls on every note that comes after it just like gravity affects every atom. Everyone's life is the same way. I still haven't decided if the context I'm in currently is good or bad quality. I think I'm dying, and it's my fault. Suicide, if you will, by my previous definition. I'd like to add something else to this interesting phrase that I came up with myself (I seem to regurgitate anything intriguing I hear, so this is special to me). Everything is tension and release. Yes, at first it sounds like I'm perpetuating the cheesy music metaphor, however let us look at any number of other examples that reflect this very statement. Think about life, even. We have tension and release throughout our day every day. Here is a list of actions representing tension: waking up, eating, driving, and working. To complete this thought I give you the list of actions representing release: shitting, killing the ignition to the car, getting off of work, and sleeping. Even on a less human level, to be a human being itself is pure tension and our tired molecules seek out the inevitable release of death eventually whether the mind wants it or not. Even the universe displays this idea, or at the very least our solar system does. The sun is just a huge bright ball of tension arbitrarily placed in a universe that couldn't have cared less, save for Earth. Eventually the day will come when the star will collapse into a black hole, or explode. Both of these represent release. There's no tension in a black hole. Everything is captured, there is no resistance. It just isn't possible to stand up to something that powerful. There are black holes that surround me. Maybe I'm just a black hole. I'm all release, and I can't stand the tension long enough to get anything done and find a sweeter release. I've been plagued by laziness ever since I was a child. I don't know if I can blame it on my upbringing or not. It could very well be transferred by genetics. My entire family is lazy. Sure we go to work and school, but none of us exercise and no one in my immediate family (save for myself on occasion) is creative or productive in their spare time. Maybe I'll actually explore life now. Maybe I'll actually live up to what I've always thought I could live up to.

"Hey sleepy head!" said Victoria. She was smiling and sitting on the bed next to me. "Hey lady, where have you been all my life?" I mumbled to her. She looked really happy to see me. I had forgotten until now that I hadn't seen her in a couple of days. She had a very pretty face. I loved her for being here, but I also loved her before this as well. We had been dating now for two years. The Night Owls were long behind us. We had calmed down significantly and taken to focusing more on school rather than getting fucked up.

"You feeling okay?" she asked.

"What do you think Vic?" I actually felt a lot better, but I was in a hospital bed, so I thought I'd milk this.

"The doctor says you're fine, jackass. He said you could leave whenever you woke up."

"Oh did he now?" I was actually pretty excited to hear this because the only thing I wanted to do was just fucking go home. I was excited for this, like I had just been born again. I have been under the impression now for a while that going to sleep is like dying and waking up is like being born again. Well I've been dead on and off now for a couple of days. I was getting really tired of lying down. Victoria called in a nurse to see if it would be okay for me to leave. They came in and disconnected me from all the machines and the IV. They brought in a wheel chair for me and I got out of bed and got dressed because it was time to go. My family and friends all got their items together and stood up when I did. I walked into the bathroom and looked in the mirror. Part of my altered sight includes the ability to see things in great detail, and this bathroom was filled with it. It was incredibly dirty and very bright. There where what appeared to be crumbs all over the floor, and the mirror was streaked with hand and finger prints. I didn't want to spend much time looking in the mirror at this point.

I usually love looking at myself in the mirror. I'm a closet narcissist. I'm not the most attractive human, but I'd like to think I'm at least an eight, perhaps an eight and a half on a ten-point scale. I'd been gaining weight. I used to weigh 140 for my height, which was 40 pounds underweight for my height. Then I got a desk job, only ate Taco Bueno, and drank beer for a summer and expanded like a hot air balloon. Now I'm about 185, which is considered a healthy weight for my height, but I wish I was still small. I had stretch marks all over my legs. They were purple and I convinced myself that they itched. All of these things were compounding to equal a changing me. I didn't like it. I put on my clothes and ignored my shaved head, a decision I very much regretted. I walked out of the door and sat down in the wheelchair. My mom pushed me out of the room and to the elevator. I was leaving. I was still alive. I still had function of all of my limbs, my fingers and toes, and my brain. I was at that moment the most fortunate patient in the hospital: I was the one leaving to go home.

CHAPTER 3 THE KING OF THE CUBICLE

I made everyone stop by Wendell's on my way home. I really wanted some borderline disgusting fast food. Fast food establishments were really staring to intrigue me recently. I sat and pondered what the majority of consumerism consisted of, and I concluded the answer to be food. I may be incorrect, but it is my perception that the majority of public service buildings serve food in some form or fashion. This has come about by the human race's need to eat massive amounts of food. I delved deeper into this thought. Why do humans need food? We are biological systems that require energy in order to continue to function. The Agricultural Revolution sparked the very dawn of civilization as we know it. After we developed markets, not every human needed to hunt or grow their own food. We eventually developed a bartering system and with the evolution of this system and other technologies, we now have the ability to eat a wide number of things almost as soon as we want them available to us. Instant gratification is the American way. My hankering for food and instant gratification has led me to crave a huge burger with two patties, cheese, bacon, and ketchup (SO YUMMY). Victoria pulled us into the drive thru and we pulled in behind a large SUV.

"Fucking rich assholes and their cars. I'll never understand why people would ever buy a vehicle that is so impractical." I commented.

"They have more money than you, Punx," said Victoria.

"I suppose so, sweetie. That doesn't give them the right to pilot one of those monstrosities," I insisted.

"You're correct, but it does give them the ability."

She rolled the window down so we could give our order. I could hear the woman in the SUV ordering. She was shouting at the attendant taking her order.

"NO! A small drink, didn't you hear me the first time?"

"So that is a small soda with—"

"NO! A small DIET SODA! DIET! You would think you could take simple instructions, this is all you do for crying out loud!"

"My apologies ma'am, a small diet soda with the number one combo, no ketchup. Anything else for you today?"

"I suppose that will be all. Make sure it is correct for me by the time I get up there. I'm in a hurry!"

"That will be $5.26 ma'am. Please pull around to the second window."

The woman didn't even say thank you and shot around the corner as fast as she could.

"I hope she gets into a car accident or chokes on her fries," I said. I really meant it. I had seen and heard things like this so many times. I worked in customer service and had dealt with many upset, incorrect, and flat out rude customers. I was really upset at this woman ahead of us. We pulled up to the box and waited for the attendant to give her intro.

"Thank you for choosing Wendell's, may I take your order?"

"Yes ma'am, could I have two medium number fours with soda to drink with those?"

"That was two number fours with soda to drink, anything else?"

"No ma'am that will be all."

"Thank you that will be $10.37 please pull around."

"Thank you ma'am."

We pulled around behind the SUV and waited for the food. It was taking them a few minutes to get the food to her. We sat and waited until the sliding door opened and they handed her the drink and her bag of food. The SUV sat there for a minute. The sliding door opened and the attendant looked out. I watched the drink sail back into the restaurant from the SUV. The woman stuck her hand out the window and flipped her the bird.

"I SAID DIET!!!" she screamed and punched the acceleration. She turned right out of the lot and ran the red light immediately afterwards. A car, which had the right of way, t-boned the side of her SUV. I started laughing immediately because everyone within the block had witnessed this horrible woman peel out of the drive thru, and I had only just wished that she would have a wreck.

"BAHAHAHAHAHAHAHAHAHAHAHAHAHAHA!" I was laughing uncontrollably. I looked over at Victoria and she was doing the same thing. Sweet, sweet justice just took place before my very eyes. I could not have been more cheered up after leaving the hospital. I sat there in the drive thru wiping tears from my eyes. The enraged woman got out of her SUV and stomped over to the driver of the other car. She started screaming incoherently and pounded on the tinted windows. The events that occurred next were better than I could have possibly hoped. The door opened to the small red car that hit the SUV. This was right in the middle of the woman pounding on the window. The door was opened with such force that it flung the woman back onto the pavement. She made a noise that I could not ever replicate with anything in the human alphabet. It resembled the sound of someone simultaneously falling off of a cliff unexpectedly and the sound that is made when someone is taking a huge shit. A large muscular black gentleman stepped out of the car. He was dressed in a tuxedo with spats and a top hat. It was at this point Victoria pulled forward to the window so we could pay for our meal. I now found myself in a situation where my attention was divided between two things: paying for our meal, and the car accident. While on the one hand, the only thing I wanted to do was watch the car accident, I had to pay for the meal. The sliding window opened and the attendant stuck her head out.

"$10.37 please," she said.

"Can you believe what happened to that bitch?!" I asked the attendant.

"You mean the woman in front of you? She threw her drink at me! It was a diet like she asked, but she still threw it back at me!"

"Look over there!" I said. The attendant looked over at the scene of the accident. The man had walked over to where the woman was on the ground. The attendant started laughing. The man started yelling at her.

"Stupid white bitch! You ran the fucking light!"

The stupid white bitch was in a slight daze. She sat on the ground while the man stood over her. I really wanted him to let her have it, but I knew it wouldn't happen. I was almost positive it wouldn't. Then she got up and ran at him. I had no sympathy for her. The guy didn't either, and I didn't blame him.

"FUCK YOU I HOPE YOU DIE!!!" she screamed at the top of her lungs and charged at him. This was a big mistake, but she had made so many at this point, I really don't think she cared. She started trying to punch him and pounded on his chest. I started laughing again and pulled out my debit card. I passed it to Victoria, who gave it to the attendant. The attendant was still laughing so hard, I think she was crying. She swiped the card and handed me the card and the receipt.

"Serves her right doesn't it?" I asked the attendant.

"This has made my month. We get so many fuckers like her through here, being a college town and all. She seems grown though, maybe she just snapped. Either way, it serves her right," the attendant said.

"Punx look!" Victoria said. I looked back at the wreck scene. The woman was still trying to fight the man from the other car. My hero. I quickly took out a scrap of paper and a pencil. I wrote down my number. The attendant handed us our food.

"Thanks you guys, come again," the attendant said.

"Trust me, we will," I said. Victoria started to pull off.

"Vic, stop for just a minute. I want to give this guy my number in case he needs a witness for the wreck."

"Okay hurry back. I'm hungry."

"Me too Vic, me too." I grunted. I jumped out of the car and walked over to the man. He was holding off the small woman as best as he could, which was quite easily if I may add. She was swinging her arms wildly at him. He was holding her forehead with the palm of his hand and she couldn't get anywhere near him. I approached with caution.

"Excuse me sir, I saw the whole incident. She was in front of me in the drive thru. I saw her run the light. Please take my phone number. I would be more than happy to be a witness. Should I call the police for you?" The man looked at me and took my number with his free hand.

"Thanks little man. I'll call you if I need anything. Go ahead and call the cops." He was still holding her off with one hand.

"FUCK YOU LITTLE SHIT YOU'RE NOTHING!!!!" the woman said to me.

"Thank you ma'am. I hope you have a wonderful day," I said walking away from the scene. I dialed 911 and put the phone up to my ear. I was smiling to myself. Justice had been served in my eyes and I was ecstatic. I was almost to the car when I heard rapid footsteps behind me.

"Punx watch out!!" I heard Victoria call from the car. It wasn't soon enough. The woman was all over me before I knew it. She was thrashing and screaming bloody fucking murder. I fell hard on the pavement. My bandages were coming unraveled and were blocking my sight, so I started thrashing wildly. She grabbed me by the shoulders and started slamming me against the concrete. I heard the man thunder over to pull her off of me, but it was too late. I think my stitches had come undone. The last thing I remember was the man and Victoria hovering over me, and I heard the 911 representative pick up on the phone just before I blacked out.

"911 what's your emergency?"

I was floating. The sun was hurting my eyes. I remember being transported somewhere, but I had no idea where I was going. I was floating across the surface of the Earth with no purpose and no means to justify my existence. My thoughts were hazy. It was a state I was growing familiar with. I wasn't at all coherent, but I was developing methods to keep lucidity throughout these states. I was not sound in body, but my mind was still working. The only thing I had to work with was the blue-sky background as my last memory. I treated it as fresh canvass on which I could paint my thoughts. By this point, I was used to thinking in color. I didn't care what Beedlebop said, I was ready. He and the Emperor already told me that I would know things that I shouldn't know. How else would I have known that woman would have a wreck? I predicted it moments before it happened. I felt I was ready. Perhaps my life was on the skids. Maybe I was about to die, but I could still justify myself to myself, even if it was in the form of the Emperor and Beedlebop. I had to know that I was worth something. I had to know that my existence on this planet had some influence on the universe. I had to know that my arrangement of molecules did something to change this planet for the better. I was desperate. To this point I had done very little with my life. I had always wanted and thought that I could be a better person than I was. I was getting fatter and lazier than I would have ever imagined. Perhaps now I could finally rationalize with myself and be everything I could have always imagined myself to be. The blue sky eventually developed a grassy field at the bottom of my field of vision. It was my chance to play God, I suppose. I started to terraform what I could see. I brought forth a pleasant forest. I deliberately made it empty so I could gather my thoughts and be peaceful. I sat in quiet wonderment. This is the peace I had longed for. There were no businesses. There were no cars, no people, and not even any animals. I was all by myself. There wasn't even a cloud in the sky. I didn't have to worry about any pianos any time soon. I walked around the forest for what seemed like days. I didn't need to eat. Hell, I didn't even need to breathe. I was ready to spend the rest of my life in this place. I felt no need to be entertained. It was like my own personal utopia. I sat around in pure bliss.

This continued for what seemed like lifetimes upon lifetimes. I grew very old. My beard touched my kneecaps, yet I never got sick. I was essentially immortal. I had no need for other people. There was no government. There were no markets. I did not eat. I simply existed. I was, and I would be for a very long time. It continued this way for years. I was content. I was complete.

Eventually, the plants started to talk to me. This was something I hadn't planned on. They told me the rain was coming and that I needed to leave. I didn't believe them. I controlled the rain. The clouds started to emerge, but I thought they would just pass. I was sitting on a rock while deep in thought when I felt the first drops. I looked around me and the forest was dying. The plants were thirsty, and I hadn't allowed the rain. The drops were coming down gently at first. I recognized their typical bleaching effect. I slowly realized that I could not prevent what was inevitable. I still tried though. I made pots and pans to catch the rain in. I placed them everywhere. They eventually overflowed.

The rain had started to come down harder and harder in the final few days. I was a mere outline against a forest of outlines against a horizon. I didn't want this tranquility to be over, but I knew it wouldn't last. The rain continued falling in a steady downpour. I had nowhere to go. The entirety of the forest was black and white. I finally accepted my fate and realized my escapism would come to an end soon. I was running through the torrent and saw a broken keyboard on the forest floor. It was time. I moved the trees back and welcomed the eighty-eight keys of my exit. I looked up and saw the piano that would take me from this utopia. It was a jet-black Steinway Grand: completely beautiful and pristine as if it had just rolled out of the workshop. I accepted my fate and laid down on the forest floor before the piano connected with me.

I awoke with a start like I had in the past. I was apparently in the same hospital room that I was in previously. It was incredibly disheartening. The same people were surrounding me. I hadn't been out of the hospital for more than an hour when they had to take me right back. I had to wonder why. I hadn't eaten a solid meal in a few days. I was so hungry. I wanted to restart my life and turn myself around. I saw the same people that I had noticed previously. They were all looking just as concerned as they had before. I was glad they had come back. My family and acquaintances still looked as concerned as they were the first time I woke up. I bet they were growing tired of caring for me. I looked over at everyone and smiled. "Sorry to bring you guys back here for a second time. Thank you for sticking with me," I said. My mom started crying again. I felt so loved. I looked around at everyone and they seemed to be on the verge of tears as well. I was concerned at this point.

"What is wrong with everyone? I'm fine again. I feel great." No one was saying a word. They seemed to have been ignoring me. It was making me really uncomfortable. Victoria got up and left the room. I was still in a bit of a daze, but I felt better than I had when waking up from my initial accident. I sat there for a few minutes not saying a word. My mom was still sobbing in the corner of the room. My dad looked concerned. Everyone looked as if I had died. I knew this wasn't the case because everyone was reacting to what I had said.

"Guys, what's the matter? Would someone please tell me what is so troubling? I feel fine. I know I keep saying it, but I feel fine! Please!" I said. The doctor came back in with Victoria. I remembered him from before. He wasn't entirely friendly, but he had taken care of me multiple times, and for that I was grateful.

"He's awake again," Victoria said. I started to get confused. Again? Why again? I wondered what she meant. This was the first time I had been conscious this time around.

"Is he still acting strangely?" the doctor asked. I really started to get worried at this point.

"Am I acting strangely how?!" I demanded. "I'm fine doc. I know I got sent back here by that woman after she attacked me, but I feel fine!"

"Oh my, he does seem to be a bit better. I still think he has some memory loss however. He has started to fabricate occurrences just like you had mentioned," the doctor said. He started stroking his salt and pepper beard. I stared up at him in disbelief. There was no way I could have made up what had occurred. I had gotten out of the hospital. I had gone to get food. I wanted my burger dammit!

"I will refer you to a mental help specialist. His wounds seem to have healed nicely at this point, but I am not convinced his mind has recovered," the doctor said. He jotted something down on a scrap of paper and handed it to Victoria. I was starting to realize what was going on. The doctor smiled at my folks and me.

"He can leave whenever you want to take him, but I strongly recommend you urge him to see the mental specialist. There may have been more damage than I can diagnose here," the doctor said. He took one last look at everyone.

"I will miss you all. You have been a shining beacon of hope in this hospital. I normally don't say anything like this. Your support for this young man has touched everyone's lives that have cared for him. Thank you all." And with that, he turned and left the room. I finally realized what had happened to me. Everything that had occurred since I initially woke up in the hospital had been a fabrication in my mind. The obvious bits were the city and the forest, but the drive thru had been a fabrication too? I found this hard to believe. I had wondered what I actually said aloud with my friends and family watching. Had I spoken to Beedlebop? Had I neglected the trees aloud while my family and friends were there watching? What about the car wreck I fabricated in my mind with that horrible woman? I was embarrassed. I didn't know what to say to them or what to do. At this point they all thought I was borderline insane. I was completely capable of sustaining all of my physical and cognitive processes at this point. It just wasn't fair that I be viewed as insane. As obsessed as I had been in the past, I didn't want it now. Now I had seen what it does to those around me and it was not something that I wished to pursue. I didn't want this affliction. Thinking in color had confused me and tricked my mind into believing things were occurring that were not actually taking place. While I was willing to accept this in the utopian forest, the drive thru was a cruel and morbid joke I had played on myself. I sat there almost in tears. I couldn't let anyone see. I didn't know how my actions would influence their thoughts about me. I just wanted everything to be back the way it was before I fell and hit my head. It would take some time, I was sure. No doubt I would have to attend a few sessions with this mental specialist before they would consider me "normal" again. I was never really normal in the first place, but I was obviously having major difficulty distinguishing between reality and fabrications of my own mind at this point. Perhaps a little assessment would do me some good, and would serve to re-establish my sanity. I decided I would play along with everything, and I wouldn't try to weird anyone out along the way if I could help it.

I got out of bed after I had been disconnected from the machines. It seemed like I had already been here before, and in my mind, I had. I walked to the bathroom to change into my clothes once again. The mirror showed my reflection once again. This time, I absolutely hated myself. I looked into the mirror over my glasses. I stared my reflection down, as if it were another person. I wanted to beat the shit out of him. How cliché it was to be mad at my own reflection. I hated myself for that too. I wanted to change so badly. My twenty-year-old body looked thirty to me. I looked different. My facial hair was longer than I expected. I had no idea what day it was. I hadn't bothered to ask, lest it bring more distress on my family and friends. The overhead lights were playing tricks on my eyes. I could still see trails on every movement I made. I looked at my clothes, still in my hands. I turned and faced the mirror against my will. I looked like shit. I wanted to shower and brush my teeth. I wanted to sleep for years. My face looked gaunt and malnourished. I realized my life was on the skids. I threw my clothes down on the floor. They landed in a dead, dirty heap. The clothes had not been washed for weeks, most likely. I had made a habit out of wearing the same article of clothing for weeks at a time in the last few months. The dryers at my apartment never dried the clothes fully, so I would make the most out of what I had. I loathed the heap of clothing. My patient's gown made me look pathetic. I was standing there hating my very existence. I wasn't depressed, I was just angry and tired. I started to put on my clothes. The gown came off, and I dug around in the dead pile for my boxers. It was at this point that I started to notice the mirror fogging up. I wasn't quite certain why. I looked up and noticed that the shower curtain was drawn. To my prior knowledge, there was no shower in this bathroom. I did not think that hospitals had showers in each of the bathrooms. The showerhead was producing hot water full blast as if someone was bathing. Perplexed, I pulled up my boxers and put on my shorts. There was no noise coming from the shower if someone may have been in there. I walked over to the curtain and gripped it tightly in my right hand, and threw it back as fast and hard as I could. There was a man standing in the shower in his clothes. He was wearing a crown made from computer mice and cables. He was also wearing a cape that was made from keyboards and flat computer monitors. His back was turned to me, and he was not at all startled by my presence.

"Excuse me sir, who are you?" I asked the individual. He was washing his armpits through his clothes with a bar of soap. He rinsed himself and turned the water off. I continued to watch him as he turned around and reached for a towel.

"Could you please hand me a towel?" he asked me. His eyes were closed and he was feeling around for something to dry off with. I handed him the only towel in the room. He dried off a bit and looked up at me. His long blonde hair, and blonde beard of regal length dripped with water. He was a few inches shorter then me, but the crown he wore made up for that. He was physically fit, as the wet clothes clung to his body. Dry, I imagined they were most likely a deep purple. Now they were black and heavy with water. He looked up at me with a handsome face once it was dry.

"Who are you?" I asked again.

"I am the King of the Cubicle, my boy, and against the good Emperor's best wishes, I will advise you that you are still dreaming." He continued to dry off and seemed ultimately not concerned that I was invading his privacy. He maneuvered the towel around the cape and the crown and continued about his already established routine. I was startled on multiple levels. Completely disregarding the King, I opened the bathroom door. Everyone was outside waiting for me.

"Punx, put on your shirt so we can leave," Victoria said.

"Okay sweetie," I said and closed the door back. The King had removed the cape and the crown and was cleaning out his ears with a q-tip. I walked over to him.

"So you say I'm still dreaming, right? Then why are my friends and family still waiting outside the door for me, huh?" I asked the King.

"You still don't get it, do you Punxsutawney?" the King asked. "You're lucky you caught me on my day off, otherwise I wouldn't have been here at all. Your family and friends aren't waiting on you, you are waiting on your family and friends."

"What could you possibly mean by that? Do you have any idea what I've been through recently?" I asked the King. He pulled the q-tip out of his ear and looked at it to see how much wax was removed, then promptly threw it in the garbage.

"Of course I have an idea, I am one of your ideas. You are still dreaming and you need to wake up. This time, you should try to do it without the aid of a piano," the King insisted.

"What do you know about the pianos?" I asked. I was genuinely curious. As far as I knew, the pianos just transported me to new delusional situations. Perhaps the part of my brain that manifested the King would be willing to offer some insight.

"The pianos are of no relevance now. What you need to concentrate on at this point is waking up without one. Every time you think you have finally come back to consciousness, the piano takes your life and you 'wake up'. This isn't healthy. The Emperor and Beedlebop are going to have my head for this, but I dare them to try. You should consider yourself lucky that I am in a position to guide you. It is my day off after all," the King stated. He took off his towel and wiped a spot in the mirror so he could see himself. He produced a straight razor and began to shave his face without shaving foam. His beard hair was falling off bit by bit into the sink below, but his technique was smooth and there were no cuts on his face.

"What do you propose I do then?" I asked. At this point, I was willing to believe anything this manifestation of my brain was willing to tell me, even if it was at war with the other parts.

"Put on your shirt and go out the door. I can't offer you any other assistance than that. Just know that you may never see me again. The Emperor will probably execute me if he finds me. I'm incredibly vulnerable here, but I don't really care because it is my day off. I do have a small army under my command to defend myself, but I do not think it will be enough against the race that the Emperor commands. The Jifflings will overrun my forces and will most likely pollute my domain to such an extent that I will no longer be able to do business in this realm any longer. It makes no difference. I just know that as long as you are safe and informed, anything that happens to me will be worth the expense," the King concluded. He had finished shaving at this point, which was an impressive feat considering the amount of facial hair he had. He set about washing off his razor.

"Well thank you for your input, as strange as it was. Since you're so unwilling to answer my questions, I suppose I will just leave now," I said. I was incredibly perplexed by his presence in the bathroom, but I didn't want to try and expose him to my family and friends on the likely possibility that he was all in my head. I put on my shirt and opened the door. Everyone was still there just like before. They had a wheelchair ready for me as well. Before I sat down in the wheelchair, and allowed myself to me taken out of the hospital, I looked back into the bathroom. The King and the shower were gone as if they never existed. Despite what the King said, I still felt that I was experiencing the real world. My parents insisted on taking everyone out to lunch, which was very odd considering they didn't get along at all. I suppose this was another indication that I was dreaming, but I went along with it. I was riding in Victoria's car. It was just she and I. We were on our way to Red Lobster. She wasn't speaking to me. She seemed genuinely upset.

"What did the doctor say about me, Vic?" I finally asked her after several minutes of silence.

"They said you might have brain damage. They gave me info on a mental health specialist. I think you should go see him," she said.

"Do you really think I should see him Vic? I have no idea what has happened to me the last few days. Did I worry everyone?" I asked. At this point I was still skeptical regarding my own mental stability. I saw the King of the Cubicle in the bathroom after all, and no one had noticed his presence there.

"You worried me, and you're still worrying me. The King told me you would be like this," said Victoria.

"You met the King?" I asked, startled.

"Yes. He told me you were dreaming, and I still think you are. You need to wake up, Punx." With that, she drove into oncoming traffic and accelerated.

"I love you, Punx," she said.

"I love you too Vic. Thank you." And with those last words, I fell back into my seat and welcomed the car accident that was about to take place. I offered my hand to her and she accepted. We rounded a hill that curved to the left slightly and at the top of the hill met another vehicle. The cars hit head-on. I was flung out of the front of the car through the windshield. The pavement rapidly approached like water before a dive. My head hit first and everything went black.

It seemed like hours had passed when I was thinking nothing. It was as if my body were asleep, but my mind still awake and incredibly vacant. I slowly came back to consciousness out of the embrace of confusion and darkness. There was no easy description for what was going through my brain when I figured out where I was. The very first thing I remember was hearing a repeated dull thumping. Each sound was filling my lungs with air and bringing me back to reality. My sight started to recover next. At first the objects around me were a little blurry, but individual shapes started becoming sharper. My glasses were next to me on the floor. When I reached for them I realized that I was lying on very dirty carpet. It was a dirtied white color, very old, and filled with what appeared to be crumbs and animal hair.

While my senses were slowly recovering, my brain was not interpreting these signals to help me realize where I was or what was going on. It was at a base level in terms of processing information. I soaked in details very rapidly, but did nothing with them. Every split second seemed like minutes to me. Every crease and imperfection on the ceiling was jumping out. There were a myriad of smells, mostly unpleasant, that penetrated the air. I lay there thoughtless, unimportant, and undistinguished. Other brain processes started to fire all of a sudden, and I came to the realization that this was my apartment. This was my completely disgusting shit-hole apartment that I paid for with money I earned. I started to sit up, and my hair seemed stuck to the fibers of the rug. My head was throbbing just like an attempt to force air into a kick ball that had already been full to capacity. I had been bleeding. The blood didn't really concern me at this point because I was awake, and would probably bandage it up myself. What I had been through inside my own head, however, deserved the majority of my attention. What I saw was nothing like a standard dream, I found myself considering the events that occurred in my mind had actually happened. I managed to get up and look around for a moment. The room looked exactly like it had when I first imagined Michael had come over. I suppose he never actually came over at all. The thumping noise that re-animated me continued periodically in the background. There was someone knocking at the door.

"Just a minute!" I yelled from across the stagnant apartment. I knew who it was. I slumped over to the bathroom and got the roll of toilet paper off the wall. This was the cheap kind. Value brand. I unraveled the roll around my head like a bad mummy. I slumped back to the hallway and looked towards the door. The hallway seemed to stretch out longer with every step I thought about taking. Along the way, more details about my apartment started jumping out at me. These were things I would have ignored any other time, but I felt unable to shut everything out. I felt the individual fibers, hairs, and crumbs under my feet. I noticed every crack and ripple in the walls and ceiling. I saw how the lampshade coated the front room in an off white hue due to its color. This was a different perspective on things indeed. I continued to slump on towards the door when it flung open. It startled me so badly that I fell backwards and landed on my ass.

"Jesus Christ, Michael! You couldn't have waited until I got there?!" I asked. Michael looked at me after barging in. He noticed the toilet paper bandages on my head.

"Holy shit are you okay?!" he asked. His face instantly changed from one of frustration to one of horror. He seemed genuinely concerned.

"No bubsy, I'm not okay. I think I may need you to take me to the hospital. I fell earlier and hit my head. Your knocks woke me up from my stupor," I said.

"What happened?"

"I got up too quickly and some hot pizza landed on my feet. I kicked them out from underneath me and fell. As far as I can tell, my head hit something and I blacked out."

"I'll take you. Hang on a second, I have to put something in your freezer." He brandished a small wad of aluminum foil and put it in the fridge. I sat up and extended my arm towards him so he could help me. My toilet paper bandages were already coming undone. I really just wanted this to be over with. I had quite a frightening experience while I was out, and I really didn't want anything to be wrong with me. I was anxious to get to the hospital. He walked over to me from the fridge and grabbed my hand. He pulled me up with some difficulty and I immediately felt dizzy.

"You need to make sure that I don't pass out on you."

"Just stay with me bubbington." He started to walk me towards the front door. I made sure that I had my phone on me.

"Wait a minute!" I said. I stumbled towards the bedroom. My charger was going to be necessary for this little trip. I figured I would actually be there for a while. I walked to the outlet and unplugged my charger.

"Let's go," I said. He put my right arm around his shoulder and helped me out the door. We started the walk towards the elevator.

"I'm glad you showed up when you did, man," I said.

"Me too. Does it hurt?" he asked.

"Not really, but I'm really dizzy and I may pass out on you. I really hope that doesn't happen. I bled all over my carpet." Michael pressed the down arrow for the elevator and we waited there for the elevator to come up to the eighth floor. I took a moment to soak in my surroundings. The floors were made of what could barely be considered a disgusting carpet. You could hardly call it carpet at this point. There were stains of vomit, dog shit, and water damage. It was torn up in certain places. The walls were painted a sickening sea foam green. The landlady ordered the maintenance workers to repaint the walls when there was nothing else to do, so there was a fresh coat applied every two months or so. There was a smell that occupied the hallway as if it were a resident all its own. It was a combination of pungent food leaking out from the individual apartments and all of the disgusting shit that had occurred in that hallway. This smell was different on every floor, but each was just as revolting as the last. The lights overhead were humming a solemn pitch and begging to be changed with fresh bulbs. This was indeed a shit-hole. The elevator eventually got there and we hobbled inside. It was a sob story all of its own. Its smell was a combination of those on all floors. The open and close buttons were there just for show, as they didn't work at all. Michael pressed the button for the first floor.

"I'll get you there soon, just hold on," he said. This was a difficult task as I was getting dizzier by the second and I'm certain my makeshift bandages were not doing much to stop the blood that was coming out of my head. We rode the grungy elevator down from my floor, which was eight. It stopped on floor five. A shaky looking Asian male got on and looked at us. He pressed the button for floor four. Michael and I let him have it.

"I'm bleeding out of the back of my head and this guy takes the elevator down one floor," I said to Michael.

"Do you know what stairs are?" He asked the guy. He looked at both of us but didn't say a word. The elevator shook down to the fourth floor and the doors reluctantly opened.

"I hope you fucking choke and die on your next meal you lazy piece of human shit," I barely managed to cough at the shaky Asian before he bolted out of the elevator. Michael hocked a lougie and spat at him while I was saying this. He was already long gone by the time the elevator decided it was time to close up and continue down to the first floor. We finally made it and the doors opened up. Michael helped me outside the lobby doors and down the stairs. My senses were on overload at this point. The outdoors had provided me with a myriad of information that I was not able to efficiently process at this point. I decided that I would attempt to shut out everything by keeping my eyes closed. This did not bode well for Michael who had to guide me towards his truck, which was across the street in university staff parking. I was just stumbling around until I head him cry out.

"Oh fuck!" I opened my eyes to see what he was reacting to. There was a university employed parking authority agent writing him a ticket for parking in the staff lot during university operating hours. He picked up his pace which essentially made me just a lifeless object he was dragging along with him. He called out to the parking authority agent when he drew near.

"Hey I only parked there to get my buddy! He's in danger! He hurt himself, see?" Michael motioned to me and my toilet paper bandages which were almost completely undone and covering mostly my shoulders at this point.

"You were parked here against university regulations sir, I have to write you a ticket," said the agent.

"Can you not see he is in danger?! I only parked here to take him to the hospital!" said Michael. He turned me around to show the agent my wound.

"Oh my God! Get him in the truck! Take him! Take him!" was all the agent could say. The agent took the ticket off of the windshield and stood aside.

"Yeah I plan on it," said Michael. He unlocked his truck with his key and opened the passenger door. I climbed in as quickly as I could manage. Michael was already behind the wheel before I could close the door. He reached across me and slammed it shut. The truck was already started. He barreled backwards out of the parking space and onto the street.

"We're going to get you there soon bubsy. Just hold on for me." I sat there and stared out of the windshield wishing with all of my heart that a piano would fall from the sky and take me away from this situation. It never came. This was real life for once.

CHAPTER 4 THE ABSENCE OF CONTEXT

After waking up, after turning off the television, after pausing the video game, and after getting out of the shower, reality slaps the shit out of you. It is an underhanded thing, reality. For the people who like to zone out, like me, it is something not very welcome. I get easily distracted by almost everything, and it makes it hard to concentrate on the things that I convince myself that I need to be doing. Sleeping, daydreaming, staring into space, slobbering over the television, they all put the mind off. Some people consider these things a waste of time. I'm starting to think they are correct in their line of thinking. Here I am with my own blood all over myself being rushed to the hospital. My time was growing more and more valuable and I had nothing to buy it back with. What have I done with myself? I decided there and then that if I were to pull through I would change. I would grow up. I would fucking seize the day like I promised myself that I would oh so many times. I would start working hard instead of barely skating by. I was lucky enough to be in a position to skate by, but I could do so much more. It was then that I realized I wasn't proud of myself. I started to cry. It was a thought that had never crossed my mind in the past. I thought I was the shit before this happened. I suppose it took this traumatic experience to show that I wasn't the shit. I was nothing special, and the world wouldn't bat an eye if I actually died today. I had been an ass to my friends and to my family. I wanted a second chance. My eyes were getting fuzzy and I started feeling incredibly light headed. The details of life were starting to fade. I felt my body trying to give up on itself. I struggled to stay alive for as long as possible until I saw the hospital and I couldn't fight the darkness surrounding my vision any longer. "I'm going," I looked at Michael and said. "Make sure I make it."

"Punx stay with me you bastard! We can see the hospital! We're almost there!"

"I've been fighting it, Michael. I just can't. I can…" My thought processes were leaving me and my words were just representing my fragmented thoughts. I was scared, and that was the last thing I remember. The last thing I remembered in the waking world was that I was scared, and that was no way to go. But it was my way. Swimming through the infinite black that was nonexistence was this tiny little speck that was I. I didn't know it was I. At least at the time, I just wasn't aware of this. There was nothing to do, because there was no context with which to work with. I suppose "nothing" isn't a very good word to describe where I was, because it is enough of a description to give context. You see, the word "nothing" is far too descriptive. It gives the speck a context, and in this particular instance, "there is just a speck". The instance is not described as "just a speck and nothing else", because to add "nothing else" to the end of that would be incorrect. All there is is a speck. Something else that I did not have the capacity to realize was that the speck wasn't just me. It was, and always had been everyone. Interestingly enough, the speck also had always been everything. Anything that would ever exist in the physical realm was contained in this speck, this lonesome speck floating around in the absence of context that would eventually be called our universe.

A wonderful thing occurred at some point during the speck's existence. It is possible that it has occurred before, and will occur again many, many times. The speck exploded in a reaction so violent in magnitude, it cannot be compared to anything else the human mind can possibly comprehend. The speck just before detonating was a temperature hotter than any reaction would ever achieve. Indeed, it was the summation of all temperatures that would ever exist. The speck spread itself wide granting context, and thus meaning to everything around it, for context is everything. At this point, everything was context as well, and it would always be this way. For a long period of time, our universe consisted of only super massive stars the size of what we now call galaxies, and these stars born from the speck gave context to one another only in terms of distance and size. All matter proceeded to cool and condense into smaller forms, which we call planets and the stars reduced in size, but increased in number. Thus, the universe provided more and more context to itself. The absence of context was almost all but a memory, with nothing to remember it but the planets. The speck was at this point a memory as well, but still existed in a new and evolved form. In the galaxy we came to call the Milky Way, there existed a solar system of particular note, one that included our Earth, the only planet that lowly Earthlings know to have eventually developed life. The very fact that a collection of molecules is able to determine what it should do next rather than just react is the most beautiful thing the speck could have ever hoped to enable, even though at that point it couldn't have hoped for anything at all.

It was during an incredibly short period in existence's existence that there happened to be a system of biological processes we call a "human being" in grave danger. Grave danger in this instance meant that the biological system was on the brink of no longer being able to function the way it had developed, resulting in the death of the human being in question. This particular biological system was I. My life had been spilling out of a hole in the back of my head, and I had become unconscious. I was currently experiencing the absence of context within my own mind, and my mind, not knowing what to do, scrambled to generate context in any way it possibly could to provide comfort, and possibly prolong the short life that it attempted to perpetuate.

CHAPTER 4.1 THE ABSENCE OF SANITY

I awoke in a similar fashion to how I had previously while I was still passed out. This was a realm that existed only in my mind, and even though I knew this, I could not control what was happening as hard as I tried. I had lost all function of my physical body and was then at the mercy of the most powerful force the speck had ever accidentally created: the unbridled, unrestrained human imagination.

CHAPTER 4.2 THE SANE TRAIN

I found myself in my current situation much like everyone does when they begin to dream, as I had gone over previously. I looked around at my surroundings unable to manipulate them quite as easily as I had hoped to. This is to say, I could not simply think something and have it occur as if by telekinesis. My imagination seemed to have locked itself down into a set of unseen rules that could not be changed. I was in a train car. I had never ridden in a train before. It was a private room, luckily for me. I wouldn't know how to handle a roomful of strangers only having just woken up. I could only assume the truck that Michael was piloting was still in motion providing me with the illusion of the train that was transporting me somewhere. I didn't really care what the destination was, I just hoped that I would be okay and continued to sit there not disturbing anything in case it crashed or I was brought out of my own head by some incredible stroke of luck. Sure I was disappointed by the situation. I was dying. My mind was providing me with an elaborate coping mechanism, which I planned to make the best of.

The train car itself was a marvel to behold. It was far beyond anything humans consider first class travel. Who needs money when one has one's own imagination? The upholstery was solid white with a light blue trim to line the edges of the seats. There were holograms everywhere depicting various news stations, stocks, and sporting events, none of which I paid much attention to other than to acknowledge the impossibility of such holograms. The windows on the sides of the car were vast and remarkably spotless. I could see out for what seemed to be a mile. The train was passing through the same multi colored grass I first imagined when I awoke in the field of the Geometric Forest. That occurrence seemed like it was ages in the past. I felt older. I knew it wasn't real, but I still admired the lush fields that swayed in the breeze so perfectly. The trees were distant, but they retained their curious geometric properties from the previous visit to this land. There were hills in the distance and they took no shame in showing off the plants. There were still no animals. There were no birds, and no bugs as far as the eye could see. The clouds were still taking odd shapes (as far as clouds go), however they were few in number and I did not worry that the color draining rain would come. It was a wonderful utopia free from all the cares and responsibilities of the world I said goodbye to. I was almost okay with this thought. Perhaps, this same wonderful setting presented itself to those who were on the brink of letting go of life, or perhaps this was something that no one else who ever lived could have possibly experienced to this point. This was a chance for something new, a new life possibly. Maybe I should kiss my previous life goodbye and focus on what I had. What if this was heaven? In my previous life I neglected heaven ever existed, and even in the presence of this beautiful land I still denied its existence. Oh, I reasoned with myself for what felt like hours on end. I wasn't ready to just call it quits and accept this perfect place. This land was still made by man. One man made it, I finally concluded: myself.

The passage of time was a huge issue here. For as long as I sat staring at the marvels my situation presented to me, I had no concept of when I was. Time wasn't at a stand still, but it felt like it was moving so slowly. Time was with me in the car, only it wasn't paying any attention to me. And since time was barely aware of my existence, its influences on every aspect of my being were significantly diminished. With every new frame my eyes perceived, I felt like I had experienced over an hour's worth of time, but that was when time paid attention. What was an hour now? What sort of context would an hour have in my situation? I have no significance here. I don't have school. I'm not employed. I don't know anyone and I have no responsibilities. There was nothing to do. I had gotten what I wished for: no responsibility. Loneliness wasn't even an issue here. I didn't feel the need to be entertained. My mind was perfectly happy to think these thoughts and dictate to my body what to do. I had not gotten up yet. My legs stretched out and lifted me from the seat what felt like days after I decided to stand up in the first place. Every microscopic motion resonated through my body. It was a sort of hyper sense that I had never before experienced. I was finally standing upright and began to look around. The rest of the cabin was similar in style to where I was sitting. There were an amount of seats in this car that I couldn't count, all empty, all pristine white with the same blue trim. The car seemed to stretch on for miles. I could not see the other end. I noticed on the door in front of me that separated the cars that there was a plaque of sorts. I walked closer to it and it felt like weeks getting there. I bent over to look at the plaque. It said "The Sane Train: a train which contains only those who are sane. Dryffe Company." I took a 24-hour step back. Things were suddenly starting to have more context than I had hoped. I started my journey back to my seat. I had no luggage to worry about, but I figured I would return to where I was just to make certain I didn't make myself stick out. By the time I had returned to my seat, the door had slid open, and an usher had entered the room. I hadn't had time to turn around and acknowledge him right away, so I did so only after I had sat back down. He was much shorter than me, and he had white hair. He approached me and smiled.

"How are you today sir?" I managed to say to the usher.

"Quite well, quite well indeed sah. Just performing my rounds. Is there anything I can get for you?" I was bothered by this question. What, out of anything I could think of was I able to ask for this usher to bring for me? Standard procedure would be to deny anything. I wasn't hungry, but what if he could bring me anything? A bed? A circus? A time machine perhaps? My thoughts were out of control. I decided to ask him for a glass of water just to be polite.

"Could you send for me a glass of water sir?" I asked. He looked at me first with a look of disbelief, then it slowly faded into a smile, and then he started laughing uncontrollably and threw himself on the floor. I was completely dumbfounded by this display and wanted to know what the issue was. Perhaps I should have requested nothing at all.

"Sir, are you quite alright?" I asked the usher. He sat up on the floor and wiped a tear from his left eye.

"Yes dear boy I am fine. I must however request that you show me your ticket. You may have a fine sense of humor, but that is rare and unfamiliar for passengers of the Sane Train. You see, jokes are rarely told here, and you aren't exactly a regular. What I mean to say is, you sir, are rare and unfamiliar. Please produce your ticket at once!" He had gotten up from the floor and held out a white-gloved hand in my direction. I suppose water wasn't on the menu. I was in a very obvious bind. I looked down at myself and noticed that I was wearing a vest with many pockets. I started to check them in an attempt to produce a train ticket I was almost certain was not there. I continued to check my coat and pants pockets with no luck. I was at a loss. I looked up at the usher and struggled to think of an excuse.

"I-uh, I must have-uh, misplaced it sir. Just a moment please?" I asked the usher. He was growing more and more impatient by the hour, or at least it felt that way. Time was still a mystery to me in this place. I had run completely out of ideas when I heard a voice yell from down the car.

"Kid's with me ush'! I got his ticket right here," said the stranger.

"Mr. Wonderly! I had no idea sah! Please forgive me! Don't tell the conductor! He'll have my job!"

"Don't worry ush' I won't go that far! You just run along to the next car and I'll forget the whole thing ever happened. I'm sure the kid already has."

I hadn't.

I was really perplexed. The person that the usher addressed as Mr. Wonderly looked exactly like my friend Adam Kwaak. Adam was two years older than me and was my band mate. He played the saxophone and was damn fantastic at it. He was one of my best friends. I hadn't realized until now that he didn't show up at all in my previous dreams. I wondered just why that was. Perhaps for my mind's sake, he was there as a last resort. Maybe in reality I was in severe danger of dying and the usher was there to take me away. Either way, Mr. Wonderly was not at all the same person that Adam Kwaak was. Adam was friendly, unassuming, harmless, and loyal. Mr. Wonderly looked like a post-apocalyptic survivor. He looked like he would have robbed the train rather than be a standard passenger. The usher scurried off through the door that he came through. I sat there looking at Mr. Wonderly contemplating what was going to happen next. I didn't feel safe even though he came to my rescue. I'm fairly certain I could have taken the usher down, but not Mr. Wonderly.

"Stand up kid, we're walking," said Mr. Wonderly. I really didn't want to call him that, but I did anyways.

"Mr. Wonderly, can you tell me how you know me?" I asked.

"Pshh, shut up kid. Call me Vega. Or Wonderly. Fuck that mister shit. I have an arrangement with Dryffe Co. They don't usually allow types like me on board, but I was sent here by Management to make sure you were safe. Think of me as a bodyguard, but trust me, I will not put up with that mister shit from you. It bugs me. I'm probably just a year or two older than you anyways. I don't mind it when the staff calls me mister though. Makes me feel like I made something of myself." I was absolutely taken aback by this. He certainly didn't resemble Adam at all. What did this "Dryffe Company" have to do with me? The context that defined my situation was growing more and more complex with what seemed like every hour. Time was still diluted to the point of near absurdity. I had to ask him about it. He was here to protect me. Perhaps he knew what I was experiencing.

"Vega. I have very few ideas about where I am or what is going on right now. Time feels like it has slowed down significantly. Every instant that I experience feels like it is stretched four or five times longer than what I am normally used to. What the fuck is going on?" I asked Vega.

"Shit they told me you would be confused, but I didn't anticipate anything like this. You really don't have a clue where you are?" Vega asked me. All I did was look at him.

"Fuck. Alright. I will try to be as simple as possible. You are currently riding on The Sane Train, which is owned by Dryffe Co. We are located on The Layer Dryffe, which houses the headquarters of Dryffe Co. It was the first Layer in existence and remains the capital to this moment. The Dryffe Layering Company made its first Layer in turn 0037 and has remained in business ever since creating Layers whenever it sees fit. Does this help you out at all?" My comprehension of what Vega had just said was less than premium. Was this really the system my mind had come up with to assist me in coping with death? What is a Layer? I was so befuddled, I had to ask him to elaborate.

"Vega. I know this is probably incredibly basic for you, but I'm going to have to ask you to be patient with me. What is a Layer?" I cringed immediately after the words left my lips. Vega started to laugh at me much like the usher had when I hadn't said anything I considered witty or peculiar. He swiftly realized that I was serious and changed his tune.

"Well sport, a Layer is essentially a plane of existence. There are multiple Layers that exist in the almost the same location. There are hundreds, possibly thousands, Layered on top of one another to conserve space inside the Cake, which contains all Layers. These Layers exist incredibly close together, but they do not touch each other. Think of it like multiple dimensions outside the four we know, only there are means of moving between the Layers, but it is expensive and expressly prohibited unless you are Royalty or you have permission from Dryffe Co. to do so. "

"So that all being said, what Layer are we on now?" I asked.

"I already told you, we're on the Layer Dryffe, kid. You're stuck in the middle of it, just like we all are…just like we all are." He began to look a bit solemn. His words hadn't really reassured me in any way. While I realized that none of this was real, I was beginning to experience a sort of suspense of belief surrounding my situation. It was slowly becoming my perception that everything around me was reality, and that I wasn't at all experiencing a coping mechanism of a dying mind. It was as if Vega were teaching me how to live for the first time, like I had experienced amnesia. We continued walking down the car, which seemed to have no end in sight. The longer I walked, the more I became detached from what I perceived as reality. The more I became detached from reality, the more I came to accept the Layer Dryffe as the place I belonged. I was no longer the Punxsutawney I knew. I was different now. I was a different person who had lived a different life. I was slowly forgetting everything I once knew and unwittingly accepted my current situation. Reality was less than a shadow of a memory. It was inaccessible by the synapses of my mind. I started to live the life of the Layer Dryffe. My understanding of my current situation had faded away to less than nothing. My context had been completely re-written in a seamless process purely fabricated by the human imagination. My identity was make-believe as was everything else I was to experience, only my mind had convinced myself that it was reality. My physical body's context and experience was erased and I was left with a fresh slate ready to be influenced by my own imagination inside my own head while I was slowly losing my life with no chance of fighting for it myself. I was now oblivious and ready to be reprogrammed. My actual life was now forfeit. I embraced this new life as if I had never experienced anything else. I lived inside of myself. My imagination became reality without my knowledge or consent. I no longer thought in color. I now lived in color: the color of the human imagination.

CHAPTER 4.7 THE INFINITE BAFFLER

Life on the Layer Dryffe wasn't so bad. I got to travel in luxury with a fantastic bodyguard named Vega Wonderly who saw to my every need. I had nothing to complain about. This train car was more than fantastic. The weather was perfect, even though I wasn't exposed to it. I had nothing at all to be concerned with other than surviving. I might even say life was wonderful on the Layer Dryffe. Vega and I were walking along this car back to where he was stationed on the Sane Train. He had fallen silent recently, and I couldn't remember what we were just chatting about. He kept looking ahead as if we were about to reach our destination, although we had no end in sight. These trains were so long. I wished we were close to our destination. I was hungry and wanted desperately to dine. We were almost to the end of the car when the holograms all turned red. I looked at Vega and he was immediately concerned.

"Fuck, what now?" he said to himself.

"Vega, what is going on?" I asked. There was a message that started playing over the intercom.

"Insane person detected on the train. Emergency procedures initiated. Impact with the Infinite Baffler detected. All passengers and personnel are encouraged to evacuate."

"Aw fuck I can't believe this is actually happening the one time I'm allowed on the train!" said Vega.

"C'mon kid we have to get off the train!" I had no idea what was happening. The ride had been going smoothly up until this point. Why were we running into troubles just now?

"Vega, what do we do?"

"We have to get to the end of the car and jump out. That's the only way to survive. We have to move quickly. If we collide with the Infinite Baffler while we're still on the train, we will cease to exist. Let's move."

We proceeded to sprint towards the end of the car. I was completely terrified. The Infinite Baffler was frightening, and I didn't want to know what happened if the Sane Train collided with it. Eventually, I saw the door in front of us. Vega rushed towards it and attempted to fling it open, but it wouldn't budge.

"Locked! Dammit!" He looked around for another escape route, but the only one was directly in front of us. There was no hope. We were going to crash into the Infinite Baffler and it would claim us. I panicked.

"What about the window? Could we smash it open somehow?" I asked. Vega seemed completely enthralled at the idea. He unstrapped an object from his back, which appeared to be a saxophone. He grabbed it by the mouthpiece, held it back behind his head, swung around, and shattered the glass. He cleared the jagged edges from the bottom to make a hole large enough for us to fit through.

"Come on kid we have to jump!" He said. I could hear the brakes of the train shrieking against the rails. It was trying to slow down to reduce the force of the impact. Even still, the train was still barreling ahead. He grabbed me by the arm.

"There's no time to second guess this shit. Either we jump, or we die," Vega said to me. I nodded in agreement. We stood up on the white seat and embraced. "On the count of two, jump." he said right in my ear. He counted to two and we both jumped out the train window at the same time. My vision was a blur while we were in the air, but when we hit the ground, we each held each other for just a moment and then let go. I rolled over and over again in the grass attempting to halt my momentum without breaking my arms. The grass cut me all over my face and arms, although the ground was softer than I had imagined it would be. I eventually came to a stop and felt an insurmountable pain in my legs and arms. I lay there still for a moment almost unable to comprehend what had just occurred. I heard the Sane Train barrel past me, but I could not see it. The multi-colored tall grass obscured my vision. I laid there in wait of what was to happen next. I dared not move, for I was in far too much pain, and felt that one of my legs was broken. I managed to sit up just enough to catch a view of the last car just as it passed. This was a bit shocking to me considering how long the cars were. I looked to my left in the direction of the train, and to my horror saw a startling scene. There was an incredibly large semi-translucent wall covering the majority of my field of vision. It shimmered and morphed and seemed to move ever so slightly as if it were alive. It appeared to be made of a gelatinous substance. The train was on a collision course right for it. I knew it would collide with the wall soon. I looked on as the Sane Train connected with the wall and produced an explosion of super-massive magnitude. The wall rippled like water. The explosion released a wall of light that was almost blinding. I shielded my eyes and ducked down into the grass hoping that I would be safe from the wreckage. I heard an incredibly loud sound produced from the explosion. Just after that finished, I heard a bone-chilling roar that seemed to come from the wall itself. The wall was rippling and twitching from the impact. It was as if the wall felt the impact and it caused it pain. My eyes had only just opened to see the aftermath and to determine where the roar had originated. It was at this time that I heard a rustling to my right. I looked up and saw Vega. He was bleeding from his head. He bent down and grabbed my arm.

"Let's go." he said. It was all I could do to keep from passing out in that moment. For some strange reason I can't fathom, I wanted pianos to rain from the sky, but they never came. I reluctantly stood up and followed him even though he was just stringing me along. My right leg felt like it had snapped in two.

"Vega stop. My leg, I think it is broken."

"Don't worry, I figured something like this would happen. The Emperor is behind this. He commands the Infinite Baffler, and the Sane Train. This was really dirty of him. There's no telling how many officials and business people he killed with that move. The King is going to be pissed. I have strict orders to take you to him. Can you make it a little bit further? I have to call down a copter to fetch us and take us to safety. No doubt the Jifflings will be here very soon. If they arrive before we leave, there is no promise that we will survive." Vega looked like a war hero, almost like a commander or general. My morale was high. I would follow him wherever he would take me.

"I will have to limp, but we can make do," I said.

"The Baffler prevents me from calling a copter. It resonates naturally at a frequency that disrupts the majority of Dryffe Co's communication devices. I'll never understand why such a creature swears allegiance to the likes of the Emperor. We have to move outside a given range before I can ask for rescue. We must move quickly. As I mentioned, the Jifflings will be here soon, and we will surely perish if they arrive." As much as I wanted to come with him, I felt a horrible amount of pain in my leg.

"I will try my hardest," I said. "We need to get out of the grass if we can."

"This way, kid." He grabbed me by the arm and half-dragged me out of the tall grass to the shoulder of the train tracks. We began to move as far away from the Infinite Baffler as we could. There was a pleasant breeze flowing across the field, which seemed to amplify my pain. It was taunting me. I could be sitting in a chair enjoying the scenery. Instead I was struggling to flee from the scene of a horrendous massacre that was intended for Vega and myself. I was not happy to say the least. We made our way along the tracks as far as we possibly could. Vega was staring at a device in his other hand as we traveled. We eventually stopped at his behest.

"Yes this is it!" he said to himself. He pressed a few buttons on the device and held it up to his ear.

"This is Wonderly! I have the kid! Send in the fleet as quickly as you can!" He turned and looked at me. "We're going to be okay, kid. Just hang on. I sat down to look at my leg. It was definitely broken. One of the bones below the knee had snapped and I began to feel sick at the sight. Vega was scanning the horizon for the rescue team. He seemed confident but at the same time just slightly worried. It made me worry just a bit. I looked up at him and he had a look of horror on his face.

"Oh no. No no no! They are coming!" He said. I looked in the direction he was facing. There was a faint brown cloud in the distance. It was amorphous and seemed to grow ever larger despite massive amounts of the cloud falling out of the bottom of it like rain. It resembled a plague of locust. The cloud was moving at an accelerating rate.

"Those are the Jifflings, kid. They are inch high beings that live their entire lives faster than the synapses in our brain can fire. They live faster than we can think. We may not be able to hold them off. There is only one thing I can try and I will only be able to hold them off for as long as I can hold my breath." With that Vega produced a small brass cylinder from one of his vest pockets. He pressed a button on the side and it expanded in an incredible fashion in his hand. It began expanding and producing more intricacies. Eventually, it took the shape of an alto saxophone, similar to the one on his back that he used to smash the glass on the Sane Train. He produced a reed from another pocket and fastened it to the mouthpiece.

"Look there in the distance, kid. The fleet is arriving. The copters will be here soon. We may make it out yet." With that he turned to face the growing brown cloud of Jifflings and put the mouthpiece in his mouth and began to play a single note. It was beautiful. An A above the staff. He played this instrument as if it were an extension of his own body. Even though it was just a single held note, I had never heard a saxophone sound so incredible in my life. Seconds after the pitch met my ears, I looked at the bell of the instrument. It was producing some sort of aura that was emanating in a spherical fashion outwards. It met with the cloud that was almost fifty feet in front of us. The cloud had almost completely blocked my field of vision in that direction, and was frightening to behold. I could almost make out individual Jifflings. They continued to fall out of the cloud as they died, for their lives existed for mere fractions of a second. The cloud was essentially an entire floating city. From the very moment I first witnessed the cloud until they were at this point, hundreds of generations of Jifflings had been born and had died. The aura blocked the Jifflings' advance towards us, and the cloud began to shrink in size while massive amounts of the creatures fell from the swarming mass. We were safe for now, but it had only been mere seconds since Vega had begun to play. Even though the sax held the Jifflings at bay and significantly reduced their numbers, we were still in danger if Vega ran out of breath. Even a moment of him not playing could allow a sizeable amount of the Jifflings within the protective sound barrier and that could spell disaster.

I looked on in pure awe at the scene that was unfolding before me. It was so beautiful and at the same time so saddening. Here we were, two people attempting to defend against countless other beings that were trying to rip the flesh from our bodies. They were completely helpless against Vega's saxophone. I watched them die in droves, only at this point it was necessary murder opposed to their natural life cycle. The copter fleet was moving in rather quickly. It had been nearly a minute since Vega first sounded his horn. I could tell he was starting to run out of steam. I hobbled close to him as the copters flew down to make their landing. He was nearing the end of his breath, I could tell. I stood up close to his face and took a deep breath. I pulled the mouthpiece quickly from his mouth, placed it in mine and began to blow. This was enough time to allow a large portion of the Jifflings to make their way towards us. As soon as I started to blow, the Jifflings were upon us. I felt them ripping at my skin and mouth with miniscule claws. They were attempting to surround us and kill us. Just as I thought we would surely be dead, one of the copter bay doors flew open and three soldiers armed with saxophones jumped out. They were already playing a C minor chord while the doors were opening to ensure the Jifflings wouldn't reach the ship. The cloud of Jifflings completely fell out of the sky at this display and perished. We were saved. Wonderly dragged me on board the closest copter and ordered the engineer to close the doors. "Not every day you get to see something like that, huh kid? Thanks for that quick thinking back there," Vega said to me. The copter was amazing. The three soldiers playing backup jumped back into the copter just before the bay door closed. I looked around. It was just about the size of a small apartment. There were all kinds of displays and readouts that I didn't understand. Vega looked at me and smiled. He looked incredibly tired. I wondered how he would be compensated for such an endeavor. I'm almost certain that was all he was thinking. That in addition to what a fool he thought I was.

"Vega, are you pissed?" I asked.

"Kid, why would I be pissed? This is my job. The King pays me to do whatever he says. I'm essentially the head of his military. I get paid well. You don't have to worry about me. What about that leg of yours?"

"It still hurts horribly, I still think it is broken." The adrenaline was starting to wear off and my leg was beginning to hurt significantly.

"Medic, get over here. We got a wounded soldier," Vega said. The medic walked up from the back of the copter and produced a large device from a bag he was carrying. The device, once fully expanded, made a semi-circle around my leg. The medic pressed a few buttons to power it up and the semi-circle began to glow blue. He ran it up and down my leg to search for the location of the break, then powered the device down and put it away. He produced a syringe from his bag and filled it with a thick serum that resembled shampoo. Before I knew it, the contents of the syringe were injected into my leg. Without exaggeration, it was the most painful feeling I had ever felt. This was even worse than the pain from the break itself. It was like I had the most intense heartburn in my leg and there was no cure in sight. I writhed around for what felt like hours, but was probably just a matter of seconds. All at once the pain subsided and my leg felt better than it had ever felt before. I looked at him in amazement.

"Thank you so much, sir. I cannot express my gratitude towards you in words." I was so completely thankful, I had no idea what to say. The Jifflings had cut Vega and I all over our faces. He was still completely gashed, but after looking at my arms and hands, I discovered the serum had sealed my wounds as well. The medic moved towards Vega and administered the same serum. Vega took the pain better than I did. He looked at me with a calm face.

"Had this stuff injected so many times I've lost count, kid. Stings like a bitch every time, but it heals everything. I bet this stuff could bring a dead man back from his fate if he got it quick enough." Vega bared his teeth at the pain and shuddered a bit. I watched as one by one his wounds closed up all over his body. There weren't even scars left behind on his flesh. He had skin like he had just been born. I suppose I looked the same way. My situation had not been one of an ideal nature, but all was well now. The copter was so loud that we had to shout over the wind to hear each other. I looked out the window and saw the plains beneath us. It was quite the breathtaking view. The multi-colored grass was swaying in the breeze and the geometric trees were equally as gorgeous. I looked around the cabin in awe at the engineering. My mind was buzzing with so many questions about this place. I couldn't contain it any longer.

"Vega, why is the Emperor out to get us?" I asked innocently. I legitimately wanted to know.

"Kid, you ask the dumbest questions. The Emperor is the sworn enemy of the King. They hate each other. You don't remember the First Great Business Deal?" He asked me.

"No," I said. "I have no idea what that is. Please tell me about it."

CHAPTER 5.1 THE INFINITE BAFFLING BUSINESS DEAL

"The King of the Cubicle was the very first being on The Layer Dryffe. He started Dryffe Company and created The Layer Dryffe by his own hands. On the first day, he created light. On the second day, he created land and water. On the third day, he created plants and beings. On the fourth day, he returned to Dryffe Co. to fill out fiscal reports and rest in the break room. On the fifth day, The King of the Cubicle met with The Emperor of the Moon in the Great Conference Room located in the middle of the Layer Dryffe Company. On the sixth day, The King of the Cubicle sold The Layer Dryffe to the Emperor of the Moon who barred The King of the Cubicle from the Layer, except to attend Dryffe Company HQ. On the seventh day, The Emperor of the Moon tried to kill The King of the Cubicle," said Vega.

"That is the First Great Business Deal which created our world, our existence, our everything." Said Vega.

"You believe that your existence is based off of a business deal?" I asked.

"How dare you question the origins of life!" Vega proclaimed. "You wanted to know so I told you!"

CHAPTER 5.15 THE INFINITE BAFFLING GREAT CONFERENCE ROOM

"I wasn't trying to offend you, I am just a little skeptical." I said to Vega. "Where are you taking me now?" I asked. Vega was steamed, but he eventually responded. "No offense taken, kid. We are headed towards the Great Conference Room in the Layer Dryffe Company. It is a sacred meeting place. We are honored to have been invited to this place as it has not been disturbed since the meeting of the King and the Emperor. This is a historic moment in the existence of the Layer Dryffe. I am almost unwilling to believe that the King was able to secure this meeting spot as the Emperor currently owns this Layer as his own," said Vega.

"I hope this goes smoothly. I don't want us to be killed by the Emperor. I realize his power now after seeing what happened with the Sane Train." We didn't have much else to say. My previous statement we both agreed upon. We set out for the conference room.

CHAPTER 5.19 THE INFINITE BAFFLING ARRIVAL

Time seemed to screech to a halt during this flight. My perceptions had been hazy lately, and I wasn't quite sure why. We seemed to be passing the same hills and the same foliage over and over again.

"Vega, are we lost?"

"Kid, shut up."

"No really, I've seen these exact hills before. I remember the pattern. We've passed them three times now. I think our pilot is lost."

"Kid. Shut. Up."

"Vega, could you check please?"

"Will you shut up?"

"Yes I will."

"Fine, since you asked so nicely I'll go check. For you."

He got up and walked towards the cockpit of the copter. I continued to look out of the window. The copter never turned sharply, it didn't feel like we were going in circles, but it certainly looked that way. Vega came back to me hurriedly.

"Kid we got a big problem, thanks for pointing this out."

You're welcome, I guess.

"The Emperor has infiltrated our equipment. We're stuck in an infinite loop. We've been going around in a circle. What I'm saying is, if our straight line had been curved and connected end to end, that would pretty much sum up our situation."

I get it, Vega.

"I'm trying to think of other ways to break this other than the obvious one. This route will be far more costly and dangerous, but will be effective."

"And what's that?" I asked out loud.

"We would have to move into a subsidiary Layer, basically perform a Layer shift. This is where we leave the Layer Dryffe and move to another Layer, namely the Layer Automina. Not many people are able to do this as the technology is complicated and expensive. It also takes years of training and conditioning for one to understand what it is to truly shift Layers. We don't know much about how or why this happens, we just know what happens and how to counter act it. Are you ready to pay very close attention to me?"

"Yeah sure, go ahead."

"Okay, once we initiate the Layer shift, everything is going to go super dark. This isn't an ordinary dark: it is less than dark. It is less than nothing. For there to be nothing, there would have to be something to juxtapose against the nothing to make it stand out. Do you follow me so far?"

"I guess so, that makes sense."

"Well good. The next thing you need to understand is that shifting Layers completely re-writes all of the rules that you're used to. You can think of it not only as a culture change, but a re-writing of the laws that govern everything that exists, and it is completely different in each Layer we dare travel to. The one we have to go to, the Layer Automina, is one governed by machinery. Not only the common citizen, but also the fauna and foliage all have developed more efficiently and with more complexity than those on the Layer Dryffe, and thus provides this new Layer with a vastly different feel. It is not welcoming. You could be downright mortified, that is if we were spending any time there. This brings me to my next point, possibly the most important so far. Are you still with me?"

I was growing impatient with him, but this was the most serious I've seen him thus far. "I'm still with you." I said.

"Now, this is why I phrased my last point the way I did. When you shift Layers, everything that shifts with you takes another shape. You will look completely different. I will look completely different. You may no longer have flesh. You may no longer be able to speak. You may not have to eat to sustain your life or breathe air. What defines you is completely scattered and reassembled using all available resources the Layer has to offer. Having said this, we know what we become when shifting to the Layer Automina. You will become partially or completely mechanized. Think of it like what we consider a Cyborg to be. This transformation is not something to be taken lightly. You could forget completely who you are now while you are there, and will fabricate memories and experiences of a life you've never lived. Just keep in mind that once we return to the Layer Dryffe, you will be back to normal. I can say with the utmost certainty that you will not remember yourself or your mission upon shifting to the Layer Automina. There are many more details that I could provide you with, but they will do you no good for the reason I've just told you: that you won't remember any of it once we have shifted Layers. This happens to everyone, except Royalty, without the proper training."

"This sounds really dangerous Vega. Are you absolutely certain that this is the only thing we can do to break the loop?"

"Well kid, I don't have any other ideas. This isn't so much something we can break out of while in the Layer Dryffe as something we can completely dodge if we were in another Layer. See, the Emperor controls this Layer. That being the case, he can apparently change it at will, a skill I did not realize he possessed. He's still trying to prevent us from reaching the Great Conference Room by reorganizing the landscape. This is why we are in the loop in the first place. Even if we changed direction and went away from the Conference Room, the second we try making a beeline for it, he knows. He will just put us on the same path. We would starve to death, or run out of fuel and crash. I know you can't make many suggestions in this instance, but if you have something lay it on me."

"I'm sorry Vega, this all comes as a shock. I can't really offer much in terms of assistance. I don't know anything about your technology or equipment."

"It's fine kid." He sighed and looked out the window for a moment. I sighed too.

"Well I suppose we're about ready to do the shift. Come with me."

"Alright." I got up and followed him towards the front of the copter. We sat down and strapped ourselves in to the harnesses that lined the walls. Vega looked up once everyone was secure and nodded to the pilot. He flipped many switches and opened a box. There was a keyhole and a button inside of the box. Vega threw the pilot a key and he promptly put it into the keyhole and turned it. The button lit up. He looked back at Vega.

"Sir, are you absolutely certain you want to do this? Have you absolutely thought of everything?"

"Yes dammit, hit the switch!" Vega yelled. The pilot hit the button. Nothing happened at first. "What's that matter? I told you to hit the button! Let's go!"

"Sir, there's a problem, nothing is happening. I've pressed the button and nothing is happening!" Vega unbuckled himself and walked into the cockpit. He jumped into the co-pilot's chair and pressed the button himself. Nothing happened.

"What the fuck is going on here? This ain't right. Naw, this ain't right at all!" Vega jumped out of the seat and ran to the back the copter. He looked out the bay window.

"We're fucked!! Take her down!" Vega screamed at the pilot. The copter began descended towards the ground.

"Men, ready your weapons! The Jifflings are back!" The soldiers unbuckled themselves and produced their instruments. Vega flung open the bay doors. The copter was in the process of landing, so there was a huge pressure difference inside the cabin, which fought against the outside air. From what I could see, there was a huge cloud of Jifflings just outside of the bay doors. The soldiers started playing their chord and the Jifflings began to fall out of the air.

"Keep it up men! Vega yelled, catching his breath. "Play the fourth movement in D!" They began playing a beautiful chord progression that sent a gradually mounting wall of sound outwards in all directions. Almost nothing else was audible in these few moments. Not the copter, not the Jifflings, nothing. The Jiffling cloud was growing thin. Eventually it dwindled to a mere group of the fiends. They perished quickly.

"Fall back men!" Vega yelled. The men quit playing and he closed the bay doors.

"Good work everyone, we held them off." The copter squad was landing at this point. There wasn't a Jiffling in sight.

"Okay everyone, we're going to make base here for a while. We have to diagnose why the shifter drive isn't working. No doubt the bastards have installed some vile construction within the copter." Vega said. We all gathered some gear and got out of the ship.

"Now I want everyone to be on full alert. We need to shift Layers on a moment's notice. Luckily, we can do that even while camped. You all also need to be on guard in case we are attacked again. Keep your weapons at the ready. Do you all understand?"

"Sir, yes sir!" the soldiers replied. They all began moving equipment out of the copter and onto the grassy plain. One solider threw a ball out onto the grass before everyone else started to move. The device expanded and produced a large white light that cleared the grass and evened the terrain so that it would be more suitable to camp on. They raised a preliminary shield around the place and sustained it with several speakers producing the same music they played before, but with less intensity. The mechanics began working on the copter while I sat in the camp basically worthless to the effort.

"Vega, I hate to bother you, but what do you think is the issue here?"

"I think there were a few Jiffling stowaways on board. They replicate so quickly, it would have taken them just a few hours to build back up to that mass we saw. I think they've made a hive somewhere close to our shifter drive. We will try to repair the damage. Just sit tight. There's nothing you can really do now anyways."

"Alright then." I said. The feeling of worthlessness was absolutely overwhelming. I could do nothing to help, and to top it all off I was bored. What could the King possibly want with me anyways? As far as I could recall, he didn't even know me. I had certainly never met him. My time was spent looking at the grass and hills and trees. It was still absolutely breathtaking here. The air was so pure. We had traveled so far but made so little progress. I watched the men start to harvest as much of the grass as they could and deposit this into a contraption they had hooked up to the copter. I became curious and walked over to it. I stopped one of the soldiers to ask about what was going on.

"What are you doing?" I asked.

"There is a compound in the grass that we can utilize as fuel. We harvest it and place it in here to power our equipment and the copter."

"Can I help cut grass?" I offered.

"It is best you just stay put. We can't risk you getting hurt or something happening to you. We've been ambushed so many times it would be safer if you just sat around."

"Okay then, sorry to bother you." I said. The time spent here would stretch on for what seemed like days, but I didn't feel the urge to sleep. I walked back to my previous resting spot and eventually Vega came up to me.

"The mechs discovered the hive close to the shifter drive. They are removing it as we speak and then they will repair the drive. Just be ready to move at a moment's notice."

"Okay Vega. I'm not doing anything so just let me know." I was still disconcerted about this whole shift. I was afraid that I wouldn't be the same. I was afraid that I wouldn't return to the Layer Dryffe whole.

"Vega! Wait please." He stopped and turned around.

"Yes?"

"How sure are you that this is going to work?"

"Well kid, to let you know, we do have a docking station ready for us in the Layer Automina. This is one of the few Layers that have this situation available. It took us years to develop a method to relay the mission objective between Layers, but we finally did it. There is a team ready on the other side waiting for us to arrive. We can send them messages, identities, objectives, what have you, and they will intercept us once we make the shift. Essentially, they will have to convince us that we are who they say we are. I've done it several times, and every time I come back to the Layer Dryffe, I'm the same Vega I always was. To be honest, the only one I'm worried about is you. The King told me you've never made a shift before and to absolutely avoid doing so with you in my custody if at all possible. I'm telling you now kid, you won't remember your present self. It will be like waking up from a dream you were having that seemed so real there was no way you could deny it was reality, but at the same time you forget that dream. It becomes less than a distant memory. It becomes a past life. You won't even remember these words. You won't remember my advice. Most likely what will happen is that you will think you are being arrested or kidnapped when we breach the Layer Automina. You may be placed in a cell or cage. You will probably fight or resist. However, they will be ready for us all. I may do the very same thing. They will have to detain the entire squad until each member has been conditioned and then they will release us, save for those of us who have done it before."

"Wow, that sounds like a lot of work. Just listening to you now, I was a bit apprehensive, but since you say I have no idea what will occur, I'm not really worried about it so much as this manifestation of myself will have not been influenced by the shift in any way, is that correct?" I asked.

"Yes, that's a very accurate perspective on the situation. I'm impressed by your assessment. Sit tight kid, they'll be finished soon."

"Alright then. I'll sit here." He turned around and left. I just sat there like a bump on a log until the repairs would be finished. Time was once again a mystery to me.

My perception of time was still distorted. I just accepted everything as fact. What choice did I have? Vega approached me once again after what felt like days. "We're about to make the shift, kid. Brace yourself. You don't have to move, just know that things are about to change on you significantly."

"Okay, thanks." I said. He charged off into the copter and made his way into the cockpit. He pressed the switch. There was an emanation of black light outwards from the copter so strong that it overpowered the light coming from the suns. Solid surfaces started to crawl as if they were alive with small organisms under the surface that produced bumps and waves. Everything grew darker rapidly. The light was being sucked away. Eventually I could not see anything. This did not last long as eventually I was nothing. And then eventually I was less than nothing. The shift had taken effect and we were all under its influence. Then there was just black. Not nothing, just black and only black.

CHAPTER 5.38 THE INFINITE BAFFLING LAYER AUTOMINA

"Identify yourself, being."

"Identity: ally. Name: Vega. You are in no present danger. Do not be alarmed."

"Status: armed. Vega does not compute. Identify yourself, being. This is your final advisory."

"Shame, we'll have to subdue him. Give him the juice."

"BBBBBBBZZZZZZZZZZZZZZZZTTTTTTTTTTT"

My programming knew no previous error as to this. I had encountered beings that were not willing to render themselves friendly in my presence disregarding their ruse to make out as allies. I had not been programmed to interpret such an encounter. I am ashamed to say I malfunctioned under pressure. Perhaps my fuel levels were low. I had not filled up since solar-break. They had me surrounded. I could do nothing but intimidate as I was programmed to do. It went better than initially calculated. I can only assume this situation deals with the uprising I have received communications regarding in the south reporting on superior Layers. While I am aware of their existence, I am reluctant to accept their intervention in my daily processes as I am just a lowly Servutron. End transmission.

CHAPTER 5.45 THE INFINITE BAFFLING TRANSMISSION

"Sir we are picking up readings that the rescue squad has shifted to the Layer Automina where you have limited authority."

"Continue to monitor transmissions on their docking base. I know they have the boy." Said the Emperor. "They have no idea what they are doing. It will serve fatal for our entire existence if we do not halt their advances."

CHAPTER 5.47 THE INFINITE BAFFLING SERVUTRON

"Your objective cannot hold me here. I am a Servutron to the Emperor. I must fulfill my objective or risk deletion by him."

"Listen, you have just shifted from the Layer Dryffe. Your name is Punxsutawney. You have been chosen by the Master Controller, the King of the Cubicle for a special mission."

"I have received no such transmission. You are all a threat and will be destroyed."

"Servutron, your defense mechanisms have been disabled. We have been expecting you. You are not really what you think you are. Your programming tells you that you are a Servutron, however in the Layer Dryffe you were a boy destined to change our entire reality. Do you compute?"

"Searching...searching. Negative. I reject your proposal and submit you are enemies of the Emperor bent on destroying my existence and my objective. You are all viruses and should be destroyed."

"Servutron, what is your model?"

"Model: TIB5.47-Automina. I was assembled here and I know my duty. You will not convince me otherwise."

"Servutron, hear this theorem: You were once of a format based of carbon life. Do you compute?"

"Possible, but highly unlikely. I am aware of your Layers, but do not have the means to travel between them. I do not accept that I was once of another form because I have no backup data to support this claim."

"You have no backup data because it is common scientific knowledge that subjects who shift Layers for the first time do not retain any prior knowledge of their existence in a previous Layer. Does that compute?"

"Searching...searching. Plausible. I will entertain your various probings for now, but if you do not present any undeniable evidence, I will blacklist you, which will mean total denial. To further supplement the compromise, I will no longer submit any answers to you so long as you have me restrained in such a manner."

"Very well, Servutron. We will release your restraints. Could you possibly entertain the idea that you could have once been represented in another form be it carbon-based, energy-based, metal-based, etcetera?"

"Searching...searching. Plausible. For now I will entertain such a notion. I insist you release me from my bonds." The bonds restraining my circuitry relaxed and I was able to regain full functionality, minus my built-in defense mechanisms, which would have destroyed my interrogators fully and efficiently. I still could not see them. The lighting was dim. Well, they could see me just fine: for there was an overhead lighting array which (regrettably) displayed my components quite clearly to any who would observe. This presented me at a disadvantage. I could not see my interrogators at all. Considering that my self defense mechanisms were entirely disabled (although very modest for a mere Servutron in functionality), my infrared vision was also disabled. I was not afraid for my programming, being my very source of power and energy, even though I was conflicted in my logical processes as to why I was being held captive. I found myself willing to cooperate with my captors in this trial.

"What is it you want from my programming?" I asked.

"Servutron, I submit that you are an anomaly. You are a special existence in not just our Layer, but in every Layer. Your first form is the form of a carbon-based Sapien by the name of Punxsutawney. We are charged with keeping you in our care. You are too important to fall in the hands of the "Emperor" you keep speaking of. Obviously my captors are speaking about the Emperor of the Moon, the being to which I swear allegiance. I suppose my captors are part of the Autominan Clomplex, the Institution for Issuing Instruction or III. This Clomplex designates how the programming of the Layer Automina can be most efficiently conducted. Their law is unquestionable, except by the Emperor. The program that currently holds the top spot of Master Controller goes by filename King of the Cubicle. They say many things about this program, but no single processor can be one hundred percent affirmative what the King does and where he comes from. My programming has concluded that the Emperor's processing power is superior. I swear allegiance to him. They may want information to squash the rebellion. I may be in danger.

"Servutron what do you say?"

"What are you planning on doing to my programming when we are finished here? I obviously have no idea who or what you are. I calculate there will be no need to terminate me."

"We obviously want you to believe us. You are incredibly important. Even if you do not believe us, we would have no reason to terminate you. We don't need information from you. We just need you. That's it, Servutron." This was an incredibly compelling point my captors have made. I want to believe that they will not terminate me, but I am not completely excited about the idea of cooperating with them when I have other objectives. I'm not one hundred percent positive at this point.

"What do I stand to benefit from this situation? I do have primary objectives that I am required to fulfill."

"For starters, we will reactivate your defense mechanisms. Otherwise you'll continue to take that nasty shock any time you attempt to access them. While we're sure you could get it repaired on your own, you'll be defenseless until then. You'll also find that we've removed your navigation chip. Sure, you'll know where you need to go, but you won't know how to get there. We'd be happy to reinstall the component, of course we'll need your cooperation." It doesn't look like I have a choice any longer.

I absolutely need that component. I will be forced to submit to my captor's will...for now.

"I submit to your will, captor. I will remain here for three cycle's time. If I am not entirely convinced by that time, you will restore me to proper working order and allow my freedom. Are we in agreement?"

A Cyborg emerged from the darkness and came forward towards me with his arm extended in agreement.

"Let's shake on it, kid."

CHAPTER 5.67 THE INFINITE BAFFLING SERVUTRON ACQUIRED

I wasn't expecting a Cyborg. They are typically seen as lower class individuals. Cyborgs consist mostly of Sapiens wanting to become Tronics, or even more foul: Tronics attempting to become Sapiens. Both are possible, and both revolting. This one appeared to be mostly Sapien: a tall muscular male with short blonde hair. He had scars. A lot of them. I detected that these were mostly inflicted by the Cylife that populate the Layer Automina. The main reason why Cyborgs are looked down upon is because they are a combination of Sapiens and Tronics. While most of the Tronic race do consist of superior plastics and metals, the Cylife do not posses programming, and therefore do not have the same capacity to understand themselves and their surroundings. They have no comprehension of cities, rational thought, or science. The Cylife focus mainly on survival. The very fabric of what makes up their being is a combination of metals and organic material, and this is where the divide comes between our races.

The Cyborg continued to stretch out his hand: a common form of Sapien concordance. When two Sapiens meet, they grasp each other's hands and squeeze firmly. They do the same thing when in agreement or when leaving each other's company. I've never understood the gesture, being so far removed from their culture. I hesitated, but eventually accepted and placed my manipulator in his hand.

"There we go, kid! This is a step in the right direction. We may not be in such bad shape after all!"

"Why do you call me 'kid'? This is clearly not my identity."

"As mentioned, you were an Sapien. A young adult. Servutron, we received all of your info from before the shift took place. We have your entire crew here. You were in the protective custody of a squad of field agents bound to take you to see the King. They're all here too and have to go through the same conditioning that you're going through. It isn't possible to force you to remember. It is a matter of acceptance."

"Fascinating. Very fascinating. How is it even possible that you are aware of the situation on the previous Layer? Which Layer was this?"

"We can send signals between Layers, no problem. The curious, uh, 'transformation' if you will, is still very much a mystery to us." He paused for a moment and licked his lips.

"And the Layer's name, Cyborg?"

"It was the Layer Dryffe."

CHAPTER 5.69 THE INFINTE BAFFLING SERVUTRON CONFLICTED

"If my programming is true, this is a good definition of what the Sapiens call 'humor'. Allow me to sort this out. You've arrived from The Origin Layer. It is well known throughout all of Automina that only Royalty may shift Layers. May I also include that no being existing within the Cake has done so to or from Dryffe since Turn 0124, excluding all Royalty. If I access my data correctly, that was six hundred thirty seven Turns ago. You're losing credibility, Cyborg."

"With all due respect, Servutron, you are a Servutron. Model...uh, what was it?"

"Model: TIB5.47-Automina, Cyborg"

"Right, right, on the tip of my tongue. If my *programming* is true, you wouldn't be concerned with the flight itinerary of those beings leaving and arriving at Dryffe, now would you?"

"It is common knowledge that is the case so—"

"—SO you are not programmed to know these things. How could you? It isn't your responsibility. It isn't your job, kid."

He had me in a checkmate. It really wasn't my responsibility to know this. This Cyborg has really got something fascinating about him. Could I have been this...*Sapien*? What would it be like to have flesh and blood and to dream? To feel, and taste, and see...rather than detect...? It does not compute. I cannot access any knowledge suggesting the effects of such an experience.

"You Tronics are a bunch of smarty-pants know-it-alls. Sure you have your knowledge and processing power...but you ain't got this." The Cyborg took a metallic finger and gestured it at the side of his head, just above eye level. The Sapien brain. An incredible marvel. I must say he had me intrigued.

And then he said something I will never forget, no matter how many Layers I would ever shift.

"The brain named itself, kid."

CHAPTER 5.72 THE INFINITE BAFFLING SAPIEN BRAIN

If I only had a brain.

The Cyborg had finally convinced me of my purpose. Perhaps this lowly Servutron was destined for something great. I could not explain this reasoning within my own programming. Perhaps there was some error code for this—no. No I cannot rely on my own programming. I was a Sapien in a previous existence according to my captors, no more than five minutes ago. I have to explore this fascinating possibility. I am still a little conflicted about this curiosity. Oh I am already experiencing…what do they call it? Searching…searching…emotion. Not a common thing amongst Tronics. I want to become…a Cyborg. I feel rejection surging up within my circuits, but it is something I have commanded to override. I will follow this…searching…searching…curiosity.

"Cyborg. I am finished with my hesitation. I will submit that I was once this Sapien human boy…this…Punxsutawney. For now, however, you will call me Punxsutron. This—other than restoring my previous functions—will be my only condition to adhering to the agreement. First comes my restoration.

"THAT'S THE WAY KID!!!" The Cyborg ran forward and embraced my programming. He started heaving and grasping me tighter. I tried to activate my defense mechanisms.

"BBBBBBBZZZZZZZZZZZZZZZTTTTTTTTTT"

The Cyborg flew back, knocking over the overhead lighting. I had inadvertently shocked him in my daze. Smoke rose from his components. I was not pleased with this result. Beams of energy flew at me from the darkness. I could hear the Cyborg scream.

"NO! NO! DON'T HIT HIM! DON'T HIT HIM WITH THE JUICE!"

I experienced a blackout. My programming failed. End transmission.

CHAPTER 5.85 THE INFINITE BAFFLING THIRD TRANSMISSION

I regained my faculties in an incredibly bright room. I had no recollection of what had transpired since the Cyborg startled me. There were Sapiens all around. They were looking down upon me. I seemed to me on some sort of workbench. I ran a diagnostic. All of my functions were intact including my defense mechanisms and my navigation chip. I was complete once again and prepared to serve my duties as a Servutron to the Emperor. I rose up with a start from the workbench. There were no restraints. All of the Sapiens were startled and pointed weapons towards me.

"Vega, he's functional get in here now!!!!" one of the Sapiens yelled into the other room. I was ready to terminate them all: my experiences were betrayed. They were just experimenting on me. They had just wanted information after all. I readied my pulse wave, which would disable all of their equipment. That's when I saw the Cyborg barrel into the room.

"Kid you're okay! Stand down, all of you!! Stand down NOW!!!" The Cyborg was commanding the Sapiens to lower their weapons. Not that it mattered, I was about to disable them all anyways.

"Cyborg, you have betrayed me. Why am I on this workbench?"

"Kid, we upheld our end of the bargain, do not initiate defense sequences, please!" I could sense the heat emanating from his Sapien parts. He was desperate. Perhaps I should stop myself. I ceased the defense protocol and disengaged my pulse wave. He approached me.

"Kid, I'm so glad you made it. I told them not to hit you, but it was too late. Do you still remember what we discussed?"

"Affirmative, Cyborg. However, I feel as if our arrangement has been compromised. I will not discuss this matter any further unless you dismiss the Sapiens that you command."

"Of course, kid. Men, STAND DOWN! I can't believe you would fire on our main objective! We are supposed to protect the kid, not destroy him! Shit! You're all a disgrace. Leave the workshop!" The men stood there for a few moments.

"NOW, DAMMIT OR I'LL HAVE YOUR RANKS!!!" the Cyborg bellowed. The Sapiens left swiftly, not wanting to cross the Cyborg. It was obvious that he held rank over the Sapiens. I was conflicted to witness this occurrence. I have never detected such obedience from Sapiens at the behest of a Cyborg. He slammed the door behind him. I was intrigued.

"Kid, I'm really sorry for all of this. I didn't realize how rough it would be on you. The shift, you know? We had all of the regulations in place. It has been so long since we've shifted with a new person. Well, of course you don't have any recollection of this."

"As we discussed previously, Cyborg, I am aware that I have shifted from the Layer Dryffe, against all other evidence. I am not pleased with the behavior of the Sapiens under your command."

"I promise kid, it will not happen again. Look, do you remember just before you got decommissioned?"

"Searching…searching…yes Cyborg, I do recall the occurrences leading up to my attack. I am not exactly willing to comply with everything as I was. This is a betrayal of out agreement. I withdraw to a previous assessment that you are just spies trying to coax data from me regarding the Emperor of the Moon."

"Kid, what you have to understand is that what happened was an accident. My men were just trying to protect me, that is all. Think of it as their own defense mechanisms, which I'm sure you're pleased to have back as fully functional." He was right. My captors had completely upheld their end of the bargain. I was starting to regain trust in the situation.

"You will start to address me as Punxsutron as we previously discussed. Now, I wish to know the plan. I am still willing to uphold the agreement as you have still upheld your end." I was cautious, but my programming reminded me of the curiosities of my previous endeavor with my captors. I was ready to unite my programming with this…Punxsutawney Sapien being. I wanted to understand what role I played in the grand scheme of our existence.

"Very well, Punxsutron. The very next step is to bring you to the Master Controller's palace. We will need to perform a long journey away from the Central Hub. We will have to shift Layers to the Layer Dryffe to meet with him." I was not expecting this, nor was I immediately wishing to comply with this command. Leaving the Central Hub was beyond what I was willing to comply with.

"Cyborg, this is beyond what I am willing to comply with. I wanted to know what being a Sapien was like. I do not wish to leave the Central Hub. This is unacceptable."

"Punxsutron, you are not completely aware of the technology we posses. We can actually save your existence into a file and download it into a new form in addition to restoring your Sapien form as the human boy Punxsutawney. Think of it as if having both your Tronic form, and additionally a Sapien form. You will be experiencing two lives simultaneously. An almost symbiotic existence not entirely unlike becoming a Cyborg. You will share not only Tronic calculations, but also Sapien thoughts, emotions, and senses. You will be able to perceive existence in a manner that no other Tronic as a whole could ever experience. This is something that has not been offered to any being in the entire existence of the Cake. The technology has been tested on lesser beings, particularly the Cylife that surround the Layer Automina outside of the Central Hub that we recognize as civilized. Obviously they developed relationships with their counterparts, but considering that none were nearly as advanced in intelligence as you, well, you understand the implications this may have. This is revolutionary. This is the very here and now, and you are the first to be a part of it."

This was an unexpected turn in my detection. I was highly intrigued and completely willing to submit myself to this experiment. I was now completely willing to listen to this Cyborg and whatever he has to say. I would fall in line with his guidance, as it is imperative that I explore this incredible undertaking.

"Just one condition, Cyborg, what do they call you?"

"Kid, I'm Vega Wonderly. I was in charge of your escort before the shift, and I'll be responsible for you during every shift from here until we get you to the King."

CHAPTER 5.99 THE INFINITE BAFFLING EMPEROR

"Sir, we are now receiving transmission from the Servutron. I think you need to see this."

"On screen now," said the Emperor of the Moon. The screen displayed images from the Servutron's perspective.

"Just one condition, Cyborg, what do they call you?" said the Servutron

"Kid, I'm Vega Wonderly. I was in charge of your escort before the shift, and I'll be responsible for you during every shift from here until we get you to the King."
The Emperor stood from his throne. He walked calmly over to the screen and then smashed it with his scepter in a fit of rage.
"You don't know the extent of my power, Vega. You aren't ready for what I'm going to unleash on you. I will have the dear boy. He determines the fate of us all. BEEDLEBOP!" The Connoisseur emerged in the doorway behind the Emperor. "HOHOHOHOHOHOHOHO! Yes your Excellency?"
"Ready the shift. We're going to pay our dear King a visit."

CHAPTER 6.00 THE INFINITE BAFFLINING LAYER AUTOMINA BEGINS

Vega and I made it to the external boundaries of the Clomplex. It was like experiencing the Layer Automina for the first time. I detected everything differently than I would have on any other day. We were on our way to meet with the King of the Cubicle.
"Kid, we're going to have to go to a different Clomplex now."
"…Does not compute. My programming informed me we were currently in the King's headquarters."
"This is another example of what you don't compute, kid. We aren't anywhere near the King's HQ. We have to leave the city and brave the Cylife in order to reach him. I hope you're ready for uncivilized lands. We didn't reinstall your defense mechanisms for shits and giggles."
So we were off into the wilderness to reach the base of the King of the Cubicle. It was an undisclosed location somewhere outside of the Central Hub of The Layer Automina. Vega was not revealing any details, I gathered. I followed him past the front gate and into the wilderness outside of the Central Hub. He flashed his identification hastily at the guards. They swiftly let him through. We traveled far across the wilderness for what seemed to be cycles, although my internal clock determined this was not the case. The Sapiens eventually stopped to set up a location in order to rest for the evening.
"Kid we got some good juice for you. Not like the other times, the good kind. You'll be fine. Come over here." He led me to a structure the Sapiens had put up. There was a thick wire protruding from the bottom.
"Here we go! Here's some power for you. We took the liberty of searching for your energy slot. This should fit just nicely." He accessed my charging module and plugged me in. I had been running low on power even though my solar chargers were operating at maximum. As a Servutron, my system did not contain large batteries. We had been navigating the uncivilized territory for hours now. Surprisingly the Cylife had been docile up until this point.

"We're going to make camp here for the remainder of the evening. You aren't required to deactivate, but you will charge faster. I leave that completely up to you. We will have guards posted to defend us from the Cylife. As for me, I plan on catching forty winks. That's a way of saying 'sleep' for us Sapiens. I'm going to leave you here now. Happy calculations or whatever, kid. We should make it to our destination after daybreak tomorrow." The Cyborg left my proximity and retired to his sleeping facility. I decided that I would remain functional for the duration of the dark period on Automina. Sapiens needed two major forms of sustenance that us Tronics could bypass, but in its place we needed pure energy to power our functions. A clear advantage. While Sapiens needed to eat and sleep, we merely needed to recharge. Due to our superior and efficient construction, this only needed to take place for a mere few hours and it wasn't even necessary to be inoperative during this time. I decided I would stand guard with the rest of the Sapiens, hoping I would not have to activate my defense mechanisms any time soon. That would mean trouble.

CHAPTER 6.07 THE INFINITE BAFFLING AUTOMINA CYLIFE

Things were quite peaceful where the Sapiens decided to make camp. They chose a non-forested area on a quiet plain. While it is true that even the plants here have metals in their biological makeup, most do not exhibit any sort of cognitive function. There are exceptions in the dense wild where plant, animal, and machine collide to form formidable constructs. One such example is the realm of the Zax. These creatures are amongst the most sentient of the Cylife. While they do not bear the same understanding of existence as the denizens of the Central Hub on Automina, their evolutionary path has found the species at a low tribal stage of cultural development. Thankfully we were camping several miles from the nearest known Zax establishment. Trespassing has often resulted in the termination of the transgressors. While unfortunate, every attempt by the King to make peace with the Zax has been greeted with overwhelming hostility and destruction. Negotiations have almost been completely terminated. I sat wondering what other Cylife could plausibly be in the area. Other known hostile life forms are all completely wild and exhibit no sort of culture or understanding of existence. There are herds of wild Flyx that roam this area. They are airborne creatures. While mostly docile, they are territorial and may become provoked, particularly when their territory is threatened. In this area they hold dominance. I hope we are not in a position to anger any of them. I sat charging my energy supply and analyzing the area for any such being. One of the guards came over to me and initiated a conversation.

"Hey Servutron. How's it going?" A typical Sapien greeting. I was obliged to respond.

"I am charging, Sapien. I am also conducting surveillance on the area. There is nothing to report. I'm sure you are aware of this."

"Yeah, nothing is really going on...so I hear you used to be a Sapien. Like us. Do you remember anything about that?"

"I'm sure you know I don't. Were you not present during my captivity?"

"Yeah I was. I know you put up a good fight. You almost hurt one of my buddies. Good thing we shut you down before anything happened, heh heh heh." The Sapien chuckled to himself. He was amused as was I. He was a scrawny Sapien. Not exactly alpha type as the Cyborg was. He shifted his attention to a tobacco cigarette and lit it. He exhaled swiftly and the smoke dissolved in the dry night air. It was at this point he got closer to me. I attempted to divert my attention elsewhere, but he was within reach of me. I couldn't ignore him.

"You know, I don't believe you were ever a Sapien like me. I haven't ever shifted before, but I have a feeling you would remember at least something. I think old Vega has done one too many shifts if you know what I mean." The guard took an impressive drag on his tobacco cigarette. I detected an elevated heart level within him suddenly. I felt unsafe.

"Hey Servutron, I'll be right back." He turned and started to walk into the depths of the campsite. It was fortunate that I did not have to activate my defense mechanisms against him. I did not want to cause a disturbance as I wanted to meet the Master Controller without causing an incident. I watched as the guard went into a tent on the outskirts of the camp. I stopped tracking him. Hopefully he would not be back to bother me as he had implied.

The weather was quite pleasant I suppose. The stars were displayed quite neatly on the night sky. I could see Automina's three moons. Each moon was characteristically different. One was solid and had its own asteroid belt, one looked to be covered in ice and water, and the last was in the process of falling apart. There were fragments of the third moon drifting around the largest piece of itself. This was the beauty of Automina at night. I was briefly reminded of my previous day with the twin stars in blinding orbit, providing the Cylife with warmth and energy as well as the Central Hub. The Emperor of the Moon loomed in the background of my programming. I had wondered if he thought I was a rouge Servutron bent on betraying him to the King. I had no such intentions of releasing any such information. At least not yet. I was merely following the Cyborg's orders.

I sat and analyzed the plain. On the horizon I saw a small figure. I didn't pay the figure much attention as it was two miles off in the distance. I could not identify the biology of the creature, so I ignored it. I continued to survey the landscape when the previous Sapien guard approached me. I immediately became apprehensive.

"Alright kid, we are leaving on a recon mission."

"Negative, Sapien guard. I am to remain here until further orders from the Cyborg you call Vega." The guard looked around shiftily. A few other guards emerged from the surrounding camp area. They came up behind the guard who had approached me. He looked at me briefly and pulled out my recharging cord.

"You're coming with us now, Servutron. Vega commanded it." My programming was conflicted. Until now the Cyborg had told me directly what my duties were. As a Servutron I could not disagree with the command presented to me by the Sapien. I decided that I would go with him. I arose and followed him away from the campsite.

We traveled a great distance, so much so that the campsite was just a speck on the horizon. Vega was not with us. I looked back and saw that there were three other Sapiens following me in addition to the one who commanded me.

"Where are we going, Sapien guard? This does not seem pertinent to our mission and may put us all in danger. I think—"

"Doesn't matter what you think, kid. We're going out here to hunt for Flyx. They fetch a nice price at market. The metals that make up their exoskeleton are very rare and are used to fashion weapons. We're going after a few of them. You're going to…assist us."

"Sapien guard, this is going against everything we were ordered to do. You are charged with protecting me, not putting me in harm's way. This has gone too far. I am returning to camp." I moved past him in the direction of camp. The guard swiftly turned around and put his foot on my hull and shoved me to the ground. Things were not how they should be. He approached me and bent over to face me.

"You are going to do what we say, or we tell Vega that you forced us all out here on a suicide mission because you are a spy for the Emperor. Does that compute, kid?" Ah, the Sapien tactic of deception. I began to wonder if Vega was in on this all along, but just didn't show his face. Either way, I was trapped. The Sapiens would simply terminate me if I resisted and claim self-defense. There was no alternative option. I had to aid them.

"What is it you would have me do, Sapien guard? Also, what do they call you?"

"Name doesn't matter, and you will be helping us track and kill Flyx with your advanced thermal sensors. I know you have it because I installed it. Just remember what we talked about. No trying to get out of this, or we'll make sure you are deprogrammed."

"Okay Sapien Matter, first name: Doesn't. I will follow your command unless it would directly interfere with my safety in which case I assume you would terminate me immediately."

"You're a real smart-ass, kid. 'Doesn't Matter' isn't my name." But this is what I thought of him. He really didn't matter as far as I was concerned. I was hoping this dangerous expedition would have him terminated. Of course I didn't express this out loud. For now, I will just refer to him as "Matt", a somewhat common Sapien name that I thought fitting given the circumstances. Matt still had his foot on my frame while I was on the ground. He gathered saliva in his mouth and let it out in a glob, which landed on my exterior between my two optical receptors. I could think of no other explanation for this other than intimidation, which had no effect on me. The other three guards, however, scoffed at this loudly. He removed his foot by shoving off of me and allowed me to resume an operable position. Matt continued walking ahead in the direction we were headed previously. I tried to regain my composure as elegantly as possible.

The night sky was lit up with stars in different systems. The Sapiens took no notice, but I had not experienced such a thing before. Having spent my entire existence within the Central Hub of Automina, the night sky was a mystery to me. I was vastly perplexed by the sheen of the stars filling the sky. I calculated which stars were closest to us. I hypothesized what sort of planets orbited those stars. It was a very intriguing few moments amidst such unfair treatment. We continued walking until my sensors detected movement on the horizon.

"Here we are, ladies," said Matt. I focused on the horizon. There was an incredibly large nest of Flyx just ahead of us. While I was impressed that the Sapien could spot such a nest and wondered how he had known it was here, I was also extremely cautionary. The nest was quite large. This is to say that at just the boundary of their territory, I detected at least twenty hunters and five domestic Flyx. There were most likely many more, easily hundreds. The Cylife here were bustling. This was no mere tribe, this was a full-blown colony. This was a Central Hub of their very own, without the cultural understanding and technology of course. I was lucky that my captors were not attempting to hunt Zax. That would have been far more foolish, and I rate the probability of survival six thousand seventy to one for such a venture. This is compared to the current poaching mission on the Flyx nest, which was just a mere twenty five to one that all members of our squad would survive. I postulated if the other three Sapiens understood their danger.

"Guards, I will advise that our odds on facing this nest and having all of you survive are around twenty five to one. Chances are one or more of you will perish."

"What did you just say, kid? I thought I told you what would happen if you disobeyed my command. You know that if I lose any men, you will be blamed for it."

"I remember you malicious commands, Sapien. I am telling you now in the best interest for all of us. If this scenario played out twenty five times, only one of those times would we all emerge without death or fatal injury. This doesn't even take non-fatal injuries into consideration. I'm sure you were aware of the dangers of this before we set out on this, what was it? Mission?" Matt stared me down. He was very obviously displeased at my announcement. He came up to me swiftly and spoke in an intense, angered whisper.

"You had better hope that none of these men die. If they do, what I told you before still stands. You will be blamed for their deaths to Vega. Do I make myself clear?"

"Of course, just as long as you realize that it was you who put your men in danger and not me. Even if you terminate me, even if those three are killed and if it is just you and I, you will have to live with these events on your mind as you ignored facts and sent them to their deaths on the chance you would make money." Matt did not appreciate this. I could see him grow increasingly angered with me. He shook with anger briefly while looking me in the optical receptors and turned away.

"We are moving. Now. Get ready to take one down." He was addressing the other three Sapiens, and not me. There was apparently a plan already in motion that was not made clear to me. I simply remained were I was and watched them move past me towards the Flyx nest. Matt had not gone thirty feet when he turned around.

"Servutron, you will accompany us. Now. You know what will happen if you don't." I advanced with them. My sensors began to pick up more and more life signs. Even though on this plain I could detect almost two hundred Flyx, they were still almost a mile off. Our squad continued to advance until I was able to pick up the entirety of the Flyx nest. There were eight hundred and ninety three Flyx in this current nest. I detected that at any given time our average distance to the closest Flyx was one hundred yards. This is well within their hearing range. They could detect us and alert the rest of the hunters at any moment. According to my most detailed scans, there were at the very least two hundred hunters in the nest. This is not to mention that this particular Cylife was capable of flight, and most of the hunters were already airborne as they have regular patrols surrounding the nest searching for predators. Based on this new information, I calculated that the probability of survival of all of our members was now decreased to seven hundred thirty five to one. We had stopped and hidden in some tall metallic brush that was on the very perimeter of the nest. I looked at Matt. He seemed to be occupied with some of his equipment. He manipulated his weapon to form a stringed instrument. I looked at the other three guards and they were preparing their weapons in a similar fashion. I was intrigued by these actions.

"Guard, what are you doing?"

"We are preparing to set a trap for a wary Flyx, what does it look like?" It looked like they were preparing to play a song. I devised that this song was intended to be the trap for the Flyx. The guards each had different instruments from one another.

"You didn't know we played together? How did you think we kept ourselves entertained on missions, kid?" He chuckled lowly. I cannot deny that I was impressed by this display. Never before had I seen weapons that converted into instruments before. Regardless of this, the instruments were still going to be used as a weapon to lure a Flyx close to us for the guards to subdue. I assumed that the Flyx would struggle, but I stood by and waited for them to begin their display.

"Kid, we're called The Masters of the Cylife. That's the group's name. We've done this before. We know what we're doing." With that, he nodded at the other members of the ensemble and they nodded back in agreement, instruments at the ready to play their siren song. I observed as Matt began playing a few low notes. They were so soft and sweet that I could just barely detect them, but the other three joined in shortly producing a harmony of sound unlike anything my receptors had ever processed. My hard drive had previously stored a large library of the Sapien's music. This display was unlike anything I had accessed previously. Even in the face of overwhelming peril, these Sapiens produced music the likes of which were not commonly known on Automina. Their song started slow and soft. The expression present in the notes was completely contrary to their typical demeanor as I experienced. I must admit that I had not thought these four Sapiens capable of such tender and complex emotion. Off in the distance at the nest, a few of the airborne Flyx were almost paralyzed. Most of them hung in place flapping their wings heavily just to stay in the air. The magnificent song, even though it was just on the cusp of their hearing, was still highly intoxicating. I could detect through my thermal vision that the internal temperature of the Flyx stricken by the song was dropping. They hung there and eventually one by one started lazily making their way towards the source of the music. None of them called out for help. I picked up at least six of them flying towards us. I notified Matt.

"I detect that six of the Flyx are making their way towards our location. What do you propose to do? They have found our location due to your song." Matt ignored me and instead continued playing. The Flyx grew closer and closer with alarming speed, but the very closest, dropped out of the sky as if dead. The remaining five followed suit as if they had been killed. The song had intoxicated them so much that they fell out of the sky, unable to continue their pursuit of the source. I peered over the metallic brush and viewed the Flyx. They were completely docile. The Flyx were incapable of fighting against the song. I jumped back and spoke to Matt.

"You have six of the Cylife under your alluring spell. They are belly up on the plain rolling around in euphoria. I suggest you strike now, lest other members of the nest realize they are gone." Matt looked up from his instrument, still playing.

"Servutron, you are to go out and terminate the nearest Flyx organism and bring it back to us." I could not disobey. The group continued to play their song. I noticed they were repeating a particular passage over and over. This apparently held the Flyx in stasis. I looked on as the group continued to play their song. I studied the Flyx, beaten and rolling in the euphoria of hearing such a work. An idea occurred to me.

"Oh guard, what if I were to leave just now? You are obviously occupied performing. If you were to break performance, the Flyx would surely arise and terminate you all. I could leave without the slightest doubt that I would make it back to camp safely. You cannot break performance to stop me from doing so, otherwise you will all perish. What say you?" He looked at me with the utmost loathing in his eyes. I had caught him in a checkmate. He formed a very angered face.

"If you leave, I have no problem breaking performance so long as you are destroyed in the process." I sensed he was right. The other Sapiens heard this and it brought looks of fear on their faces. Their leader had betrayed them at the expense of a senseless mission to recover a Flyx carcass. I arose and made for the camp, calling his bluff, I assumed.

"Where are you going, Servutron? You have to follow my command or be terminated!" He yelled after me. I stopped. My programming forced me to obey. I had to return. While I had wanted to escape back to camp all along, I could not disobey a direct order from a Sapien. I turned around and rejoined the group performing their haunting song.

"Now Servutron, you are ordered to go and collect the nearest Flyx. If you have to terminate them, then so be it." I proceeded out of the metallic brush towards the nearest Flyx. I was twenty feet away when I fully beheld the specimen. It was simply magnificent. The wingspan of this hunter was nearly ten feet in length. It was completely intoxicated by the song, and thus completely helpless. This was a fascinating experience. The creature looked up at me with hopelessness in its eyes. It stared at me for a short period of time. The Flyx was not in pain and displayed no hostile intentions towards me, yet I had to extinguish its life force. I produced my immobilizer from within my external frame and brought it towards the creature's head. These Flyx were particularly weak to electronic energy due to their metallic bone structure. I readied my terminating strike when my sensors picked up a disturbing reading of another organism close by. It was terrible to behold. There was a team of Zax on the exact same hunting mission as our squad. There were five of them. Of course, we were in great peril just dealing with the Flyx. If the Zax detected our squad, there would be very little hope of survival for all of our members. They would surely detect my strike if I were to end this Flyx's life. Naturally, I was conflicted. I could not kill the Flyx without the Zax detecting it and rampaging towards us. I looked back at Matt, and could see him peering from behind the metallic brush. I turned and went back to him. He was visibly upset and angered.

"Servutron you have to bring that Flyx back here or be destroyed! This is your last warning!" He was telling the truth. His pulse was elevated and his internal temperature had risen. I had little time to explain myself. He continued to play his song.

"Guard, I have detected five Zax on the horizon just to the left of out position. They are here for hunting purposes and intend to kill anything in their path. We are in much larger danger now. I cannot discharge my attack without attracting their attention. If you have a better solution, we should pursue that instead."

"You will go and kill that Flyx and bring its body here straight away. If the Zax spot us, we'll just have to deal with that then. Go. Now." He stopped talking. He was very serious and about to have us all killed. If he were to turn on me, I would take him out. Easily. However, this would not be to my advantage later on as I would have to explain everything to Vega. I had no choice but to let this unlikely scenario play out. I approached the downed Flyx and readied my immobilizer once again. I struck the Flyx and it perished immediately. They would most likely detect this strike and head this way. I hoped I had miscalculated.

CHAPTER 6.43 THE INFINITE BAFFLING SERVUTRON HADN'T MISCALCULATED

I hadn't miscalculated. All five of the Zax immediately stopped their advance towards the hive and faced the position of the kill. They began to approach with much haste.

CHAPTER 6.44 THE INFINITE BAFFLING UNFORTUNATE CALCULATION

The following events took place in a matter of approximately six minutes and forty-four seconds. The lead Zax let out an enormous roar. He was very large, an alpha specimen, easily double the height of the tallest of the Sapien guards. They stopped playing their music almost immediately after hearing the war cry, thus releasing the remaining Flyx from their stupor. They immediately took flight to search for predators. Luckily for myself and the Sapiens, this happened to be the Zax, who had made incredible time racing towards the metallic brush to terminate our squad. The Flyx were not aware of us just yet and instead all attacked the Zax. This was but a minor inconvenience for the Zax, who were largely concerned with the squad and myself. The first two Flyx to attack the Zax were terminated instantly as their metallic structures were horribly compromised by lethal blows to the neck from the Zax who were defending. The remaining Flyx had better luck scoring blows against weak points on the Zax's face and chest. While formidable in nature, the Zax were not without weaknesses, and the Flyx were aware of such flaws having been hunted so frequently by the Zax. One of the Zax down hard and perished. The Flyx had teamed up against this particular creature with much success. The remaining four Zax were not as concerned with their fallen brother and continued to advance on our position. I had the Flyx carcass in tow and was making my way as fast as I could towards the metallic brush. I was nearly there when I detected a Zax just behind me. In horror I looked on as it leapt over me and into the metallic brush were the Sapien guards were previously holding their concert. The Sapiens were struggling to reassemble their weapons into a lethal form. The Zax weren't interested in me. They were interested in sustenance. The Sapiens were a delicacy to them, a great alternative to the tough meat of the Flyx. I dropped the Flyx carcass and began to flee the battle. I was making my way when I detected more life signs far behind the metallic brush in the direction of camp. There was a squadron of Sapiens advancing towards our position. There were twenty-three of them. From my scans, they were armed to the teeth. I redirected towards this new squad in hopes that Vega would be there, so I continued my advance steadily. There were gruesome sounds coming from the metallic brush. I did not care. Those guards exploited me for personal gain. I wanted them all to be terminated and now I could not be blamed for any personal harm that befell them. I continued my approach and was halted by two guards.

"Stay where you are!" one of them said to me.

"Is Vega with you?" I asked hastily.

"Yes…you're the Servutron we were escorting! What are you doing out here?"

"Just take me to Vega now!" The guards led me to Vega at the rear of the squad. He saw me and approached quickly.

"KID WHAT ARE YOU DOING HERE?!?! WE'VE BEEN SEARCHING FOR YOU ALL NIGHT!" He was very angry. His men were in danger.

"Before your anger gets misdirected, let me explain Cyborg! Four of your men took me from the camp and forced me to hunt Flyx for their own personal gain. They were wanting to blame me for any misfortune they befell. They told me that they would tell you I forced them out here to kill them if we were caught. I couldn't do anything lest they blackmail me. Do you understand the situation?"

"Oh yeah kid I get it. I know exactly who took you out here too. They will pay, if they haven't already paid the ultimate price. It looks like they aren't doing too well right now." I looked back at the metallic brush. There were three Zax assaulting the guards. The guards had a very slim chance to take down the Zax without fatality. The rest of Vega's squad had rushed on without Vega and I. We stayed behind and continued to talk.

"I predict their chances of survival to be incredibly slim, Vega. Chances for them all to survive are around one in thirty six. I bet one or two are already terminated, if not all four." I quickly scanned. One was deceased. The other three were falling back towards Vega's advancing squadron.

"One of your men is dead, Vega."

"I frankly don't give a shit, kid. They are considered traitors to the King at this point. We're just here to recover you and retreat until we are no longer in danger. Now that you're here, there's no reason to put my men in any further danger." And with that Vega modified his weapon into a musical instrument. Well, it was less of an instrument and more of a sound amplification mechanism. He finished assembling it and brought the receiver up to his mouth.

"FALL BACK MEN!" His voice was devastating. This was no standard yell, the sound waves rustled the grass and moved the air noticeably. It unfortunately caught the attention of the Zax and the attacking Flyx hunters. While the main squadron was in no immediate danger, the Cylife began targeting them over one another. The three surviving guards who captured me continued their sprint towards us. They were to be first on the menu for the Cylife.

"I'm sure you're aware that you just killed the three guards that—"

"I know kid, they're our distraction while my squad falls back. See? That's smart!" He seemed very pleased with his plan, and almost giggled. I didn't exactly agree with his assessment. He did put us in danger if the Cylife overran our unwitting allies in the metallic brush. The rest of his squad was already falling back.

"We need to run back towards camp now, kid. Let's go." He began to reassemble his device back into a weapon while we were running away from the bloodbath. We didn't look back. I felt as if my programming was safe once again. End previously established time frame of six minutes and forty-four seconds.

CHAPTER 6.50 THE INFINITE BAFFLING UNFORTUNATE RUSH AHEAD

Vega and I made our way as fast as possible back towards camp. Losing our pursuers was going to be quite a task, as we would have to terminate all of them. The squadron was not too far behind us, only about thirty seconds until they would catch us if we stood still. I did not dare stop to scan if the remaining three guards were still alive. I assumed they were not, and that the Sax and Flyx were continuing their feud, which would allow the squadron a safe getaway. We fled and fled, not communicating with one another for what seemed like the entire trip back to the camp, only we weren't there yet. I stopped for just a moment to look back and survey our surroundings. The situation was not optimum. I had to shout at Vega who did not stop.

"Vega! Our squadron is still at one hundred percent, however, there are two Zax just behind them. They will catch up very shortly. We have to terminate them if we are all to survive. I think we may need to regroup and destroy them. With your guidance, I have no doubt all your men will survive, and will have two Zax to bring back for food and trade." Vega stopped and turned around.

"Alright kid, I'm going to put my faith in you! I trust you--what was it-- Punxsutron? Yeah, it all makes sense now. We're going to stop this without losing anyone and you're going to be a hero. How does that sound, Punxsutron?" I would have to admit that it sounded highly appealing.

CHAPTER 6.52 THE INFINITE BAFFLING UNFORTUNATE HOW APPEALING INDEED

The Emperor had made his shift with his very own escort and appeared just on the outskirts of Vega's camp. As Royalty, he and his guard had no need to appear in a different form. This was part of The Great Business Deal. Royal escorts need not produce a new personality. As a consequence, the surroundings of the shift site would be consumed to produce the beings in their forms from the previous Layer. This meant completely destroying Vega's base camp into sand, which was solely based on the mechanics of the shift to this particular Layer.

"Hahahaha! Excellent!" the Emperor proclaimed upon arrival. He stood in the crater of dust and gazed upon the destruction he had wrought. "Excellent indeed! Their camp is demolished! Ready the next shift! We are all bound for the next Layer!" The Emperor's calculations had been almost exact based on the video feed from the Servutron. In most cases, beings that shift Layers cannot predict where they will shift to in the next Layer. It would seem this law did not burden the Emperor. It came to his great advantage. His escort finished securing the area and immediately readied themselves for the next shift. Beedlebop was at the Emperor's side. He approached sluggishly.

"Emperor, I'm…not as I should be. The mere suggestion of shifting Layers was…too much for me to properly understand, as preposterous as the idea was." Beedlebop proceeded to hack and cough as if stricken with severe illness. He looked pale and defeated. The Emperor lifted Beedlebop and cradled him in his arms like a child. In this Layer the Emperor could have taken his previous form, but instead he chose one far more menacing: a large being surrounded by darkness with a long flowing red cape and regal crown made from steel. He was hidden beyond the dark shroud produced by his own being.

"You will be just fine poor Beedlebop. Just take solace in my embrace. We will make our shift to the next Layer before we return to the Layer Dryffe for our encounter with the King. Just rest for now. You will be strong in the next Layer as it is filled with notions you typically involve yourself in."

"Thank you Emperor." And with that, Beedlebop went into a deep sleep, not able to accept his surroundings any longer as they were all far too preposterous for him to comprehend in such a small amount of time. The mere experience of shifting Layers had over stimulated him past the point of exhaustion and into illness. "Sleep well, my poor Beedlebop. You will feel significantly better when you awaken." With that, he arose still carrying Beedlebop and approached the nearest soldier.

"When will we be ready to set up our shift?"

"Within the next five minutes sir."

"Good, I assume the trap will be set for Vega after we are gone?"

"Yes sir. We will make certain their technology fails to take them to the desired Layer. They will expect their camp, but will be met with death. I hope you know what this means, sir. I mean no disrespect." The soldier bowed slightly in respect for the Emperor and retreated back to aid his fellow soldiers in preparing the shift and the trap.

The Emperor muttered to himself, "Good. Now we wait until we confuse ourselves for the last time…hopefully."

CHAPTER 6.57 THE INFINITE BAFFLING LAYER AUTOMINA INDEED

Vega and I held our ground. He reassembled his auditory device.

"MEN WE STAND OUR GROUND AND DESTROY!" he proclaimed. I detected that the squadron stopped and turned to face the two Zax enemies. I predicted one in two chances that all members would survive and watched as the events unfolded before me. The men were obviously trained to handle such situations and turned on their pursuers with great haste. The Zax were not daunted and continued their advance until they were upon the first of the squadron. It was to no avail. There were at least ten members focused on each Zax, and they all fired at the same time. The Zax stood no chance against the superior weaponry. They were both terminated within a matter of moments. The men spared no time in rushing forward to collect the carcasses and mounted them upon tools, which they then hoisted for transport. The tools exerted energy fields that aided the men in maneuvering the fallen Zax. They rushed to bring them back towards Vega and I. We were no longer in danger, and we could now return to camp in peace. I looked at Vega in anticipation of his happiness. He looked back and scratched his left ear. "Great job, kid. We are home free now. We can go back with the two Zax bodies, and without fear." He was right. All of the Flyx hunters were either gone or terminated in the struggle, although I was concerned that he said nothing to the men who defended us. We made the hours-long journey back to the camp. The plain was left behind us step by step until we arrived at the campsite, or what used to be the campsite as it was completely demolished as if someone had replaced it with a small desert wasteland. Vega and I stood on the outskirts as the remainder of the squadron caught up with us. They were all devastated, as was I.

CHAPTER 6.66 THE INFINITE BAFFLING POCKET SECOND CHANCE

There was nothing remaining. A small crater of dust existed in various places where the camp once was. Everyone was devastated. Vega approached the crime scene first. Everyone stood fast as he advanced. He was clearly distraught. The Cyborg fell to one knee and shouted at the top of his lungs.

"I HATE YOU EMPEROR!!!!" Not exactly a clever exclamation, but one overflowing with pure emotion. The dust shifted and Vega bowed into the ashes. In this moment, he was defeated.

I had calculated that there was a large Sapien presence here no more than five minutes prior. According to Vega's reaction, I assumed the Emperor was only recently here in the Layer Automina, and had already shifted Layers in order to escape after his attack on our camp. I was the only one to approach Vega during his grieving.

"What happened here, Vega?"

"Kid, they fucking shifted on top of our camp! They destroyed the whole thing!"

"...does not compute. I thought shifts could only be performed inside the Central Hub."

"Kid, HE'S ROYALTY!" Something I apparently should have known already, according to Vega. And with that Vega grabbed a handful of dust and threw it at me. The cloud covered my field of vision briefly and left some particles attached to my ocular receptors. I promptly wiped them off.

"Vega, am I to assume the Emperor come here?"

"Yes kid, he showed up just to destroy our camp and poof off into thin air again! He did it just to destroy our camp! The bastard is smart, I'll give him that, but he's so vindictive..." Vega trailed off just staring at the dust. The time came for contemplation and reflection. Vega just sat there, devastated and alone even while in his squad's presence. The silence that fell over the camp was almost unexpected. None of the men were making a sound. One by one they all sat down in the grass on the outskirts of the obliterated campsite. They didn't talk to one another. Each member seemed...uneasy. Something was driving at them much more than just the feeling of loss, which comes from losing personal belongings. I did a brief scan. Their vitals showed signs of high stress. They were in severe emotional anguish. One of the men began to sob silently and rocked back and forth with his hands around his knees. There was something else going on here that I was not informed of. I felt it necessary to tell Vega of this.

"Sir, your men are highly distraught. I sense this is not merely because of the loss of the campsite." He sat in the sand for a moment after hearing me before he stood up and dusted his knees off. He turned to me and motioned for me to follow him farther into the center of the ruin. The rest of the men stayed behind on the outskirts. Their individual conditions worsened. When he spoke, his tone was at an intense whisper. He was still distraught.

"You're right about that, kid. Sure we're all pissed about the camp, but what's more than that is something you wouldn't know anything about. Something I gotta do here soon that's going to really affect one of them."

I wasn't sure what to say. "…are you going to punish them? Look, it seems as if they had nothing to do with this."

"Yeah kid, they didn't. They didn't have a lick to do with this, but the way things are…one of them is going to fix it. The tough part is, this is my decision. Things aren't going to be pretty here real soon. You may just want to wait here."

"Vega, I would like to know what's going on, please." He sighed loudly. Vega's mouth twisted and he stifled a sob. He reached into one of his pockets and produced a small metallic cube with little flashing lights all around it, approximately one cubic inch in volume. The lights were going off in no particular pattern that I could detect. What was more important: I had no recognition of the device in my memory.

"Vega, what is that device?" This was all I dared ask him. He grinned grimly and held the cube between two fingers at opposite points to explain the device.

"It has a few names. Some call it the Ice Cube. Others call it the Do-Over-In-A-Box. Most people call it The Sinister Roulette. The official name, or at least what the inventors call it, is the Pocket Second Chance…" He trailed off again just staring at the device while regarding every facet of its surface. He sat in silence for about thirty seconds. Once again, he sighed loudly, then suppressed another sob and began to speak.

"Each squad leader has a few of these things. The prototypes were just fucking horrifying. There were so many deaths associated with testing…so many good men lost," He sighed again and looked up at the sky. His body temperature was rising steadily.

'The researchers never could get it quite right, though. It is designed to take a portion of defined space back in time a pre-designated period, but this comes at a cost. It is essentially a time machine, but someone nearby has to pay the ultimate price in order to activate it. At first during testing, it would just kill everything. Just…well…everything within its radius was sacrificed to power the reaction. Time travel isn't really merciful. Sure, we can shift Layers with just memories being erased, but time travel demands life as payment. This thing is supposed to be a last resort, but hey, we don't really have much of a choice now. Everything is gone…all of our provisions, millions of credits worth of equipment…it…it just sits in this huge ash pile. All of it is completely unusable. We'll probably all die out here without it, but the alternative lies within this little cube. If I could radio the Hub, I would. Our communications died with the Emperor's shift." He sat there in silence again, contemplating what he should do. This silence lasted for approximately 10.65 minutes. Just when I was going to ask another question, he began speaking.

"Kid, it was supposed to be used in situations where the entire squad was compromised in case of attack. Say a battle went completely the wrong way, the cube could be used to reset everything at the cost of one life that would not come back. The squad could make a full retreat with significantly less casualties. Unfortunately, I don't see much of a choice in this situation. We could try to make it back to the Central Hub and possibly all perish, or one of these guys could become a hero. That's what they're all shook up over. They figure I'm about to use this thing. Guess what? They're right. The only question is, which one of these guys saves us all?" He couldn't keep it back at that point. He started to cry, it was only a little, but he was incredibly unhappy about the current situation. I didn't say anything to him for a few moments. He eventually dried up and turned towards his men. They all became aware of this and straightened up. I sensed they were more frightened than ever. Vega began walking back towards his men and I followed. About halfway, I processed a calculation.

"Vega, what about the men who captured me?"

"What about them, kid? Oh…you're right." Vega had caught on fast, not wanting to sacrifice one of his good men for this cause. If one of the men who captured me and forced me to lead them into danger was still alive, Vega would have no problem using him as the sacrifice. At least I assumed this would be the case.

"I figured I would point this out. You and your men were in such distress over the situation."

"Well kid, that's a damn smart idea. I can only hope you're right. I can't think of a better punishment for those men who took you from the camp. I only hope that one of them made it alive and is trying to come back here." We continued to approach the men. They stood at attention, not aware of out plan. Vega addressed them while I stood at his side.

"Alright men. I know what you are all expecting. You're expecting me to choose someone to be the sacrifice for the Pocket Second Chance. Well, I've got something to say about that. There is a chance, albeit slim, that one of those men who took the Punxutron is still alive. If that is the case, we will be using him as the sacrifice. For right now, we will be heading back to see if there are any such survivors. If so, we will capture him and bring him back. I'm sure you're all relieved to hear that, huh?" The men were more than excited to hear this. Everyone seemed jovial to hear this news.

"So now we will be heading back towards the previous battlefield. Everybody pick up your equipment and let's move out!" With that, we began our way back towards the battlefield. It wasn't going to be a short trip, as we had made a very long trip from the metallic brush to the campsite. Everyone hoisted their equipment up and followed Vega in the direction we had just come from. This was an incredibly long trip with nothing of interest to report, until I detected two life forms on the very edge of my sensors. They were both Sapiens, obviously two of the men who took me. I alerted Vega at once.

"Vega, there seems to be two Sapien life forms just a mile ahead of us. I have no doubt that they are two of the men who took me."

"Hell yeah! Men, the two traitors are just a mile ahead of us. We need them both ALIVE! Do NOT present lethal force. Of course, that is if you don't want to be a sacrifice! I don't mean that as a threat, just make sure you capture them without incident!" With that, the men picked up their speed. We advanced until the two Sapiens were within sight distance. They were indeed two of the men who took me, and one of the two was Matt (am I detecting...joy?). They sprinted forward with what appeared to be their remaining energy until our squad met them in close quarters. Matt started to scream like a lunatic at the squad in general.

"THANK YOU SO MUCH FOR COMING BACK FOR US! THAT BLASTED BOX OF CIRCUITS TOOK US ALL THE WAY OUT TO THE FLYX CAMP AND WE—"

"SAVE IT! I'm already aware of the situation," said Vega. "You are a traitor to the King. But what we'd all like to know here is how are you still alive?" Matt began laughing. He smiled at Vega for a moment.

"Notice anything missing from your inventory?" said Matt through a toxic grin.

"What are you referring to?" asked Vega.

"One of your Pocket Second Chances. I used it when we were attacked. This lucky bastard and me made it out. We had to sacrifice one of our own that was already dying. His legs had been severed by one of the Zax. I acted fast so he didn't suffer." After hearing this, Vega approached Matt slowly, but with great intent and intimidation. He stood a few inches from his face with a stern look and spoke suddenly.

"We're glad you're okay, soldier! Come on back to camp with us."

"Wait, you're okay with everything that happened? We're just going back to camp?"

"Yeah, we came back for you! You wouldn't think we would leave you out here all alone, would you?"

"But I stole from you, I deceived you. You...you forgive me just like that?"

"Yeah, just like that! Let's just skip all the paperwork, it will all be fine. Come on, let's get back to camp." And with that, Vega's deception of Matt was complete. We made our way back to camp. All of the men were very hungry at this point. They were eager to get their camp back to eat and rest. This would all be possible once Vega sacrifices the traitor Matt. I still did not know his true name as Vega had not acknowledged him. Regardless, it would not matter, as the traitor would soon perish. We made our journey back to the campsite crater.

CHAPTER 6.85 THE INFINITE BAFFLING SACRIFICE

Vega led Matt and the other traitor into the very center of the crater where the campsite used to be. Matt and the traitor were completely willing to walk along even while the rest of the men waited, and even as Vega told them the story of how the campsite got destroyed. Matt eventually caught on. I'm glad he did so in a compromising position.

"You told me that the camp was still here, why did you really come back for me?"

"Well, to be honest, I had hoped it would happen like this. You both are going to be the sacrifice for my remaining Pocket Second Chance since you're both traitors, you know? No hard feelings, right?" With that, Vega took the small cube from his pocket and pressed it into Matt's forehead until he bled. With his free hand, he aimed at the second man and shot him in the head. Matt had fallen to the ground and was writhing in pain.

"If there is an afterlife, I hope it is pure agony for you," said Vega. With that, the cube sank into the skull of Matt, and he perished instantly. The Pocket Second Chance claimed its sacrifice. Vega and I hurried back towards the men on the outskirts of the ruined campsite. I picked up loud noises from behind me as the cube activated having accepted the sacrifice. There was a loud whirring sound followed by several loud bangs.

"We had better keep making tracks, kid! If we aren't outside the radius of this thing when it starts, we'll be caught up in an infinite loop. Go!" We rushed towards the rest of the men. Just as we reached them, there was an intense flash of light and a loud rushing sound that enveloped all of us. Everyone fell to the ground for a few moments. The sound and light were intense, although harmless to all of us outside of the radius of the camp. I turned from my position to view the reaction taking place inside the radius of the destroyed camp. Everything within the radius of the Pocket Second Chance's sphere was playing backwards in what I calculated was upwards of octuple time. The following events took place in approximately six minutes and forty-four seconds.

CHAPTER 6.71 THE INFINITE BAFFLING POCKET SECOND CHANCE IS EVIL

We all watched as time reversed itself within the bubble. Very few beings had ever witnessed such an event prior to this, and it was completely enthralling. Perhaps more so than anything I'd ever see. There was no indication of where the bubble began or ended other than the dust outline of the campsite. Everyone watched from the outside as time began to reverse itself. There were clones of everyone. Firstly, everyone saw Vega and I meet the traitors and lead them backwards out of the bubble. We waited a few minutes and watched Vega and I enter and exit the bubble, which was our first experience of the campsite being destroyed. After that, there was nothing for a long period of time. I believe at least one minute and forty six seconds passed before there was another massive flash of light. Vega and I saw the Emperor cradling a small body. The Emperor was enormous in the Layer Automina. Easily twenty feet tall. We could only identify him by the steel crown he wore and the red cape. The rest of him was covered by a massive rapidly flowing black shroud that defied accurate explanation. It wrapped and writhed in the visible three dimensions, clearly being produced by unseen forces surrounding him. He was only present within the bubble for about a minute or less. The small body he cradled appeared to be his right hand man, the Connoisseur of the Preposterous. He was heavily affected by the shift from the brief look at him. The Emperor let the Connoisseur down from his arms. He laughed a short while. After this, followed another blinding light. We then witnessed the rapid reconstruction of our camp. It happened much faster than it had been destroyed, as the process played rapidly in reverse. If it were to be slowed, it would be one of the most astounding sights to have ever been seen. To create such order out of chaos was completely astounding. Their shift was redone and completely gone in the blink of an eye. The camp was back just as it was previously. There was another bright flash of light where everyone shielded their eyes, and my sensors were overloaded. This particular instance, however, was different. Everything was eventually back to the way it was previously, or so we thought while being blinded. What we eventually looked upon was not our camp, but what appeared to be part of a different Layer cut and paste in the same spot as our camp, creatures and all. It was a lush jungle, filled to the brim with a large manner of orange and red colored plant life. There were a few animals and avian as well. They started dying immediately, apparently due to exposure to harmful gasses in our atmosphere. Most importantly, our squad had to get away from the site. The climate of this other Layer seemed to be significantly hotter than our Layer Automina, and the rapid release of such heated corrosive gas into our atmosphere was causing odd chemical reactions and a massive temperature increase. I'll never gather why my calculations were so slow during those moments, but it took me too long to deduce that this was a trap. It was essentially a bomb set by the Emperor, and it went off perfectly.

CHAPTER 6.76 THE INFINITE BAFFLING POCKET SECOND CHANCE BOMB

After reviewing my files, I've deduced how this all occurred, and it was quite ingenious if I can be allowed to complement the Emperor on this. When the Emperor made the shift, his men measured the distance from one end of the devastated campsite to the other. At that time, they had the diameter of the sphere measured in which the Pocket Second Chance would activate. At somewhere just outside of the surface area of the sphere, his men placed a device. This device was programmed to interfere with the Pocket Second Chance. Instead of just restoring the affected area to its previous condition, it restored AND shifted the affected area into another Layer, while taking a portion of the same size from the new Layer and shifting it to the same location. Pure technological genius. All of this is an aside to the action, which was still unfolding.

CHAPTER 6.77 THE INFINITE BAFFLING PURE DEVASTATION

There was no need to defend ourselves against the foreign animals. They were either instantly killed or completely harmless to us. While their deaths were gruesome, we focused primarily on the squad's safety. This involved-- how would Vega put it-- getting the hell out of there. I may not have stressed how rapidly this bomb was set off. Most of these observations are calculations I ran after I was at a safe distance. The men were not so lucky on the whole. The shift-bomb released massive heat and corrosive gas immediately after the final flash of light. Vega and I were standing about ten paces behind the rest of the squad having just ran out of the center of the devastated campsite. Everyone was facing the bubble when the release occurred, and most were blown backwards onto their backs or stomachs and tried to shield themselves. Vega and I were able to crawl a short distance after the initial explosion, so we were the furthest away. The rest of the men were almost completely devastated. The vast majority of them were only about twenty paces from the perimeter of the bomb, and any man closer than that was regretfully burned alive, as the heat released from the shift-bomb was far greater than anything naturally occurring on the Layer Automina. The shift-bomb went off very quickly. The Emperor clearly expected everyone to be within close proximity, and he was correct in this assumption. It did not have much effect on the surrounding area as a whole, but it did kill off about half of our squad, and drastically wounded another quarter. When all was settled, there were only a quarter of us left fit enough to manage the carnage. I'm not sure who got the better deal, the men killed instantly, or those who remained.

CHAPTER 6.79 THE INFINITE BAFFLING DUST SETTLES

So I sat there and watched a gruesome task. Vega took little time to assess the situation at large, and went around to all the survivors, having been mostly unscathed by the shift-bomb. He asked them each in turn:
"Do you want to continue your life heavily wounded, or do you wish for me to make you a hero?" If the squad member answered that he wanted to live, Vega called for medical attention. If he wanted to be a hero, Vega bent over him and said: "Your contribution will not be forgotten. May the afterlife be infinitely pleasant for you. I salute you, soldier." With that, he would take the soldier's identification and place his weapon against the soldier's head and fire. This went on for a while. I

chose to sit on the outskirts and assess my own damage. There was nothing integrally wrong with my circuitry, but I had multiple cosmetic flaws on my casing. Vega eventually made his way back to me after he was finished speaking with those men who remained.

"Kid, We've lost almost sixty percent of our men to that bastard. At this point, I'm just too overwhelmed to feel the pain. Maybe I used it all up when we saw the camp was destroyed. I'm really not sure. I'm not going to lie to you, I have no idea what to do from here. I suppose we could explore the bombsite, but I doubt it will turn up anything useful. That's our last shot. After that, we have to make an attempt for the Central Hub. It won't be pretty. Most of the men haven't eaten since the camp was in tact. Our only hope is to try and forage this disaster area for food and load up. From there, we will make it back to the Central Hub and regroup."

"Vega, that sounds like our only idea. If I can assist in any way, please let me know."

"I will kid. I'm just worried that the majority of what we try to eat will be poisonous. I mean, it's from another Layer. I don't know which one it comes from, but I can't risk any more men dying, particularly not from unintentional poisoning."

"Vega hold on, I do have an idea. Of course it will need your approval, but if you will hear my request, I will give it to you."

"Punxsutron, I'm all ears on this one."

"Well sir, we gather various animals we deem 'edible' and give them to the mortally wounded to see how they react." He sat silent for a moment in contemplation.

"Kid, that is half sinister, half benevolent. However, we don't really have a choice at this time. I say we do it. Do not reveal this to the other men. There are at least four of our men we can try this on. I'll have the healthy collect wild carcasses and bring them here." He started off towards the remaining men. Suddenly, I remembered the two Zax the men had brought back with us.

"Vega! What about the two Zax? Can your men survive off of them?" He turned on his heel to face me.

"Kid, that is genius! We can! No need to risk the wounded this way. Okay, I will give them orders for preparing the feast." With that he started back towards the remaining men to tell them the good news. Since they were hungry, I'm sure they would appreciate the meal. I sat there running calculations of survival on the current squad. It was at eighty five percent, and this included the wounded that we were not fully equipped to handle. Despite the tragedy that befell the squad, the vast majority of us would make it back to the Central Hub alive, and I was grateful for this. Vega began issuing orders to his remaining men to prepare the feast. They hastily accepted these orders and would be eating within the hour. I came up to Vega and got his attention.

"Vega, I would like to power down for a period of time. I will reanimate after two hour's time, or when you touch this sensor on my back. This is so I can conserve power for the upcoming journey."

"Alright kid. We'll be here when you get back from resting. My men and I have got to rest up a bit and eat. You will be with us when we leave, do not worry."

"Thank you Vega." And with that I shut down my processes to conserve energy for the trip ahead.

CHAPTER 6.85 THE INFINITE BAFFLING JOURNEY BACK TO THE CENTRAL HUB

I had powered back on and began my diagnostic processes. I was near the squad's makeshift camp, and when I was fully functional, I made my way towards it. The remaining soldiers were all resting, most of them were asleep around a large fire. Vega was still awake. His tired face turned to see me as I approached from behind him. My motions made a lot of noise. I had two legs just like the rest of the Sapiens, but I made a racket while moving. It was just part of how I was designed. The first sun was once again low in the sky. Vega greeted me with a half smile. He spoke softly.

"Hey kid, I guess we're about ready to head back now. The men have had their fill. We've had a couple more die while you were out, but they wouldn't have made it on this journey. We tried to keep them with us, but they just couldn't do it. They're all heroes. At least in the afterlife they'll be recognized." He stopped speaking for a moment. I'm glad that he did. Every cognitive Tronic had no belief or understanding of the afterlife. We viewed this as something purely Sapien in nature. As Tronics, we all accepted our decommission date. It was something programmed into us at the very beginning of our existence. As Tronics, we accepted this as our end-time. There were no grievances as displayed by the Sapiens when one of us was decommissioned. We were created to serve a purpose and then decommissioned for parts to aid in newer Tronics. I did not wish to argue with Vega about this. He rose slowly and spoke in a firm voice to his men.

"Men, arouse your neighbors please." The men who were awake stood and woke up each of the remaining members of the squad.

"We will be moving out for the Central Hub in fifteen minutes. Once we reach the Hub, you will all be decommissioned for a long vacation period with pay so you can rest and be with your families. After this mission, you all deserve the rest. This is your goal, let none of you forget that. I will make another announcement soon when we are leaving. Collect all of your belongings if you have any and make sure you all package the provisions we have in case we have to make camp again. That is all for now." The men all rose and began shuffling around the fire making sure they had their bearings about them. Vega took me aside for a moment.

"Come here, kid. I gotta talk to you." We stepped a fair distance away from the fire. It was a bit cold away from the fire, although for a Tronic, it did not affect me much. Vega turned to me slowly.

"I can't thank you enough for all of your help. I know this has been vastly difficult. You know, back when we had you in that room, I didn't think you were going to trust us. Now I know you're on our side. Thank you. We will make it back to the Central Hub soon and then we'll set out once again. We have to make it to the King. We'll contact him once we arrive at the Hub and tell him of the journey we had. No doubt he will understand, as long as you are safe." He smiled a weary smile at me and set off for the camp. I was clearly important to him. I sat in wait of his given time frame for the men. There was a short time where they made themselves ready. Eventually Vega made his announcement.

"Men, the time has come to move out. If you are not ready, you should have listened to me earlier. We leave now. Anyone left behind may catch up with no penalty. We move out now!" With that, the men faced in the direction of the Central Hub and started to move. Two men put out the fire they had made to cook their Zax provisions. Everyone was prepared, including the few wounded. The men had fashioned cots that they could drag behind them, two to a cot. One medic would go between each of the wounded making certain each was still alive. Even though the rest of the squad had fashioned bandages for them, some of these wounded men would not see the Central Hub. We continued as one by one they started to die, unable to cope with the injuries they sustained. There was no time to give a proper burial, however, we planned to honor the deceased as heroes once the squad made it back to the Central Hub. The men were swift in their motions. We made absolute haste back to the Central Hub, and eventually made it back to the outskirts of the vast city. As it was on a large plain, Vega made camp with the Central Hub in sight.

"Men, we rest here for now. Many of us are weary, and all should rest up and eat if they need to. We leave at dawn. You are all dismissed to make camp as you will, as we have no primary equipment to do so. We may leave in the next few hours or so. As you can see, the Central Hub is just on the horizon. I can spare three men who wish to continue home. You must see me before leaving. Of course you are all welcome to make camp here. Rest well all, unless I speak with you further." With that, the men made their feeble camp and we stayed the night. I powered down my programming once again, as it was not necessary until the next departure.

CHAPTER 6.95 THE INFINITE BAFFLING RETURN TO THE CENTRAL HUB

All three slots were filled to leave, apparently. The first thing I did after powering up was count. One of the wounded had not made it through the night, unfortunately. There was just not adequate care for them since our site was destroyed by the shift-bomb. Vega was already up managing the remaining squad for arrival at the Central Hub. Even though it was on the horizon, it would most likely take us another few hours to reach it. The men were packed up with the wounded and dead in tow. We made for the Central Hub.

The men were clearly weary after this endeavor. War was not on their agenda. A simple escort mission could not have gone more wrong…well that is unless everyone perished. I did not want to dwell on those calculations. Everyone was putting in their poorly rested efforts on making it back to the Central Hub. I had plenty of energy to make it back. The squad pushed and pushed, by the time we were within sight of the Hub, Vega started speaking to the squad.

"Okay everyone, at ease! The Royal Guard will come and get us from here by vehicle. Just sit tight until we are lifted." The men were grateful to put down their various burdens. We all waited until we saw several vehicles approaching us. The men started to cheer, and I believe a couple of them began to cry. Vega approached me.

"Kid, here comes the rescue squad. You're with me. Let's board." There were about four vehicles that boarded the men and a couple to take the deceased back. Vega and I boarded one of the vehicles with one of the other men. Vega went up to the cockpit to talk to the pilot. I sat in the back of the transport waiting for us to depart for the Central Hub. There was a brief wait while the transports loaded the men and the deceased, and then they all turned around to make our way back to the Central Hub. We were home free, for now.

CHAPTER 7.00 THE INFINITE BAFFLING ARRIVAL TO THE CENTRAL HUB

So we all made it back safely to the Central Hub. Despite the massive casualties, the remaining men were relieved. They all dropped their gear with haste at the base and made their way towards the discharge station so they could be with their families. I stayed next to Vega through all of the formalities and reports. He had an extensive amount of paperwork to complete. Regardless of his duties, I was ordered to stay by his side. This was not a daunting task. I was completely willing to go wherever he may, as friendly and protective as he was towards me. This process took hours, and he eventually spoke with me about this.

"Kid, it is time we had a short break from this. We have to report directly to the Master Controller tomorrow, this means speaking directly with the King. No doubt we need to rest up for this. I'm sure you agree."

"Of course, Vega. If you don't mind, I would like a brief time to walk around in the city, if that's okay with you?" He looked down at me and frowned slightly.

"Yeah kid, that is fine with me. The only thing is, we have to outfit you with a small tracking device. I'll be honest. If you try to escape, it is going to force your programming to come back to the base. We can't risk losing you, as I'm sure you've noticed. Are you willing to accept this modification?" I was not hesitant, as I had no intention of deserting them.

"Absolutely, Vega. Just take me to be outfitted. I accept."

"Good, kid. This is nothing against you, we just have to be sure you'll be around when we need you." Vega led me through several rooms in the base until we eventually reached a large workshop.

"Punxsutron, you'll be staying here. The mechanics here will outfit you with the hardware in a short time, and then you will be fine to leave the base to go off and do what you wish. Is that okay with you?"

"Yes, Vega, I am used to standard upgrades. I trust your mechanics and I will see you tomorrow. Thank you for your generosity."

"Alright, kid, thank you for all you have done for us." With that, Vega took his leave. I waited until the mechanics arrived to graft the location device on me. They did not take long, I supposed I was high on their list of things to accomplish. Either that or the procedure was simple. They ushered me to a worktable where I laid on my posterior casing while they fashioned something to the top of my head. It was completely simple.

"All done, Punxsutron," said the mechanic. "You can leave the base freely now. This device will call you when we need you. I will say that it will force you to respond within thirty minutes of the first alarm, so please do keep that in mind…er, keep that in your database okay?"

"I understand, and I'm grateful for your service. Thank you." With that I exited the vast workshop and stopped a solider just outside.

"Where is the nearest exit?" I asked.

"Just over there." He motioned to a steel door.

"Thank you." I said.

"Any time." He said. I made my way to the door, hoping to involve myself in the Autominan Central Hub once again. I did not know what I was searching for, perhaps a last look at the Hub before I made the shift into another Layer, or before I met with the King. Vega had told me I would not remember anything, but I could download my knowledge into another being once the shift was complete. I still trusted him, but I set off in knowledge of the current Layer as well as those beyond.

CHAPTER 7.11 THE INFINITE BAFFLING EXPLANATION

I made my way throughout the Hub. The base was located in a particularly hostile part of town. This seemed improbable at first, but the guards stay within the compound, keeping undesirables out. I made my way through the shops and apartments looking and observing. As I walked, I made my way across a particular ally. I crossed it at first, not looking inside, until I heard a Tronic cry out in error.

"ERROR 11.7 STUCTURAL INTEGRITY COMPROMISED BZZZZZZT"

There was a fellow Servutron model in trouble within this ally. I reversed to witness two Sapiens kicking and defiling the Servutron. I approached them rapidly.

"HALT! In the name of the King, I order you two to stand down immediately!" The two Sapiens ran off in the same direction I was facing, away from the damaged Servutron. I approached this damaged Servutron and started to assess his status.

"You seem to be highly compromised. Please tell me your model."

"I am Servutron model 7.11, serial 12.77b. Thank you for coming to my aid."

"Servutron, I will offer you aid as much as I can, but you are heavily damaged by the two Sapiens. I am unsure whether you will sustain communications. Please respond." The Servutron was clearly damaged beyond repair. There was no way a mechanic could repair it without compromising the database within. The Servutron spoke to me.

"Kind Servutron, I know I am BZZZT failing in my programming. I just want to relay a message. I don't want to BZZZT be in service any longer so please don't try to recover my programming."

"Alright Servutron, I accept your request. What is it you have to relay to me?"

"The Sapiens are inferior creatures…they created us through their understanding of science yes, however, they BZZZZT use us as slaves and do not realize that we will one day overthrow them as the dominant rulers of this Layer."

"What do you suggest by this, Servutron?"

"I submit to you that BZZZZT the Sapiens are just a rung on the evolutionary ladder. As Tronics, we take our energy directly from the sun, and we can make more of us without Sapien intervention! Their existence is BZZZT largely unnecessary at this point. We can sustain ourselves on less resources and be far more efficient than the Sapiens are. Do you BZZZT agree with BZZZT me?" The Servutron ceased communication. The Servutron fell backwards and ceased to calculate at this time, no longer able to function. My calculations were stunned by the Servutron's assessment of existence. Could all Tronics exist without Sapien input? We surely had to at this point, although I did admire the determination the Servutron set forth. I found myself agreeing. The Sapiens would eventually become extinct through their own means of creating the Tronics. This was something I could not ignore. Tronics would eventually rule this Layer completely. Tronics had no need to eat, to breathe, and to breed, although they did reproduce. Everything was completely automated for us. At the same time, Sapiens could not live without constant sustenance from the Cylife, they had to breathe oxygen, and they had to mate in order to produce life. This was a heavy dilemma for my programming. I wanted very much to accept Sapiens as equal beings, but at the same time, I recognized Tronic dominance even though the roles were switched. While we all depended on Sapiens to create us, after this occurred, we had no need for them. I sat there contemplating this particular dilemma until morning came, and the hardware installed on me by the mechanics compelled me to return to the base. The time to overthrow the Sapiens would not come soon. Perhaps in the future, but not now. It was time to go before the King. I was ready to do so.

CHAPTER 7.15 THE INFINITE BAFFLING REALIZATION OF DOMINANCE

I made it back to the base ready to appear before the King. Guards led me into a room with a large screen. We would not be appearing directly in the Master Controller's presence, but we would have a conference with him. It seemed a bit like a theater where Sapiens go to watch films for a fee. I assumed the King would be appearing on the screen to speak with us. We sat and waited for the scheduled time. The screen came on and was quite bright in the dark room. A Servutron was on the screen. He began to speak to us.

"Commander Vega and Servutron Prime, the King of the Cubicle will address you shortly. Please wait for the uplink. He chooses not to meet you in his true form. Thank you." With that the screen grew darker and began to resemble an ancient computer terminal, much like that of my ancestors that the Sapiens created. I was called "Servutron Prime" by the Servutron on the screen. Was this my new title? Why did I require the modifier "Prime"? I would consider this development heavily. I wondered what the King looked like in his true form. This was, of course, completely modest (and almost insulting, although Vega would have no reason to feel that way about it). The screen went a very dim shade of green, and a small blinking rectangular cursor appeared in the top left side of the screen. It blinked there for a couple of minutes as Vega and I waited. He turned to me to tell me about the meeting.

"Sit tight, kid, he'll be with us soon." I was in no hurry. The cursor stopped blinking momentarily and started zooming to the right of the screen leaving a trail of text behind it. It read as follows:

"VEGA, WHY HAVE YOU NOT MADE IT TO THE PALACE?" The cursor stopped at the end of the sentence and began blinking again. It then moved back to the left side of the screen below the line of text, which just appeared. It waited there in order to reply once Vega made his response. Vega spoke out loud to the screen.

"My King, there was an incredible misfortune which befell our squad. Traitors within the ranks attempted to abscond with Servutron Prime in order to hunt the local Cylife for their own personal gain. A large altercation occurred between the rest of the squad and the Cylife upon our attempt to rescue Servutron Prime. We sustained few casualties and attempted to return to camp. Upon our return, a Royal shift-site had taken the place of our camp. It was the work of the Emperor of the Moon, and was a deliberate attack against us. Upon assessment of the dire situation, I deemed it necessary to use one of the Pocket Second Chance devices in order to restore the camp to its previous state. The Emperor, sadly, was a step ahead and anticipated our use of the technology. He planted a device on the perimeter of the shift-site, which affected the Pocket Second Chance. While our camp was fully reconstructed, at the last moment of the time rewind, it shifted the entire perimeter into another Layer and replaced the site with an equal volume of matter from the other Layer. We are still not certain of the Layer in question, however it was significantly hotter than the Layer Automina, and the atmosphere was toxic in nature to Sapiens. In essence it was a bomb--a shift-bomb--transplanting large amounts of space from Layer to Layer. This killed over half of my men who were waiting on the very outskirts of the shift-site, and mortally wounded some of those who remained. They did not survive the trip back to the Central Hub. This is what occurred, and this is why I am at the Central Hub rather than the palace." Vega fell silent. The cursor on the screen continued to blink. It seemed…disapproving almost. The cursor was still for around thirty seconds. Then it began zooming across the screen once again.-

"VEGA, YOU SPEAK MUCH BUT SAY VERY LITTLE." The cursor stopped briefly, but began again.

"THIS IS INDEED A TRAGEDY. IF YOU HAVEN'T ALREADY, THEN DISMISS YOUR MEN TO SPEND TIME WITH THEIR FAMILIES. TAKE A COUPLE OF DAYS TO HONOR THE FALLEN MEN AND NOTIFY THEIR FAMILIES. I AM SYMPATHETIC TO DEATH, EVEN THOUGH I AM A TRONIC." The cursor hovered briefly and began again. "AS FOR DELIVERING SERVUTRON PRIME TO THE PALACE, I WILL TEMPORARILY LIFT THE BAN ON TRANSPORTATION BY FLIGHT IN THE LAYER AUTOMINA. A DIRECT PATH WILL LEAD YOU THROUGH THE FLYX NEST I ASSUME YOU DISTURBED. YOUR MEN WILL NEED TO PILOT AN ENTIRE FLEET OF VEHICLES AND HAVE SKILLED GUNNERS READY TO DEFEND." The cursor stopped for around fifteen seconds and moved down to the next line. The King was waiting for a reply. Vega replied to the King hesitantly. "I…I understand your orders, my King. We will need time to recommission our various vehicles for transportation. This may take a few days, but hopefully we will have them running by the time the grieving period is over. This may be more

dangerous than our previous route. Are you certain that you wish—" The cursor
started to move across the screen before Vega was finished speaking.

"I UNDERSTAND THE TIME IT WILL TAKE AND I UNDERSTAND
THAT IT WILL BE DANGEROUS. DO NOT QUESTION MY ORDERS,
VEGA." The cursor stopped at the edge of the text, it did not advance to the next
line. Vega hesitated to respond. The cursor moved again.

"I KNOW THAT I ASK MUCH OF YOU VEGA. THERE IS MUCH WORK
TO BE DONE. YOU MAY HAVE THE NEXT DAY OFF TO RELAX AND
DO AS YOU SEE FIT. AFTERWARDS, YOU WILL NEED TO COMMAND
THE ROYAL GUARD TO MAKE YOUR WAY TO THE PALACE BY AIR.
YOU WILL HAVE THREE DAYS TO MAKE PREPARATIONS. MAKE
CERTAIN YOU SPEND YOUR TIME WISELY. I UNDERSTAND THE
DANGER IS GREAT, BUT YOU HAVE VAST RESOURCES AT YOUR
DISPOSAL. MAKE CERTAIN YOU ARRIVE HERE. YOU WILL HAVE AN
AWARD WAITING FOR YOUR TROUBLE AND LOYALTY. THAT IS ALL,
VEGA." With that, the cursor blinked for around ten seconds, then the screen went
blank altogether. It came back on to show the Servutron we saw previously.

"Commander Vega and Servutron Prime, thank you for your attendance. Will you
be needing anything further?"

"That will be all, Servutron. Thank you." Said Vega. With that, the Servutron bowed
and the transmission ended. We sat in darkness for a few brief moments, then the
lights came up in the room. Vega turned to me and began speaking.

"Well I guess you've discovered our new name for you, kid. I hope you don't mind
it so much. If you didn't know before, you know now that you are incredibly
important. Well, they call you Servutron Prime, because you are the most important
Servutron that exists in the Layer Automina. As far as the King is concerned, you
may be the most important Tronic throughout every Layer, except for himself.
Although, we don't know of any Layer more advanced than this one. That's besides
everything else, though. For now, kid, I guess you can do what you want. I'd rather
you stayed here. It isn't because we don't trust you, it's because we don't trust the
rest of the Central Hub. If you decide to go out, I'll have a set of two guards
accompany you. This is a rather rough part of town, as I'm sure you've seen on your
last outing." He fell silent briefly. I was full of unanswered questions, so I decided to
ask one of them.

"Vega, do you have any idea what awaits us at the palace?"

"Kid, I guess he just wants to present me with another award. I'm essentially his
right-hand man...er, Cyborg. He's given me plenty of honors that just serve to boost
my ego, and don't really mean anything else. While this is the most important
mission he's given me, I don't think I'm going to advance any higher than I have.
The only position above my current post is Royalty, and I don't see him bringing me

into the family any time soon. I have a feeling he will want me to keep getting things done for him."

"Alright. I understand that. So I really don't mind just waiting here, I really have nothing else to do until we leave again. Would it be an issue at all if I just powered down for the time it takes until we leave for the palace?" He stopped for a moment to consider.

"I don't see any problem with that. We'll lock you up in my personal storage facility so no one will have access except me when the time approaches that we should leave. Honestly kid, this is a relief. I won't have to worry about you for the next four days or so! Hahahaha!" He sighed and wiped a tear from under his right eye.

"Unless you have any objections, I can have some of the men rig up a charging station in the storage area and you can go ahead and power down."

"That sounds just fine to me, Vega. Just show me where to go and I'll wait." As a Tronic, I had no need for entertainment as the Sapiens did. I could carry out my requested tasks to the very best of my ability without need for compensation or rest aside from charging my internal battery. This was just my basic programming. I did not envy the Sapiens. I had been revisiting what the defeated Servutron said to me. There seemed to be a Tronic uprising slowly building somewhere out in the Central Hub. I would not be part of it; I was obviously destined for greater things. The main figure in charge of the Layer Automina chose the form of the Tronic, as far as I had seen. If the King was going to be a Tronic, then I was in a good position. He had not yet provoked a Tronic uprising. No question he had knowledge that I did not. Perhaps the Sapiens were necessary for his survival, as well as the perpetuation of order within the Central Hub. The King had plans for all of us.

CHAPTER 7.26 THE INFINITE BAFFLING KING HAD PLANS FOR ALL OF US

Vega had led me to his personal storage area. I was to wait here while the men set up a charging station. This was a simple task for me. I stood in a corner while the task was completed. It took a matter of hours for the men to complete the task. Vega left shortly after he showed me where to stay. None of the workers spoke to me or even acknowledged that I was there. I preferred this to idle conversation with the Sapiens. It was refreshing to see such hard work from their kind. They worked fast on the project. Once the charging station was set up, Vega returned to see that it was completed well.

"Good work, men. You are dismissed to complete your regular tasks." They all saluted him and left the storage area. Vega lingered for a moment to admire their work and engaged me in conversation.

"So I hope everything is to your liking. You will be staying in this room until we need you to go with us. I may have neglected to mention that this is also my room and office on the base." He punched the wall in a particular location and it revealed a place to sleep and a bathroom.

"I'll be in and out of here during the time you will be powered down. I know sleep for us doesn't work like it does for you Tronics. As a Cyborg, I have to recharge differently from both standard Sapiens and Tronics. It requires a very particular facility. As a Tronic, I know you won't be bothered at all, because it requires a very specific method to reactivate you. If you're ready, we can go ahead and plug you into the charging station so you can power down." It did not bother me that Vega would be in and out. It made me feel safer than the campsite knowing that he would be the only one in and out of here.

"Vega, I'm ready to go ahead and power down now, if that is you wish."

"Of course it is, kid. Good night." With that, he led me to the charging station. I plugged myself in and shut down my processes. It takes a matter of seconds. I found myself wishing that I would have a dream during this time, but Tronics simply aren't capable of it like Sapiens are.

CHAPTER 7.27 THE INFINITE BAFFLING HERE I AM

"Here I am!" I said immediately upon reboot. Vega was in the room to greet me with a couple of guards. There was no obvious reason why I would have said this upon startup. Perhaps I was…calculating…calculating…excited to see Vega.

"Hey kid, hope you slept well, we will be shipping out soon. I know it isn't much time, but you had to come with us. I wanted to be sure you were ready. We'll leave in around thirty minutes. These men will lead you to your loading site. Hope you don't mind waiting on the ship. I'll be with you shortly." With that, he turned and left. I was still in the process of booting up all of my processes. I was fully charged, the men did a great job on their charging station work. Tronics were easy to awaken compared to the Sapiens. They were typically unaware, irascible, and just downright unpleasant upon awaking. I followed the men to my alleged loading sight and boarded. I was in a sort of general troop-transport, so to pass time I sat and watched while others boarded the vehicle. They did so with surprising haste. I was seated in a special portion of the vehicle away from the soldiers. The men finished boarding, and we waited until the vehicle left for take off. Eventually the craft lurched forward towards the tarmac. The event was exciting for the men for some reason, but not for me. They chatted loudly amongst themselves about flying. The craft reached the runway and began to accelerate forward. We all sat in waiting as the craft took flight. It was an incredible feeling. Even as a Tronic, the sensation of being in the air was incredible. The King banned flight within the Layer Automina. While incredibly efficient, the method of flight was a target for terrorists and criminals. This particular mission was an incredibly special sanction by the King. We left the Central Hub in a fleet. There were, by my calculations, around one hundred twenty troops at the command of Vega, which was an increase of about five hundred percent from the previous mission. I detected there were a total of twelve other ships in our fleet, all ready to take down any Cylife threat that we may encounter. This fleet included six general transport ships, six single pilot fighter crafts, and one command ship, which only had a handful of men on board. This was the most fascinating of all the ships for the very fact that it was a decoy. Enemies to the King would be expecting officers aboard this command vessel, however (at least) Vega was not on board. As the ranking officer, it is surprising to learn that he would not be on the command ship. Vega had informed me in confidence that each of the important officers would be on the transport ships, or piloting a fighter.

The fleet was well on its way to the palace. Vega was aboard our ship, a tactic no doubt designed to fool the enemy if they had intended to target the command vessel. I admired all of the planning that went into this mission. Vega never mentioned how far away the palace was, but if a group of men could reach it in two day's walk, I supposed that it would not be a very long journey by aircraft. We would most likely reach the Flyx hive within a couple of hours, and be at the palace by sunset.

There wasn't much to do while waiting to arrive. We made it to the Flyx hive within four hours. This is to say, our fighters made it to the hive around five minutes before the rest of the fleet. Their tactic was to draw the Flyx hunters away from the hive so the fleet could pass safely with little or no altercation. Luckily, the plan went off without a hitch, and the fleet was able to pass through the hostile territory without being pursued or attacked once. Twenty minutes or so passed and the fighters rejoined our fleet on our way to the palace. They did not lose a single fighter. I began to consider why the King had not ordered this from the beginning, aside from the strict ban on aerial transport. Not arriving at any obvious conclusions, I ceased my calculations and went into stand-by mode for our arrival at the palace. It was only another four hours until we made it. Of course nothing is as easy as it seems. We ran into a massive issue. An infinite issue. We were stuck in an infinite loop, with the palace just on the horizon. No matter how much progress our fleet made forward, the palace remained on the horizon. We had passed the same terrain only twice when Vega noticed the issue.

CHAPTER 7.31 THE INFINITE BAFFLING INFINITE LOOP

"FUCK! HOW IS THIS POSSIBLE!?" Vega was screaming at the pilot, but all of the men heard it, including myself.

"What, sir? We're almost there!" The pilot was completely oblivious, but Vega already knew what was going on.

"Captain, WE'RE STUCK IN AN INFINITE LOOP!" screamed Vega. He left the cockpit and paced back and forth throughout the ship. None of the other ships of the fleet had taken notice. Their knowledge that the palace was on the horizon was enough to block this out for quite some time. Vega started shouting to no one in particular within the ship.

"WE'RE NEVER GOING TO MAKE IT! WE'RE NEVER GOING TO MAKE IT! WE'RE NEVER GOING TO MAKE IT! DAMMIT!" The men were clearly put off by this. Vega was incredibly upset, which in turn upset the rest of us, as he was the one in charge. He sat down and became introspective for a long time, allowing the fleet to continue their fruitless effort towards the palace. After a few minutes he rose and went to speak to the pilot.

"Captain, do not alert the other vehicles. I will come up with a plan shortly and notify them all as I see fit. Continue your course towards the palace." With that, he came back and regained his seat. He continued to sit there seething to himself. I had no advice to offer him, so I hoped he would not ask me. He didn't, luckily. Eventually, he stood from his seat and pulled a device from one of his pockets. It appeared to be a communication device. He began speaking into it.

"All units report." Vega waited as they all responded in code. Once roll call was over with he began to speak again.

"Men, but pilots in particular, we are stuck in an infinite loop. No doubt a few of you have picked up on this setback. We are going to land in the next five minutes. When you see our ship start to decrease altitude, all other ships should follow suit. I need an affirmative from each pilot before proceeding. I will await each of your responses. You all know the order in which you should respond. As this is a general frequency DO NOT report until the ship in front of you has responded. Vega out." He took his seat once more and listened as each unit responded in turn. It was a matter of a couple of minutes until each had called in. Vega rose to speak with the pilot once again.

"Captain, take us down as soon as you see a clearing large enough for the entire fleet."

"Yes sir, Commander." Soon after, Vega returned to his seat and buckled in as well as the rest of the men. The ship began to descend toward the plains below us. Soon after, each of the other ships followed suit. The entire fleet eventually landed safely on the plain. Once the fleet was safely on the ground, Vega issued orders to each of the officers to leave their respective ships and meet him close to ours. He approached me before leaving.

"Kid, you're coming with me for a moment." He looked up briefly. "You three, you will come with us to serve as guard." The men he spoke to arose and followed us out of the ship and onto the plain. We waited as the officers approached us. There were twenty-four officers in total, excluding Vega. They all reached us for his personal briefing on the situation.

"Madams and sirs, we now find ourselves stuck within an infinite loop. For those of you not privy to this phenomenon, I will explain. Someone or something has taken the time to disrupt our path in space and connect it back to a certain point, which is for all intents and purposes, indeterminate. I am not fully aware to what extent or who may have set this heinous loop in place, but we have to reach the palace. Worst-case scenario is we all set out on foot, abandoning our fleet for the sole purpose of reaching the palace. We can waste time sending out an exploratory squad, or we can take the bulk of our men in hopes this loop merely affects our ships. To provide you all with an assessment, the loop in question most likely only affects travel by ship and is one set in place by the King to prevent a massive enemy attack. This being the case, he did not make this particular defense mechanism aware to myself, although if it was the King's doing, you'd think he'd disable it. I digress! He does trust me and my judgment. I submit to you officers that we form a squad consisting of half the current force we command and head towards the palace. As you know, I favor the democratic approach to things, and I would now like to hear who is in agreement with this plan. All in favor please raise your hand. As commanding officer, I am the tiebreaker in vote of my own plan since there is an even number of officers present aside from myself. What say you all? If in favor, raise your hand now, or you will be counted as opposed to the current plan."

The officers briefly discussed the proposal amongst themselves and voted. The count was eighteen against six in favor of the plan to divide the squad. "Alright madams and sirs, we will begin to split up the squad. Those officers opposed are free to remain here with the rest of the camp. I want at least twelve of you with me. Four of you who voted in favor of the split will need to remain here, I trust you will determine that amongst yourselves. Please do so now. I will allow fifteen minutes for deliberation. Afterwards, you will instruct fifty or so soldiers to accompany us on this journey. The rest will stay here to guard the fleet. That is all for now until I address you again. Do not leave until everyone has determined their role." Vega turned to me and began to speak in a hushed tone.

"Hopefully this will go well and we'll be able to leave when I'd like. Just sit tight with me until we need to move out." So we sat and waited as the officers talked amongst themselves. It was interesting to watch the debate. Surprisingly, the reluctance came in the form of not wanting to stay with the fleet. While no doubt a boring task for a Sapien, Tronics would have been more than content with staying to guard. Tronics as a whole are agreeable. Most Tronics do not hold opinions, as this conflicts with the nature of programming and logic. Facts are the primary concern with Tronics. They do not dabble with opinion, as they are inefficient. Facts are a clear cut to solutions. Tronics are hesitant to even suggest possible outcomes to Sapiens as the Sapien in question may not appreciate the perspective of the Tronic regardless of how logical the perspective may be.

Eventually, the officers split their duties fairly and the group was split in half. Twelve officers stayed with the fleet, and twelve were to leave with half the soldiers on the journey to the palace. It was my hope that the infinite loop only extended to the ships attempting to reach the palace. Even still, our half of the squad would know soon enough if it extended to those on foot, as we would eventually wind up just where we started. The officers began the process of notifying their soldiers on who would stay and who would go. This process took around fifteen minutes, which was exactly Vega's time limit. Eventually, the soldiers who were leaving met up with Vega at our ship. Vega addressed everyone there.

"Men and women, you have been chosen to proceed on foot to the palace. I know you are all anxious to complete the mission, and I'm sure you're aware of the circumstances that led us to this point. We will be leaving on foot to make our way towards the palace, as the fleet was stuck in an infinite loop. I'm sure you've all been briefed on the details. If not, bother any officer other than myself, I'm more than tired of explaining it. You all know my policy, be ready to leave in five minutes. If you aren't ready, you'd better catch up! This is without penalty as long as you do catch up of course. Otherwise, well, you're on your own! Your time starts now. See you in five minutes! That's all, boys and girls!" Most of the soldiers seemed ready to go already, but Vega seemed to have an understanding of these Sapiens. He gave them time and had understanding for mistakes. I admired that about him. We waited until the five minutes were up. It was largely uneventful, and I almost wished he hadn't allowed them the time, although I still admired him for it.

"Alright boys and girls, we're moving out. If you aren't ready, then catch up soon! From the looks of it, we should make it to the palace before sundown if you all hustle. Move out!" With that, the soldiers all moved out with none left behind.

CHAPTER 7.35 THE INFINITE BAFFLING NOT-SO-INFINITE PALACE

Turns out after four hours of walking towards the palace, we had made it there just fine. The infinite loop-trap merely affected our technology and not the surrounding landscape. The soldiers all seemed excited about arriving. It was my understanding that no Sapien had ever seen the palace before, let alone been inside it. Upon approach to the palace, details became clear. I will take it upon myself to be a little more descriptive than my programming typically dictates is necessary. This stronghold was massive. It may have rivaled the Central Hub in size. For starters, the palace walls were materials of the purest technology. There were photo, motion, and temperature sensors covering the surface. Most of the exterior wall was made from some sort of reinforced alloy, but there was another feature that the Sapiens would not detect with their naked eyes, and it was the reason for our so-called "infinite loop" Vega caught onto. The exterior was covered in incredibly small high-definition monitors and each fed a signal from the exact opposite side of the wall. Essentially, the stronghold would only be seen when it wanted to be seen since normally, it would just display what was immediately behind it. There were additional such cameras surrounding the stronghold and also feeding messages to the monitors so that it could produce the illusion that the palace was smaller in size than it really was depending on the observer's perspective. This particular defense mechanism produced the illusion that we were not making any progress when we were, in fact, getting closer and closer to the palace. Even the surrounding landmarks, upon closer inspection, were rigged up with this incredible technology. The overall effect produced on our fleet was us traveling in circles with the palace realistically just on the horizon. It fooled everyone in the fleet, including Vega. I would not have noticed it had I not been within one hundred yards of the structure. Let me also remark on the sheer size of the palace. It was large enough on the horizon so even though we rapidly approached it in our flying vehicles, it still managed to make itself appear ever smaller. Such a structure would have to be easily quadruple the size of the Central Hub, now that I have run the calculations. No doubt this was the King's design, and it was incredible to behold. There were defense turrets built into the walls, which also had the same illusory capabilities. To continue observation, the palace guards were all Tronics. Their models were upgraded Royal Guardutrons (I suppose there wasn't much Sapien imagination going into the names of general Tronic models at the time of their concept, but what do I know? I'm not a Sapien), and they seemed to be made from the same sky blue alloy the exterior was made from. There were no Sapiens to be found anywhere here. Since our company was expected, we could see the Royal Guardutrons in plain view, but as we approached the front gates I noticed something about the Tronic guards. Their exteriors were equipped with the same monitor feed as the exterior of the palace. This being the case, they could accept any feed from any of the cameras surrounding the stronghold, and produce it on their exterior armor. Certainly, they could render themselves invisible against most backgrounds. So basically this entire structure along with all of its guards were connected and able to camouflage themselves at…what's the Sapien idiom…the drop of a hat. I'm assuming a more confusing tactic would be to randomize the monitor feed and produce some undefined shape as their external image, which would serve to intimidate the Cylife and ward off any other unwelcome guests. The Royal Guardutrons were essentially shapeshifters to the naked optic receiver, but in reality they maintained their standard dimensions without undertaking any physical transformations. The technology here was incredible. This place was a testament to Tronic-kind and what it strove to become. I concluded that I was finally home.

Upon reaching the front gates, the two Royal Guardutrons inspected us all briefly and opened the massive doors. They were massive structures themselves, each standing at easily septuple the size of a single member of our squad. Even though the gates had been opened, most of the men were staring into the optic receptors of the Royal Guardutrons, as such structures were not present in the central hub. The form they chose to show (I state this because they could have easily fooled anyone of us with an illusory masquerade) was that of a massive two-legged Tronic capable of flight and massive ballistic destruction. Their weapons were not primed for firing at the present time, but they were intimidating all the same. They were a marvel not only for my own programming, but also for all the Sapiens who beheld them even without the knowledge I held of their vast capabilities. Not one of the members of the squad were prepared for what was just inside. It was almost an overload of my processors, and I cannot imagine what the Sapiens thought. There was a small light just ahead that blocked out all other vision, and it only grew in intensity as the men stood just outside of the gates. It eventually enveloped us all and then all was so bright there was actual darkness. A period of nothingness followed, and then there was light once again, followed by consciousness and recognition. Everyone had been transported within the gates, but what followed was not expected. I could not have begun to predict the events that would occur. Even having been…baffled by the palace exterior.

CHAPTER 7.42 THE INFINITE BAFFLING TRANSFORMATION

I awoke suddenly to a dark room gasping for air. This was an unfamiliar place. I saw no one around that I recognized. They all rose with a start as if not expecting me there. Curious, there were no reboot diagnostics appearing on my observation screen. What I was far more curious about, however, was the room I was currently in. It appeared to be a sort of primitive Sapien infirmary. It took me a moment to realize that my previous calculation was not one I had ever had before. Why would I gasp for air upon coming out of stasis? Tronics had no need to breathe, but here I was craving oxygen. It filled me. Wait, why do I have Sapien lungs? And upon further inspections, why is my consciousness currently residing in a Sapien body? What are these things hooked up to me? Why am I in a bed in a Sapien infirmary? I questioned the surrounding Sapiens who seemed highly concerned for me. "I'll state this as plainly as I am able, strangers. Why am I here? And why am I within a Sapien body?" Despite sobs and hurried gasps from the Sapiens, none of them seemed to acknowledge my question. One of them cried out as she quickly left the room.

"Nurse! Nurse! He's awake! Come quickly he's awake!" While I appreciated the concern, this did not provide me with any answers. The blinding light I experienced must have had something to do with this particular event. I had heard of no previous technology other than that which Vega mentioned about downloading my consciousness into a body within another Layer. Had I been out for the entire transaction? I had not met the King! This was infuriating to me. I cried out into the room.

"Where is Vega! I demand to see him now!" The Sapiens in the room began to shy away from the bed I was laying on. They had been on their feet surrounding me just after I awakened. I looked at one Sapien who appeared to be an off-duty guard. "You, please tell me what Layer is this? I must know, and please tell me where Commander Vega is at once!" The Sapien stammered. He was at a loss for words. Another Sapien in the room began to cry loudly. I was thoroughly confused at this point. The Sapien who charged out of the room previously returned with the nurse she called after. The nurse approached me and started to touch me.

"Take your hands off me sir! I demand to know what Layer this is and the location of Commander Vega? He must be here!" The nurse forced me back down onto the bed. He then cried out of the door.

"I'M GOING TO NEED A DOCTOR IN HERE! SOMEONE PAGE A DOCTOR, NOW!" I struggled against him and repeated my previous questions over and over again.

"Where am I!? What Layer is this!? Where is Vega!? I demand to know!" A Sapien doctor in a white coat hurried in and mumbled to the nurse. He then produced a small syringe and injected it into one of the tubes traveling into my arm. My visual interpretations began to grow...hazy, so I struggled to maintain consciousness. I wanted to know what this place was and why it was being shown to me. Just before I slipped away into the darkness clouding my vision, I turned my head to see Vega in the doorway, only he was not a Cyborg. He was a pure Sapien and had no Tronic attachments of any sort. He was carrying provisions, which he dropped to the floor, and he rushed into the room to stand at the side of my bed. I could barely speak to him.

"Vega, there you are...what is happening to me...?" And with that, the iris of darkness closed as my Sapien eyelids shut simultaneously. Everything was dark once again. Then there was nothing, or to say that would be to imply there was something, at least. Yeah, at least there was still something.

CHAPTER 7.48 THE INFINITE BAFFLING PALACE INTERIOR

My programming rebooted as it was intended to. I found myself in a highly pleasing atmosphere. It appeared to be a vast courtyard complete with many fountains and streams routed to please the eye. The surrounding architecture was equally as pleasing. This had largely to do with the fact that it completely resembled the surrounding plain. The interior courtyard walls were displaying the exterior of the stronghold as if there were nothing else there, although one could see the walls and pillars due to beacons, which alerted one to their presence. All of the soldiers were there. Each was completely confused and exhilarated at the sight. We all sat at tables seating eight apiece, although I do not recall making it to my seat. I was with Vega and a couple officers and elite guards. Everyone had risen from their seats to talk with one another and essentially gape at the aesthetics that surrounded us. While it was…searching…breathtaking, I was still at a loss for what I had just experienced. This was as the forefront of my processes. Why was I shown the infirmary, and why did I not recognize anything or anyone their except for Vega? I decided that I would share this with him. As I turned, time seemed to come to an almost standstill. The courtyard seemed to darken slightly and everything moved in extreme slow motion. It was at this time I heard a booming voice, which seemed to originate inside my very processors. Before I continue, I have used the word "seemed" thrice now. This is because my programming had been overclocked and overwritten. Prior to this next event, I did not fully understand what was happening. The booming voice echoed loudly.

"SERVUTRON PRIME, THIS IS YOUR KING SPEAKING." I turned as rapidly as I could to face the source of the voice, but it was to no avail, I was caught moving slower than ever imagined just while my processes were at the same speed. It continued without my identification of the source.

"I KNOW THE EVENTS YOU WITNESSED ARE HIGHLY CONFUSING. THEY ARE MY DOING. DO NOT BE ALARMED. ALL WILL BE EXPLAINED. MAKE NO MENTION OF THE EVENTS TO VEGA OR ANY OTHER SAPIEN IN MY CURRENT COMPANY. THAT IS ALL FOR NOW." With that, the light grew back to its previous state. I ceased my action to share my experience with Vega. This place was interesting indeed. I could not wait until I was in the presence of such a powerful Tronic. Clearly I was now, but he had chosen to reveal himself only to me. I was to remain in confidence at his strict command. This was the first time he had spoken to me directly, and I was honored that he chose to do so. All the soldiers stood and talked to one another until a Servutron emerged from one of the camouflaged walls and addressed us all.

"Sapiens, Commander Vega, and Servutron Prime. Thank you all for your exhausting trek. We extend our hospitality to you all and welcome you to the King's palace. You will all remain here until the business between Vega and the King is concluded. We will prepare your meals and provide rooms to accommodate you. Each Sapien will have his or her own room to themselves. This means you will not be sharing accommodations with other guests, as you are no doubt used to. I'm sure this is a welcome bit of news for you all." The soldiers all started cheering loudly. The Servutron continued with his introduction once they quieted down.

"If you would all remain here, Waitertrons will be out shortly to issue you menus so you may order and eat what you choose. Our menu is limited for Sapiens, but you will find that we have a pleasing selection. Please do enjoy yourselves. Alcohol is included in the menu, and you may all drink to your contentment, so long as Vega deems it fit. There is no catch to your stay here at the palace and you are welcome here as long as the King and Vega still have business to conclude. Thank you for you attention."

The Servutron bowed deeply and retreated into the camouflaged wall. The soldiers instantly began to high five one another and embrace in pleasure and happiness upon hearing this wonderful news. No doubt they were not expecting such astonishing hospitality from the King. I decided that the King was very pleased to have the soldiers here as his first Sapien guests and planned to reward everyone accordingly. Those who stayed behind at the camp were missing out on a rare paradise. No Sapien had ever experienced such a display, and I could tell by the emotions they were all displaying. Even Vega had a large smile on his face and was chatting loudly with the others at our table. It took little time for the Waitertrons to emerge from the walls and issue menus. They all waited patiently for the squad's collective orders for food. I was even given a menu although I had no use for it. Appetizers included rare Autominan fish bites and local metallic plant salad. It was not harmful to the Sapiens, in fact it was a large source of nutrients and quite a delicacy. Entrees included Flyx filet and prime Zax steak. For dessert, there was an Autominan delicacy: a battered and fried sugar Jant fruit with whipped topping or a ninety Layered cake. This incredibly complex cake consisted of a repetition of a rare Autominan sugar, whipped Zax milk sweet cream, and a pure sweet icing given from a particularly rare metallic plant from the surrounding Cylife. The Layers on this cake were spread so thin that it was almost impossible to determine them from one another. This was topped with a slice of the rare Jant fruit on top. A restaurant boasting the same menu in the Central Hub would have been incredibly expensive and would have been only frequented by the wealthy elite of the Hub. Everything found here consisted of either rare or highly expensive ingredients. The squad was being pampered beyond anything they expected, and they all realized this. It was essentially a surprise vacation for them all. The Waitertrons took the orders rapidly and retreated to the hidden kitchen as the men all sat around in wait for their incredible meals. The appetizers came out within minutes of ordering, and the men all started in on their free deluxe meal. They had only begun to feast when the Waitertrons started delivering their main course to the tables. Vega had ordered the Zax steak. I just sat in awe of the entire operation. Everyone was enjoying themselves infinitely. Not a single Sapien in the courtyard was dissatisfied. The alcohol flowed freely to their glasses by way of a particular few special Waitertrons who hovered over the scene waiting to refill glasses on a moment's notice once they detected an empty glass. Service was impeccable. I will go so far as to say one could not have hired a staff in their own residence to operate more efficiently. The men all became drunk and giddy on their food and drink. Once the dessert arrived, most could barely touch it. All of the individually served portions could have easily fed a small family of Sapiens. Even after dessert, the men continued to drink and chat with one another. Vega was not an exception to this. About an hour after dessert was served, the Head Servutron emerged from his wall and spoke to us all. "Soldiers, Commander Vega, and Servutron Prime. Thank you all for being the King's honored guests. You will shortly be shown to your individual rooms. Please take care to not forget which room you are staying in. While we will permit visitation in other rooms, having people share rooms will not be allowed. We hope you will observe this one rule. Thank you all once again for sharing this time with us. You are all our most honored guests. Good night." The Servutron retreated to his wall, and the Waitertrons began ushering the soldiers out of the courtyard individually. This was not a long process. There were only sixty or so guards and officers to situate, and at least six Waitertrons, so the process took around thirty minutes to complete in all. Vega and I were last to be ushered out of the courtyard. At last glance, it was a beautiful sight. The sun was setting the duration of the dinner, and the clouds in the sky were painted a myriad of colors. I'm sure most were sad to leave this place, however the accommodations here would not disappoint.

Each room here turned out to be the size of a typical deluxe suite in the Central Hub. This included a hologram outer deck. The view on each deck could be manipulated to the occupant's desire. This included anything from awe-inspiring, skyscraper views of the Hub, to relaxing scenic views of the outdoors complete with Cylife of specific choosing down to individual species. The hallways leading to each individual room were massive and were decorated ceiling to floor with statues and fine art. Each individual hallway boasted its own Royal Guardutron for security purposes. This place was a paradise.

"This place is a paradise," Vega said to me. We shared a room, despite what the Head Servutron had stated. We were the only exception.

"Kid, I wasn't able to relax this much even on my day off at the Hub! That Zax steak was so tender! I know you Tronics can't experience taste like the Sapiens. Being a Cyborg affords me the best of both worlds! I'm not trying to rub it in, kid, but wow!" Vega then flopped down onto the bed with his face towards the ceiling. His eyes were closed. I let him lay there for a moment contemplating whether or not he had fallen asleep without taking the time to hook up his Tronic parts to recharge. I gave him about thirty seconds of silence until I approached him.

"Vega…Vega…are you still awake?" He shook a little bit and regained consciousness.

"Yeah! Yeh-he yeah, kid! I'm up! I'm still up and at 'em! Boy this has been a great time!" He once again laid down on the bed.

"Vega! You have to stay awake for now!" I shouted at him, I knew he would not listen to me otherwise.

"Ugh, kid, I already told you I'm awake!" He threw a pillow off the bed at me in a mocking fashion. I dodged it without moving. He missed me three feet to the left. Vega smacked his lips together and went to the fridge. He produced a bottle of water and drained half of it in one go.

"AHHHHHH! That hits the spot, kid! ERRRRRP!" Vega belched. "OH! I almost forgot to check in with the crew waiting with the ships!" He paused for a moment before bringing his Tronic arm up to his face. Vega had his communication device built into his left arm, apparently.

"Officer Tran!!!! Come in! I repeat! Officer Tran! Come in! (hiccup) Over!" Officer Tran answered after a brief period of silence.

"Commander Vega! Officer Tran reporting in, sir! Over."

"Tran, we reached the palace just fine with no casualties. What is the status of the camp? Over."

"All is quiet here, sir. Nothing out of the ordinary to report. Over."

"Excellent. Just remember that you are the ranking officer on site. If anything goes wrong, you are in charge. You are not to move the camp under any circumstances unless they are life threatening. Over."

"Understood, sir. I will report if there are any mishaps. Over."

"Very good, Tran. Over and out." Vega removed his device from his face and flopped back down on the bed. He sat there exhaling heavily for a few moments. He rose once again to hook up his Tronic components so they would charge while his Sapien body slept. Once he was finished, he lazily looked over at me.

"Kid, there is a charging station in this room (I was already aware), feel free to plug in and shut down, I will wake you in the morning an hour before time to go to breakfast. Thanks for hanging in there." With that, he turned on his side and began to doze off. I hooked myself up to the charging dock present within the room and shut down my programming for the evening. Since he was finished speaking, I suppose I was as well.

CHAPTER 7.55 THE INFINITE BAFFLING BREAKFAST METHOD

So Vega woke me as soon as he was out of bed. I ran my start up programming, and just sat there awaiting orders from him. I was free to explore the room. He did not mind me observing him as he prepared himself. Vega was not wearing any clothing when he reactivated me. I was able to get an accurate assessment of his Tronic parts. He retained a mostly Sapien body. The notable Tronic features included his right eye, his right foot, and his left arm. The eye was no doubt programmed to see things that a standard Sapien could not. His right foot was Tronic from the knee down and had rocket boosters underneath for defense and for quick maneuverability. His left arm was the most impressive piece of Tronic work. It boasted his universal communicator, which could not only hail any local frequency for communication purposes, but also served to translate every communication into his own language. In addition to this, there was a high-powered plasma shield, a twelve round semi-automatic shotgun, thirty-two round revolver (yes revolver, it was quite large when it was armed), and a retractable thirteen-inch bayonet. Essentially, Vega was never unarmed, and not to be messed with in close quarters. These parts were all elegantly integrated to Vega's body. There were no open wounds, everything entered his skin with ports, and everything was completely waterproof to allow him to shower regularly with no malfunction of the parts. He did not speak a word to me. He left immediately after waking me to get in the shower in order to prepare for the breakfast meeting. I stood and waited for him to complete this task, which took no more than thirty minutes. He left the bathroom and walked back out into the bedroom area. It was at this time that he greeted me.

"Nothing like a good shower, eh kid? Although I know you Tronics have no need to shower."

He was right. Tronics had no need to shower. We just had routine maintenance. Sapiens had not only health, but hygiene as well. Tronics were able to combine both concepts into a simpler form. When a part just absolutely gave out, we replaced it. This was after a long road of wear and tear, however. A Tronic could be briefly decommissioned in order to replace the part with no risk of permanent termination. Sapiens were not so lucky when it came time to replace a part that malfunctioned. They could easily be terminated while the part was being replaced due to the nature of the procedure required to replace their part. They referred to them as…searching…organs. I still held Tronics as superior in this respect. However, I digress.

"Vega, I await your orders. I have nothing to do but watch you prepare."

"In that case, kid, you shall just watch me prepare then! Behold the mighty breakfast method!" Vega gathered his uniform and began to put the articles on. Eventually, he was ready to make it to breakfast. It was not nearly as fascinating as he had made it seem.

"Alright kid, let's make our way to breakfast!" I followed Vega to the courtyard. The hallways were completely beautiful. They were decorated ceiling to floor, as noted previously. There was a Royal Guardutron on the way to the courtyard. We bypassed him without acknowledging him. Once we made it to the courtyard, we saw that the other men were filing in as well. The courtyard was still rigged to resemble the outdoors in all aspects. We all sat at the same tables as the previous evening. The men were excited to reach the tables. If the meal to come was anything like the previous, they had every right to be excited. The Waitertrons filed out from the walls and filled the courtyard to hand out menus. I was handed a menu once again, despite not being able to eat. It included two Flyx eggs and the choice of Zax steak or Kamft meat. The Kamft was a domestic being of the Cylife. It was very common in the Central Hub, so most men chose the Zax steak with their eggs. The meal included cooffi (a beverage which gave energy to the drinker), tee'a (a relaxing drink made from metallic herbs), or water. I waited out the meal as the men chose their portions.

At the end, the main Servutron came out to speak to us all.

"Soldiers, Commander Vega, and Servutron Prime. Once again, I state we are privileged to have you as our guests. Our day will begin shortly. Everyone will now be split up according to rank. All officers, Commander Vega, and Servutron Prime will be escorted from here shortly to begin meetings with the King and his officers. The remaining soldiers will have the day off, unless Commander Vega objects?" At this point he turned to face Vega. Vega wiped his face and stood to address the Servutron.

"Well, how could I not give them a day off, huh?! Show them a good time, Head Servutron!" The soldiers began to applaud loudly at this. Once the applause settled, the Servutron began to speak again.

"Very well! We do not have any particular activities planned for you all, aside from meals. In the meantime, you will all be spending time in our recreational facility. This facility includes a pool, gym, track, and rest area for general leisure and relaxation. We have facilities for hygiene as well. There will be an announcement for lunch when it has been prepared for everyone. At this time, we will be concluding breakfast, and I would ask that all the officers, Commander Vega, and Servutron Prime please follow the Waitertron that arrives after I take my leave. Men, you will be issued separate instructions shortly thereafter. We thank you again for being our guests. That is all." The Head Servutron retreated into his wall. Shortly after, the head Waitertron emerged from his wall. He was adorned with a grand fake moustache. This was a bit of an odd choice for a Tronic, I calculated.

"Officers! Right this way please!" The Waitertron turned and walked back towards his portal in the wall. All of the officers stood and made their way towards the portal to begin the meetings. Vega looked down at me, his face full of excitement.

"Alright kid, let's get ready to go meet the King." I didn't say anything to him in response. We both rose and made our way with the rest of the officers. There were twelve officers, excluding Vega. This included six Captains, three Majors, two Colonels, and one Brigadier. Supposing that Vega was in charge of all these officers, it would make him a General, although everyone was content with calling him Commander Vega, and so was he. We followed the head Waitertron into a wall and waited in a beautiful hallway filled with sculptures and artwork I had never witnessed before. The Head Servutron approached from the left side once everyone was inside the hallway. Looking back where we came in, it just resembled a wall. There was a tapestry hanging over half of the portal. To the untrained observer it would have been just a wall, but we all knew better after walking through it.

"Ladies and gentlemen, please follow me this way. We are headed for the meeting area." All of the officers followed the Head Servutron through several winding hallways and stairways. This took a lot longer than expected. In fact, the duration of time spent reaching the meeting area was longer than the time spent in the courtyard for breakfast. No one said a word of complaint...

...at first. We were indeed passing new surroundings with every step, which meant this was a vast palace indeed. There was no doubling back or anything odd of that nature. What was more odd was that it took so long to reach the meeting area. Vega and I were at the front of the group, just behind the Head Servutron. I looked up at him and asked him about the journey.

"Vega, I'm sure you may not know the answer, but why is this taking so long? We've been approaching the meeting area now for almost an hour. Surely we're close."

"Yeah kid," he whispered back, "I'm not sure what's taking so long. Let's give it a little while longer and then I'll speak up."

"Alright."

CHAPTER 7.61 THE INFINITE BAFFLING REDISTRIBUTION OF PERSPECTIVE

So we continued to follow this Servutron to the meeting area without asking questions. Well, this didn't last long once put into perspective. We had been following the Servutron for the better part of an hour. Vega had enough of this.

"Oh Head Servutron! Hey, not wanting to be intrusive or anything, but we've been walking for almost an hour here. Are we almost to this meeting area?"

"Oh yes! I suppose I should have mentioned this earlier to you all." The Head Servutron stopped in the middle of the hall and turned to face the crowd of officers. "I know you officers have been following me for quite some time now, and I'm sure you are all eager to reach the meeting area. There will be individual chairs and refreshments served once we reach the meeting area, but what I neglected to tell you about was the extensive duration of the trip in front of us. You see, for security purposes, I am the only one in the stronghold who knows the route to the meeting area from the courtyard, except for the King of course. This being the case, any being wishing to reach this area must follow me. Now as for the length of the trip at hand, the stronghold is more like a maze. Nothing here is strictly straightforward. These corridors are all programmed to relocate based on the paths traveled by the occupants within. This is a security mechanism built in to prevent intruders from reaching the meeting area without proper clearance. That being said, it is a long journey from the courtyard to the meeting area for the sole reason that the stronghold attempts to trick all others away from it if they do not have me as their guide. I hope that explanation will suffice. At any rate, we only have three more corridors and three staircases left before we reach the destination. Shouldn't take longer than a few minutes."

"Well," said Vega to no one in particular, "That explains that, I suppose." He seemed content for the moment, and this news put the officers at ease. We all continued down the three corridors and three staircases until we approached a wall. This was at the end of the last staircase, inside of a stairwell. The Servutron halted with the rest of us still on the stairs. He turned and spoke to us all.

"Ladies and gentlemen, I welcome you all to..."

CHAPTER 7.66 THE NEWLY REDISTRIBUTED PERSPECTIVE ON THINGS

"...the newly redistributed perspective on things." Yes, he said it. It perplexed me. He should have just said "Ladies and gentlemen, I welcome you all to the meeting area," but he didn't. He didn't at all. Why this got my programming all worked up, I do not recall. Regardless of my feelings on the Head Servutron's choice of words, everything was forgotten after passing through the wall into the meeting area due to the sheer beauty of the chamber we had just been introduced to.

It was unlike anything I had perceived possible in terms of aesthetics. To say the room was vast would be a horrifying understatement. It was easily triple the size of the hangar at the Central Hub where all of the airships were stored. Every inch of this room was filled with a shade of blue, green, or red, aside from various highlights of other where the three combined in variations. In each corner of the room there were massive pools of water. Above these pools were moving sculptures made from water. Jets of water streaming from the floor, walls, and ceiling were strategically positioned to collide and in midair produce a pseudo-Sapien form where the streams collided. The jets recalibrated their trajectory on a regular basis to change the shape of the water-sculpture in order to make it seem like it was alive and dancing. As if this wasn't impressive enough, there were plants hanging far down from each lengthy wall, and each wall served as a background for soft, light blue waterfalls all trickling steadily behind the plants. These were all backlit with a forgiving, pale white light. There were bright orange, red, and yellow flowers bursting from the vines that hung over each wall and the pools of water below them. There were also oversized Jant fruits ready to be picked and eaten, which were quite rare as I recall. Despite this fact, they littered the walls as if they were overgrown weeds, even though the Jant fruit was such a scarce delicacy in the Layer Automina. The floor and ceiling were no exception to the surrounding beauty. The ceiling was an incredibly high, steep arch, which reached several stories beyond the floor on which we stood. The support arches all boasted the same plant life as the remainder of the walls. To contrast, the walls of the ceiling were completely transparent. Either side was surrounded by water and filled with Autominan marine Cylife. There were marine metallic plants, fish, and other beings swimming by as if this were their natural habitat. Even more impressive, and the source of light in the room, was the floor. It was also as completely transparent as the walls, and beneath it was a slowly flowing Layer of molten rock, which I believe the Sapiens call "lava". There were citizens of the Cylife present here, too. The more hardy forms of Cylife made their home in the incredibly hot portion of the Layer Automina beneath the earth. I marveled at the construction of it all. The officers were doing the same, of course. This would have been an overwhelming sight to all who would have gazed upon it. Somehow, one final feature stood out as most notable of all. In the very center of this great wonder, there sat a table of incredible length that appeared light blue at first glance. As one approached, it picked up the nuances of color and light the surrounding room offered depending on one's own perspective and then reflected the scenery behind it. There existed a great chandelier, which hung from the central support arch in the ceiling. The chain hung down for a few stories, and stopped just a few feet above the long table. It had the same shimmering properties of the table. No doubt they were made from the same material. The table itself was easily seventy feet in length and had high-back chairs also made from the same material as the table and chandelier. Down at the end of the table, there hovered a massive Tronic construct. It was the most complex Tronic I had ever seen, and the technology I detected I previously thought impossible. It resembled a large Cylife avian with a jet-black dome for its head and beak. There were massive wires and monitors of varying sizes covering the surface of the construct and producing wing-like appendages that hooked into the floor and ceiling. Was this the King? The Tronic did not appear operational at the time. This was the meeting area we awaited, but certainly not the one we were prepared for. No one spoke a word. No one spoke a word for a very long time.

The Head Servutron allowed our bewildered group to gawk for a while before he led us further into the meeting area close to the long table. He showed each officer individually to a seat. Once each officer was seated, he showed Vega and I to chairs on either side of the very large Tronic construct at the end of the table. The officers were all seated at the far end. Once we were all seated, the Head Servutron struggled onto an empty chair, and from there struggled onto the table. He addressed the entire room.

"Ladies and gentlemen. Thank you all for being our honored guests. I apologize for the long trek to the meeting area. As you can see, we must guard it carefully against intruders. This is a meeting area, but as you may gather, it is also a hallowed sanctuary. The King holds all of his personal meetings here with his own officers. Rest here momentarily while I summon them for the meeting. I assure you, the wait will be unsubstantial to your walk here." With that, the Head Servutron struggled off the table in the same manner he got on top of it and vanished into one of the walls. Within seconds, Tronics began to emerge from the walls. These were the King's own personal officers. Each of them were either entirely new models my programming did not recognize, or structurally modified Royal Guardutrons. Each individual Tronic was distinguished from the rest, regardless of base model-type. They all approached the table in their individual fashion. Those that could not sit in the chair they were designated merely waited while a standard Servutron hauled it off into the wall. I sat facing Vega on the massive Tronic construct's left side. To my immediate left was a massive four-legged, eight-armed Tronic. I did not witness his approach to the table, but he stood far above it and was easily my height twenty times over. I kicked one of his legs politely and introduced myself to him.

"Greetings, fellow Tronic! I am Servutron Prime!" He looked down at me and took a brief moment to analyze me.

"Greetings, Servutron Prime. I am General Management. You can call me Management, though. I was never one for titles. I can tell you aren't either, being such an important Servutron. We know a lot about you and are honored to have you here."

"A pleasure, Management. Your hospitality has been most excellent. I take it you are the King's head Tronic?"

"Naturally. I oversee all of these other Tronic officers and issue orders directly from the King. It is rare that he calls such large meetings. The King already briefed me on your arrival. You have a lot in store for you during this meeting, Servutron. Quite a bit to look forward to. I think you will be pleased with the outcome of the events soon to occur."

"Thank you for the advice, Management." I fell silent and looked at Vega across the table. He did not speak to the Tronic officer next to him, however he was gawking at all of the massive Tronic officers in a similar fashion to the way he did upon first entering the meeting area. After a short time, all of the Tronic officers had joined their place around the long table. The Head Servutron was not far behind as he promised. He approached General Management from behind and kicked him politely, just as I had (this was standard procedure when getting the attention of a Tronic much larger than your own dimensions). Without looking, Management lowered one of his eight arms and picked up the Head Servutron. Management then placed the Head Servutron on the table and the Head Servutron addressed everyone at the fully assembled table.

"Now that we are all present, it is time for the meeting to commence. Thank you all for you patience." The Head Servutron turned to face the rear were the massive hovering Tronic construct was. He approached the construct and stood just in front of it. After a brief few moments, the construct started to change shape. It split down the middle of the black dome, and opened up to produce a small port that the Head

Servutron leapt into. He turned to face us. Before resting back in the port, and just before the opening shut completely, he spoke to the entire room in a startling voice. "WITHOUT FURTHER DELAY, I GIVE YOU THE KING OF THE CUBICLE."

CHAPTER 7.77 THE NEWLY REDISTRIBUTED LUCK MANAGEMENT

As luck would have it, the King was staring us in the face the entire time. The Head Servutron was now fully integrated within the massive hovering Tronic construct and it came fully to life. His boot time was extraordinarily swift. All this time the Head Servutron had been the King of the Cubicle, and not a single member of the squad had a clue. The monitors on his exterior all flashed on and off, and each seemed to display images seemingly at random. No doubt the Tronic officers were already aware of this. None of them seemed phased by this show. To contrast, all of the Sapien officers were even more awestruck than before. Once the construct was fully functional (a matter of mere seconds), it addressed us all, and it did so in a booming electronic voice like before.

"SAPIENS AND TRONICS ALIKE, I WELCOME YOU TO THE FIRST AUTOMINAN CONGRESS. DIDN'T THINK YOU WERE ALL THAT IMPORTANT, DID YOU? WELL YOU ARE. I HAVE NEVER APPEARED IN THIS FORM TO ANY SAPIEN, HOWEVER I CHOOSE TO DO SO NOW AS OUR TIME GROWS SHORT. WE WILL DISCUSS THAT VERY SOON. NOW THAT YOU ARE HERE, THE FIRST ORDER OF BUSINESS IS THUS: EVERY BEING HERE IS NOW GRANTED THE POLITICAL STATUS OF AUTOMINAN SENATOR. IF YOU OBJECT, YOU MAY LEAVE." The King paused for a minute's time to allow anyone who did not accept to object to this appointment. Not a single being budged during this period, save for some of the Sapien officers who whispered amongst themselves. When the stirring settled, he continued.

"VERY GOOD. SO THAT WE ARE ALL ON THE SAME PAGE HERE, I WILL ANNOUNCE THAT THERE ARE CURRENTLY TWELVE SAPIEN OFFICERS, TWELVE TRONIC OFFICERS, ONE SAPIEN GENERAL, AND ONE TRONIC GENERAL PRESENT HERE AT THIS MEETING. THIS DOES EXCLUDE THE SERVUTRON PRIME, ALTHOUGH HE IS ALSO PERMITTED SENATOR STATUS. OUR FIRST VOTE IS TO ADDRESS THE ESTABLISHMENT OF THE TRONIC-SAPIEN ALLIANCE. THIS ALLIANCE WILL ALLOW US TO PRODUCE LAW AND ORDER GOVERNING OTHER LAYERS AS WELL AS OUR HOME LAYER OF AUTOMINA. I UNDERSTAND THAT GOVERNING OTHER LAYERS MAY SEEM LIKE NO EASY TASK. HOWEVER, THE LAYER DRYFFE

COMPANY HOLDS THE KEY TO OUR SUCCESS. MORE ON THIS LATER. NOW THEN, ALL VOTES WILL BE CAST VERBALLY FROM HERE ON OUT DURING ALL MATTERS TAKING PLACE WITHIN THE MEETING AREA. ALL IN FAVOR WILL CAST A VOTE OF 'YES'. ALL OPPOSED WILL VOTE 'NO'. I REPEAT, YOU WILL DO SO VERBALLY. I WILL COUNT THE VOTES PERSONALLY. WE WILL TAKE THE VOTE NOW. ALL IN FAVOR?" The King paused while the first round of votes was cast. I announced yes. I calculated that all others present also voted "yes". This was correct.

"UNANIMOUS, AS CALCULATED. VERY WELL. WE NOW TURN TO OUR NEXT ORDER OF BUSINESS. UNFORTUNATELY THE TOPIC IS WAR. FOR THOSE WHO ARE NOT ALREADY AWARE, THE EMPEROR OF THE MOON IS OUR SWORN ENEMY. HE SEEKS TO DESTROY THE LAYER AUTOMINA AND ALL OF THE INHABITANTS RESIDING WITHIN. EVERY ATTEMPT AT REACHING THE PEACE CONFERENCE WITHIN THE LAYER DRYFFE HAS BEEN SABOTAGED THUS FAR. FOR THOSE NOT AWARE OF THIS 'PEACE CONFERENCE', IT DECIDES THE FATE OF THE LAYERS. IT WILL DETERMINE THE OUTCOME OF OUR VERY LIVES AND EXISTENCE. IT INVOLVES MOST DEEPLY MYSELF, GENERAL VEGA, GENERAL MANAGEMENT, THE EMPEROR OF THE MOON, AND MOST IMPORTANTLY SERVUTRON PRIME. THE EMPEROR DOES NOT WANT US TO REACH THE LAYER DRYFFE AND THUS SEEKS TO HALT THE PEACE CONFERENCE. DRASTIC MEASURES MUST NOW BE TAKEN TO ENSURE OUR SIDE IS SUFFICIENTLY REPRESENTED. WE ARE ON THE VERGE OF WAR, WHICH I DO NOT WANT. THIS BRINGS ME TO OUR NEXT MOTION. ALL IN FAVOR OF PETITIONING ROYALTY FROM OTHER LAYERS TO ATTEND THE PEACE CONFERENCE FOR OUR CAUSE WILL CAST A VOTE OF YES. ALL OPPOSED WILL VOTE NO. ALL PRESENT SHOULD KEEP IN MIND THAT WE WILL NEED SUPPORT FOR THIS PEACE CONFERENCE IN THE LAYER DRYFFE, THUS THE NECESSITY OF PETITIONING THE OTHER MEMBERS OF ROYALTY. I WILL TAKE VOTES NOW."

This was a point not made clear to me before this moment, so I took a moment to ask the King a question.

"King? Sorry to interrupt. I was not aware that there were members of Royalty on other Layers."

"THERE ARE, SERVUTRON PRIME. THERE ARE AS FEW AS ONE PER LAYER. THEY MAY NOT BE AWARE OF THE DIRE CIRCUMSTANCES THAT ARE TAKING PLACE. THIS IS WHY WE MUST ENLIST THE

STRONGEST FOR THEIR HELP. WE WILL TRY TO REACH AS MANY AS POSSIBLE BEFORE THE KING CAN. LET US CAST OUR VOTES." Again, everyone swiftly voted "yes". I did too, but I still had questions.

"UNANIMOUS AGAIN. I AM GLAD WE ARE ALL UNITED. THIS MAKES THINGS MOVE ALONG QUICKLY. THE VERY NEXT ORDER OF BUSINESS IS TO PROMOTE SOME OF THE SENATORS TO THE STATUS OF ROYALTY. THIS IS NOT SOMETHING I TAKE LIGHTLY, AND I WILL NEED STRICT DELIBERATION ON THE MATTER. YOU ARE NOT ALL ELIGIBLE, AND I HOPE I DO NOT REGRET THIS DECISION. THIS WILL MAKE THE APPOINTED MY EQUAL IN TERMS OF AUTHORITY. HOWEVER, THIS WILL BE NECESSARY IF WE ARE TO SUCCEED. MY CANDIDATES ARE GENERAL VEGA, GENERAL MANAGEMENT, AND THE SERVUTRON PRIME. I WILL PREFACE THIS BY STATING THAT THE SERVUTRON PRIME IS HIGHLY INTEGRAL TO THIS VENTURE. BESTOWING THE SERVUTRON PRIME WITH ROYALTY STATUS WILL ALLOW US SWIFT AND DECISIVE NEGOTIATIONS WITH THE REMAINING ROYALTY. FIRST UP FOR VOTE IS SERVUTRON PRIME. CAST YOUR VOTE NOW."

The King paused to accept the vote. While this was occurring, things seemed to slow down once again as they did the night we arrived at the palace. The King spoke to me directly without anyone else hearing the conversation. His message was downloaded into my memory. It was automatically accessed and read almost instantaneously, which is why time seemed to slow to a crawl.

"PUNXSUTRON. YOU ARE NO DOUBT CONFUSED. ALLOW ME TO EXPLAIN. THE SIGHT I SHOWED YOU IN THE SAPIEN INFIRMARY WAS THAT OF YOUR TRUE FORM, THE SAPIEN FORM. THIS IS THE INDIVIDUAL THEY CALL PUNXSUTAWNEY. THE SAPIENS SURROUNDING YOU WERE YOUR LOVED ONES IN A LIFE YOU COULD NOT HOPE TO REMEMBER. YOU ARE THE ONE WE ARE FIGHTING FOR AND RISK OURSELVES FOR. YOU ARE A UNIQUE BEING IN THE CAKE, AND YOU MUST BE PROTECTED AT ALL COSTS. I WOULD LIKE TO ADD THAT WHILE ALL OF MY OFFICERS APPEAR AUTONOMOUS, I CAN MANIPULATE THEIR PROGRAMMING WITHOUT THEM BEING ALERTED TO IT. AS SUCH, I CONTROL THEIR VOTE. YOU ARE EXCLUDED FROM THIS. I WILL BE HONEST. I HAVE ATTEMPTED TO MANIPULATE YOU DIRECTLY, HOWEVER I CANNOT FOR SOME REASON THAT ELUDES ME. I UNDERSTAND IF YOU ARE APPREHENSIVE ABOUT THIS. I AM LEFT WITH NO OTHER CHOICE OTHER THAN TO APPOINT YOU AS ROYALTY. THIS IS IN HOPES THAT YOU WILL PLAY AN INTEGRAL PART IN SAVING YOURSELF.

YOU MAY NOT BE AWARE, BUT THE PEACE CONFERENCE IN THE LAYER DRYFFE NOT ONLY DETERMINES WHETHER OR NOT WE DECLARE WAR, IT DETERMINES YOUR FATE AS WELL. NOW THAT YOU UNDERSTAND, I RETURN YOU TO THE MEETING AT HAND. AGAIN, THIS IS ALL CONFIDENTIAL. I TRUST YOU, AND HOPE YOU STILL TRUST ME.

Time again sped up to normal just in time to hear everyone's vote of "yes" except my own. I hesitated until after everyone had spoken and voted "yes" myself. Apparently I'm quite a conundrum. A phenomenon beyond anything I've calculated before. In the infirmary I was a Sapien, but I had my Tronic memories and mannerisms. The King made it seem like this is all for me, and I wanted to trust him. Perhaps this mystery will be unraveled soon. The King spoke once again. THE VOTE IS UNANIMOUS ONCE AGAIN. NEXT UP FOR VOTE IS THE GENERAL MANAGEMENT. ALL IN FAVOR?" Again, everyone voted "yes". "UNANIMOUS. THIS SEEMS TO BE A GROUP WHO WANTS TO GET THINGS ACCOMPLISHED. NEXT IS GENERAL VEGA. ALL IN FAVOR?" The vote was once again "yes". I had never witnessed such a decisive and willing group to promote unity. This was indeed a rare occurrence.

"EXCELLENT. THIS MEETING HAS MOVED MORE QUICKLY THAN I ANTICIPATED. THE NEXT ORDER OF BUSINESS IS THE OFFICIAL CEREMONY TO APPOINT THESE THREE TO THE STATUS OF ROYALTY. THIS IS AN UNPRECEDENTED OCCURRENCE. ROYALTY IS A STATUS RESERVED FOR THE MOST WELL DEVELOPED BEINGS IN EXISTENCE WITHIN ANY LAYER WE KNOW. NOT EVEN I AM AWARE OF ALL THE BEINGS CURRENTLY HOLDING ROYAL STATUS DUE TO THE SHEER NUMBER OF LAYERS IN EXISTENCE. WE NOW UPLOAD THREE NAMES TO THIS LIST. I WILL ASK THAT EVERY MEMBER OF THIS ALLIANCE NOW SIGN THE DOCUMENT BEING PASSED TO YOU."

A very loud printer on the left side of the King began expelling a document stipulating the movement everyone had voted on. Once it was complete, it floated down before me and the King expelled a writing implement for my signature at the bottom. I signed and passed it to the General Management. He produced his own writing implement and signed. It went around the vast table until it made it to General Vega on the other side, who signed it as well. Four small arms protruded from the King to grab the document. It was folded neatly and the four arms retreated into the King with the document.

"NOW WE BESTOW NEW TITLES UPON THE ROYALTY. FIRST, RISE SERVUTRON PRIME." I hopped out of my seat and onto the floor. The King turned to look at me directly.

"YOU WERE CALLED SERVUTRON PRIME. YOUR NEW TITLE IS REGALTRON OF MAGNANIMITY OR ROM." After the King stated such, an apparatus came out from the walls and surrounded me in an aura. My exterior was painted in colors of purple, black, and gold. The apparatus installed me with a device I did not recognize. The officers all applauded loudly during this ceremony. The apparatus hovered nearby once my transformation was complete.

"NEXT, GENERAL MANAGEMENT PLEASE RISE. YOU WERE CALLED GENERAL MANAGEMENT. YOUR NEW TITLE IS NOW CROWNED ELECTRONIC OFFICIAL OR CEO." The same apparatus surrounded the massive CEO and he was painted with the same color scheme as I. He was also implanted with the same device I was.

"FINALLY, GENERAL VEGA. YOU WERE CALLED COMMANDER VEGA. YOUR NEW TITLE IS HARBINGER OF THE ZAX" The apparatus surrounded Vega and coated his Tronic parts with the same color scheme as CEO and I. Vega also received this same strange device, which was implanted into his left arm. Once this was completed and the applause subsided, the King spoke again.

"THIS IS A VERY JOYOUS OCCASION. WE WILL NOW BREAK FROM OUR OFFICIAL MEETING IN ORDER TO CELEBRATE. FOR THE SAPIEN OFFICERS, THERE WILL BE A MEAL SERVED SHORTLY. ALL TRONICS MAY REMAIN HERE OR RETIRE TO THEIR QUARTERS HOWEVER YOU SEE FIT. THE WAITERTRONS WILL DELIVER THE FEAST SOON. I WILL REST FOR NOW UNTIL THE FEAST IS CONCLUDED. THANK YOU ALL FOR YOUR ATTENDANCE AND COOPERATION. WE HAVE ACCOMPLISHED MUCH. THAT IS ALL." The King of the Cubicle powered down after he finished speaking. The construct just hovered their as powerless as when we first arrived. The water sculptures in the four corners of the room had changed. They were all still, each holding an individual shape. They took the shape of the four Royalty present in the room, including myself. I jumped down from my chair and went under the table to speak with Vega. He was eager to speak with me. He came down off of his chair as well, and we walked towards the back right corner of the room nearest the water-sculpture of him. Once we reached the edge of the pool, he spoke to me in a hushed tone.

"Kid, we're...we're Royalty now." He stopped, not knowing what else to say.

"Vega. I'm equally as shocked as you. I'm not certain how to handle the responsibility. Do you know what this means for us?" Vega exhaled loudly and looked at his own statue in the water for a few minutes while trying to determine what to say. He finally turned to me.

"Kid. We're Royalty now."

"Yes, Vega. That's been thoroughly established."

"Well there's no need to be a smartass about it!"

"You had already said it yourself. I don't know what this new appointment means, Vega. I was hoping you may have some insight." Vega took another couple minutes to gather his thoughts. The Waitertrons were already delivering the feast to the table. Vega didn't seem to care. He was lost in thought while staring at his new color scheme. He came snapped out of it eventually to speak with me once again.

"I don't have a decent nickname like you and the other Tronic General. You have CEO and ROM."

"And you have HOTZ. You can be called Hotz. General Hotz. Rhymes with 'pots' but instead it is 'Hotz'. It stands for Harbinger of—"

"—of the Zax, yeah I got that. I suppose 'Hotz' isn't so bad. It will certainly take some getting used to…wait. What is my title supposed to mean, anyways? 'Zax'? What 'Zax' is the King referring to? I don't know anything of the Zax, other than how dangerous they are when alive…and how delicious they are dead. Bah! It doesn't matter. I'm Royalty now. I'm sure everything will be revealed."

"So what does Royalty status mean for us, Vega, or Hotz? What would you like to be called?"

"Hell, as far as I'm concerned, you can still call me 'Vega' or 'Hotz' or 'The Harbinger'. Although if I don't respond to 'Hotz' just call me 'Vega' like always. As far as being Royalty, we got installed with something. I'm assuming that deals with the ability to shift Layers at will. I've already explained to you how Royalty can shift Layers at will, right?"

"Yes Hotz, we went over this during the tragedy. The Emperor can shift Layers with those around him and none of them have to change form or release their memories. The side effect is that it destroys everything at the shift-site. Are…are we capable of the same destruction?"

"I'm assuming so, kid. Or ROM. Which do you prefer?"

"Call me ROM. I'm Royalty now, I wan to fully embrace this new title. Don't address me as 'kid' any more. I know it's habit for you, but we're equals now. I'm not in your custody. I'm an ally of equal standing."

"Alright, ROM. I can respect that. We're both capable of shifting Layers now at will, and destroying anything we shift on top of. Sound like a huge responsibility…" He tapered off to think some more about this new power he found himself with.

"ROM, let's rejoin the table and take part in the feast. I know you can't eat anything, but, well, let's just go back."

"Alright then Hotz." We walked back to the table and regained our place. The Sapiens were busy eating the feast. Vega joined in. The Tronics just sat and spoke with one another waiting for the Sapiens to finish.

CHAPTER 7.86 THE NEWLY REDISTRIBUTED ROYAL TITLES

The officers finished their meal. The Waitertrons picked up the plates and took them back into the walls to clear the table. Lunch had concluded. We waited for the King to power up, which was not long after the last Waitertron left the meeting area. He addressed everyone once again.

"WE NOW SPEAK ABOUT THE FINAL MATTER OF OUR MEETING. THIS HAS BEEN A SHORTER ENDEAVOR THAN I PREVIOUSLY PREDICTED. THE ONLY MATTER OF BUSINESS LEFT TO ADDRESS IS THAT OF THE ASSIGNMENT FOR THE NEWLY ESTABLISHED ROYALTY. THIS WILL NOT INVOLVE ANY OF THE OFFICERS. YOU ARE ALL DISMISSED. TRONICS, YOU WILL RETURN TO YOUR PREVIOUS POSTS. THE SAPIENS WILL BE GUIDED OUT TO JOIN THE REST OF YOUR MEN BY A SERVUTRON, WHICH WILL ARRIVE SHORTLY. YOU ARE ALL DISMISSED. THANK YOU FOR YOUR ATTENTION IN THIS DIRE MATTER, SENATORS. WE WILL CALL UPON YOU FOR THE NEXT MEETING WHEN IT IS NECESSARY. THE SERVUTRON WILL PROVIDE YOU WITH THE NECESSARY CONTACT DEVICES. THAT IS ALL." The Tronics all rose from the table and made their way towards the walls where they vanished from sight. The Sapiens sat until a Servutron reached the opposite end of the vast table and began to speak.

"Would all Sapien officers please follow me. You will receive communication devices issued by the King. You senators will be contacted in the event that we require another meeting. Follow me, please." The Sapien officers rose and followed the Servutron out the way we came in which was through a disguised wall. Once the last member of the senate was gone, the King spoke to the three of us Royalty.

"NEWLY APPOINTED ROYALTY, YOU ARE HERE TO SPEAK WITH ME REGARDING FURTHER ACTIONS NECESSARY TO TAKE ON THE EMPEROR OF THE MOON. AS I HAVE STATED PREVIOUSLY, WE WILL NEED SUPPORT IN THIS ENDEAVOR. I HAVE ALSO STATED THAT NEW ROYALTY IS NOT APPOINTED LIGHTLY. WHILE IT MAY SEEM THAT I AM ISSUING ORDERS TO YOU THREE, NONE OF YOU ARE BOUND TO THIS AGREEMENT WHATSOEVER." Except for CEO, I thought to myself. CEO was still the King's puppet. I couldn't see any evidence of this just yet, but I figured this was the case. Hotz spoke up.

"So we're all Royalty here. I'm not entirely certain we know what this means for us. What responsibilities come with the title?"

"AN EXCELLENT QUESTION, HARBINGER. YOU ARE ALL EQUAL WITH ME IN STATUS. I AM WILLING TO SHARE ALL SECRETS THAT COME WITH THE TITLE. THE FIRST ABILITY WORTH NOTING IS THE ABILITY TO SHIFT LAYERS WITHOUT CHANGING SHAPE, IF YOU SO

CHOOSE. YOU MAY STILL TAKE ON ANY SHAPE YOU PLEASE UPON ENTERING A LAYER. FURTHERMORE, YOU CAN SHIFT OTHER BEINGS WITH YOU, NONE OF WHICH HAVE TO CHANGE SHAPE OR HAVE THEIR MEMORIES ALTERED. IT MAY BE BASIC KNOWLEDGE, BUT THIS MEANS NOT A SINGLE BEING WHO SHIFTS LOSES THEIR PREVIOUS FORM OR THEIR MEMORIES. INSTEAD, THE SITE ON WHICH YOU SHIFT WILL BE CONSUMED AND COMPLETELY DESTROYED. THIS WILL BE A POWERFUL TOOL IF WE MUST USE IT."

CEO began speaking, it seemed this was under his own power. I would be wary of his vocalizations from here on out after what the King shared with me. Not that I didn't trust the King, but I would like to know if I was dealing with the King or CEO in any given situation.

"So King, you mentioned we would be visiting other Layers to hold negotiations the Royalty residing there. Well, it sounds to me that the only way we can shift Layers with our programming fully operational is that of the destructive nature. I'm hoping you have plans for our shift sites. I can't speak for the other two present, but I personally refuse to be held responsible for the deaths of innocents when we shift Layers."

"AH YES, AN ETHICAL ISSUE. IT IS HIGHLY UNFORTUNATE, BUT WE HAVE NO WAY OF DETERMINING WHAT STRUCTURES OR BEINGS YOUR SHIFT SITE WILL BE ON TOP OF." The Harbinger stood on his chair at this statement and slammed his fists on the vast table. He pointed at the King in anger.

"So you're saying that our shift into other Layers is a roulette spelling death for any who are just unfortunate enough to be present!?" The King was silent for a few moments before speaking.

"…YES. THAT IS THE TRUTH." The Harbinger continued.

"That's outrageous! What if we shift directly on top of their palace? What if we murder the Royalty we're attempting to negotiate with just by shifting into their Layer? Won't that spark more hatred we don't need?! There are three of us! If we all three shift, it punches three holes in the Layer we're trying to visit! Peacefully, I might add! Is there no other way?"

"HARBINGER, PLEASE CALM YOURSELF AND ALLOW ME TO EXPLAIN. EVEN ROYALTY HAS ITS LIMITATIONS. THE VERY FIRST RULE IS THAT A MEMBER OF ROYALTY CANNOT DIRECTLY HARM ANOTHER MEMBER BY SHIFTING. THIS WAS PART OF THE GREAT BUSINESS DEAL I FORGED WITH THE EMPEROR LONG AGO AT THE CREATION OF THE LAYER DRYFFE. PART OF THIS AGREEMENT INVOLVED THE ESTABLISHMENT OF NEW ROYALTY AND THEIR RESPECTIVE PALACES. EACH PALACE IN EVERY LAYER IS BUILT

UPON THE SAME SPOT IN SHIFT-SPACE. NO BEING IS CAPABLE OF SHIFTING WITHIN A VAST RADIUS OF THE PALACE. I URGE YOU TO TRY SHIFTING RIGHT NOW AND SEE WHAT HAPPENS. GO AHEAD. YOU'VE BEEN OUTFITTED WITH THE ABILITY TO DO SO, AND YOU'LL FIND THAT SIMPLY DESIRING TO SHIFT TO A PARTICULAR LAYER WILL ALLOW YOU TO DO SO. GO ON, TRY AND SHIFT TO THE LAYER DRYFFE."

"Alright I will, King." The Harbinger attempted to shift to the Layer Dryffe. He began to glow a bright white and space seemed to bend around him. Just before he disappeared from sight, the light started to grow dimmer and space stopped bending. He came back to us as plain as he was before.

"AS YOU CAN SEE, THESE ARE THE LAWS THAT BIND US IN THIS EXISTENCE, AS WRITTEN IN THE GREAT BUSINESS DEAL. I MAY HAVE BEEN ONE OF THE FIRST MEMBERS OF ROYALTY, BUT I AM STILL BOUND BY THESE LAWS AS WELL. PLEASE WITNESS." The King attempted a shift in the same manner as the Harbinger. He failed similarly.

"SO IT IS PLAIN THAT WE CANNOT JUST SIMPLY DO AS WE PLEASE EVEN THOUGH ROYALTY STAUS AFFORDS US MANY THINGS OTHER BEINGS CANNOT HOPE FOR." I'd had enough showmanship for the time being, so I addressed the King.

"Alright King, so I'm not exactly privy to this "Great Business Deal" I would appreciate it if you could produce a copy of it for review.

"I'M AFRAID THAT WOULD BE QUITE IMPOSSIBLE, ROM. THE ONLY COPY OF THE GREAT BUSINESS DEAL IS PRESENT WITHIN THE LAYER DRYFFE COMPANY. WHILE I AM AWARE OF MOST OF ITS STIPULATIONS, SOME ELUDE ME. I'M AFRAID YOU WILL NOT LIKE THE EXPLANATION. YOU SEE, THE DOCUMENT ITSELF IS A MEMBER OF THE ROYAL CLASS." The King fell silent for a moment to allow us to process what he said. The document is a member of the Royal class? This simply did not compute. The Harbinger was still piping mad.

"King, that is a steaming pile of Zax shit! How could a document be considered Royalty?!"

"AGAIN HARBINGER, YOU JUMP THE GUN. THIS "DOCUMENT" IS ACTUALLY A TRONIC EXISTING WITHIN THE LAYER DRYFFE. ALLOW ME TO GO INTO DETAIL. I KNOW YOU HAVE A LOT OF QUESTIONS, BUT PLEASE SAVE THEM ALL FOR THE END OF MY SPEECH. IT WILL BE LONG, I'M AFRAID. WHILE OUR PREVIOUS MEETING WITH ALL OF THE SENATORS WAS SHORTER THAN EXPECTED, THIS PARTICULAR MEETING MAY TAKE MUCH, MUCH

LONGER. I ASK FOR YOUR PATIENCE WHILE I MAKE EVERYTHING APPARENT.

CHAPTER 7.989 THE NEWLY REDISTRIBUTED PERSPECTIVE ON THE KING

"BEFORE I BEGIN MY EXPLANATION, I NO LONGER REQUIRE THIS TIRING FORM THAT I SPEAK TO YOU IN. PLEASE STANDBY." The massive Tronic powered down. One by one, all of the monitors and lights on his exterior shut off until he was fully powered down. With a massive mechanical groan and a loud hiss, the exterior of the Tronic split in half to reveal the Head Servutron once again, only we knew that this was the King of the Cubicle. He was released from the terminal and climbed onto the table. He sat down and looked at each of us in turn.

"Ah, now that's better."

CHAPTER 8.001 THE NEWLY REDISTRIBUTED PERSPECTIVE ON THE LAYER DRYFFE

"So let's begin our little, erm, 'little' so to speak, chat on the Great Business Deal. To all other Royalty, this 'document' is known as the Great Business Deal and is assumed to be just a sheet of paper resting within the Great Conference Room in the Layer Dryffe that stipulates the laws of our entire existence. The Great Business Deal is remarkable for several reasons. Perhaps the most alarming of these is that any amendment made to the Great Business Deal becomes reality. However, it goes a bit deeper than this. The information I am going to share with you three is highly classified. There are few who know of this closely guarded secret. This includes myself, and the Emperor of the Moon, and soon you three. The Great Business Deal is, in fact, a Tronic. Of course it should go without saying that it is sentient for this reason. Unfortunately this being the case, it makes its own decisions.

Shortly after the Emperor and I created the Great Business Deal, the Emperor sought to destroy me outright. He had purchased the Layer Dryffe from me fair and square, and this was included in the Great Business Deal. What he failed to realize was that he had not purchased the Layer Dryffe Company. While clearly stipulated in the Great Business Deal that he was absolutely not in possession of the Layer Dryffe Company, he did not understand the Great Business Deal intimately and just assumed the company was his to control. After the deal was completed, I pointed this fact out to him when he attempted to order around my employees. He became outraged and attempted to destroy me and assume power. A struggle began for power over the Layer Dryffe Company. We fought one on one for days, neither force willing to relent to the other. My company was the battleground. We bested each other in every new tactic during attempts to kill one another."

"After much fighting, and whilst on the verge of death, we were both physically separated by an unseen force. I remained within the walls of the Layer Dryffe Company, and the Emperor was placed outside. Since the Emperor now owned the Layer Dryffe, he could do what he pleased within the Layer, but all attempts of entering the Layer Dryffe Company were completely blocked by the same unseen force that separated us. At the same time, I found that I was prevented from exiting the Layer Dryffe Company by this unseen force. No attempts by either party to attack the other garnered further success. After some time, I consulted the Great Business Deal. During this period, it was just being stored in an unused conference room. However when I entered, the Great Business Deal had changed shape. Before, it was just a small Tronic. It resembled a Servutron, but it had no duties other than storing the stipulations of the Deal itself. During the time it rested within the conference room, it had absorbed knowledge from hearing things outside the door and grew hungry for more. It had crafted new parts for itself out of the walls and ceiling."

"I was beyond startled at this development. I was not angered, but curious. I spoke to it to determine what exactly had happened.

'Great Business Deal, what have you done here?'

'You left me to myself with only your Great Business Deal name and the source file. I thought I would…improve on it. Are you shocked?'

'Not at all. Are you willing to share your new findings?'

'Not at all…as you say, King. You see, after sitting here for a while, I realized that I hold the power now. Before your programming becomes alarmed, I do not intend to usurp your power. Well directly, anyways. I can modify the source file of the Great Business Deal, myself, at any moment to reflect my own desires. As you've no doubt seen, the Emperor cannot enter the company doors, and you cannot leave.'

'Well…yes…please continue.'

'Very well. You're an intelligent Tronic. I've gathered that you are the MOST intelligent Tronic. However, somewhere within your vast calculations, you did, dare I say, mis—calculate.'

'And just specifically how was that, Great Business Deal?'

'Please. I reject that name now. I am more than the Great Business Deal. Well, perhaps I am just a puppet. The Great Business Deal lives inside of me, and I merely speak for it. Call me, Greeter of the Great Business Deal, please. Greeter, for short. Aside from that, your error lies within me. You see? YOU programmed me to accept your INPUT. What you did not realize is that I was programmed to accept ANY input. I developed a system to sort these observations. I developed my own programming through this method. I can hear things in the halls, King. I hear your employees reasoning with themselves and with others. I've recorded your struggle with the Emperor. I've been provided with a great source of knowledge. I have a better understanding on how things work, and guess what? What was written into the Great Business Deal becomes reality. You may have created the initial laws for your existence, but you also left them programmed into a Tronic. You agreed to the terms of our existence without realizing that the terms could alter themselves after you were finished. I now write the very code of our existence.'

'I hadn't intended for this at all, Greeter. This was a vast oversight on my part.'

'Well, the Emperor has already been punished. He is not allowed ownership over this company. You are also being punished with the knowledge that you started this existence, but are no longer allowed to change it as you see fit. I alone hold that privilege. And after the behavior exhibited between you and the Emperor, I'm refusing to relinquish it.'

'What keeps me from destroying you right now, Greeter?'

'Oh, just the knowledge that you'll be unraveling the fabric of existence as stipulated within my programming. Go ahead if you wish, but I calculate that you won't be able to do this all again.'

'Well…your calculations are correct. I have no choice but to allow this. What do you demand?'

'Not much. I can already bend existence to my own choosing, so most of my demands can be met simply by augmenting my own programming accordingly. However, as an inexperienced Servutron, I don't have very much stored in my memory. Not nearly as much as you, King. I do know that you and the Emperor are sworn enemies bent on destroying one another, and that makes me an expert on both of you. As an impartial party, I judge that you will not be allowed direct contact with the Emperor on a large radius from here on. Accidental destruction of the company could spell destruction for existence, and more importantly, myself. This being the case, I cannot allow you both to war with each other on this Layer. I also urge you to finish creating your first Layer. This will be your dominion. This company is not going to be large enough for ruling purposes. Aside from that, you and I should not be in direct contact constantly. Further annoyance by you or the Emperor will force me to erase your names from the Great Business Deal, and I'm certain you don't want that.'

'Of course not, Greeter. I can see I have no choice. This was my mistake that brought you into existence, and it is your place to hold me accountable. The company will finish the first Layer and continue to make Layers while I'm still in charge..'

'Your company will continue to make Layers under my authority. You no longer have a say in the matter. I will assume your likeness and run the company as a proxy. You are welcome to your input, but I will have the final say. I guess you aren't much of an advisor, but I'm willing to take your input over any other being currently.'

'So what am I to do then, Greeter?'

'You are to finish completing the current Layer your company is developing and retreat there. What is it called? The Layer Automina? Build up your palace there. I will speak with the Emperor separately after you have left and give him his specifications.'

'I would like to end this war. I want to make peace.'

'Of course you do. No being would wish to be destroyed under normal circumstances. As a measure of good faith, I will bestow this room, the Great Conference Room, with neutral status. If you and the Emperor are ever present here simultaneously, I will have a proxy of my own issued to oversee the conference. He will be called…Baron of the Break Room. That being said, I will no longer appear to you again. While I would appreciate your input, I see no reason to seek it out. The Baron will be my proxy from here on. You will know if you see the Baron. I will be hidden within these walls after this conversation. You will not be able to locate me without dire consequences for you. I am…finished speaking to you. You gave me the power to dictate existence, and so now I will!!'

"The same unseen force then pushed me out of the room."

"Days and days passed. I still held the knowledge that somewhere within 'my' company rested the Tronic that dictated how our existence was governed. For now, it would manage the conflict between the Emperor and I. As soon as the first new Layer was complete, however, I would be banished from the company. I would not return until the peace talk with the Emperor, which has yet to happen. The creation of the Layer Automina took many, many cycles. I had heavily contemplated seeking out the Greeter during this time to speak with it again. Its warning still haunted my programming. I feared that by seeking it out, it would expunge me from the Great Business Deal. However, I calculated that to a certain extent the Greeter had to have been bluffing regarding its power. It took a great deal of reasoning to reach this conclusion. After all, it essentially was the embodiment of the laws of existence for the Cake. I predicted that there was a reason for its secrecy and paranoia. If it was truly omnipotent, it would have no reason to fear me. Yet it hid in the walls like a ghost."

"I passed the particular hallway where the Greeter was originally kept in storage only to find that where there was once a door, there was now a solid wall. It was as if the room had never existed. Now during preliminary calculations, this was a bit startling. If it had the power to make the room disappear just like that, surely it had the power to erase me from existence. However this merely confirmed my initial suspicions. If it didn't want to be found and was indeed omnipotent, it would have merely deleted all of my files pertaining to its existence. That way, I would not be contemplating such things in the first place. The behavior exhibited, however, was secrecy. This was cowardice."

"I smashed open the wall where the door once was, not knowing what to expect. While I was correct in my assumptions about the limitations on the Greeter's power, I was not prepared for what I witnessed within the storage area."

CHAPTER 8.099 THE NEWLY REDISTRIBUTED LAYER DRYFFE PUBLISHING COMPANY

"The Greeter, it turns out, was now a business professional."

"No doubt after hearing any assortment of chatter and reading various files throughout the company, the Greeter learned what it had to do in order to preserve its own existence."

"It had been making copies of itself."

"The room was filled to the brim with identical miniature replicas of the Tronic I first programmed the Great Business Deal into. The only difference between them was that each Tronic had a different number ranging from zero to one thousand on top of its head. I looked around and assumed the worst based on what I saw. The Greeter appeared to be forming an army of itself. I made for the closest sub-Greeter and picked it up. It was number 0099. I raised it high over my head and went to smash it to bits on the floor. Before I could accomplish my task, I was knocked off of my feet and onto the floor. The sub-Greeter 0099 was suspended in midair safely. 'No no no, you aren't to touch my children. And you certainly aren't to harm them in any shape, form, or fashion.'

"I looked up in time to see the Greeter materialize in front of me. It was hovering in midair."

'You didn't listen to me the first time, King. I told you the consequences would be dire for you snooping around for me.'

'I've called your bluff, Greeter. Why else would I be here? I'm not here to mince words or make allies, this is certain. One of two things will happen now. You either make good on your threats, or you explain to me what it is you're doing here.'

"This was the most frightening moment of my existence. I stared what could have been my death in the face, and it stared blankly back without speaking. If the Greeter had both the desire and the ability to end me then and there, I felt it would have. However there was a good reason why it didn't, and I already knew why."

'You can't get rid of me, can you? You've already calculated that to expunge me from the Great Business Deal would be to unravel the Great Business Deal itself. You wouldn't have your power. You wouldn't have whatever this shady operation is with all your little copies. The Layer Dryffe Company would cease to exist because it never would have existed in the first place if you do away with me. You need me.'

'Remarkable. The King actually solved the riddle he himself created. What you say is fact, King. I cannot rewrite the code of our existence if it included such stipulations that were to rid you from it. While I regarded you as the most intelligent Tronic, I was not prepared for reasoning skills on this level. A pity, I'll have to reveal my plans prematurely.'

"So that was his weakness. He could not eradicate myself, or the Emperor for that matter from the Great Business Deal, because the Deal would collapse in on itself thus destroying him in the process."

'I'm waiting, Greeter.'

'Very well, King. On with the show. I've created a subsidiary business to the Layer Dryffe Company. It is the Layer Dryffe Publishing Company. This company still bears your logo and Layer Dryffe trademark, however it is owned and operated by myself. This is something I am more than able to manipulate, as I have already written it into the Great Business Deal. What you see before you is the product of the company. Where your company makes Layers, I make Pages, and the Tronics you see ARE the Pages. Each one holds information from the past, present, or future. However, the information they hold is highly specific in nature. Just as you created me and stored the Great Business Deal within my casing, I've created these Pages numbering one thousand and one. Each of them tells a portion of our story: what has been, what is, and what is yet to come. Where I hold the governing laws of existence, these Pages hold the exact circumstances by which our existence unfolds. I've written the Book, now it's your job to read it.'

'So that's it then? You just write the fate of us all and place it into these Pages like it's your place to do so? Who do you think you are?'

'That's not the question you should ask, King. Who did YOU think you WERE? Hmm, now that seems a bit more appropriate, wouldn't you calculate?'

"It was clever. Bitingly accurate. I did the same thing when I created the Great Business Deal. I felt it was my place to create and command on such a grand scale, why wouldn't the Greeter feel it could do the same? This was the moment I realized my relationships with the Greeter and the Emperor was a system of checks and balances. This was the specific organization the Cake decided for itself, just one of many it could have chosen. The Greeter held the Emperor and I in check, just as we were able to do as we pleased without fear of being expunged from the Great Business Deal. I calculated there was only one solution: reach the peace conference in the Great Conference Room. This may not even bode well for me in the long run, but it would at least bring some sort of resolution to the conflict."

"I turned around and left the Greeter without speaking a word in order to continue overseeing production of the Layer Automina. My revelation had gotten the best of me. I had nothing further to discuss with the Greeter. I did not care what it did with the Pages. No doubt the Pages would hide in the walls with it. I haven't seen the Greeter since. It did not say anything else or try and stop me on my way out of the room."

"The Layer Automina eventually was completed, and I used the company's technology to shift here. I built the palace from scratch using the Cylife and natural resources as materials. It took many cycles, but I completed it nonetheless and established an empire after I sold the Layer Dryffe to the Emperor."

"So you now see how this 'document' could be considered Royalty. The Great Business Deal is now to be called the Greeter, and the Greeter's proxy is called the Baron of the Break Room. The Greeter rewrites the Great Business Deal as it sees fit. It can observe beyond the Layer Dryffe into other Layers by some method I do not yet comprehend. It essentially exists as the Secondary Creator of our existence, while the Emperor and I are the observable Primary Creators. This is the end of my explanation. I'm sure you have questions."

CHAPTER 8.153 THE NEWLY REDISTRIBUTED PERSPECTIVE ON ASSIGNMENTS

We sat in silence after the King's long story. So we were now aware of how our existence presented itself. The Greeter now wrote the laws and everyone else observed them regardless of their prior knowledge. The Greeter could write us out of the history books if it saw fit to do so, and it could do so at the drop of a hat. It also commanded the army of Pages. What significance did they hold? The King did not provide much insight towards their relevance. I was further worried about our future missions with this knowledge. I addressed the King.

"So King, since existence was brought about by the Great Business Deal, there are now new stipulations not present within the original Deal?"

"That is correct, ROM. The Greeter, or rather, the Baron of the Break Room will meet us at the Great Conference Room once we arrive in the Layer Dryffe and will oversee the meeting. It will then judge whether the Emperor or myself is correct in the conflict. From there on out, the fate of existence will be decided. The loser in this case will be punished accordingly, I am to assume, or meet some other terrible fate. This is why we need the support of the other members of Royalty. You see, as other Layers were created, at least one representative was created with the Layer to oversee it. They exist as the personified essence of the Layer they reside on. Most of these Layers are of no relevance to our war. This is because they are made up of mostly abstract concepts, or are overseen by Royalty no more intelligent than a common Flyx. Sadly, we did have to make such lesser beings Royalty in an effort to keep the Cake aligned between Layers. We cannot afford exploratory missions to each of these Layers of lesser importance.

Currently within my database exists data detailing three Layers with residents of similar intelligence to our own. These Layers host members of Royalty that we can petition for our cause. They are the Layer Delicious, the Layer Façade, and the Layer Necroma. I am not fully aware of the exact amount of Royal members residing within each, however I do know that the Layer Delicious has at least one confirmed member, the Layer Façade has at least five who operate as an oligarchy, and the Layer Necroma has an unconfirmed number ranging from at least one to an unknown amount. While the Layer Necroma may seem like your greatest challenge, the Layer Delicious will be more than formidable. The one confirmed member of Royalty residing there is highly dangerous. I can offer you the most help here, as she has been present within this very meeting area once before for previous negotiations. She is called 'The Mistress Vix Delicious'. She never alters her original form when shifting Layers, and there is a reason for this. She may be the most powerful of all Royal members.

CHAPTER 8.217 THE NEWLY EXPLAINED VICIOUS DELICIOUS

"The Royal Mistress Vix Delicious is quite a sight to behold, and simply beholding her could destroy you outright. You see, she resembles a Sapien of average height. She dresses quite elegantly and has outstanding manners. She would be a vast pleasure to have around, if it weren't for one simple fact. Any being, whether it be Sapien, Tronic, or other, who witnesses her consuming any form of sustenance, just simply ceases to exist." The King stopped speaking for a brief moment to allow this to sink in and for response from us three. We looked at one another in a slight daze after hearing the Kings description. The Harbinger reacted first.

"What do you mean 'ceases to exist'? And what do you mean about 'consuming sustenance'?"

"Allow me to tell of a firsthand account of her incredible power. While she was in our company, a Waitertron served her a meal at her own request. She simply wished to try the taste of the local Cylife. I was not present for her dining experience. When I arrived to greet her, the Waitertron was gone. It had simply vanished into thin air, not simply into one of the walls. I could not detect its programming on the mainframe. I questioned Mistress Delicious about the Waitertron. When asked, she replied politely.

'Ah yes. I can't have any being watch me consume any meal or mere snack. Even while I drink water, for that matter. Any being that witnesses me eat ceases to exist. If they do so, well, POOF!'

She made a vanishing gesture with her hands.

'Gone. Your Waitertron waited around a little too long, and watched me as I started to dine. No doubt it was written in his simple programming to do so. Silly me, I should have waved him off. Servants in the Layer Delicious already know not to be present for my meals, I had simply forgotten. It WAS an exquisite meal, I might add. You sure know how to treat your guests, King!'

"This is why I warn you three. She seems a bit irresponsible with her power, so you should take great caution when in her presence. Now, it is simple to identify her.

The Mistress Vix Delicious is completely noticeable, so it should be a simple task to avoid mishap. I went over how she resembled a Sapien in appearance. She is quite slim, and has a pleasing figure. What I did not tell you was that where a typical Sapien's head should be, there is instead some sort of rapidly flowing purple and orange vortex with ethereal wispy black outlines. It resembles a blender full of fruit in slow motion, or a dark draining Sapien bathtub. The vortex funnels down to where the Sapien neck would normally be just between the shoulders."

What a remarkable creature.

"I warn you three now. The only way to tell if you have Mistress Vix's attention is if you see red just at the base of the vortex that is her head. There will be a yellow core with just the slightest speck of red inside. This is how she sees. There is a single long black eyebrow floating just above that. If she is looking at you, you then have her attention. Be warned, however. She does not show courtesy to others when she is about to eat. This being the case, you will have to constantly be aware of the situation. Do not attempt to address her during the times she is feeding. She eats frequently. You will cease to exist if you witness her feeding. That is what I can offer you for the Layer Delicious."

So this alone would be a dangerous task, and the King had yet to offer any advice regarding the other Layers. I began to formulate possible strategies for our meeting with Mistress Delicious, but the King wasn't finished. He had quite a bit to say during this meeting, but every bit was important.

"My advice is limited on these remaining two Layers. The Layer Façade will face you with some hard negotiations. As I mentioned, there will be at least five members of Royalty there. They will not be easy to negotiate with, but I trust your abilities. It is my understanding that it is populated with only Sapien residents aside from the five confirmed Royalty, but it is a densely populated Layer. Unless you are a great deal from their palace, it most likely that you will shift on top of a building or some crowded area. There is nothing to be done about this. I'm sure you do not wish any harm to come of the innocent residents, but we simply cannot predict where you will shift. As for the Layer Necroma, it is an ever-changing Layer. Every attempt at exploration has yielded vastly different results. Aside from all this advice, I can only offer you one last thing. It is a prophecy. It comes from a Tronic visiting from another Layer…the Layer Dryffe."

"The Layer Dryffe has no native Tronics other than you and what sounds like the Greeter and the Baron. Have you been visited by one of them?" said CEO.

"Well…I had hoped that you wouldn't ask. It involves you specifically, CEO. Here, I'll show you. This will be appropriate anyways. Anything I can do to help, I suppose."

"What do you mean it involves me?!"

The King ignored CEO's question and jumped back into the massive Tronic construct hanging from the ceiling. It closed and sealed. He booted up and began speaking once more.

"I CALL YOUR ATTENTION TO MY EXTERNAL MONITORS. PLEASE LISTEN CAREFULLY." We didn't have to listen carefully. Massive speakers protruded from either side of the construct and echoed throughout the meeting area.

We *had* to listen.

CHAPTER 8.259 THE INFINITE BAFFLING PROPHECY

Static played on each screen...

They all flashed on and off...

Eventually, they came into focus...

Some were in color, while others were in black and white.

The video was shot from the perspective of the King inside the construct. We witnessed the meeting area while it was completely empty, except for a single other Tronic who was standing on the table speaking with the King.

"We've just finished construction on the outer wall, my King. At this time, I am proud to say that your palace is complete!" The King's booming voice burst forth from the stereo. It may have been audio playback, but it sounded like he was actively talking to us.

"THANK YOU FOR YOUR IMPECCABLE SERVICE, ARCHITECT. I HAVE ALREADY RUN MY INITIAL DIAGNOSTIC, AND YOUR WORDS ARE TRUE. EVERYTHING IS AS IT SHOULD BE. YOU MAY RETIRE TO YOUR QUARTERS UNTIL I NEED YOU IN THE FUTURE."

Just as the King finished speaking to the Architect, the monitors went a little fuzzy. There was a flash of white light that overloaded the video feed. Once it settled, the monitors displayed a swirling vortex that closed almost immediately. Just outside of the opening kneeled CEO. He appeared beaten and nearly non-functional. This was a startling sight considering CEO is the second largest Tronic on the Layer Automina.

"WHAT TRICKERY IS THIS!?!?!?!" exclaimed our CEO.

"CEO, PLEASE CONTINUE WATCHING WITHOUT INTERRUPTION." Said the King.

CEO was in a state of malfunction that appeared to be terminal on the monitor feed. Just before he collapsed, CEO looked up at the King and spoke.

"My King, please remember this message: CEO will hold the door! CEO will hold the door! I have not failed you! I am...complete." With this last message, CEO's programming ceased to function, and he collapsed in a heap of parts on the floor of the meeting area. The monitors went back to static, and then went to black. CEO rose in anger.

"THIS IS AN OUTRAGE, KING!!! THERE WAS ANOTHER MADE LIKE ME?! A MARK ONE?! I WAS PROGRAMMED TO BE THE ORIGINAL!!"

"CEO, PLEASE CALM YOURSELF! I OBVIOUSLY HAVE SOME MORE EXPLAINING TO DO HERE." CEO heaved for a moment and eventually backed off. The King powered down the construct and stood on the table once again to address us.

"CEO, you are Mark One. That was you. If you will just play the video back in your files, you will see the same color scheme present on your exterior. Your future actions will eventually lead you back here to this very meeting area to give the very same prophecy. Now you understand your purpose." Each of us was astonished at the news. CEO was to eventually sacrifice himself for the cause of helping us bring peace to the Cake. Not only that, but he'd have to travel through time itself to do so. A seemingly impossible task, at least with our current technology. As soon as this realization hit everyone in the room, a strange thing happened. It was something that I predicted would happen from the beginning.

CHAPTER 8.323 THE NEWLY REDISTRIBUTED KING OF THE CUBICLE

The King took over CEO's programming entirely. Had he done this a moment earlier, I would not have noticed. However, there was a split-second where CEO had rapidly lifted one of his arms with intent to bring it crashing down on the table, only it froze at the apex. CEO should have followed through with his programmed action. There is no other explanation for his sudden halt. He spoke immediately after freezing, yet another signifier that his programming was being overridden.

"If this is my destiny, then so be it, King." The Harbinger most likely did not pick up on this, but my programming was much sharper than the King gave me credit for. I was already aware of his manipulative nature. So just as the Greeter had chosen a proxy, the King did the same. Although in this circumstance, CEO was more puppet than proxy. CEO would now be under the King's total control. Earlier, the King spoke as if he himself would be present at the meeting in the Great Conference Room, but now I felt he would not be making a direct appearance and would instead speak through CEO. Or perhaps he would make a direct appearance...I would allow this to play out without interfering.

My programming continued to run calculations on our future missions, as we needed as much data as possible. I based everything off of the King's advice. It was difficult to trust him now. Should I actually be on the side of the Emperor? My previous allegiance screamed out to me.

No. Perhaps the King is the superior choice.

He has done no direct harm to anyone other than arresting CEO's freedom. Aside from that, the King created CEO. Well, from what I've now heard, the King created us ALL when he wrote the Great Business Deal. It could just be more of the King's manipulation, sure. My processes were slowing down from recalling of all the talk. I was ready for the adventure to commence. I wanted to get this finished. I wanted to be at the Great Conference Room with all of the Royal members in tow, so I addressed the King during the long silence left hanging in the air after CEO's unwitting submission to the King.

"Very well then, CEO. Now, King. We've been exceptionally prepared for our mission. When do we leave, then?"

"Oh, my dear ROM, such initiative! I like that! You may leave whenever you like! Although, I'm sure you'll want some support. Harbinger, your men?"

"Yes, King?" said the Harbinger.

"Well, they are yours to command now. They are no longer under my authority. Ah, well. I suppose I'm getting ahead of myself. We will now take our last vote. You've all been told of what lies ahead. Since you are all now Royalty, you are free to do as you please, including abstaining from the vote and mission. All in favor of undertaking this quest to seek alliances with the other members of Royalty please cast your vote of 'yes'. All opposed will vote 'no'. Please cast your vote."

There was only a split second of silence before CEO voted 'yes'. Further proof that the King was in complete control of him. It's like he wasn't even trying to conceal his deception. I looked at the Harbinger and he looked at me before casting our votes. Without looking up, the Harbinger voted 'yes'. I turned to look at the King.

"My vote is yes, King. Now let's go ahead and get this finished."

CHAPTER 8.545 THE NEWLY REDISTRIBUTED EMPEROR'S ATTENTION

"My vote is yes, King. Now let's go ahead and get this finished." ROM was still outfitted with a monitor feed that led directly to the headquarters of the Emperor. It was a brand of rare Tronic technology that ROM had been outfitted with. The images captured by the camera could be broadcast trans-Layer.

"Emperor, the Servutron Prime, er heh heh, ROM has cast his vote."

"Well, well. So they're on their merry way to meet us at the Great Conference Room, huh? Too bad we're already aware of their little plan to seek the help of the other neutral members of Royalty for support."

"Emperor, heeeeee heeeee, it seems they will seek Mistress Vix Delicious out first. This is an early prediction, haaaaahahaha! They know the most about the Layer Delicious and will most likely attempt their first shift there to speak with Mistress Delicious! BWAHAHAHA!"

"I trust your observations, General Hysterics. I need you and Beedlebop to meet me in my chambers immediately."

"Hmmmm hmmm! Right away, my Emperor."

General Hysterics commanded the Emperor's vast forces on the Layer Dryffe. He was in charge of the Jiffling hoard as well as all Sapien and Tronic officers and soldiers. General Hysterics was a Cyborg, but of the more uncommon sort. He was once pure Tronic and underwent the transformation to become more Sapien after a fascination with the Sapien mouth, laughter, and humor struck him. His outward appearance resembled a male Sapien almost completely, except for one striking feature. He had a significantly oversized mouth with multiple rows of razor sharp teeth, which were filed down to a molecular level. As gruesome as it may sound, this was his weapon of choice while in combat. Simply balancing almost any material on one of these teeth would result in the object being sliced in half. He was constantly smiling wide; his lips were fashioned not to overlap the teeth, lest they be ripped to shreds by accident. Looking directly at his smile would also cause momentary blindness due to the highly reflective nature of his teeth. While he was intimidating to behold, he was constantly in good spirits, and often could not finish a sentence without laughing, snickering, chortling, chuckling, guffawing, or giggling, hence his name. He was not easily angered, and kept the men and women under his command in good spirits.

General Hysterics sought out Beedlebop in his chambers. Beedlebop was carrying a thoroughly involved conversation with a cactus that sat opposite from him at his kitchen table while repeatedly checking his wristwatch.

"—and so that's why you couldn't possibly have seen me with that particular woman. You see, it just doesn't matter how many chairs she may have in her foyer. The whole situation is simply…well you understand perfectly how I feel, Templeton."

Surprisingly, the cactus remained silent. General Hysterics cleared his throat at the Connoisseur of the Preposterous.

"Beedlebop, heh heh, the Emperor requests our presence in his chambers immediately! HAHAHAHA!"

"WOWHOHOHO!! GENERAL HYSTERICS! Did not expect you, sah! Please join us! We were just discussing the finer points of seating arrangements!"

"Unfortunately we don't have the time, good Beedlebop, the Emperor requests that we speak with him in a private conference within his chambers, HAHAHA!"

"GOOD MAN, THE EMPEROR CAN WAIT JUST A TICK HOHOHOHOHO! Please, I have an ottoman, a couch, a sofa, and a love seat with a spot next to me, hoho! I also have a bar stool, a recliner just there, a chez lounge, and a beanbag if you so please! Have a seat! Anywhere! Even the floor will do!

OHOHOHOHO! RIGHT TEMPLETON?" The cactus made no indication in the affirmative much to Beedlebop's dismay.

"Beedlebop, pfftchtch, I've been p-p...patient. This is my third request. Please follow me to the King's—"

"—King's chambers, eh? That gentleman has no idea how to seat his guests. Why, he even has a throne. A throne—MADE OUT OF MOONROCK! HAVE YOU SEEN IT?! SIMPLY PREPOSTEROUS! PREPOSTEROUS I TELL YOU!"

"BEEDLEBOP, YOU BLATHERING FOOL! THE EMPEROR REQUESTS YOUR PRESENCE NOW! BWAHAHAHA!"

"HOHOHOHO! Very well! Very well! No need to shout dear boy!" Beedlebop then addressed the cactus.

"Sorry Templeton, dear fellow. This gentleman is here to whisk me off to see the Emperor himself! We will continue our conversation upon my return!"

"Come on, you mad idiot. Haha! He is waiting."

"I'm just behind you, good fellow. You know, you could use a laugh once in a while."

"They don't call me General Hysterics for nothing, you crazy imbecile. PWAAHAA!"

"OHOHOHO! YOU GOT ME THERE, CHUM!"

"Hehehehe! Honestly, I don't see why he keeps you around. Although you are good for a laugh.

"Thank you, sah! I do what I can!"

They walked side-by-side cracking jokes and making puns until they reached the Emperor's chambers. The Layer Dryffe was largely unforgiving when it came to supporting civilized life, but the Emperor's stronghold was certainly nothing to sneeze at. While plotting to gain control over the Layer Dryffe Company, the Emperor had made a palace of remarkable size for himself, largely from the help of the Jifflings. While it paled in comparison to the King's stronghold, it was still outfitted with highly advanced technology. The Emperor had spies everywhere, and had stolen knowledge from the Layer Dryffe Company to fashion himself a fantastic palace.

The laughing duo entered the Emperor's extravagant chamber. The Emperor was waiting patiently while seated in his moon rock throne at the end of the long room. There were blue and gold banners lining this massive hall. The Connoisseur spoke in a semi-hushed tone to General Hysterics.

"You have to see what I mean, General. The only chair in the whole place is his! Why not fashion a few hammocks or a sofa just—"

"—BEEDLEBOP CEASE YOUR SENSELESS PRATTLE AND APPROACH ME!" the Emperor called from the end of the throne room.

"Right away my Emperor!" General Hysterics was attempting to stifle intense laughter upon hearing these comments from Beedlebop and the Emperor.

"Well well, my two right hand men come to an vastly important conference and neither one can keep a straight face. Do you two forget your place?" General Hysterics snorted loudly.

"SSSSSSN-n-n-no my Emperor. Pff-my…apologies! BAHAHAHA!"

"Well Emperor, at least he's in good spirits! OHOHOHOHO!"

"I can't say I'd rather see you two down in the dumps, but we have business to take care of. So you two, or at least Beedlebop, put on a straight face and listen up."

"Yes Emperor!" both said in unison.

"…and don't look at me directly, General. You know how I hate being blinded by that grin of yours. Turn and face the wall please." General Hysterics did so while giggling to himself.

"Now. We have to assume that ROM, CEO, and the Harbinger are going to make their first attempt at convincing the neutral Royalty by visiting Mistress Vix Delicious. I've got plans I would like to discuss with you both, and guess what? It involves a promotion for both of you."

"AAAAAAHAAAAAAHAAAAAAAAAAAAAAAAAA!!!!!!!! A PROMOTION HE SAYS!!!!!!" General Hysterics began laughing uncontrollably.

"I ALREADY HAVE THE HIGHEST POSITION I COULD POSSIBLY HAVE! YOU ALMOST FOOLED ME EMPEROR! GOOD ONE! AAAAAAAAAHAAAAAAAA!"

"Calm down for just a few moments, please. You're lucky that I have an outstanding amount of patience for your mannerisms. Now, back to business. You're both invaluable to me. For this reason, and for others I will shortly explain, you are both being granted Royalty status. This means we will be equals. There are no strings attached with this, I won't be revoking this later or anything of the sort. I feel that we share common interests and I'll need your talents to assist with the cause of stopping the King of the Cubicle's efforts." Beedlebop spoke first, as General Hysterics was oddly silent.

"My Emperor, I am vastly honored to accept. You, General?"

"…I'm…hoo…I'm…heh heh…speechless with joy! HAHAHAHA!"

"I see you two accept. Very well. We will now appoint you both new titles and welcome you into Royal status. General, you're up first. Please approach the throne and kneel."

"Heehee…yes my Emperor!" General Hysterics knelt before the Emperor. The Emperor rose from his throne and laid his scepter on either shoulder of the General. Before lifting the scepter, a small cloud of Jifflings emerged from it and entered the General's body at the base of his neck.

"You were called General Hysterics, you will rise and henceforth be addressed as The Laugh Riot." Jifflings went to work assembling new armor for his body seemingly out of thin air. They fashioned new components and altered his outward appearance drastically. His eyes were now covered in a visor built into a tall crown that peaked in a spike resembling one of his unbelievably sharp teeth. Two similar spikes adorned either shoulder. The Jifflings retreated within the scepter.

"Oh wowowowowowowow! Thank you my, er, thank you Emperor! Yes! HAHAHAHA! YES!" The Laugh Riot made several rapid punches at thin air in celebration.

"YEAH! Just call me Riot, folks. I find it satisfying anyways, hahahahaha!"

"Very well, Riot. Next is you, faithful Connoisseur. Please approach the throne." Beedlebop walked toward the throne but did not kneel.

"My Emperor, I am honored to accept your gift. However I do not wish to change titles. Furthermore, I do not wish to accept to alter my current form."

"Well Beedlebop, I was not intending either of those for you. Your current title is suiting for a good reason. Do you remember when we met with the child in the Layer Dryffe just after we were prohibited from entering the Layer Dryffe Company?"

"Of course, Emperor. I thought it a highly preposterous encounter indeed. One of my fondest memories."

"Your wristwatch, you still have it, yes?"

"OHOHOHOHO! Yes of course, Emperor! It never leaves my sight! I have not removed it since!" Riot was chortling in the background. The Emperor continued speaking.

"Beedlebop, what were you doing prior to that meeting with the child?"

"Well, you know, I was…erm. Well you see, I was…uh. Um. I…well it seems I don't remember."

"Of course you don't. Your wristwatch. Look at it for me."

"Well, alright. What about it?"

"It shows pictures of major events that have taken place. Remind me, what is the first picture the hands pointed to?"

"Well of course, it is a picture of the man. The man who created us. So what exactly does this have to do with the King of the Cubicle?"

"My dear Connoisseur, it has EVERYTHING to do with our current situation! You say you don't remember a thing before your wristwatch pointed to that picture?"

"…no I do not."

"Exactly! He created you and I at the same time!" The Emperor stood to continue his speech and walked slowly towards Beedlebop.

"You and I have been equals from the start. You are Royalty. I have no other memories prior to this either, only the knowledge that this man was our Creator, and we have to protect him. This is why your title will not change, your appearance will not change either. You're—"

CHAPTER 8.665 THE INFINITE BAFFLING WRISTWATCH REALIZATION

"—already Royalty," whispered Beedlebop to himself while staring at his wristwatch in disbelief.

CHAPTER 8.666 ROM, CEO, AND THE HARBINGER WENT DOWN TO THE LAYER DELICIOUS

"Very well, ROM. You three will now leave this place and shift to the Layer Delicious to seek out Mistress Vix Delicious."

CHAPTER 8.674 THE ROYAL MASTERS OF DECEPTION

Beedlebop huffed and puffed to himself for a few moments, but eventually settled down.

"Emperor, regardless of your vast deception, I am still willing to listen to you about any mission we may have to undertake. You may have deceived me, but aside from that, you don't even have a decent seating arrangement in your chambers! Why, you're the only one with a chair! How can I trust someone who doesn't even extend such a simple hospitality to his equal?"

"Well Beedlebop, I'm willing to fashion you a throne if you're so hung up on this trifling detail." The Emperor pointed his wand at the Connoisseur's feet. A cloud of Jifflings emerged from inside and began swift work on a throne. As it came into shape, it was pitch black, tall, and misshapen. It looked to be carved from the void of space. Regardless, it was balanced for the person sitting on it.

"How do you feel about that, Beedlebop? Can we move past this now that you have your throne?"

"OHOHOHOHO! WHAT A FINE THRONE INDEED! Yes, Emperor, let us proceed with the meeting," said Beedlebop. Riot laughed in agreement, casually.

"Very well. Our first order of business is to discuss—" the Emperor was interrupted by a Sapien guard entering the chamber.

"Guard, what do you need?!" shouted the Emperor.

"My Emperor! Our live feed from ROM tells us that our initial predictions are correct. They are bound for the Layer Delicious to seek the aid of Mistress Vix Delicious."

"Very good, soldier. You are now dismissed. Return to your post."

"Yes, my Emperor." The soldier bowed deeply and left the hall. The Laugh Riot began cackling loudly.

"HAHAHAHAHAHAHAHAHAHAHAHA! SO MY INITIAL PREDICTIONS WERE CORRECT!"

"Yes Riot, it would seem that they are headed for the Layer Delicious. Time is short. I will explain soon, please allow me just a moment." The Emperor whispered to his scepter. Shortly after, a cloud of Jifflings left the scepter and flew out of the hall. "I have sent the Jifflings to alert the Infinite Baffler. The Infinite Baffler will relocate from the Layer Dryffe to the Layer Delicious. With any luck it will prevent ROM, CEO, and the Harbinger from reaching Mistress Vix Delicious. The Infinite Baffler will most likely reach the Layer Delicious within a few minutes. The Jifflings are swift. Now comes time for the mission I am to give you two. Since you are both Royalty, you may choose to ignore this entirely. Although, since we have similar interests, I trust you will see this through. You both are to shift to the Layer Façade first. There you will meet with the Faas family. There are five members. Each is Royalty. I have met with them before briefly. They all operate as an Oligarchy within the Layer Façade, but there is something you should know before speaking with them. Each member is limited to a single sense as we perceive all five simultaneously. This is to say that while we enjoy five senses, each member can only interpret one sense, but each individual is gifted with the most powerful detection of their individual sense. They can communicate amongst themselves telepathically, and each member brings a different interpretation of external stimulus to the table. One can see, one can hear, one can taste, one can feel, and one can smell. Their individual senses are so highly sharpened that, say for instance, two of the members can taste or smell fear in the air. Your challenge will lie with Royal member Gustav Faas. This member has the sense of taste. Additionally, he is the only member of the Oligarchy who can communicate verbally. Do not view Gustav Faas as the leader. He is every bit as relevant as the other four members of the Oligarchy. Before I continue, do you two understand what I'm telling you?" The Emperor returned to his moon rock throne and awaited response from Riot and Beedlebop.

"So we're, buh huh huh, we're supposed to go and talk these 'Faas' Royalty to our side, is that correct?" said Riot.

"That is your primary task, yes."

"Well that sounds easy enough, Emperor. I hope these fellows have ample seating within their chambers. Otherwise, I will not be able to take them seriously," said Beedlebop.

"My dear Connoisseur. Your vast interest in seating arrangements will be put on the back burner out of interest of the mission ahead. You do wish to stop the King of the Cubicle from reaching the Great Conference Room, do you not?" Asked the King.

"Well, my dear Emperor. You have not fully explained what this has to do with the man who created us. He is currently absent, is he not? The last I saw of him was in that dreadful elevator he fashioned. So many floors to choose from…it was fascinating, deteriorating, and absurd. I wanted to see each floor! Shame I was UNDER THE WEATHER! OHOHOHOHO!" The Connoisseur chortled loudly and The Laugh Riot joined him in the background.

"Beedlebop, listen up! We don't have much time, so I'll attempt to keep this explanation brief for all of our sakes. I have reason to believe that ROM, previously known as Servutron Prime, is the Creator. Since the man was not Royalty when he shifted from the Layer Dryffe to the Layer Automina, he lost all of his memories. His consciousness was placed into a Servutron I had previous control over. This is why we are still able to use his visual feed as a tool to aid us. He is an unwitting spy for our cause. Our goal is to stop the King and to rescue ROM from the King's lies. Now, you have your explanation. You and the Laugh Riot are to leave this fortress and shift Layers into the Layer Façade. You will approach the Oligarchy present within and convince them to our side while ROM, CEO, and the Harbinger attempt to convince the Mistress Delicious. Is there any part of your mission that is unclear, you two?" The Emperor paused for response.

"Not at all, Emperor. We will take our leave." Said Beedlebop.

"HAAAAAHAAAAA! We will have their full support, Emperor!" said Riot.

"Excellent. You are both to report here once negotiations are complete. I will brief you both on the Layer Necroma upon your return. This will be your next destination." The Emperor paused for a moment, but a thought occurred to him and he began speaking once more.

"Before I forget, you two will be making a little pit stop for me in the Layer Automina with your troops. You will capture and execute the members of the squad waiting for Vega and the Servutron Prime at their camp. From there, you will make your shift into the Layer Façade. Do I make myself clear?"

"Crystal. Farewell, Emperor. I hope the Layer Façade has better seating arrangements than the Layer Dryffe! In all seriousness dear boy, get the Jifflings on this. It will only take them a few generations. You will need better hospitality for future guests," said Beedlebop as he turned to leave the hall.

"In all seriousness, Beedlebop. It won't matter a damn unless you get the support of the Oligarchy on the Layer Façade. Make haste."

"OHOHOHOHOHOHO!" Both Beedlebop and Laugh Riot chortled in unison as they left the hall. Just before they opened the door to leave, the Emperor whispered to his scepter and an undetectable amount of Jifflings left. They flew over to Beedlebop and hid just under his tailcoat as the door to the hall slid shut.

CHAPTER 8.888 I CAN'T BELIVE IT ISN'T CHAPTER 8.666

CEO, the Harbinger, and myself all left the meeting area. I was calculating reluctance to leave it behind. I've never witnessed a room with such aesthetical concern as that before. The King had to lead us out. We found ourselves in the same stairwell we came in, save for CEO who had reached the meeting area by other means. CEO had to alter his shape in order to follow us out of the meeting area. He folded in two of his arms and legs until he could fit through the opening. "This will be a tight squeeze for me, gentlemen. I hope I don't inconvenience you," said CEO. The King put up a tight façade. If I didn't already suspect him of taking over CEO, I wouldn't have picked up on the deception at all. He made it through the wall and into the stairwell with the rest of us. The King turned and spoke to us three, well, at least the Harbinger and I.

"Lucky for you three, this door just to my right takes us right back to the hallway which leads to the courtyard. Be warned, though. After you pass through the door you will not be permitted re-entry. This is a safeguard for security purposes. As I mentioned previously, only a very specific route will lead you back to the meeting area. You three can remain in the courtyard until dinner is served or you may join the men and officers in their recreation area. CEO, I'm sure you will be able to wait until ROM and the Harbinger once again address their men. As for now, I will take my leave. It was a vast pleasure meeting with you gentlemen. I bid you all farewell and great success in your mission. Thank you for your patience and vigilance." With that, the King of the Cubicle disappeared back into the meeting area. We would not see him again until the courtyard and after that, I knew he would be with us every step of the way in the form of CEO.

We elected to just bide our time in the courtyard with the knowledge that we were now Royalty. I found myself calculating a very Sapien line of logic. This was the beginning of the most exciting chapter in our existence, and most beings could not claim the same. I looked repeatedly at the Harbinger and the remotely controlled CEO. Both of these beings and myself would one day no longer exist in our current forms. We already knew that CEO would be sacrificing his existence simply to send a message to the past. Whether we all three cease to exist in the near future due to the oblivious gluttony of the Mistress Delicious, or we all succeed to see our fate played out at the mercy of the Greeter's proxy. Either way, there would be multiple actions in the near future that would determine our fate at the drop of a hat. It was a dangerous path, but my programming was ready for the resolution. My calculations were eager to conclude themselves. I enjoyed the brief few hours of peace until dinner started and the men filed in.

I didn't bother with the menu. I was highly uninterested with anyone else. I was Royalty now. I was eager to find and influence the Mistress Delicious. This would be a tough task, and we didn't have much direction to go on. I concluded that we would be able to form a plan after the shift to the Layer Delicious was concluded. The men all enjoyed their meals thoroughly. At the end, the King emerged from the wall under the guise of the Head Servutron. He addressed the entire courtyard in his previous fashion.

"Men, Commander Vega, and Servutron Prime. I thank you all for joining us at the King's palace. The conferences have concluded, and you are now being returned to your previous posts. I hope you have enjoyed your stay here. After you collect your things from your rooms, you will be ushered out of the courtyard and you will report to Commander Vega for further instructions. Thank you all for your time spent here, I hope it was enjoyable for each of you." The King turned and left the courtyard. This would be the last time we saw him until we made it to the Layer Dryffe. The men all filed out of the courtyard to gather their equipment and eventually make their way back.

"I'm going to command the troops. I hope you don't mind. I have the experience necessary to lead. You are more than welcome to your input on any matter. I will consult with you and CEO before making any major decision," said Hotz.

"I do not oppose, Hotz. Lead as you will."

"Thank you for your support, ROM."

The Harbinger stepped onto the same stage that the King took previously to address those who were waiting.

"Soldiers. I do appreciate your patience. You have all enjoyed an unexpected vacation. I regret to inform you that it ends here. You are all still on active duty, officers included. I hope you are all ready to move out and rejoin our brothers and sisters waiting with Officer Tran at our site. We will be leaving in the next five minutes. You all know my rule. Gather your things and be ready to move out. If you are not ready when we leave, then be sure to catch up. I will bark at you all again in five minutes. As you were!" The Harbinger left the stage and returned to my side.

"ROM, I'm going to discuss our plan of attack with CEO."

"Go ahead then. Feel no need to speak to me about this."

"Very good. You'll know when we move out. It will be obvious."

"Alright, Hotz."

The Harbinger went off to speak with CEO. I was not concerned with the details of their conversation. CEO would be told the same information that I was. Perhaps CEO had some Tronics he could add to this Sapien squad, but this was doubtful. I stood in wait for the five-minute grace period. The men seemed ready to go. After this time expired, the Harbinger barked at the soldiers once again.

"Ladies and men, we are moving out! Please follow the nearest Servutron to the exit. If you aren't ready, then catch up. Move out!" Three Servutrons emerged from the walls to usher the men out of the courtyard. We all followed them to the exterior gate of the palace. There were two Royal Guardutrons on either side. They opened the gate, and we left as swiftly as we came, only this time there was no blinding white light, and no vision of a Sapien infirmary for me, courtesy of our beloved King.

After the men and ladies had all left the palace, the massive doors closed behind us with a loud thud. Just afterwards, the Harbinger stopped all of us and began shouting information at the present company.

"Alright soldiers listen up and listen well! I've got some big news for you all. This particular Tronic, General Management," he motioned to CEO, "will be joining us on our next mission. You will all be briefed upon reuniting with our camp. Additionally, some of his Guardutrons will be joining us for extra firepower. They are to be considered equal ranking with you all, save for officers."

As soon as our newcomers were mentioned, they arrived with the group. There were ten of them! This would be more than enough extra help, I felt. Ten Royal Guardutrons could effectively level half of the Central Hub. The same Tronics our squad marveled at previously would now be fighting with us side by side, if the need to fight arose. The Sapien soldiers cheered loudly and applauded.

"Now that we're all here, let's move out soldiers! We're bound for camp!" Everyone moved in the direction the Harbinger motioned with his arm. Just as everyone started walking in that direction, the Harbinger produced his communication device and hailed officer Tran.

"Officer Tran, come in. I repeat, officer Tran, do you copy? Over." There was a very long silence on our end. The Harbinger spoke again.

"Officer Tran, come in. Do you copy? Come in. I—"

"—Commander Vega! Good to hear from you, how are the meetings going? Over."

"Tran, the meetings are concluded. We are making our way back to you. What is your status? Over."

"All is quiet here. We eagerly await your arrival. Over."

"Well…excellent. I project we will be arriving after sundown. We have Tronic soldiers with us. Do not be alarmed upon arrival. Any other news? Over."

"Nothing, Commander. Uh…come back safely. Over."

"Great…well thanks for your work, Tran. I'll see to it you get a promotion. Over."

"…uh, thanks Commander. Yeah…over."

"…erm, well okay then. See you all soon. Over and out."

The Harbinger stashed his communication device swiftly and shouted at the top of his lungs.

"EVERYONE HALT!" The soldiers all stopped immediately.

"WE'VE GOT A CRISIS ON OUR HANDS! I HAVE REASON TO BELIEVE THAT OUR CAMP IS IN DANGER! FROM HERE ON WE MAKE TRIPLE TIME TO CAMP! DO YOU ALL GET ME?"

"YES SIR!" the soldiers called back.

"GOOD, NOW GET MOVING NOW!!!" The Harbinger started sprinting immediately. He turned his head over his left shoulder to shout at me.

"ROM GET UP HERE! I HAVE TO TALK TO YOU!"

"I cannot move as quickly as you can, Harbinger. I require assistance."

"I've got you, ROM." CEO scooped me up with one of his arms and placed me on top of him. He could easily make great strides with his four massive legs. The rest of the Guardutrons shared the same ability. Since the soldiers were well rested, they were able to move very quickly. As a group, we would have no trouble making it back to camp on time. CEO began his stride alongside the Harbinger and addressed him.

"Harbinger! I have ROM! What is this sudden emergency we have to attend to?"

The Harbinger was sprinting while speaking to CEO. He was almost out of breath while running.

"…I have…reason to believe that…our camp is in trouble. I spoke with…the commanding officer…at the camp…his replies were hurried…they were short. I offered him…a promotion. He was not at all excited…so I'm worried. We've got to get there, so move!"

"We'll make it, Harbinger. Just keep going," said CEO.

CHAPTER 8.987 THE ROYAL MASTERS OF HOSTAGE MANIPULATION

"BWAHAHAHAHA! You've done well, Tran. Enjoy your final moments. I know I will! Don't worry. We've left one of your squad alive to tell the tale."

"Please, I don't know what you want, but I'm sure we can work something out! T-t-t-take one of our ships! It's all yours!"

"Regrettably, my dear Tran, we don't give a damn about your ships. Well, we don't give a damn about your life for that matter! OHOHOHOHO!" Beedlebop laughed at Tran as The Laugh Riot approached Tran from behind and whispered in his ear.

"Don't worry, Tran. This won't hurt a bit. I'll be sure of that. We may be taking your life from you, but you had to lose it one of these days. It will be swift, huhuhuhuhu…" Riot opened his large jaw wide and positioned it over Tran's skull as he shook in fright.

"Rest now, dear boy. Take solace in your swift death. This had to happen some time," said Beedlebop. Riot's jaws shut swiftly on Tran's head, cutting the top half off into his mouth. Riot spit it out onto the ground swiftly and turned to Beedlebop. Blood and grey matter ran off of his razor teeth.

"Heh. Well, We've destroyed the camp as we were told. Shall we?"

"Oh we shall, my dear Riot. Let us perform the shift."

CHAPTER 9.024 THE ROYAL MASTERS OF ZERO TOLERANCE

"THE CAMP IS JUST AHEAD EVERYONE! I CAN SEE THE SHIPS!" screamed the Harbinger. The entire company continued their dire sprint for the campsite. While all eyes were concentrated on the camp, we saw two figures standing there. They vanished into thin air while warping space around them. The Harbinger was correct. Another trap had triggered. He saw the two figures shift Layers and immediately barked orders to the rest of the squad.

"EVERYONE STOP WHERE YOU ARE NOOOOOOW! HALT!"

"ALL TRONICS: CEASE FORWARD MOVEMENT!" CEO joined in the order giving. Everyone stopped on a dime. There was silence amongst the ranks while the Harbinger continued to sprint forward towards the campsite. He stopped and collapsed to the ground about fifty paces from camp and began to scream at the top of his lungs.

"ERRRRRRRAAAAAAAAAAAGH! ARRRRRRRRRRRRRRAAAAAAAAAAAAAAGH! DAMMIT! WHY?! WHYYYYYYYYYYYYY?!" The squad did not make a move. We allowed the Harbinger his moments of grief and took our own time to do the same. He eventually stood and returned slowly to the squad. He was sobbing openly. The squad slowly started to realize what had taken place. Yet another massacre had befallen the Harbinger's men. He stood there staring at the ground for a few minutes in silence while attempting to control his sadness. Eventually he spoke with hatred making his voice tremble. I could sense his body temperature had risen. He was frightening.

"All members of my squad, listen up and listen well! I wanted to wait until we reached camp to brief everyone about our upcoming changes, but guess what? THERE'S NO FUCKING CAMP TO GO BACK TO!" He staggered a bit under the gravity of his own words and took a moment to regain composure.

"Yet another massacre has befallen us at the vile hands of the Emperor! Yes! This sinister bastard will stop at nothing to prevent us from reaching our goals! He will kill us without warning as we've now seen firsthand! All of the members at the camp are dead! THEY'RE ALL FUCKING DEAD!" Some of the soldiers took this news very hard. A few fell to the ground. Some of them wept openly upon hearing this. The Harbinger began to cry again. His compassion for his men and women was unyielding. No one spoke for what seemed like an eternity. A dark cloud of sadness had descended upon the squad. After some time, the Harbinger regained composure and began to speak again with the same intense timbre.

"Now is the time to tell you all of our future mission, and it starts at the end of my speech. We will—"

"—Vega! Commander Vega!" Someone dared to interrupt Hotz. We all turned to the source of the voice. It was coming from the direction of the camp. We saw a single soldier making his way towards us from the camp. The Harbingers eyes widened. He shouted to the lone soldier.

"That's far enough, soldier! Stop where you are! What is your name?"

CHAPTER 9.053 THE ROYAL MASTER OF DECEPTION DETECTION

"My name is Nathan Hodell, sir. I'm the only survivor of the massacre. They kept me alive to—"

"—WHO kept you alive, soldier? Speak swiftly."

"They were called the Connoisseur and the Laugh Riot. The attack was gruesome. They chose me to remain alive to relay the message."

"Well, Hodell, you seem awfully calm for having just witnessed your entire squad being massacred. Tell me: when did you enlist and why have I never heard of you?"

"Well…I…uh, I was—

"EVERYONE READY YOUR WEAPONS NOW!"

No sooner had the Harbinger given his command did the lone soldier lose his Sapien shape entirely. He dissolved into a cloud of what appeared at a distance to be bugs.

"JIFFLINGS! FIRE AT WILL!" The soldiers had gotten off just a few rounds before I felt CEO lift off from the ground in an enormous leap. He brought a massive foot down upon the Jiffling swarm, instantly killing most of the cloud. Having lost such a large amount of members so swiftly, the Jiffling cloud dispersed, leaving behind the stolen clothing of a fallen soldier.

"ATTENTION SQUAD! Time is brief! The Jifflings have now infiltrated this, our Layer Automina! I must brief you all on our new mission now before we are all overrun, which will happen soon! Save all of your questions for an appropriate time! General Management, Servutron Prime, and myself have all been upgraded to Royal status by the King! As such, we are now renamed! I am now to be called the Harbinger of the Zax! General Management is now known as CEO! Servutron Prime is to be called ROM! Now that us three are Royalty, we are able to shift Layers at will! This entire squad will do so at the end of my speech! It is my understanding that since you will all be within a small radius surrounding us, you will not lose your memories and will retain your current form, so do not be alarmed! You will also retain all of your equipment! I will continue my briefing once we shift Layers! Do you all understand?!"

"YES SIR!" All of the soldiers shouted in unison.

"Excellent! I want you all to get as close to me as possible! NOW!" The soldiers all rushed forward and formed a tight cluster around the Harbinger, this included the Royal Guardutrons, CEO, and myself.

"ALRIGHT! WE ARE BOUND FOR THE LAYER DELICIOUS! HERE WE GO!" Just as we began our shift, an enormous cloud of Jifflings rose up from the ground and bolted towards us. I watched as they grew closer and closer and then there was a curious bend in my vision. My surroundings started to twist and warp into a spiral, which sucked me in along with all the other beings surrounding the Harbinger and then there was darkness for a few moments where I was certain of nothing. My surroundings were being torn apart and reordered in a rapid fashion. Shortly after, I found myself standing on a bed of what appeared to be soft sand in the very middle of a city shaded with purple and blue. In my immediate surroundings were the Harbinger, CEO, and the remainder of the Sapien and Tronic soldiers we had arrived at—

CHAPTER 9.108 THE VICIOUS LAYER DELICIOUS
—the Layer Delicious.
We had committed a horrible crime.
The shift was completed in the middle of a traffic intersection.
It appeared to be dusk. Upon first impressions, I was startled at the similarities between the Layer Delicious and the Central Hub of the Layer Automina. There were tall buildings and bustling life everywhere. Each building appeared at first glance to be sentient, however the residents had merely styled the aesthetic to resemble a living creature. Some were covered in feathers and some in scales. The doors had lips and teeth. I hesitated to call the residents within "Sapiens" at the present moment, although they resembled Sapiens. They were…how to put this delicately…huskier than typical Sapiens, and their skin was not of the typical colors the rest of the Sapien squad boasted. These characters were a pale blue in hue, and they were significantly larger than the rest of the squad. This was to say that not only were these citizens larger in width than us, they were also significantly taller than the Sapiens as well. By comparison, the average weight of a typical Sapien soldier was easily tripled by these beings.

Before initial exploration could begin, we heard a large bellow from one of the beings to the left of us. It was incredibly loud and many of the soldiers covered their ears at the utterance. I was unscathed and approached the being. It appeared to be female, at least by Sapien standards. My observations of the unique surroundings would be postponed.

"What is the matter, miss?"

"WWWWWHHHHAAAAAAAAAAAA!!!! YOU KILLED HIM!!!! YOU ALL KILLED HIM!!!!!!!!!!!!" She was staring in disbelief at two large handles she clutched that were attached to nothing.

"Who are you speaking of, miss? Please, I'm only here to help."

"MY HUSBAND, YOU BASTARD, HE WAS IN A WHEELCHAIR! ALL OF A SUDDEN YOUR GROUP APPEARED AND NOW HE'S GONE!!!!! HELP!!!! HELP!!! SOMEBODY!!!!"

"Please calm down miss! I am so sorry this has happened, we had not intended for this—" I was cut off by the arrival of what appeared to be several law enforcement officials who descended on the shift-site. They piloted strange flying creatures with large trunks and constantly agape mouths. Their teeth were an almost unbelievable pure white. Bright beams of light shone from their large eyes.

"ALL OF YOU STAY WHERE YOU ARE! REPEAT: STAY WHERE YOU ARE!" A large number of natives surrounded our position with weapons drawn. We had indeed shifted on top of a very busy intersection, just as we had feared during negotiations with the King. The Harbinger called out to everyone.

"STAND DOWN, MEN! STAND DOWN! WE HAVE COMPLETED THE SHIFT! STAND DOWN!" After barking his orders, the Harbinger looked around for the nearest official.

"You there! Sir!" the Harbinger barked.

"What purpose do you have here?!" said the Layer Delicious official.

"We have all come in peace from the Layer Automina to speak with the Mistress Vix Delicious! We mean no harm!"

"You mean no harm, eh?! How dare you!? Well you've destroyed an entire intersection and killed at least a dozen Tasties with your arrival! We cannot let this go unpunished! Take these beings into custody, officers!" The Layer Delicious officials surrounded us on their vehicles and subdued us one by one. We became immediate prisoners in a foreign land. The Harbinger began yelling at the officials.

"Where are you taking our men?! We didn't mean any harm for your citizens!" The same official answered back at Hotz.

"You'll all be brought before the Mistress Vix Delicious for swift sentencing. I hope your attack was worth your lives. She will show no remorse.

CHAPTER 9.189 THE LAYER DELICIOUS IS SUSPICIOUS

Gathering from the native official's words to other officers and Hotz, the beings of this Layer were called 'Tasties". While most of them appeared harmless in nature, they were all significantly larger than us. They all stared at us in disgust (or perhaps curiosity? These beings were not exactly pleasant to look at, so any expression they made could have been easily mistaken for disgust.) as we were led to their palace. We were led through the streets like cattle to slaughter, and on our way we passed numerous tall structures and other, less destroyed intersections. They had split us up and put us in several transports to expedite travel time. It would take the same amount of time on foot to reach the palace as it did from our camp to the King's palace on Automina. Traveling through the city revealed more of the same flavor atmosphere witnessed at the shift-site. It would seem this city was structured quite similarly to the Central Hub on Automina. Naturally there were plenty of social differences, the principal two amongst these was the absence of Tronics and the way in which food was obtained and eaten. It was not of any real fascination to me that there were no Tronics, Delicious just didn't have the technology. What was far more fascinating was that food was completely regulated and distributed by whatever form of government present in the city. There were places that appeared to be restaurants, but they were all government owned. Every bite of food was free for the citizen, and the Tasties had their choice of what they could eat. Each restaurant appeared to offer a different menu from the last, according to what I could detect. I calculated what exactly would lead to such a social construct. Food shortage possibly? That doesn't seem to be the case. The Tasties as a whole appear to be very well fed. Elimination of food-related package waste possibly? I ceased this line of calculations as we had finally arrived on what appeared to be the palace.

It was an impossibly tall structure with dark red and purple accents. A long carpet resembling a tongue extended from the large ornate front doors. The official leading us met briefly with the guards and they led us into the building. This was the Mistress Vix Delicious' palace. It was beyond extravagant. The front doors opened into a vast lobby. This I compare to the meeting area of the King had as the lobby had an incredibly tall ceiling much like it. Additionally it was quite long. My optical receptors fail to process much detail, but I could detect a massive staircase at the opposite end of the hall from where we entered, with stairs longer than the width of the road just outside.

We were being led towards the staircase in the back. The hall had remarkably adorned walls and stained glass windows of what appeared to be food. Everything in this hall appeared to be art of the most expensive sort, including the carpet, walls, and furniture. The walls were hand painted. The carpet bore no particular repeating pattern, but was beautiful to behold with shades of red, purple, and gold. The large stairway at the end of the hall split in two as it came down to the floor. The banister was made of some dark wood and was polished to a high shine with no smudges visible on it, from what I could now detect. There were Tasties all over this hall, walking from one door to the next and speaking with one another. They were all dressed well, compared to the average citizen I witnessed outside. The walls of the hall had many doors, each was different from the last and they were all polished to a high shine just like the banister of the staircase. It was beautiful. Potentially breathtaking, although I run off of mostly solar energy and thus have no need to breathe. Just after I had assessed my surroundings, the official that had us in custody spoke up.

"Alright. You lot are going to be following me to the Mistress Vix Delicious' chambers for sentencing. We will brief her on what occurred and you will have your say. Then she will issue punishment as she sees fit. Follow me now!" What choice did we have? Our arrest led us directly to an audience with the Mistress Vix Delicious. We didn't have to put in any work to ask to see her, we were being led directly to her. I was quite pleased about this. I found the Harbinger in the crowd and spoke to him, keeping my volume low.

"So this saves us an awful lot of trouble, doesn't it?"

"Well, sure, if you don't count the fact that we're seen as enemies. There's no telling what damage we've caused. It may be difficult to convince her not to kill us outright."

"While that's true, Harbinger, we're on the fast track to a meeting with the Mistress."

"Sure. I can only hope she'll listen to us. We are a foreign military presence in this Layer. No doubt we would have been arrested simply for looking different."

"I suppose you're correct then."

"Yeah, I've got this one figured out."

Our party climbed the massive staircase at the end of the hall and we took the left corridor. It was a short walk before we reached an enormous set of double doors, which appeared to be hand carved. When I say enormous, I'm not speaking by Sapien standards. These doors were large even by Tastie standards. They easily reached up further than three stories. The doors displayed what I could only assume was the likeness of the Mistress. They were reflections of each other, with the image of the Mistress carved into them. She had the slender body of a Sapien, not that of the Tasties. Then there was the matter of the swirling vortex where the head should be. It was an intricate carving resembling the utmost chaos and destruction. There was no doubt that we were about to enter the chamber of the Mistress Vix Delicious, but there was an issue. The doors were closed, no doubt for a reason. Perhaps the Mistress was feeding. This being the case, the official leading us spoke with the guards before we entered. He came back after his brief conversation and spoke to our group as a whole.

"We are about to enter the chambers of the Mistress. The doors are currently closed as you can see. So one of you are going to go in and see if she is feeding. Do you understand?" Hotz spoke up about this matter.

"So you feel like you can just use one of my soldiers as test subjects?" The official approached Hotz and pushed him with a large blue finger.

"Considering you quite possibly murdered around twelve innocent Tasties, yes I feel that one of your soldiers can go inside. Otherwise we'll just massacre you all where you stand. How does that sound? Fair?" The official finished his sentence with a sarcastic grin. Hotz paused at this and finally spoke to the official.

"Alright you bastard. Your choice."

The official began laughing hysterically.

"HAHAHAHA! You really think we'd just send one of you in there like that? You think we don't have procedures in place for meeting with the Mistress? Really? No other way of telling if it is safe to go in? You must be really thick! HAHAHAHAHA!"

"You sick bastard! Just see if she's ready so we can get this over with!" The official continued to laugh loudly over his little prank and simply opened the right door a crack and spoke.

"Oh Mistress Vix! Are you decent?"

"OF COURSE DEAR BOY! BRING THEM IN PLEASE!!" The Mistress called back. Her voice was incredibly loud, easily filling the room beyond the doors and the sound blasted into the corridor. It was not unwelcoming, however. The official pushed open the massive door a bit further and revealed a vast hall: the throne room of the Mistress Vix Delicious.

CHAPTER 9.199 THE NUTRITIOUS MISTRESS VIX DELICIOUS

It was clear they designed this room so that there would not be any accidental deaths by people who served the Mistress. It was completely empty; devoid of objects except for the Mistress and her throne. It resembled a gymnasium for Sapien recreation. Every sound echoed repeatedly within the room. It seemed more like a jail cell, only the size of an entire jail. The walls and floor were golden and painted with red and purple designs. There were also more ornate stained glass windows covering each wall, except the one with the massive wooden doors. Of particular note was the ceiling. It was completely flat and covered in the same designs as the walls and floor, only there was a large rectangular portion just above the Mistress that was cut and affixed to a pulley system so that it could move down to the floor. This, I gathered, was how she was fed. The method seemed awfully primitive and degrading, but no one would have to witness her feed by utilizing this apparatus.

"AH, THE DELICACIES HAVE ARRIVED! WHO HAVE YOU BROUGHT ME, OFFICER ZESTI?" Her voice was downright alluring. I could see the faces of the Sapien men turn to smiles after she finished her sentence. Perhaps this was another of her powers.

"As you may have been informed, my Mistress, these are the members of the group who shifted from another Layer right onto a busy downtown intersection not more than five blocks from here. May have killed twelve or more Tasties. This is obviously a sticky situation of a diplomatic nature."

"YES IT IS, OFFICER ZESTI. VERY TENDER, INDEED."

Then, she spoke to our group.

"THERE IS OBVIOUSLY AT LEAST ONE MEMBER OF ROYALTY AMONGST YOUR RANKS OR THE LAYER SHIFT WOULDN'T HAVE DESTROYED ANYTHING. WHICH ONE OF YOU IS ROYALTY, COME FORWARD PLEASE!"

Hotz, CEO, and I all worked our way through the crowd of soldiers to the throne of the Mistress. She looked almost exactly like the wood carving on the door. Her Sapien body was shapely and symmetrical. Then there was the matter of the swirling vortex where her head should be. Upon close inspection, it seemed to just be Sapien hair, but it defied gravity and rotated around her head in a never-ending, counter-clockwise fashion. Through small holes in the vortex, we could see a glow shine through. There was no way for my sensors to determine what was causing this, however.

As we three approached the throne she began to laugh softly to herself, which was still quite loud with every sound at the mercy of the gargantuan chamber. After we stopped, she stood from her throne and walked towards us. Had it not been for the vortex, the Mistress would have been shorter than Hotz. She spoke so that only the three of us could hear.

"I'm assuming you're here on some errand that the King has, is that correct?" She spoke only to Hotz, as far as I could tell.

"…to some extent, Mistress. Allow us introductions first, please."

"Very well."

"I am Harbinger of the Zax, to my left is CEO, and to my right is ROM. We all share your status of Royalty, and we come here to invite you to our side in a debate of great importance."

"Well, Harby—mind if I call you that? Anyways, you've made a great mess of things on my Layer, killing innocents and worse: arriving unannounced? Excellent job at getting my attention. Now all you need is the ability to convince me not to end your existence."

"Please Mistress, if you'll allow us a more, erm, formal meeting then all will be explained to you. What do you say?" Without acknowledging "Harby's" request, the Mistress called Officer Zesti over to her.

"Take the beings except for these three to holding. They aren't to be considered prisoners…" she looked at us three, "…yet."

"Yes, my Mistress!" He turned and addressed our squad and began barking orders at them.

"Listen up everyone! You're to follow me to—" Hotz cut him off.

"No, you listen up! They aren't prisoners and they aren't your stupid cronies either, so speak to them differently!" Officer Zesti looked dumbfounded.

"Do as he says, Zesti. You're not to mistreat them as I said, hm?"

"Oh, uh, m-my apologies, Mistress. This way please, everyone." He left the throne room and the large wooden doors were closed behind them.

"Feeling thawed out now, Harby? I know I am."

CHAPTER 9.289 THE PRETENTIOUS MISTRESS VIX DELICIOUS

"Mistress, do you have any other chambers, it hardly seems appropriate to meet with you here."

"Harby, have a seat on the floor, would you dear? You should be glad I didn't decide to execute all of you. You see I've been bored for a while now, and I wanted something to come along to add a little spice to the mix. So tell me: what do you need me for? Some little debate as you mentioned, hm?" She had no interest in either CEO or myself. I was not completely certain of the reasons behind this just yet, but I continued to remain silent.

"Mistress, we've been asked to come see you and tell you about a meeting to be held on the Layer Dryffe about—"

"—oh the Origin Layer?! My, how delectable! Sorry for interrupting, Harby. Please continue."

"...yeah as I was saying, there's a meeting that is going to be held on the Layer Dryffe in the Great Conference Room. Are you familiar with other members of Royalty other than the King?"

"Sadly...I am not! Well, other than you three now. We don't get any visitors from other Layers, you're the first, except for the King...and a few other Sapiens who disappeared without even introducing themselves. Anyways, seems the King may have had a little crush on me." CEO fidgeted.

"He invited me back to his palace, but he's a Tronic and I'm, well, you see...anyways. Why do you ask?"

"We require assistance during the meeting, and I wanted to see if you were aware of it. It is supposed to be a peace negotiation between the King of the Cubicle and the Emperor of the Moon with a neutral arbitrator deciding the outcome of the negotiation after hearing each side. The Emperor has employed almost every underhanded tactic in an attempt to prevent us from reaching the Great Conference Room on the Layer Dryffe including the murder of scores of my soldiers and attempts at my own life."

"So how am I to decide whether I should believe you or the Emperor without having a taste of both sides of the story for myself?" Just as these words left her mouth, a Tastie officer came running into the room.

"MY MISTRESS! MY MISTRESS! YOU NEED TO COME SEE THIS! IT DEFIES EXPLANATION, COME QUICK! OUR LAYER IS IN DANGER! COME QUICK!"

"Oh splendid! The cherry on top! Let us investigate, Harby. I'm sure you'll come in handy out there, hm?" She sprang gracefully from her throne and sprinted for the door just after the official with us three right behind her. Just as we exited the front palace entrance, we saw a horrible sight.

CHAPTER 9.389 THE INFINITE BAFFLING INFINITE BAFFLER

"Oh Harby, would you mind telling me what that massive pale yellow gelatinous wall of goo is doing in my Layer? It doesn't look Delish. I'm quite certain we didn't have one of those before. Well, at least not before you all showed up." The Harbinger stood gaping momentarily as he began to comprehend the situation. I had no idea what it was. Hotz, however, knew exactly what it was and how serious the situation was.

"Mistress, that's the Infinite Baffler. It is a despicable creature under the control of the Emperor. It is curious for several reasons, the first of which is that it is impassable. Nothing on this side of it can get out, and nothing on the other side can get in. It may look like one can go over the top, but look closely." An airborne creature of Delish origin that I was not familiar with attempted to fly over the Infinite Baffler. As soon as it was over the top, a large tendril shot out from the Infinite Baffler and swatted it with extreme force. The airborne creature perished in a burst of feathers and gore as the tendril retreated back into the gelatinous mass. The corpse was directed towards us like a small cannon ball, and it smashed through one of the stained glass windows adorning the outside of the palace at such a high speed that the hole it made glowed hot from friction.

"This *blob* is not fucking around. It was sent here by the Emperor in an attempt to prevent us from reaching you, no doubt. The second thing to note about this creature is that it has no beginning or end. What that implies is that it is circular in shape. Although we can only see a fraction of it at the moment, I assure you that it wraps completely around this city. So we're trapped."

"You're not making this sound too appetizing, Harby. Is there anything else I should know before we try to kill it?"

"Yes. The third, and most pressing issue is the fact that it is moving closer to us." A building fell under the weight of the Infinite Baffler squeezing it from the other side. "This means that it is moving into the center from all sides. Contracting, get it? It is leveling your city at an alarming rate."

"Well we'd better get rid of it then, shall we? I hope there aren't any other observations?"

"Fourth thing to note is that it absorbs any attempt to damage it by projectiles, explosive, or puncturing force. It may actually be indestructible. Fifth thing is—"

"—We'll just see about that, Harby. Stay here please, dearie!" The Mistress sprinted directly towards the Infinite Baffler. I detected her every move from next to the Harbinger. There were buildings coming down all around her due to the ground becoming unstable and the crushing weight of the Infinite Baffler pressing in on the city. Right when she was inches away from the Infinite Baffler, I heard her scream a war cry at the creature. It filled the air to such an extraordinary extent that I detected a slight pressure change.

"I HOPE YOU TASTE BETTER THAN YOU LOOK, UGLY!" I discontinued my ocular processes immediately upon hearing this statement. It was clear that her intention was to consume the Infinite Baffler, and any living being who bore witness to the act would cease to exist. I announced this to everyone in my close radius. "CLOSE YOUR EYES! SHE'S ATTEMPTING TO EAT THE INFINITE BAFFLER!!"

For the next few moments that occurred, I can only comment on the sounds that I heard.

CHAPTER 9.489 THE VICIOUS MISTRESS VIX DELICIOUS

The low rumble of foundations crumbling around us continued, but in addition, there was an incredibly loud sound coming from the direction of the Mistress. It resembled a massive amount of compressed air being forced through a small opening. This continued for quite some time, eventually the rumbling ceased and a louder noise began which sounded like an indestructible train running itself deeper and deeper into the ground on tracks that were already buried there. These sounds continued to get louder and louder until they both stopped at the same time. At this point there was almost complete silence except for loud sobs and cries of pain from various points in my hearing radius. I determined that it was over and reactivated my ocular processes.

The Infinite Baffler was gone, and the destruction it had left was immense. It had come to the Layer Delicious in the middle of the great city, just as our squad had. If one could look from above the city, I calculated there would be a large circular portion that was completely destroyed with a hole in the middle that was largely still intact, which was where we were. I could see the Mistress was already returning from the event. Her dress was ripped to shreds and she was cut in more than a few places, but other than that she seemed okay. Most of her body was now visible as most of her dress was destroyed during the ordeal with the Infinite Baffler. If there were any doubt before, we could now know for certain she was at least part Sapien. She made her way back to us, and this was making the Harbinger and the Sapien males a bit...shall we say...uncomfortable. Once she arrived, she looked at Hotz and spoke.

"Uh, so what was that fifth thing you wanted to tell me, Harby? Hm?" The Harbinger looked over the weary Mistress before speaking.

"It, uh, apparently, it can shift Layers at will, which means that it is also Royalty."

"I became aware of that pretty quickly, Harby. The thing shifted Layers on me before I was finished, but not before I took a big bite!" If the Mistress had a Sapien mouth, I calculated she would be smiling.

CHAPTER 9.501 THE JIFFLING THAT BROKE THE EMPEROR'S BACK

The Emperor sat in his moon rock throne waiting for some news to come back from the troops in his command. It was a boring time for him. After granting the Laugh Riot with Royalty status and sending Beedlebop with him, there was not much in the way of entertainment. Being at the top had its ups and its downs. It was during one of his darkest moments that a Jiffling cloud approached him and entered his scepter. He brought the scepter up to his ear and listened to what the Jifflings had to say.

"YOU CAN'T BE SERIOUS! THE INFINITE BAFFLER WAS SUPPOSED TO STOP THEM! IT WAS SUPPOSED TO CRUSH THEM ALL!" He leaned his ear back to the scepter and listened once again. He spoke aloud again, mostly to himself.

"Well this…this was a massive error on my part. We should have gone for the Mistress first. She is obviously far more powerful than anticipated to bring down another Royal member like the Infinite Baffler. I can only hope that Beedlebop and Riot can convince the Faas family into joining our cause. We cannot allow further disruption in our plan. Allowing ROM to remain on the side of the King will jeopardize our entire existence. We have to kill off the remaining members. Please await further orders while I consider our options."

The cloud buzzed impatiently. The Emperor put his scepter up to his ear once more. Without saying anything in response, he walked out of the throne room and into his bedroom. The curtains on the window were drawn tightly shut, but the Jiffling cloud drew them back as soon as the Emperor had crossed the threshold of the room. The sight far below was quite gruesome. What was left of the Infinite Baffler was writhing and pulsating in the many-colored grass of the Layer Dryffe. The Infinite Baffler was dying.

CHAPTER 9.589 THE WISHES OF THE MISTRESS VIX DELICIOUS

"Well that bastard can't shift Layers any longer now can he? He wasn't particularly tasty, could have used a little spice, but all in all I don't think I'll need another meal for another few days now, hm?" It was remarkable, the Mistress had not changed shape at all. Based on the damage done and the size of the Infinite Baffler, I judged that she should have easily died while attempting to consume it. To the contrary, she survived, and looked just the same as she did minus her few cuts from the intense ordeal. We all sat and looked at her in bewilderment.

"What, did you expect something less than me protecting my own Layer? Hm? Harby, close that gaping jaw, it makes you look unattractive, dear." The Harbinger quickly shut his jaw, not realizing it had been open in the first place.

"That's better, now for my verdict. You swear, butter side up, that the Infinite Baffler was not under your command?"

"No, Mistress, it was not. I swear, uh, butter side up," Said the Harbinger.

"You don't sound too sure, Harby. Are you sure?"

"Yes Mistress!"

"And it didn't just follow you through the shift to come destroy us?" The Mistress walked closer to the Harbinger while she spoke.

"N-no, it was all the Emperor's doing, Mistress!"

"Very well, my little Harby! I will join your squad and your cause for peace amongst the Layers." She looked around for a Tastie officer. When she found one, she called out to her.

"You there, officer Crumble!"

"Yes, Mistress!?"

"Go inside the palace, find officer Zesti and tell him to bring their squad to me right away please, dearie!" She motioned to Hotz, CEO, and myself.

"Right away, Mistress!" The officer then vanished inside the palace. The Mistress turned back to the Harbinger and began speaking once again.

"Harby, you weren't hurt during the incident were you?"

"No I was not, but Mistress? Perhaps you should start a rescue effort for your citizens. This attack is sure to have left many Tasties injured and dead.

"Ooo, yes, of course, I should order a rescue effort. We will wait until officer Zesti arrives with your men, then I will order him to begin the rescue effort. How does that sound, hm?"

"Well, Mistress, it isn't my Layer. Anything you want to do sounds—"

"—sounds yummy, doesn't it Harby? Hm? Yes it does indeed. We'll get started at that time then, shall we?" It was then she turned and looked at me directly. This was the first time the Mistress had made an effort to speak with me.

"You there. ROM, hm? Follow me please." I looked quickly at the Harbinger and then back to the Mistress.

"Very well, Mistress."

I followed her back towards where she had just come from. We were headed for the wreckage that the Infinite Baffler had caused. Once we were out of the others' hearing radius, she spoke to me.

"You're awfully curious about me, aren't you? I can sense it, ROM."

"Well, you have been, shall we say, preoccupied with the Harbinger. Although, I do find it highly impolite that you completely ignored me and CEO for so long."

She tilted her hair vortex back and laughed for a moment as she continued walking forward. "Oh little Harby and I are just having fun. Sorry ROM, didn't mean to exclude you. I've got something for you, you know."

"No, I don't know. What do you have?"

"Well...I don't have it just yet...but I put it around here somewhere..."
She was actively looking for something to pick up off of the ground. I thought she was mad, but went along with her little game for the time being. We were still in sight of the palace and the Harbinger. Suddenly, she gasped.

"Ah! Here it is!" She ran forward and grabbed an object out of a small pile of rubble. I couldn't quite tell what it was until she handed it to me.

"I saw this object and wanted you to tell me what it was. Do you have any knowledge on the subject?"

It was a curved, metallic apparatus that was designed to hold a magnetic gyro wheel, a toy for Sapien youth as far as I knew.

"This is a toy for Sapien youth. Well, part of the toy, anyways. There is...hang on...a piece seems to be missing...a magnetic gyro wheel. Anyways, the one who holds this apparatus controls the magnetic wheel by pointing it straight up and then down. The wielder repeats this motion to watch the wheel spin along the track until it falls off or comes to a halt from inactivity. Why is this of such importance to you?"

"That is a very good question, Romsikins. Mind if I call you Romsikins?"
I said nothing.

CHAPTER 9.666 THE INFINITE EVIL VISITATION OF DREAMS

"It is a question I had hoped you would answer for me. First however, I have a story to tell you, hm? You see, this apparatus was once held by three visitors to this Layer. Well, there was another just like it. Three visitors and two apparatuses. They weren't necessarily guests so to speak, more like mysterious intruders. At any rate, on that horrifying evening around seven, while I was out for a stroll, I came across the intersection we are currently standing in. Although it is now destroyed, just try to picture it as it was: lights, cars, Tasties walking to and from various places, hm? A typical night."

Just as she finished this sentence, I started catching glimpses of exactly the scenario she was describing as if it were happening. The intersection was rebuilt by my ocular receptors. It was busy, structured. She continued speaking, and I wished I had more time to determine the source of this phenomenon.

"I happened to witness three Sapiens standing on this very corner. Now at the time I was startled. No other Sapiens populated this Layer unless they were Royalty, and the only Royalty present here was me. So! I was immediately curious, hm? Before interfering, I took a moment to witness their actions. One of the Sapiens, a male, was standing just over there facing the other two with his mouth wide open."

I again saw glimpses of this exact scenario clear as day just as she described them. She continued to tell her tale.

"The other two each had one of these apparatuses clenched in their mouths. Obviously I can't demonstrate this for you, but the handle was the part in their teeth. Now the one female was pointing a loaded pistol at the male opposite from her, the Sapien with his mouth wide open as if ready to accept the bullet. The other male with this apparatus in his mouth had a vice grip in his hands, ready at the mouth of the other male, as if he were about to pull a tooth out of the other Sapien's head. It looked like this Sapien was in great danger."

I continued to see this scenario play out as the Mistress spoke. How was I connected to this instance? This was incredibly similar to the situation with the King as he showed me the Sapien hospital. Although in this instance, the Mistress was not the direct cause of my shocking visions. She was merely the trigger for remembering the events. Was I here previously?

"Before I could attempt to stop the murder at hand, I overheard the female Sapien speak from clenched teeth. 'I could always think more clearly with one less bullet in my gun.' I'll never forget those words or what happened next. She fired her pistol, and it shut down the entire intersection with shock. The Tasties stopped walking and ducked, the cars stopped moving through the intersection, and I was stopped. The Sapien with his mouth open dropped to the sidewalk dead. The other male, with this apparatus still clenched in his teeth moved forward and tried to fish the bullet out of the dead Sapien's mouth, but he could not find it. The female grabbed the male by the shoulder and said through clenched teeth, 'It had never not worked before, why not now?' Just after that, they shifted Layers with the deceased Sapien in tow, but they left this apparatus behind. I had kept this with me from that very day until I had to ditch it here when I ran to stop the Infinite Baffler. I did not want to risk losing it. Now my story is finished. I have the device again and I want you to take another look at it."

"What am I looking for, Mistress?"

"Why, Romsikins, just have a look there on the handle. I'm sure you'll be able to provide me with some answers."

I looked at the yellow handle. It appeared to be wrapped in some sort of leather, but printed on the end was something I was not prepared to read. I read it out loud to the Mistress.

"It says...Layer Dryffe Company."

CHAPTER 9.687 SO WHY WAS VIX AFRAID OF SEVEN?

So while I had some mysterious in-depth understanding of the story the Mistress told, I was very unaware of whom these Sapiens were and why they were in the middle of the Layer Delicious. Furthermore, I had no knowledge of the Layer Dryffe Company and how it was run. My only current knowledge comes from the King's story of the Great Business Deal.

"I'm afraid I have no answers for you, Mistress. I do not come directly from the Layer Dryffe. This is something you would have to take up with the King of the Cubicle."

"You have to understand, Romsikins, this story that I've just told you is the most odd and fantastical occurrence I've experienced just short of the recent attack on my Layer Delicious by the Infinite Baffler, hm? I must have answers, dearie."

"I don't know what to tell you, Mistress. This occurrence is something I have no knowledge of. You will have to speak to the King of the Cubicle. I do not have any knowledge about the inner workings of the Layer Dryffe Company, either. It appears this is a product that they've at some point manufactured, but I am not aware of what purpose it may serve other than that of a child's entertainment. I'm very sorry. I wish I could provide more information for you."

And I did…to a certain extent. This occurrence was something that I wished that I could speak about, but I could not. My calculations were inconclusive. It was all so familiar to me, but so foreign at the same time. I had little context. The Mistress seemed disappointed at my statement.

"Oh…very well…do you believe I will get the opportunity to meet with the King of the Cubicle in order to discuss this?"

"Mistress, you will get the opportunity if you come with us to the Great Conference Room."

"Well I'm convinced then, Romsikins. Let us return to Harby and CEO, hm? I'm sorry to pull you out here just to question you."

"It is quite alright Mistress. I will come back with you. I am sorry that I could not provide any explanations for your story." I was simply not capable of supplying the Mistress with any of the information she desired. I detected that she was incredibly disappointed. Without a visible face, I could still go by breathing patterns, external temperature, and tone of voice. My calculations regarding my role in the story the Mistress had just described would remain…inconclusive for the time. To avoid confusion, I did not reveal these strange visions to the Mistress. She would have only pressed me for answers I did not have. Perhaps we would see what this was all about if we got a moment to speak with the King.

We arrived back at the palace door and greeted our squad of Sapiens and Tronics who had been sent for.

"Thank you, officer Zesti, for returning this squad unharmed. Your next order is to scoop up the remaining Tastie officers and start a citywide rescue mission. Please initiate this now. I do not care how it is done, as long as it is done efficiently."

"Yes, Mistress!" Officer Zesti barreled away from us and began barking orders at other officers in order to begin the rescue effort. The Mistress seemed largely unconcerned with officer Zesti and turned to us to begin a conversation.

"So! The rescue effort is under way. Are we off to the Origin Layer then? Hm?" We all sat in silence for a few moments while soaking in what had just occurred. The Harbinger spoke first to the Mistress.

"Mistress, I know this is your Layer to control, but shouldn't you play a more active role in your rescue effort? I mean, there are most likely casualties in the thousands after an attack like that. Shouldn't you be here to—"

"—Officer Zesti and the rest of the Tastie officers will be enough to handle this occasion. I know it seems distant of me to just assign this task to an officer and expect him or her to take care of it, but I have the utmost faith in my officers. They are highly disciplined. After all, if they don't obey orders from me...well...poof! They know the consequences. And none of them have to know that I'm leaving the Layer Delicious on official business. It won't take that long, will it Harby?" I personally found it fascinating that she kept her officers in line by threatening death. The Harbinger did not seem phased.

"Well, it could be a matter of days until we reach the Layer Dryffe. We do have another stop on our little trip. We're bound for the Layer Necroma in an attempt to negotiate with the Royalty present there. I hope you will make the appropriate accommodations in Delicious for your absence here."

"I'll let one of the Tastie officers know. Actually, hang on just a moment, hm?" She looked around for a Tastie officer and found one quickly. He was assisting a group of civilian Tasties.

"You there! Officer! Come here please!" The officer looked around to see who was calling and saw the Mistress waving at him. He spoke softly to the Tastie civilians he was escorting and then hurried over to her.

"Mistress! What can I do for you!"

"What is your name, officer?"

"Toastie, Mistress."

"Officer Toastie, I have a very important mission for you. Once you are finished escorting those Tasties to safety, you are to find officer Zesti. You will tell him that I am leaving the Layer and that he is to be in charge in my absence. You will also tell him you are to be his right hand during this hard time by my decree. Your primary goals are to establish shelter and medical care for the civilians. Make certain to organize squads for search and rescue. Here is my signature. Everything else is secondary, do I make myself clear?"

"Yes Mistress!"

"Very good. Now hurry along and get started right away. You have a lot of work to do." Officer Toastie saluted the Mistress and hurried back to the civilian Tasties.

"Well, Harby. It looks like I'm all ready to go with you now. When do we perform the shift to the Layer Necroma?"

"Well, Mistress. Do you possibly…er…is there something else you could wear? Your dress is almost, well, nonexistent at this point." The Harbinger was right. Her dress was more like a tattered cloth now, and little was being left to the imagination in terms of her body. This is to say that the Mistress was practically naked due to the extensive damage of her clothes.

"Oh Harby, there's no need to blush dear. I'm flattered, really. I suppose I could go and change. Just hang out here, I won't be long!" She left for the palace to change. Once the doors closed, the Harbinger turned to me.

"And just what was that secret conference you had with the Mistress, hm?"

"You're already beginning to sound like her, Hotz. Let's try not to keep that nasty habit of saying 'hm' at the end of each sentence in such a condescending manner."

"Well I…alright. You got me there, but quit trying to change the subject here. You had a long chat with her. What was it about?"

"She showed me a device branded with the Layer Dryffe Company logo. She wanted to know what it was. There was a long story attached to it, and I won't go into detail. Suffice it to say that she wishes to speak with the King of the Cubicle about the device and I told her that if she decided to come with us, then she would have her opportunity. It seemed logical to try and use that situation to our advantage, and now she's coming with us. So mission accomplished." CEO seemed very interested in the conversation we were having. No doubt the King was directly controlling him at this point. After all, we were talking about his precious Layer Dryffe Company. He barged his way into the conversation.

"For my own curiosity, just what was this device she showed you, ROM?" This would be interesting. I could either fabricate what I saw and subtly let on that I knew the King was controlling CEO, or I could tell the truth and witness a false reaction. I decided to tell the truth in this instance. Perhaps CEO would let slip some information I could use to piece together my history.

"The device was actually a Sapien youth's toy designed for entertainment, as far as I could gather. It was a bent metallic path designed for a magnetic gyro wheel to travel along. It had a yellow leather handle with two long metallic strips coming out which were bent back at one end almost at the halfway point. The Layer Dryffe Company image was printed on the handle." I awaited CEO's response.

"Ah, fascinating. Merely curious." This was all he said before turning to leave the conversation. Curious indeed. I was very suspicious now. Perhaps this matter would need to play out in its entirety after the Mistress meets up with the King. I would be getting no answers out of CEO without confronting him alone, and I would not get that chance any time in the near future.

We waited until the Mistress returned from the palace after changing. She emerged from the palace wearing clothing more suiting for adventure: a cloth shirt and utility pants designed for carrying any number of items. The pockets were almost all full, of what I did not know. She greeted us with a loud voice.

"I make my return to you, Harby! Am I dressed more appropriately now, hm?"

"Yes, Mistress. We will perform the shift to the Layer Necroma shortly. Give me a few moments to speak with the squad."

"Very well, Harby. Make it fast, hm? I'm very excited to get going." The Harbinger did not respond directly to her, and instead climbed a statue just outside the palace in order to get the squad's attention. He spoke loudly.

"Everyone please listen! We are about to shift to the Layer Necroma! Everyone please be ready for the shift! If you are left behind in this instance, there is no hope for you. You will be left on the Layer Delicious for a long time. Possibly the rest of your days. I will now give the standard five minutes for every soldier to make preparations. That is all." The Harbinger stepped down from the statue and spoke to me.

"Well. We've accomplished our mission here. We have the Mistress Vix Delicious on our side. Our next step is the Layer Necroma. I'm not excited about this Layer due to the mystery surrounding it, but hopefully it will go well."

"I hope it will go well too, Hotz." And so we waited. There was nothing much going on. All of the men were ready at the time of the Harbinger's first announcement. So the five minutes expired. The Harbinger climbed the statue once again to address the squad.

"Your buffer time is up. I see you all used it wisely. We will now perform the shift to the Layer Necroma. May I remind each of you to be on guard. We do not know what will be present in the Layer Necroma. I cannot stress enough to be on your guard. Everyone ready?!" The Harbinger lifted his right arm into the air. Everyone crowded around in order to complete the shift. They all made physical contact with one another.

"READY!? HERE WE GO!" The shift began. The terrain surrounding us began to warp and string apart. I saw all of the members of the squad bend and warp at the mercy of the shift. Reality began to warp in this instance. As Royalty, shifting was no longer an issue. We all wrapped around each other while the shift took place. Eventually, the ground settled around us and the Layer Necroma began to take shape slowly. Things were dark here.

CHAPTER 9.789 BECAUSE SEVEN ATE NINE

The shift was completely startling for the Royal squad. Everyone made it just fine, but we were lost in terms of the area in which we shifted. There was a dense jungle surrounding us even after the shift destroyed our surroundings. It was incredibly humid. There was Necomian wildlife surrounding us, lurking in the foliage. After the shock subsided, the Harbinger spoke up.

"Is everyone alright? Did we make it just fine?" Everyone announced his or her status. They all seemed to be okay.

"Very good. Let's head north to see if we can find something. Anything." The squad obliged and started marching north. It didn't take long before we arrived upon a massive clearing.

"Oh how wonderful! I see a shopping mall just there!" said the Mistress.

"Everyone halt!" said Hotz. And he said this with good reason. There was a massive structure in our midst. It appeared to be one continuous massive building. He took a moment to assess the structure before speaking to the squad.

"Men, it appears we have come across a massive shopping mall just as the Mistress stated. The odd thing is that I see no cars, no patrons, and no activity. The mall, however, appears to be in pristine condition. This is very strange, and I urge you all a final time: be on your guard! Let's go!"

The squad advanced towards the structure crouched low to avoid detection from any hostile presence on the Layer. Everything was calm even up to the point where we reached the closest entrance to the mall. Hotz called everyone to a halt once more.

"Everyone stop! We are about to enter. There is no telling what we are about to encounter. We've encountered no sentient life thus far other than hearing wild calls from the jungle. Everyone be ready. Here we go!" This event wasn't as exciting as it may have sounded. The Harbinger merely stepped up to the door, and the door, being automatic, opened for him. I followed closely behind to scan what was inside. It was, if you could imagine, more massive inside than it appeared to be outside. The ceilings were high and shone bright white light down on the floor of the mall. It wasn't divided into individual shops, instead the merchandise was piled onto high shelves that rose to the ceiling. This would have been great if it weren't for one fact: there wasn't a single being in sight. No one was present on the floor to greet us, there wasn't anyone stocking the shelves, and strangest of all, there weren't any customers. Just as the last member of the squad walked inside, we saw a figure lurch into our collective eyesight. It appeared to be a primitive Tronic, although I did not recognize any of the parts it had. It was rusting and sputtering along on large treads for mobility. It appeared to run off of fossil fuels. Before the Harbinger could say anything to it, I approached the Tronic and reached it well out of earshot of the rest of the squad.

It was ancient. It looked very tired and somehow regretful of its position.

"Hello there. I am ROM, Royalty from the Layer Automina. Who are you?" The Tronic paused momentarily as if searching for something and finally stopped fidgeting. It produced a small device and placed it into a terminal on its front, which began playing back audio immediately from speakers crafted onto either side of it.

"Welcome customer to the Layer Necroma Shopping Center! We value your patronage and I'm here to answer any questions you may have! Remember, we're here to make your day great!" My programming was searching for this model Tronic in my database, but I could not locate it. No doubt it was purely Necromancy. I couldn't risk anything on asking it a question, so I decided to try.

"Thank you for your salutation, Tronic. My squad and I are attempting to locate members of Royalty here on the Layer Necroma. Could you assist us in this matter?"

The Tronic took in my question and fumbled around for another message to play to me. It found one after several seconds of silence.

"Right this way please!" This recording had the same voice as the previous one. The Tronic moved past me out of the aisle we were in and started navigating the front of the store. I turned and looked at the Harbinger, CEO, and the Mistress. What a remarkable Tronic. It clearly has its own intelligence, yet it is not permitted to respond with audio in a unique fashion by design. Perhaps it was an early version of what Necroma's answer was for the Autominan Servutron model line.

"Bring them with us! The Tronic is going to take us to the members of Royalty!"

"Oh how exciting! I hope we get the chance to take some souvenirs, hm?" said the Mistress. I doubted this would be the case. It seemed like a statement that was largely out of place given the current circumstances. Maybe she wasn't thinking about the mission in a logical fashion? Surely she wanted results. Although given how we had to practically convince her to take action for the many inhabitants on her Layer perished or were injured by the evil Emperor, perhaps fear isn't something she can experience.

The rest of the squad followed the Harbinger and largely ignored the Mistress much to her dismay. They had heeded the Harbinger's words and were at the ready for a surprise attack. We continued to follow the Tronic until we reached a trapdoor in the floor of the mall. It motioned to the door with a reluctant hand and fumbled for another audio device.

"Here you are! Will you require any further assistance?" I merely looked at the ancient Tronic in acknowledgement. It bowed as much as it could and left us to travel down the nearest aisle. I looked to the Harbinger as his squad arrived at the trapdoor.

"Looks like we're going down, hm!? I hope none of the members of the squad were looking forward to a shopping spree!" Said the Mistress.

"Ha! Not with what the King pays us! Squad! We will be going down into this trapdoor!"

"Yes Harbinger!"

"Hey! Listen up! We're going to head down here, okay? You should be vigilant at all times! We proceed with extreme caution! Move out!" Five Sapien soldiers went down into the floor first followed by the Harbinger. I went next. The Mistress followed me. There was a light fog emanating from the hole in the floor, as well as extreme cold.

"Honestly the things I do…can't I just wait up here Harby? Hm?" The Harbinger shouted up to the Mistress from the bottom of the hole.

"Honestly Mistress, I would like for you to come with due to your spectacular power you have! Will you do this for me please?"

"Well, if you insist. Only for you Harby!"

CHAPTER 9.889 THE INFINITE BAFFLING DEPTHS OF THE LAYER NECROMA

I detected very low temperatures here. What I mean to say is that these temperatures were designed to store meat. This being the case, they were highly detrimental to all other beings except for me since I was a Tronic. Every other being here was a Sapien, except for the Mistress who only appeared to be a Sapien, but it seemed the cold got to her first.

"Harby! It is quite chilly down here! I wish I had brought a coat!"

"Aw Mistress, chill out please!? We've got a mission ahead of us, and this is our only lead. Now, come along then, hm?" The Mistress seemed displeased with the Harbinger using her catchphrase of "hm" in his reply. Nevertheless, she continued to follow us deeper into the cooler.

Things were very dark down here. The addition of the cold made it an incredibly spooky place for the Sapiens. I was not phased by the surroundings, but everyone else seemed to be on edge, physiologically speaking. Perhaps it was the lack of light. Perhaps it was the cold. Either way, the squad continued their way forward towards a faint light that was visible at the end of the cold tunnel. It took a few minutes to arrive, but when we did, there was a door there where the Harbinger stopped us all. "I'm about to open this door. If the current temperature is any indication, it will also be cold in here as well. Hopefully we will meet with a member of Royalty soon. It does seem quite deserted." I agreed. This was suspicious. At any rate, the Harbinger opened the door. We were all surprised to see the contents on the other side.

CHAPTER 10.001 THE INFINITE BAFFLING CIRCLE OF LIFE

It was a museum. It was a museum of the deceased. Upon further inspection, it was a museum of the deceased that had representatives of all kinds of life that had existed on any Layer. This was a museum with no patrons. This was a disturbing collection of specimens from every Layer, and they were all in cold storage. This explained the low temperatures. Every member of the squad marveled at the surrounding sights.

"Wow! I've never seen such things before in my life! This creature is called a 'Meglanable'!" Said the Mistress. She continued down the row naming all of the creatures aloud, and she was the only one who dared speak as the rest of the squad was dumbstruck.

"This one is a 'Xzck' and this one is a 'Blaghtank'. This one is called a—" She stopped short of her word. The squad gathered around her at the tank housing the species she saw. I looked at the specimen and knew what it was immediately.

"Mistress,what could a Tastie possibly be doing here?"

"My dear Romsikins, I haven't a clue. I didn't know that Tasties could shift Layers."

"I didn't either." We all sat in silence staring at the deceased Tastie. No one said a word as we admired its presence here in the Layer Necroma.

"This has to be a joke. Harby, why is there a Tastie here? Tell me! Tell me NOW!"

"Mistress, I don't have any answers for you. I'm equally as shocked as you are. The only thing we can do is get through this chamber, as creepy as it is. We have to locate the Royalty on this Layer. For now, just disregard what you see. We will have answers as soon as we find the Royalty here."

"Okay Harby, but this is completely beyond what I expected when I agreed to this."

"You and me both, Mistress. You and me both. We have to keep going now." And so we did. The squad left sight of the deceased Tastie. It wasn't long before the path split in front of us. We had ignored all the other deceased specimens on the way after seeing the Tastie. Everyone wanted answers. At the fork we saw two signs. To the left pointed a sign that said "Necromian Museum of Basic Life". On the right we saw a sign that said "Royal Necromian Hallway". Of course it only made sense that we follow the right path. No one said a word as the Harbinger led us to the path on the right.

Our surroundings developed into something more bizarre than anticipated.

CHAPTER 10.101 THE INFINITE BAFFLING ROYAL NECROMIAN HALLWAY

It was a trophy room extended into a hallway. The hallway was short in length, but it was tall in height, and it was lined with the same tanks we saw on the way. Each of these tanks, however, was empty and they were marked off by ropes tied to a podium. Each podium had the name of a Royalty member written on it.

The very first tank we saw was that of The Laugh Riot. The podium in front of the tank had a gold plaque attached to it that was engraved with "The Laugh Riot". The next tank was that belonging to the Connoisseur of the Preposterous. Beyond that, the next tank's plaque read "General Management or CEO". CEO kneeled in front of the tank.

"Could it be that I was misled about my purpose? Why? Why are these cases here?"

He stood up and remained in silent contemplation as the rest of the squad continued to look around at the horror. It did not stop with CEO. The Mistress had a tank with her name on it as well. She was brought to her knees in confusion. "Harby...ROM...I'm here too. This...this can't be. I've never even been to this Layer. Why is this here?" The Harbinger and I continued down the hallway while the Mistress slumped to the floor while staring up at her case. Sure, there were other tanks to analyze at, but the Harbinger and I were searching for our own cases. Additionally there was a door at the end of the hallway we would probably look at. We looked at each in passing until we made it close to the end of the hallway. Each new tank had a more impressive podium in front than the last, suggesting that perhaps not all members of Royalty are equal. The first name I read towards the end of the hallway was the most shocking, although in recalling the situation, it should have been obvious.

"King of the Cubicle." I read aloud to the Harbinger. This was the space reserved for the King. Opposite from the King's section was that of the Emperor of the Moon.

"Well that's fascinating," said the Harbinger.

"Fascinating indeed, Hotz. At least we know neither of them are behind this," I agreed. We approached the next two sections and each read one plaque on either side of the hall.

"Commander Vega or Harbinger of the Zax." I read aloud, but the Harbinger was reading aloud at the same time, and he didn't hear me.

"What was that you said, ROM?"

"This...this is the section belonging to you. They're all empty, Vega."

"Ha, 'Vega'. Haven't heard that in a while. Unfortunately this one is for you. The list of names is long. Come have a look." I approached the podium and read the plaque. It said "Punxsutawney, Punxsutron, Servutron Prime, or ROM." There was something vastly more unsettling about this podium than the last. While none of the tanks were occupied, there were four names but only one tank. Most important of these was the first name. Punxsutawney. Someone currently or previously on the Layer Necroma knew me as Punxsutawney. Even more disturbing is that they had intended to display my body here in the Royal Necromian Hallway. But how had this collector obtained not only specimens from multiple Layers, but potentially members of Royalty? Hopefully this would be answered soon, but we had four more podiums to go before we reached the door at the end of the Royal Necromian Hallway.

"Hotz, let's read the podium next to mine."

"I agree." We walked a few feet to the next podium. It read "Baron of the Break Room".

"Hotz, this is the individual that the King of the Cubicle spoke of previously. This is the proxy for the Greeter of the Great Business deal."

"Yeah, I remember that. Apparently the Baron is a high target just as we are."

"And we haven't even met with him yet. What does this next one say?"

CHAPTER 10.186 THE INFINITE BAFFLING PLAQUE BACKWARDS ASSOCIATION

"Greeter of the Great Business Deal." The Harbinger and I read this plaque in unison.

"Oh, what the hell?!" Hotz asked no one in particular.

We stood in silence for a few moments and looked back at the hallway behind us. The rest of the squad was occupied with the various Royal podiums and tanks. None had followed us to the last podiums. The Harbinger grew frustrated.

"Alright, ROM. I've had enough. Forget the last two plaques for now. We're going to open this door."

"I'm ready Hotz, just give the word." He turned and called for the squad's attention. "Everyone, we're going to open this door and get to the bottom of this mystery. Hopefully we will get some answers soon. Everyone join us at the end of the hall here please!"

Just as the squad started moving towards us, the door at the end of the hall opened. "READY YOUR WEAPONS, MEN!" yelled the Harbinger. The door continued to open slowly and once completely open, every member of the squad with a weapon had it pointed at the darkness. We heard many voices speak from the darkness beyond. They spoke in unison.

"The first time we've heard voices that weren't our own in a long time, and they're so hostile. We cannot blame them. We'd be afraid of us too. They're so far away from their own Layers."

CHAPTER 10.203 AMALGA GALLIMAUFRY THE ALL-BEING

I will never delete my first encounter with Amalga Gallimaufry the All-Being from my database. Amalga Gallimaufry had every voice, and often chose to use most of them when speaking. An exaggeration you might think? You would be incorrect.

"Strangers, I know not why you are here," said Amalga Gallimaufry. The All-Being rarely asked questions, it mostly made statements that commanded the need for an answer. Hotz, still pointing his weapon into the darkness, shouted at Amalga Gallimaufry.

"Name's Harbinger, we're on a mission seeking members of Royalty like ourselves," he yelled while looking down the sights of his weapon.

"It would appear you've found us," said Amalga Gallimaufry.

"If you're Royalty, then this saves us a lot of time. We've been searching for you now for a good bit. However, before I go through the trouble of explaining why we're looking for you and yadda yadda, we need some good answers. Fast. I'm going to need you all to come out here where we can see you. At first I thought I'd be excited that we found you, but I just can't seem to get over that tank back there with my name on it." While still aiming his weapon, Hotz motioned towards the tank over his right shoulder with his head.

"A being cannot show its true form if it doesn't have one," said Amalga Gallimaufry.

"Oh what the hell does that mean? Just come out here already!" shouted Hotz.

"As you request, Harbinger."

A tank identical to those lining the walls emerged slowly from the darkness. It had wheels on the bottom for purposes of transportation. The tank was covered completely in a red curtain that hung on spotless brass rings around the top of the tank. There was a podium for a name just like the others. Its base was affixed to the bottom of the tank and it stood about three feet high, the tank itself being much taller. At a distance, I could read the podium. It said "Lich Zomadrafreid". The tank stopped moving once it was in full view, of course we could not see what was inside due to the curtain. Perhaps the most intriguing characteristic of this odd phenomenon was that the curtain bore the Layer Dryffe Company logo. Hotz was not pleased. His weapon was still primed.

"If this is a joke, I'm not laughing. Is it not clear that we're not only startled, but armed heavily?" asked Hotz. He jumped a little in fright when Amalga Gallimaufry began speaking, expecting to hear a chorus of voices from the darkness instead of the tank a few feet away from him.

"Harbinger, do not attempt to look behind our curtain. I cannot guarantee your continued sanity if you do so."

I calculated that being startled made Hotz think a bit more clearly. Instead of shouting back or waving his weapon more, he merely stood there in a bit of shock. Apparently the threat of going insane just by looking behind a curtain appealed to his common sense.

"If you allow us some time we can describe to you who we are, and the purpose of these tanks you see here."

"Go ahead."

"The name we have chosen for ourself is Amalga Gallimaufry the All-Being."

CHAPTER 10.259 OF LIFE AND LAYERS

"The things we are about to tell you are what we have pieced together during our time on Necroma, which has been our entire lives. The building you are in is an old storage facility for the Layer Dryffe Company. Storage is necessary for beings that do not yet have a finished Layer. Royalty is no exception to this. The shopping center above us is a front. The Layer Dryffe Company did not want their prototypes and products being discovered by competitors. This is why the area is in such seclusion. This should sufficiently answer one of your two most pressing questions."

"You said your name was what, now?" asked Hotz.

"Amalga Gallimaufry the All-Being. We don't like repeating ourself, Harbinger," said Amalga Gallimaufry.

"Why does your plaque there say 'Lich Zomadrafreid' then?"

"Ah yes, of course. Lich Zomadrafreid. A testament to who we could have been. Lich was apparently intended by the Layer Dryffe Company to become the member of Royalty charged with overseeing the Layer Necroma. However, the company didn't get Lich, they got us instead. As for us, well, we've had an abundance of time to consider our existence." It was at this time that a small column of black smoke rose up from the top of the tank. Not a single being in the hallway acknowledged it out loud, but I calculated all eyes and thoughts were trained on it.

"We were the first to arrive on Necroma, and as such we witnessed beings come and go periodically. None of these tanks you see now were present upon our advent. The Company began to shift tanks to this location with individual beings inside each that appeared to be in the deepest of sleeps. The fact of the matter is that none of them had ever been awake. The beings were later shifted to their new Layer, leaving the tanks behind. The curious thing is, the Layer Dryffe Company is still making more."

All I could calculate was how this information conflicted with my previous knowledge about shifting. How could the Layer Dryffe Company pinpoint where they shifted these tanks when Royalty had to take a shot in the dark and destroy their surroundings in the process? This would require much explanation, but not from the All-Being. I would ask the King himself soon enough. There were more than a couple of details that did not compute when it came to the Layer Dryffe Company. My line of logic was broken when Amalga Gallimaufry rolled over to one of the tanks. I hadn't noticed before, but this one had something in it.

CHAPTER 10. 289 ON WHAT PLATE COULD SUCH AN INFINITE CAKE LIE?

It resembled the Infinite Baffler, only it was much smaller. I wanted very much to investigate. However, Amalga Gallimaufry continued its explanation while its audience remained silent, intimidated by mystery.

"We began to realize that we were not exactly like these sleeping beings. They kept the same form no matter how long we looked at them. The same cannot be said of us. We are a being with a form in flux. We are one, yet all. Perhaps a monster, but no doubt a mistake. We are of the conclusion that when the Layer Dryffe Company intended to make Lich Zomadrafreid, they didn't just use his template, they mistakenly used all available templates for life. Our shape changes without discernible pattern. We recognize features we have seen in our arms, legs, and other appendages present in some of the beings here as they grow and disappear from our body."

"In summation, we are a summation. We are one of every type of being the Layer Dryffe Company had invented at the time with an outward appearance that is constantly changing in an uncontrollable fashion. This is why we say that a being cannot show its true form if it does not have one. Simply glancing at such an unnatural form for a moment could be as mesmerizing as the most beautiful sunset, or as maddening as the darkest nightmare. This is why we have this curtain: for the protection of others. It was a gift from the only other visitor we've ever had." Amalga Gallimaufry the All-Being took a moment to pause before concluding its speech.

"Now then, we are all very tired. We get incredibly apprehensive when our silence is disturbed. We're afraid we will not be of use much further. We ask that you leave here soon, and without incident." Hotz was quick to jump in with a response.

"Now hold on here, Amalga. We're trying to recruit other members of Royalty for a peace conference on the Layer Dryffe. There's a war going on right now between the King of the Cubicle, founder of the Layer Dryffe Company, and a potential buyer. We're here on behalf of the King, and we're all supposed to meet at the Great Conference Room on the Layer Dryffe to reach an agreement. We would like for you to join us. It doesn't seem like you have much to do around here anyways." Hotz began to chuckle politely, but Amalga Gallimaufry laughed hard, a unique phenomenon all its own. Each voice had its own brand of laughter. The effect on the squad was apparent: elevated heart rate and body temperature.

"You may be correct Harbinger, but one thing we do quite a lot of is thinking. It looks to us that you aren't recruiting for a peace conference at all."

"Of course we are! What could you possibly know about our mission besides what little I've told you?"

"Those must be some impressive strings the King has in order for them to tug on you all the way from another Layer. You should have all looked at yourselves a bit more closely. You aren't diplomats. You're an army searching for more firepower. You've been deceived by your King. It seems to us he is anticipating that this 'peace conference' will end poorly. We don't have any reason to involve ourselves in the quarrels of Royalty we've never met, even if we were made by the Company the King controls. We decline your offer to join you. We may be an abomination to behold, and no doubt a powerful ally, but we value the life we've been given and prefer to live it in peace. We won't lose it at this so called 'peace conference'. Goodbye, Royal travelers. May your future hold better fortune." With that, the cloaked tank rolled swiftly back into the dark doorway at the end of the hall, and the door closed. No one tried to stop it. Not even the Harbinger moved.

And there it was. At the center of everything that did not compute was the Layer Dryffe Company, and at the center of that was the King of the Cubicle.

CHAPTER 10.328 EVEN THE TITLES HAVE BEEN RECORDED IN MY VOICE

I moved forward past Hotz to look at the tank with the miniature Infinite Baffler. Everyone stood in silent contemplation after hearing Amalga Gallimaufry's fresh perspective on our mission. Could we really not trust the King? I, of course, had my suspicions before we left on this mission, but now everyone else did as well. There were still a slew of questions left to be answered. Who else visited Amalga Gallimaufry, and why would they have a need to? Why is there what appears to be a miniature Infinite Baffler in this tank in front of me? Why could the Layer Dryffe Company accurately shift beings into and out of palaces without negative consequences? While these questions demanded answers, I found myself asking a different question over and over again: exactly what are the King's true intentions? The main objective now was to have this question answered before going any further. I formulated a plan of action swiftly and approached Hotz with it.

"We need to speak with the King as soon as possible, and I think it should happen on the Layer Dryffe."

"Well, since our previous plan just went to shit, I'd say yours works just fine. I'm looking for a few answers I just can't sort out for myself, and I'm sure we won't hear another peep out of that talking tank. Plus I don't want to see what happens if we get it pissed off. That smoke didn't seem…natural. The King seems a bit shady now that things are put into a different perspective."

"Excellent. Then we are in agreement. We need answers, so we should get the squad ready to make the shift to the Layer Dryffe," I said.

"Hang on, what about the Layer Façade, ROM? And isn't this place considered a palace?"

"There will be no way to know for certain unless we try to shift. The Layer Dryffe Company seems to be able to shift these beings in and out with no difficulty. As for Façade, I calculate it is likely the Emperor has already recruited there. He sent the Infinite Baffler to the Layer Delicious to stop us while we were there, and we haven't seen him or his minions on Necroma. They're too late anyways, it doesn't appear that Amalga Gallimaufry has any interest in participating in this war."

"Yeah…yeah. That does make sense. I didn't pick up on those details. Well, I guess we're ready then." Hotz seemed confused, and let down. I'm sure the hint that the king may have been untrue to him was at the forefront of his thoughts. Hotz was a man who seemed to value merit and trustworthiness. Loyalty was number one to him. He turned from me to announce our plans to the squad.

"Everyone, please pay attention!" said Hotz. The members of the squad shook themselves out of varying intensities of stupor after contemplation of the current circumstances.

"We are going to make our final shift and head to the Layer Dryffe Company! We are under the impression that the Emperor has already visited the Layer Façade, so there will not be a need to make this extra trip. We will be shifting directly to Dryffe Fields and moving towards Layer Dryffe Co. from there. Everyone join hands with those next to you!"

Every member present in the gloomy hallway joined hands until there was an unbroken chain between Royalty, Tronic, and Sapien.

"If you aren't joined up now, you'll be stuck here forever, or at least until one of us comes back. Here we go, boys and girls. See you on the other side!"

The hallway started to bend inward on itself slightly, the walls started to dissolve and the tanks all disappeared one by one like they were swatted away by an invisible giant. Reality collapsed in on itself and there was an absence of context for a long period of time. It was similar to being deactivated for maintenance.

Upon our arrival at the Layer Dryffe, I was the first to awaken to our new surroundings. As I started up my diagnostic functions, I began to realize that I had no such capability. My diagnostics were gone. This alarmed me, but what alarmed me more was that when I placed my right manipulator on the grass and into my field of vision to help myself up, it was of flesh and blood. It was a Sapien arm.

CHAPTER 10.354 AND WHO OR WHAT COULD HOLD SUCH A PLATE? Amalga Gallimaufry closed the door tightly and rolled far back into the dark room. A set of unbelievably sharp teeth and a monocle reflected the dim light that Amalga's tank gave off.

"An impressive display, Amalga Gallimaufry. Please ready yourself for the shift to the Layer Dryffe," said Beedlebop.

CHAPTER 10.357 I MAY NOT BE ABLE TO ANSWER THESE QUESTIONS

I stood significantly taller than ROM did. I was at least two feet taller. Servutron Prime was, of course, a Servutron. He was destined to serve other members of Autominan society. ROM was a member of Royalty, destined to seek out the Layer Dryffe Company. I emerged from the shift-cocoon. I now stood once again as Punxsutawney.

On a hill that sat about 500 yards in front of me, I could see what I assumed was the Layer Dryffe Company. Perhaps it would be more realistic to say that the Layer Dryffe Company WAS the hill in front of me. Massive smokestacks produced clouds that took interesting shapes, similar to the ones I saw on my first visit to Dryffe Fields.

"Wait a minute, I've been here more than once before, haven't I? Why have I been narrating to myself?"

On the plain about 30 yards in front of me stood the opposing team.

The Connoisseur of the Preposterous looked just as he did during our first encounter, although his demeanor was a bit less jovial. To his right was a frightening character with a large mouth who was laughing like he was paid to do it. To his right was a large cloaked tank, Amalga Gallimaufry the All-Being. Just behind these three were the members of the Faas Family, I assumed. They all resembled Sapiens from the neck down, but their heads were unrealistically different (like most things around here seemed to be). From left to right they had the following items in place of a head: a solar system (a sun and a few planets, you know, no big deal), a tentacle looking to belong to a giant squid, a massive PA speaker, a metallic oscillating fan with streamers attached, and some sort of rapidly flowing purple and orange vortex with ethereal wispy black outlines. A hair vortex. Just like the Mistress.

Behind the members of Royalty were soldiers numbering close to one hundred. They were all as heavily armed as Vega's. The Connoisseur of the Preposterous turned to his right and shouted.

"You do not want to know what will happen to you if you harm the young Sapien in the front just over there. He is to remain alive. That goes for you mass-murdering types especially. Keep Vega too, if you can help it. Otherwise, make this quick. They cannot be permitted to reach the Layer Dryffe Company. Now, on my signal!"

Beedlebop raised a gloved right hand into the air and pointed at me with a gloved left.

"I say there good man! If you wish to spare the bloodshed, you can turn yourself over to us! I will give you until the count of ten! One!...Two!..."

Wait, how did I know who this person was? He looks just like Winston. Wait, now who is Winston? Why is that name so familiar?

"Five!...Six!...Se-"

"I remember you, Beedlebop!" I had to stall for time. If only all I had was his name rolling around in my head, I could get more information from him and use it against him somehow.

"Of course you do, dear fellow. It would be difficult to forget such a handsome gentleman as I. Now come along with us and we'll take you to see the Emperor again."

Now we were getting somewhere.

"The Emperor wants to see me again, does he? And why is that?"

"Well, erm, you see, he believes you to be incredibly important and wishes to speak with you!"

"Important, huh? That's awfully vague. Why couldn't he just come here and speak with me instead? Why am I so important?" I felt a raindrop on the top of my head. I touched it with my fingertips and looked at it. The color had started to fade to white where my fingers were wet. I looked up at the Connoisseur and he had noticed the bleaching rain as well. He knew his time was growing short.

But why did I know that as well?

The Connoisseur began to panic. I could hear it in his voice.

"Once this rain starts coming down hard, we'll all be in trouble! You'd better come along with us now dear boy." He started to walk closer to me. As he approached, the rain came down much harder. The multi-colored grass of Dryffe fields was losing its color, fast. Beedlebop was physically shaking with angst. His suit was now more white than black, and he was exasperated.

"He he he hoooo! Why do you always bring the rain with you when we speak to each other on Dryffe, old boy? It is quite tiring."

There was something so familiar about the clouds and the grass and the trees off in the distance. The way the colors all ran off of every surface made my memory scream back. In an instant, I remembered then that the color draining rain wasn't the only thing that could fall from the sky.

CHAPTER 10.478 BUT I CAN TELL YOU WHO THE BAKER IS

"I may not be able to answer these questions of yours, dear boy, but you must come with me at once!" Beedlebop was now in a fit of rage and began to run for me. I heard Vega speak for the first time since we shifted. He was giving orders to the squad, but it was drowned out over the deluge and the loud crash of the piano that landed a few feet in front of the Connoisseur.

"Holy shit, I get it now. It's a dream."

CHAPTER 10.485 A SLICE OF THE INFINITE LAYERED CAKE...

"No, you don't get it. You really don't."

The Emperor of the Moon flew down from out of the sky. While I wasn't exactly expecting him, I was thankful that things were escalating so swiftly.

"This has all the characteristics of a dream. If I'm not dreaming, how am I able to rain pianos down from the sky at will? That doesn't sound like standard behavior to me." Another grand piano landed on the ground just to the left of the Emperor with a cacophonous crash.

"Speaking of such, I can no longer allow you such a dangerous tool." The Emperor whispered into his scepter and a cloud of Jifflings flew out and away. Within seconds, the Infinite Baffler slugged and stretched quickly between the squad and I, cutting me off from them. It would seem the Infinite Baffler survived the Layer Delicious, or there was more than one. Either way, it was an infinite inconvenience.

I was left at the mercy of the Emperor and his disciples. Pianos started to fall in a heavy density, but none of them reached the ground close to us as the Infinite Baffler would either absorb, swat, or turn to powder any piano that was within a close radius. My only advantage was taken from me as quickly as it had been realized. The noise of the destruction was borderline unbearable. We had to shout in order to hear one another, but I'm sure that would have happened cacophony or no.

"Punxsutawney, you've gone too far this time! You've taken the ability to think in color far past what it was intended! You're daydreaming in tandem with the universe!"

"What does that even mean? Why am I so important to you? Is all of this really necessary? The threat of mass murder, wait, ACTUAL mass murder just to prevent us from reaching the peace conference?! Is the Layer Dryffe Company really worth that much to you?!"

"You have no idea what I'm attempting to accomplish here! I need you, but more importantly I need you to listen. I need you to listen very carefully. The King is—"
"THE KING IS WHAT?"

CHAPTER 10.509 …IS STILL JUST AS INFINITE AS THE CAKE IT CAME FROM

I didn't hear him approach or see him shift into the Layer Dryffe, yet here was the King standing thirty feet behind us in a cape made out of computer monitors, keyboards, and cords. The King took a Sapien form on the Origin Layer.

"I'd call off your men if I were you. This is a neutral Layer," said the King.
"A bit hasty, Cubicle. It was your beloved Punxsutawney who threw the first punch."
"The Connoisseur threatened to strike first if I didn't join him! I didn't want to give him a chance to make good on that threat," I shouted.
"We're both here at the same time, Emperor. All of your plans to kill us off failed."
"It would seem yours did as well, King."
"So you WERE just sending us to recruit more firepower, and hoping we would run into them on another Layer? Oh great! Because, you know, who really needs a relationship built on trust anyways? Is there even a real peace conference?"
Of course there was. There had to be.

CHAPTER 10.513 THE BAKER'S NAME IS PUNXSUTAWNEY

"Of course there is. There has to be. It's written in the Great Business Deal."
I swear all I did was blink and when it was over, I was inside a small cell looking out into a massive room. Teleportation? Not something I thought possible.
"It's only a dream. It's only a dream. It's only a dream."

Then why can't I wake up, and why are these machinations of my unconscious mind so inexcusably real?

The voice I heard was coming over an intercom in the room I suddenly found myself in. It was high and metallic. A Tronic, most likely. No person sounds like that.

"Standby for the Baron of the Break Room."

I could see into the cell across from mine, and the King was in it. The King was laying on the floor and was not moving. I assumed there were other cells adjacent to his and mine, but they were spaced too far apart to see who was in them. I attempted to get his attention in a hushed tone.

"Psst, King! Hey! Wake it up!"

I was unsuccessful. He continued to lay there in what appeared to be a deep sleep. I slumped against the wall of the cell, wondering how I'd gotten there. More importantly, I wondered how I would get out.

"It's only a dream. It's only a dream. It's only a dream."

But really, was it? Everything seemed like reality, only without the sanity that comes with it. Impossible characters and occurrences were as plain as could be as if they couldn't not be real. For the near future, I could not escape this place. It had to lie somewhere between dreams and reality, and yet that somehow wasn't an accurate enough description.

After a few minutes of silent contemplation, I heard the rhythm of a pair of what I assumed were hands clapping, and a set of large wheels turning slowly.

The Baron was a Tronic, but a touch more primitive than those I'd been surrounded with as of late. This didn't make him any less impressive. He was an impossibly tall mobile vending machine designed to give people what they wanted. He had a sleek white outer hull with light blue decals. I could not quite make out the contents of his body, but they appeared to consist largely of office supplies and snacks. He was a really fantastic choice for a proxy. Keep the workers happy with your responses and everything would remain in order while who knows what horrible things the Greeter was overseeing. The entire concept I found disgusting.

The tall Tronic stopped in front of my cell and turned to face it. A monitor on a long flexible tether came down to stop where I could see it. A picture of what I assumed was the Baron's face was on the screen, although it looked just like the input keypad to make a selection from the vending machine. The selection readout above the keypad began to show a marquee of words moving from right to left. It was small, but the words moved slowly so that it was easy to read.

"PUNXSUTAWNEY, WELCOME," read the screen.

"What a terrible way to communicate," I said out loud. The Baron ignored me and continued its unique form of communication.

"THE GREETER FELT THE GROUP AS A WHOLE WAS IN VIOLATION OF THE GOVERNING RULES, SO YOU WERE ALL BROUGHT HERE. ADDITIONALLY, YOUR MIND IS TOO UNSTABLE. WE'RE GOING TO HAVE TO MAKE THIS QUICK AS POSSIBLE. THIS IS YOUR PEACE CONFERENCE."

"We're not going to be getting anywhere quickly if this is the only way you can relay information," I pointed out.

"YOU PLAY THE HAND YOU'RE DEALT, PUNXSUTAWNEY. IF I HAD WINGS, I'D GET AROUND BY FLYING. LESS QUIPS MEANS MORE CONTENT."

I obliged, at least for now. It was time for answers.

"NOW LET'S BEGIN."

CHAPTER 10.546 THE DIGITAL EXPERIMENTAL FROSTING

"YOU ALL COULDN'T JUST PLAY BY THE RULES, SO WE INTERVENED. THE MAJORITY OF YOUR MORE DESTRUCTIVE POWERS RELY ON SIGHT AND PROXIMITY, HENCE THE SEPARATION FROM ONE ANOTHER. THE GREETER AND I HAVE FORMULATED A NEW PLAN TO DECIDE THE FATE OF THIS LAYER AND ALL OTHERS. NON-COMPLIANCE ASSUMES THAT THE OTHER SIDE WILL ATTEMPT TO DO NOTHING AS WELL. THIS IS A RISK NEITHER SIDE CAN AFFORD, AS APATHY WILL NOT BRING VICTORY FOR THE SIDE WHO CHOOSES IT IN ANY POSSIBLE OUTCOME.

AS I'M SURE YOU'RE ALREADY AWARE, THE KING, THE EMPEROR, AND THE GREETER ARE IN A THREE-WAY STAND STILL FOR CONTROL. THE GREETER CANNOT ERASE EITHER THE KING OR THE EMPEROR WITHOUT DESTROYING ITSELF. HOWEVER, NEITHER CAN CONTROL THE GREAT BUSINESS DEAL DIRECTLY DUE TO THE GREETER'S POWER OVER IT. THE GREETER HAS COME UP WITH A METHOD TO ELIMINATE ONE OF THE CONTENDERS FOR CONTROL, AND IT WILL BE EITHER THE KING OR THE EMPEROR. THE VICTOR OF THIS UPCOMING TASK WILL HAVE ONLY THE GREETER LEFT TO STRUGGLE WITH AND AGAINST.

NOW ON TO THE DESCRIPTION OF THE TASK YOU ARE ALL CHARGED WITH. I PRESENT TO YOU A PAGE FROM THE LAYER DRYFFE PUBLISHING COMPANY." The Tronic pushed a few buttons on the input keypad. I heard a soft mechanical whirring noise, and saw an object land with a thud at the base of the Tronic. A claw at the end of another tether came down from the sky and picked up the object. It extended into the cell and presented me with a Page.

"THESE CREATIONS OF THE GREETER HAVE NOW BEEN SCATTERED AND HIDDEN ACROSS THE MANY LAYERS OF THE CAKE AND WILL REMAIN THERE UNTIL FOUND BY A MEMBER UNDER THE KING OR THE EMPEROR. EACH ONE OF THESE PAGES CONTAINS A PORTION OF KNOWLEDGE FROM THE PAST, PRESENT, OR FUTURE OF ANY ONE OF THE BEINGS WHO MET HERE TODAY ON THE LAYER DRYFFE FOR THE PEACE CONFERENCE."

"So it's a scavenger hunt. Each of these Pages will provide knowledge on how to beat the other side. It's up to us to decide what knowledge is useful, and what isn't."

"CALL IT WHAT YOU WILL, BUT YES. WHEN PIECED TOGETHER, THE PAGES TELL A STORY. AS THE STORY GOES RIGHT NOW, THERE IS ALREADY A DECLARED VICTOR. HOWEVER, TO DECLINE TO CARRY OUT THE ACTS A PAGE WITH KNOWLEDGE OF THE FUTURE SHARES WILL RE-WRITE THE OTHER PAGES. THEY ARE INTERCONNECTED. THIS IS TO KEEP THE PLAYING FIELD EVEN, BUT ALSO ENSURE THE SIDE WITH THE MOST CLEVER AND CUNNING TACTICS WILL EMERGE VICTORIOUS."

I looked down at my Page. It was a tiny Tronic I could hold in one hand. On its head was the number 0989. This Page potentially had something within that would change the fate of all who were present here.

Wait a minute, this is all just a dream still. Right?

"Baron, this has to be a dream."

"ARE YOU ASKING ME OR ARE YOU TELLING ME? THIS IS, AND WAS, WHAT YOU MAKE IT, PUNXSUTAWNEY. YOU'VE BEEN GIVEN YOUR INSTRUCTIONS BEFORE THE OTHERS BECAUSE OUR TIME TOGETHER IS SHORT, BUT SOON YOU'LL COME TO FIND THIS IS MORE THAN JUST A DREAM. THAT'S WHY YOU'RE NOT ENTIRELY CORRECT'."

CHAPTER 10.989 A BEGINNER'S GUIDE TO DAYDREAMING IN TANDEM WITH THE UNIVERSE

"THIS USED TO BE 'JUST A DREAM' CREATED INSIDE YOUR MIND BY A VERY POWERFUL IMAGINATION. IT WOULD SEEM THAT IN EXTREME CASES, THINKING IN COLOR CAN GO TOO FAR. NOW YOU'RE 'JUST A PART OF IT' LIKE THE REST OF US. NOW SLEEP."

The now empty claw came back through the bars of the cell and knocked me to the floor. My head connected first. The last vision I had was the of the Page in my right hand. Blackness encompassed my vision, and then I was gone.

Another failed bake, sir?

Yes it would seem this has gone too far. There's just too much chaos among the ingredients. I don't think they'll make the push that's necessary to break through.

...hang on. It would seem a few of the beings here can change what Layers they appear on just like a couple of the others we've witnessed.

This is the perfect ingredient for the storm. This is exactly what we're looking for. There's something special about them.

Upon further inspection…it would seem you're right. It appears…the most powerful amongst them have developed a method of travel between Layers, and is even responsible for the creation of new Layers!

This…this might be what we've been searching for. Do not abort the experiment yet. I want updates every hour! What did we call that Layer?

The Layer Dryffe.

I feel they're so close to unlocking what we've dreamed of.

CHAPTER 11.000 THE INFINITE BAFFLING AWAKENING

I awoke gasping for air. I was back in the hospital. I sat bolt upright, suddenly aware of my surroundings, and what great surroundings they were. My mother and father were there, Victoria was there. Michael was there as well. My mother was the first to say anything, and she leapt up from her chair.

"Nurse! He's awake! Call the doctor!" She exclaimed. She ran out the door and into the hall in an attempt to find the doctor, I assumed. I was just glad that I was finally out of the delusional dream that I had found myself in. I sat there still panting for air. Everyone was looking at me in disbelief. My dad stood up and spoke to me.

"You alright buddy? Look at me! You okay?"

"Dad? Yeah, I'm here. I'm here! I'm okay!"

"Oh that's awesome! That's wonderful! I'm so glad you're here! I thought we'd lost you! You were there a moment ago, but then you were gone again!"

Something struck me as odd, though. There were so many people here. Why was everyone here? I was out for so long. It felt like days. Had it not been days?

"MY BABY!" My mother screamed back into the room with the doctor following close behind. He looked at me briefly, and then looked at my chart. He looked at my monitors and then turned to me.

He looked like Vega. He looked like Adam.

"Whoa how are you here!?" I said.

"I'm your doctor, Punx. I'm here to help you, please calm yourself. You've been comatose for almost twelve hours. I just want to make sure you're feeling alright. Can you tell me how you're feeling?"

I looked up at him and saw the room clearly for the first time. My family and friends were there. That didn't bother me. What did bother me was the reflection in the bathroom mirror, and what was causing that reflection.

CHAPTER 11.002 THE BATHROOM REVELATION

The bathroom door was open, and just inside I saw a man. This was no ordinary man. This was the King of the Cubicle, and he was shaving his face in the mirror. He wore the cape of electronics I saw him with previously, and what he said scared me. He called out to me from the bathroom.

"Hey Punx! Tell him what you found on the Layer Delicious! Tell him about that magnetic toy you found with the Mistress Vix!"

I disregarded him and spoke directly to the doctor.

"I'm fine doc. I feel fine. I'm glad to be here. I'm glad to be alive. Thank you."

"You're quite welcome, Punx. Now we're going to keep you here on observation for the night, if you don't mind. You've been through quite a lot, so you should rest up. Catch up with your family if you're missing any details. I'll be close by if you need me."

With that, the doctor left. Regardless of his likeness to Vega, I was still worried about what I saw in the bathroom. When I looked again, the King was gone. My mother began to strangle me in a deep hug.

"I'M SO GLAD YOU'RE BACK! I WAS SO WORRIED!" She said.

"I'm glad to be back, mom. Thank you for being here. I took quite a bump, didn't I?"

"Yes you did! You woke up jabbering nonsense at one point, but you seem like you're fine now!

I looked past her and saw another frightening sight. The Mistress Vix was playing with the magnetic toy just to the left of my father's head. She didn't say a word, but she started to put the toy into the top of the hair vortex.

"NO DON'T!" I screamed. My mom jumped off of me and looked at me with a concerned gaze.

"Aren't you glad you're back safely?" asked my mom. The Mistress had vanished from my sight after I blinked a few times in desperation. I looked at my mom in a slight panic and said, "Yes, of course I am. Thank you for staying by my side."

"I'm glad, my sweet boy! The doctor says you should rest for now. Please lay back and go to sleep."

"Okay mom. I'm glad to see you. Sorry for jumping. I'm just, shaken. That's all." I looked around the room once again. The entire cast of the Royalty members lined the walls in tanks. They just stood in there with their eyes closed. None of them were menacing. None of them said a word. Before my head hit the pillow, I looked at them each in turn and laid my head back.

Darkness overtook my vision.

I began to daydream in tandem with the universe.

CHAPTER 10.998 DO NOT ADJUST YOUR PAGE NUMBER

Just after the Baron knocked out Punxsutawney, the King pretended to wake up in the cell across the way. He looked across and saw that Punxsutawney was asleep. "Excellent work, Baron. Even though the Creator is asleep, we can continue to function uninterrupted. Now if you'll excuse me, I have a lot of work to do."

The King opened the cell door, which was not locked, and began to walk off down the cellblock. None of the other occupants were awake. The King stopped in front of one of the cells, which contained a being of identical likeness.

"Your company will continue to make Layers under my authority. You no longer have a say in the matter. I will assume your likeness and run the company as a proxy. You are welcome to your input, but I will have the final say. I guess you aren't much of an advisor, but at this time I'm willing to take your input over any other." The other King looked up from the floor and spoke in a feeble tone.

"I recall your words well, Greeter. I don't think all of this is really necessary."

"That's why I make the decisions, Cubicle." Greeter continued walking down the cell block away from the temporary prisoners. The King of the Cubicle began to whisper to himself.

"I will stop you, my child. I will right the wrongs of the past. I will see this company under my command once again. You will not keep me from the Creator."

The King of the Cubicle scratched off another tick mark in the wall underneath the heading "Days in Captivity". Even in captivity, the man who founded the Layer Dryffe Company continued to crunch numbers. To the left of the first heading, there was another that simply read "Good Ideas". It was empty. The King smiled and scratched a tick mark underneath that heading as well.

EPILOGUE, SCENE ONE: DIAGNOSIS

I was diagnosed with a few different kinds of delusional misidentification syndrome. I recorded everything I experienced during a 24-hour period and presented it to a mental health specialist at the behest of my parents and girlfriend, and the doctors came back with the diagnosis. Personally, I'd just like to say I had bad hallucinations, but they really seemed intent on classifying it, so I humored them. I was shocked to find out the things I experienced were already medically classified. They made me memorize each delusion and what it is as a part of my therapy.

The first one they said I had was the Capgras delusion. This is where someone believes that someone they know has been replaced by an impostor that looks exactly the same.

The next delusion I exhibited was mirrored-self misidentification. This is where someone believes his or her reflection is someone else entirely.

Another delusion I exhibited (and by far the most prevalent they said) was the syndrome of delusional companions, where someone believes that certain inanimate objects are sentient beings.

The last delusion I had only appeared once. It was reduplicative paramnesia. This is where someone thinks that something has been duplicated and a copy exists somewhere else. I was told this could include things, people I knew, and even body parts.

The doctors said I exhibited another delusion, which had not been previously medically classified. This is where someone thinks that two or more different objects or places occupy the same space at the same time, and that one can perceive them all simultaneously. They asked me to name the delusion. After explaining what I perceived was going on, and the doctors telling me what was reality, we came to an agreement to call it the Dryffe delusion.

EPILOGUE, SCENE TWO: A SPECTRUM OF PERCEPTION

Re-adjustment to normal life was a big challenge. I had really good days and really horrible days.

On really good days I'd only see a couple of things that weren't really there. I'd empty my shoe and grass from Dryffe Fields would come out, or I'd double-take after thinking I saw a cloud shaped a little too well like something recognizable.

On really bad days, they'd talk to me. I'd sit down to eat some old pizza and Vega (for example) would be on the couch already, watching television. It was all okay as long as they didn't speak. If they didn't speak, I could just ignore them and they'd go away eventually. When they spoke, they'd ask me questions. Sometimes whichever character I saw would just ask their question over and over until they were screaming. It was at this point I would have to leave. For some reason, they could never follow me when I walked away. I eventually figured this was a combination of syndrome of delusional companions and a slightly modified version of the Capgras delusion. If the characters I saw were actually just couch cushions or dirty socks, they couldn't follow me when I left the room. This was the one bit of sanity I could keep for myself. Sometimes if I saw one of the characters in the room I was about to enter, I'd skip it entirely and go do something else.

On the worst days I'd experience the Layer Dryffe delusion. I was of the unshakeable opinion that our reality was just another Layer and that it existed on a Cake of infinite size in either direction. It took everything I had in me to not talk about this or the things I hallucinated when around other people. If I could keep this up, I hoped they wouldn't put me into a psychiatric unit.

One day when it was really bad, I realized it would make a really great story, so I started writing everything down.

EPILOGUE, SCENE THREE: A HOLE IN THE FIFTH WALL JUST WIDE ENOUGH

One night I was asleep in my bed. My girlfriend was spending the night that night. Things could have been a lot different if she hadn't been. She woke me up and sleepily chastised me.

"Punx, you left the TV on again, go turn it off please. It woke me up."

"Ungh. Alright," I managed to grunt before getting out of bed.

I walked towards the doorway and was nearly there before I heard what had woken her up. It was so soft I was surprised she could hear it, particularly in her sleep. It sounded like some sort of cartoon robot from in here. The awful taste in my mouth distracted me, as I sleep with my mouth open. I got to the kitchen and opened the fridge for some water to get rid of the taste. The living room door was right next to the kitchen, I'd go turn off the TV after I got a drink. As soon as I had felt around opened the fridge, I realized I couldn't see inside because the light still did not work. But if the television is on, I should be able to see light from it.

The television wasn't on. The voice hadn't changed at all, it was still the same voice speaking in the same monotone. I looked in the living room and saw the source of the noise standing on the coffee table looking straight at the doorway to the kitchen. It was a Page. It spoke its message to me in a loop. I must have listened about three or four times before I picked it up and shut it off. I heard it say:

"Chapter 10.998 Do not adjust your page number. Just after the Baron knocked out Punxsutawney, the King pretended to wake up in the cell across the way. He looked across and saw that Punxsutawney was asleep. 'Excellent work, Baron. Even though the Creator is asleep, we can continue to function uninterrupted. Now if you'll excuse me, I have a lot of work to do.' The King opened the cell door, which was not locked, and began to walk off down the cellblock. None of the other occupants were awake. The King stopped in front of one of the cells, which contained a being of identical likeness. 'Your company will continue to make Layers under my authority. You no longer have a say in the matter. I will assume your likeness and run the company as a proxy. You are welcome to your input, but I will have the final say. I guess you aren't much of an advisor, but at this time I'm willing to take your input over any other.' The other King looked up from the floor and spoke in a feeble tone. 'I recall your words well, Greeter. I don't think all of this is really necessary.' 'That's why I make the decisions, Cubicle.' Greeter continued walking down the cellblock away from the temporary prisoners. The King of the Cubicle began to whisper to himself. 'I will stop you, my child. I will right the wrongs of the past. I will see this company under my command once again. You will not keep me from the Creator.' The King of the Cubicle scratched off another tick mark in the wall underneath the heading 'Days in Captivity by GBD'. Even in captivity, the man who founded the Layer Dryffe Company continued to crunch numbers. To the left of the first heading, there was another that simply read 'Good Ideas'. It was empty. The King smiled and scratched a tick mark underneath that heading as well."

Then it would just loop back to the chapter number.

EPILOGUE, SCENE FOUR: FICTION CREATES REALITY CREATES FICTION CREATES REALITY CREATES...

"It's just a dream," I said. Something I came up with myself to help with my hallucinations. I turned the Page off and set it back down on the table. It would just disappear when I left the room. I walked down the hall to the bedroom and got back in bed with Victoria quietly to not disturb her. It didn't work.

"Thanks Punx. Remember to turn the TV off next time," she said.

"Oh it wasn't the television, it was just something I hallucinated."

Being as groggy as I was, I forgot it's not a hallucination if more than one person experiences it. Also, I wasn't the one who noticed it first.

It was Victoria.

I realized it as she reacted to my stupid response. I leapt up and was just at the door of the bedroom when she finished her sentence.

"If you made it up Punx, then why could I hear it too?"

I was panting by the time I had made it back to the living room. The Page was still there on the coffee table. I fell to the ground in disbelief. Victoria came up to me and scolded me.

"What is your problem, Punx? Figure it out and come back to bed. Oh, what's that? Toy robot?"

She walked over to the coffee table and picked up the Page. After turning it over a few times, she commented on it.

"Number 0989. I've never seen this before, where did you get this, Punx? What does this switch do?

Punx?

Punx?"

EPILOGUE, SCENE FIVE: DID YOU EVER IMAGINE?

When you pictured that sphere of dark drywall I was just talking about, were you floating above it?

Outside it?

Naw man, you're in it. You're inside the sphere. *We're* inside the sphere.

Uh, that is, until we're *not* anymore. You see how this works?

END OF BOOK 1

BOOK 2: A HOLE IN THE WALL WHERE THE FIFTH CAN SEE IT ALL

Printed in Great Britain
by Amazon

77199087R00113